# VALUED FOR MURDER

## A DOTTY SAYERS ANTIQUE MYSTERY

### VICTORIA TAIT

KANGA
PRESS

# CHAPTER ONE

"The lies that fool me," sang Zenobia Richardson, and as her voice rose in pitch, twenty-eight-year-old Dotty Sayers cautiously placed her glass of sparkling water on a walnut sideboard. Staring at her drink, she wondered if it was true that an opera singer's voice could shatter glass.

"Isn't Zenobia amazing?" whispered Aunt Beanie beside her. "Even though she claims to be in retirement, few singers have her vocal range."

Aunt Beanie, whose full name was Bernadette Devereux, was not Dotty's real aunt, but she'd provided Dotty with a cottage to live in and continued to offer her support, guidance and friendship.

They were standing at the back of a beautiful room in Windrush Hall, a large Georgian country house, nestled in a valley in the rolling hills of England's picturesque Cotswolds.

The new owner, as Dotty considered Zenobia Richardson, stood in a semi-circular alcove at the front of the formal room, bathed in soft spring sunlight pouring through the floor to ceiling windows which looked out over the colourful garden beyond.

Last week, Dotty had read a magazine article detailing the transformation Miss Richardson had made to the formal gardens, and she longed to walk through them admiring the tall delphiniums, delicate aquilegias and striking agapanthus.

Zenobia finished her song with a clear, high note, and the group of American tourists who'd listened in rapt silence broke into applause. Those who'd been sitting on ornate chairs stood and clapped and someone at the back of the room hollered, "Encore."

"Come on," muttered Aunt Beanie, tugging Dotty's sleeve. "I need to familiarise myself with the contents of the drawing room before I conduct the first house tour."

As they left the music room, or morning room as it had been called in the sale prospectus, they met Zenobia's red-headed and fiery-tempered Italian personal assistant, Serena De Rossi.

Serena announced, "Madam will finish with a short aria. After, guests eat high tea or go on tour of house. Bene?"

"Bene," replied Aunt Beanie as she strode away.

Dotty stood in the stone flagged entrance hall of the large Georgian house and gazed up the circular staircase. On her first visit, which was only last November, the house had been forlorn and neglected, with dust covering the now glittering chandelier.

More had changed in the past eight months of her life than in her entire twenty-eight years. Her husband, Alasdair, who'd been fifteen years older than her, had died while on a peace-keeping tour in Africa with his British army regiment, 8 SCOTS.

The regiment had amalgamated last December and moved back to Scotland. She'd been tempted to move with them and continue to receive their support until she'd realised how sheltered and smothering such an existence could be, and that she did in fact have the strength and determination to tackle life on her own.

She'd been assisted by her colleagues at a job she'd inadvertently acquired at Akemans Antiques, and by her new friends in the Cotswolds.

She tucked a strand of mousy-blonde hair behind her ear, and glanced across at a mahogany table where Serena was arranging Zenobia Richardson merchandise beneath a tall vase of pink lilies. The fragrance of the lilies was strong and pungent.

"Come and look at this," called Aunt Beanie.

As Dotty crossed the entrance hall, a grey-haired butler, wearing a black tie, waistcoat and tailcoat, with formal grey trousers, appeared from the dining room carrying a silver platter.

"Do I smell sausage rolls?" enquired Aunt Beanie.

"Yes, madam. Straight out of the oven."

Aunt Beanie stepped forward, plucked one from the platter and popped it into her mouth.

Red-faced, Serena De Rossi stormed across and in an aggressive whisper declared, "Those are for the guests."

"Delicious," muttered Aunt Beanie through a mouthful of flaky pastry. "Compliments to the chef."

The butler's lined face wrinkled into a smile as he replied, "My wife's own recipe."

As he headed towards the music room, Dotty followed Aunt Beanie into the drawing room. She gasped. When she'd first seen the room it had been an echo of its former splendour, but the peacock-blue silk wallpaper had been renewed and as she touched the curtains, whose fibres did not part as the original ones had, she noted the delicate embroidered flowers.

Even the gilt wood sofas and chairs had been reupholstered.

"Beautiful, isn't it?" declared Aunt Beanie.

"Of course," remembered Dotty, "Miss Richardson bought most of the furniture, and some of the paintings and ornaments, as well as the house. But it must have cost a fortune to return it to its former glory."

"She has money," mused Aunt Beanie, "but she's also smart. How much do you think this group is paying for a private performance, high tea, and a tour of her new house?"

Serena De Rossi strode into the room and announced, "Madam finish last song, so you begin tour."

Aunt Beanie examined her reflection in a gilt mirror above the fireplace. She adjusted her green headscarf, tightened the bow which held it in place, and tucked a strand of grey hair beneath it. She turned towards Dotty, smoothing down her green smock over her charcoal grey trousers.

For Aunt Beanie, she was conservatively dressed, as she loved bright colours, often wearing a combination of them together.

"Wait here while I fetch the tour group," she instructed Dotty. "You can listen and learn, so you'll be ready to assist me the next time Zenobia hosts an event." She turned and strode past Serena.

Dotty was left alone in the drawing room and she heard applause, which she presumed signified the end of the performance.

A brightly coloured display of ceramic figurines, animals, and objects arranged in a mahogany glass-fronted display unit caught her eye. She stepped closer and her gaze was drawn to a model of two pairs of dancers in a colourful art deco design.

She jumped as an elderly male voice said, "Madam's original and favourite collection." She had not heard the butler enter, but he stepped forward and pointed to a statuette of a black cat holding a bunch of flowers.

"That one started her collection. She was given it on opening night when she first performed on stage in the West End. But I doubt it, or the rest of the collection is worth much, unlike the majority of the contents of this house, which is probably why I like them so much."

Dotty turned to the old butler and smiled.

He inclined his head and continued. "Our housemaid, Esme, has taken to her bed complaining of stomach ache, and my wife is struggling with the last-minute preparations for tea. Mrs Devereux told me you are an excellent cook and that you'd be willing to help out in the kitchen. Is that so?"

"Of course," replied Dotty, realising she was relieved to be doing something useful, and she did enjoy cooking.

She followed the butler across the stone flagged entrance hall and into the dining room. Little had changed since the sale of the house and the auction of its contents, most of which Zenobia had bought, including the Duke of Ditchford's family portraits which still hung on the walls.

The kitchen was a different story. The old Duke had used the space as his living quarters with a kitchen area, and a circular dining table and chairs arranged at one end around a log-burning fire.

But the fireplace was no longer visible, as a wall had been constructed across the room, and the modern kitchen into which Dotty stepped was half the size of the old one.

A dumpy woman wearing a pair of yellow-tinted glasses entered the kitchen carrying a wicker basket full of bread rolls. She exclaimed, "Benson, what am I to do? Madam demands freshly prepared sandwiches, but I cannot make them and fry the tempura prawns and vegetables at the same time."

She deposited her basket on a counter and scampered across to a gleaming stainless-steel range cooker from which she pulled out a tray of mini quiches. She placed them on a metal rack beside the oven and wafted them with a tea towel. "Ouf! They are not burnt, but Madam will be furious if we don't serve everything immediately."

Benson crossed the black and white chequerboard tiled floor and gave the woman a huge hug. "Françoise, this lady has come to your rescue."

"Chérie, quick, quick," gestured Françoise to Dotty.

Dotty worked quickly but diligently. As instructed, she prepared open sandwiches with an array of toppings, including smoked salmon and cream cheese, smoked trout pâté and dill, and blue cheese, fig and walnuts with a honey drizzle.

Benson arranged the sandwiches on chrome platters and carried them away, while Françoise fried prawns and slices of vegetables in two deep fat fryers. The noise of an industrial extractor fan dominated the kitchen.

After half an hour of continuous work, the red-headed Serena appeared and declared, in a haughty voice, "You can stop now. The guests have enough savouries, so you need to start on the sweets."

Seemingly oblivious, Françoise placed another handful of vegetables into a deep-fat fryer, which spat and hissed. Serena shouted, "I said that's enough! We need the cakes. Now."

Françoise spun round and stared at Serena through her steamed up glasses. She removed them and began wiping the lenses on her apron.

"Oh, who's this?" exclaimed Dotty as a large furry grey cat wandered into the kitchen from the main house.

"Who?" exclaimed Françoise. She finished wiping her glasses and put them back on. With a note of relief, she cried, "Mario. There's no food for you here at the moment. Out you go."

The cat stopped and examined the cook and then Dotty.

He was just like Earl Grey, her cat, who had originally lived in this house with the old Duke, but she was sure Earl Grey had never worn a diamanté studded collar. Presumably they weren't real diamonds. "Mario?" she enquired.

"Tosca's lover," snapped Serena as she roughly picked up the cat and carried him out of the kitchen.

After a few seconds, Serena cried, "Ow!"

Françoise smiled and exclaimed, "Bravo, Mario."

# CHAPTER TWO

After Zenobia Richardson's guests had departed, Dotty and Aunt Beanie returned home to Meadowbank Farm on the edge of Fairford, a small, attractive Cotswold town, ten miles east of the larger Roman town of Cirencester.

As she relaxed in her bath, Dotty reflected that she'd had a fascinating day. She loved visiting other people's houses, and it was her favourite part of her job at Akemans Antiques.

Most properties were not as grand as Windrush Hall, nor did they all contain so many expensive antiques, but the way people lived their lives, and the items they cherished, intrigued her.

Aunt Beanie had invited her to the main farmhouse for a light supper, although this would now be enhanced by delicacies left over from high tea which Zenobia's cook, Françoise, had smuggled into Aunt Beanie's car, under the ever-watchful and disapproving gaze of Serena De Rossi.

"So, has she made many changes?" Norman Climpson asked as Dotty entered Aunt Beanie's farmhouse kitchen. Even though Norman was in his sixties, there was no grey in his sandy-coloured hair, but the broken veins in his permanently tanned face betrayed a man who'd spent the majority of his life outdoors.

He sat at the pine kitchen table watching Aunt Beanie pull a large black kettle to the edge of a hot plate on her Aga range cooker.

"And we really must find a better place for Agatha to sleep," he added.

Agatha was a black Berkshire pig who'd been a small piglet when she'd been given to Aunt Beanie the previous autumn. Although her breed was not large, her prostrate body extended across the entire front of the Aga, absorbing as much heat as she could.

Norman shook his head. "One of these days, we'll drop something hot on her. I think I'll remove those shelves beside the Aga and build her a bed. Then she can sleep on or under it, whichever takes her fancy."

"Earl Grey will like that," noted Dotty. Her furry grey British blue cat lifted his head and stared at her with his bright yellow eyes. He was laying on top of Agatha. The two had become great friends since Dotty had moved into the adjoining farm cottage. Most of the time, she left the door open between the two properties so Earl Grey could wander in and out at will.

"Tea?" asked Aunt Beanie.

"Yes, please," replied Dotty as she sat down next to Norman. She glanced across at the conservatory extension to the kitchen where Aunt Beanie's husband, Uncle Cliff, sat in an armchair, wearing a pair of headphones. He had dementia, but listening to podcasts about farming or nature seemed to keep him calm and content.

"So back to Windrush Hall and its new owner, Zenobia Richardson. What is the house like?" asked Norman.

"You really should come with me next time I'm taking a group around," replied Aunt Beanie as she placed cups of tea in front of Dotty and Norman and sat down.

"Who'd look after Cliff?" responded Norman. He'd moved into the farmhouse at the same time Dotty had taken the farm cottage and he helped Aunt Beanie care for Uncle Cliff, and undertook odd jobs around the farm.

He'd also persuaded Aunt Beanie to hire contractors to run the main farming business, something Uncle Cliff was no longer able to do.

"I think she's done an amazing job," said Dotty, brightly. "I'm so pleased the drawing room has been restored, but I think it's strange that she kept the old Duke's family portraits on the dining room walls."

"I believe it gives her a sense of heritage," declared Aunt Beanie, "although I explain exactly who they all are on my tour." She looked across at Norman.

"Thank you for recommending me as a tour guide, and for persuading me to come out of retirement. I really enjoyed today, and American tourists aren't nearly as stupid as people make out. There were one or two questions where I had to fudge the answers. I'll need to prep more before Zenobia's next private event."

"Well, it won't be next weekend. Akemans are hosting *The Antique Tour* television show at Charbury Castle Hotel," announced Norman.

"Of course, but how will my niece, George, cope with that?"

Georgina Carey Boyd, known as George, ran the auction side of Akemans while her warm-hearted but disorganised sister, Gilly Wimsey, ran the antiques centre.

Norman shrugged. "She'll be calm and professional once the event starts and the cameras roll, but a neurotic nightmare in the run up to it next week. Which is one reason I've been asked to work all week, if you remember?"

"Of course. I've already asked Mrs Todd to sit with Cliff on Wednesday morning so I can visit Fairford market." She stood up. "Time for supper."

Dotty unwrapped the foil parcels Françoise had given them and arranged their contents on blue and white Wedgwood patterned plates.

"What about you?" Aunt Beanie asked her. "What are your plans for the week?"

"I'm not involved in the TV show, thankfully, as they have their own production team and receptionists. That's what they call the ladies who meet and greet the public, and direct them to the most relevant professional valuers. So I'll be keeping my head down in the office and organising Lots for this month's auction."

"You've dodged a bullet there," agreed Aunt Beanie.

# CHAPTER THREE

M onday morning was bright and warm as Dotty parked in a staff only space on the gravel yard outside Akemans Antiques. As she climbed out of her green Skoda Fabia, she lifted her eyes to the cornflower-blue sky and felt the warm rays of sunshine.

The sand-coloured Cotswold stone of the three-storey converted mill building, which housed the antiques centre, looked mellow and welcoming, but the single-storey auction house, in whose shadow it stood, appeared cold and uninviting.

Dotty pushed open the large oak door at the front of the antiques centre and strode across the vast, high-ceilinged room, which was divided into individual booths selling an eclectic range of bric-a-brac, art and collectables.

The walls were covered with pictures and mirrors and countless objects hung from the ceiling, including wicker baskets, cast iron light fittings, and retro signs advertising soup and baked beans. When she had time, she loved rummaging around the different stalls.

Outside auction week, the front door to the auction house was kept locked and access was via an interconnecting door from the antiques centre. Dotty stepped through the door into the auction office-cum-reception area and placed her wicker basket on the worn green leather top of the mahogany reception desk.

Pausing, she thought how lucky she was to have this job. The work wasn't difficult, although sometimes the paperwork became monotonous, and generally it was interesting. As were her colleagues.

Dotty walked to the rear of the small office area, which extended behind the reception desk, and switched on the kettle.

"Excellent, coffee time," exclaimed a short lady who had followed Dotty from the antiques centre. Gilly Wimsey pushed her orange-rimmed glasses back up her nose and flicked an unruly lock of her curly orange hair out of her face.

"How was Zenobia Richardson's private performance?" she asked. "I was so jealous when Aunt Beanie told me she was taking you along as her assistant."

"She's a fabulous singer," replied Dotty as she made Gilly a cup of coffee and a Yorkshire tea for herself. There had been a few months, after she'd been attacked and hospitalised with a head injury, when she'd only drunk herbal teas to help ease her headaches.

Her late husband, Al, had insisted on only having Tetley tea bags in the house, even though he usually drank coffee, so she was enjoying trying out different types of teas.

She turned and handed Gilly her coffee. "And it was wonderful to see the house again, restored to its former glory. I'm only sorry I didn't get a chance to visit the garden as I was assisting the cook in the kitchen."

Gilly laid a hand on Dotty's arm. "You're always so kind and thoughtful. Helping out wherever you can."

Dotty blushed.

"It's such a wonderful day, and almost feels like summer. I think we should air the auction house," Gilly declared. She placed her cup on the reception desk and bustled across to the front door, which she unlocked and swung open.

"That's a start, but do close it if it gets draughty. I don't want you catching a chill."

Between the mahogany reception desk and the front door was the reception area with a wooden coat stand in the corner nearest the antiques centre, and a grey sofa and tub chairs surrounding an oval, reclaimed elm coffee table in the opposite corner.

There was a door in the partition wall beside the sofa and chairs, beyond the reception desk, which led into the main auction house and it opened now as Norman Climpson walked through.

"Just the man I need," cried Gilly, as she clasped Norman's arm and led him back into the auction room. Dotty heard her explain, "Let's throw open the doors and get some fresh air in here."

Dotty settled herself at the reception desk and started examining the week's schedule of auction item deliveries.

David Rook strode through the open front door and declared, "I take it Gilly has commenced her annual late-spring clean." He was a distinguished-looking gentleman with short grey hair, a high, pronounced forehead, and a salt and pepper moustache and trim beard.

His darker-toned skin was even more noticeable after his recent trip to somewhere in the Far East. He had been surprisingly vague when Dotty had asked him about it.

"That's right," announced Gilly, as she returned from the auction room. "It's time to clear away the cobwebs." She picked up her coffee cup from Dotty's desk.

"And not only in the auction house." David's large dark eyes were playful as they regarded Dotty and she realised she'd been yawning. "A late night in the metropolis of Fairford?" He grinned.

She smiled and shook her head. "I was busy yesterday helping out at an event at Windrush Hall."

"You met Zenobia Richardson?" David's large eyes opened even wider.

"No. But I did hear her sing, and I had a look around the ground floor of the house."

"Zenobia Richardson," echoed a haughty voice, and George Carey-Boyd strode through the front door. She was tall and elegant, with long blonde hair and she wore a powder blue trouser suit. "She's the celebrity guest expert for our episode of *The Antique Tour*."

"I thought she was an opera singer. What does she know about antiques?" asked Gilly, as she tugged her ear.

"Quite a lot, actually," replied David. "I attended a talk she gave at the British Museum in London on Italian Renaissance sculptures. When she was performing in Italy, she spent much of her free time viewing the country's statues and artwork and she had some novel ideas." He turned to George. "What is she an expert for on *The Antique Tour*?"

"Sculptures." George's phone rang, and she fished around in a large, black handbag before stepping outside to take the call.

Gilly Wimsey leaned back against Dotty's desk and asked, "Who are the other experts?"

"Jennifer Boyle is on jewellery, Casper Dupré for furniture, Gilmore Chapman is giving his expert opinion on paintings and pictures, and I have the dubious title of 'Miscellaneous Expert'."

"And George is the guest presenter?"

"Yes," confirmed David.

"I know this weekend will be a disaster," George declared as she reappeared in the entrance doorway and flicked her long blonde hair out of her face. "That was Max, the producer ..."

Gilly giggled.

"What?" demanded George.

"He took rather a liking to David when he visited last summer."

David brushed off the comment and smiled at Dotty as he replied, "What can I say? He's a man of taste."

Dotty smiled back, but George wore a thunderous expression. "Never mind that. What are we going to do for a new show receptionist? One of the regulars has to attend a family funeral."

"Dotty could stand in," replied David, still regarding her.

"Oh, yes," agreed Gilly in a breathless voice. "She did a fantastic job at the last auction when you and Marion were away, David."

"And I'm sure Marion wouldn't mind coming in to help in the office this week, if needed," added David.

"But," spluttered George, "She can't appear on TV looking like that."

# CHAPTER FOUR

Dotty felt nervous when she arrived at Akemans Antiques on Tuesday morning. In the office she was greeted curtly by Marion Rook, David's wife.

Marion was efficient and organised, and worked in the auction house during the week preceding an auction, and she helped out when there was extra work or a special sale or event.

As always, Marion was immaculately turned out. Not a hair of her grey bob was out of place and she wore a pair of tailored grey trousers with a pink cashmere top and matching cardigan. She examined Dotty over her tortoiseshell-framed glasses.

Dotty shrank back, feeling self-conscious in a powder-blue blouse she'd found in a second-hand shop and an old denim calf-length skirt.

"Hair," announced Marion, in her rich gravelly voice. "That's the first area to tackle."

Dotty tucked a strand of her mousey-blonde hair behind her ear and bit her lip as Marion picked up her phone. She felt like a small child again.

"Giovanni, Ciao. I have a friend who's hair is in desperate need of restyling. Do you have a free appointment this morning?"

Marion listened to the response before replying. "We'll come straight over."

She drove them competently to Cirencester in her silver VW Golf and Dotty soon found herself being ushered into a boutique hairdressing salon in a narrow street, behind the gothic-entranced St John Baptist Church.

She sat in a black leather chair, facing a wooden-framed mirror which spanned the length of the salon area, and watched the shaven-headed Giovanni lift strands of her hair, before letting them fall through his fingers. He curled his lip before pronouncing. "So dull and lifeless. It needs colour to lift it, but I don't have the time today. You come back tomorrow?"

"No, Giovanni," answered Marion. "You'll have to do the best you can with a cut. What style do you recommend? She needs to look approachable but professional."

"Like you?" remarked Giovanni as he glanced across at Marion, who sat in an identical black leather chair which she'd swivelled round to face Dotty. Giovanni moulded Dotty's hair around her face. "A bob, si, but layered at the back to create beautiful shape."

He pulled a strand of hair forward and then tucked it behind her ear. "And graduated at the front, and feathered so she can tuck it away and it doesn't fall in front of her face."

"Perfect," agreed Marion.

Dotty's chest tightened. She had no idea what was about to happen, but she'd have to trust Giovanni. At least he sounded competent.

After her hair was washed by Giovanni's teenage assistant, Dotty gripped the armrest as clumps of hair fell to the wooden floor.

Giovanni's scissors whispered against her cheek as he snipped away, and she felt bare and exposed. After twenty minutes, he picked up a hairdryer and slowly dried her locks into a sleek bob.

Then he picked up his scissors again and snipped and feathered the ends so the sharp bob shape softened around her face. She marvelled at his expertise and his total confidence in his own work.

He held a mirror behind her so she was able to admire the neatly curved shape of the cut as it graduated into the nape of her neck. Turning from left to right, she examined her reflection with wonder. She didn't recognise the sophisticated-looking woman in front of her.

"Bella," exclaimed Giovanni, stepping back. "Next time we add highlights. That make it perfect." Giovanni unfastened the Velcro at her neck and whisked off the black nylon cape.

"Much better," agreed Marion as she brushed stray strands of hair off Dotty's arm. "Now for a new outfit."

They walked along the street, away from the town centre, towards Cirencester's 3,000 acre deer park.

Marion peered through the window of the first women's clothes shop they reached and then waved dismissively with her hand. "Too casual."

A young man with rich-dark skin loitered beside the window of the next boutique they came to. He turned away quickly as they approached the front door and Marion pushed it open.

"Can't you read?" demanded a female voice Dotty recognised.

Serena De Rossi blocked the shop entrance with her hands on her hips. "It says 'closed for private fitting'. Madam, not like to be disturbed."

Dotty felt Marion tense, so she placed a hand on her shoulder. "Why don't we try somewhere else? We can always come back later."

Marion hesitated and she and Serena glared at each other. Then Serena noticed something behind them and a shadow crossed her face. She turned quickly, slamming the glass-paned door in Marion's face. It quivered and Marion reached forward to open it again when Dotty grabbed her arm.

"Really, it's not worth it. That was Serena De Rossi, Zenobia Richardson's assistant, and I learnt at the private event on Sunday that there's no point arguing with her."

The man who'd been hovering outside the boutique was now examining cakes and bread in the bakery on the opposite side of the street. For an instant, Dotty locked eyes with his reflection and she felt sympathy for the troubled young man.

Marion gripped Dotty's arm. "Danielle's. I'm sure we'll find something suitable there." She pulled Dotty forward, away from the bakery and the man who was still staring through its window.

Dotty liked Danielle's the minute she stepped inside. It was neither too country set, being without rails of tweed skirts and jackets, nor too trendy, as there were no leather trousers and dresses with minimal amounts of fabric.

Marion marched across to a rail and lifted the hanger of a pale green wrap-around dress with short flutter sleeves. She held it in front of her. "What do you think?"

It looked rather racy and wasn't a style Dotty normally wore. "I'm not sure," she stuttered.

Marion threw the dress towards her. "Try it on, and I'll see what else I can find."

Dotty did as she was told and reappeared to find Marion talking to an elegant woman with spiky grey hair, who wore a flouncy chiffon layered top.

The woman approached Dotty and ran an admiring eye over her.

Dotty felt the blood rush to her cheeks.

"So simple, but elegant. And it highlights your wonderful curves."

Dotty lifted her leg and looked down at the parted material. She wasn't sure about the gap created by the wrap design.

"You've such long, shapely legs," added Marion with a note of awe. "Why do you always hide them away with long, tent-like skirts?"

Dotty dropped her eyes to the floor, but she felt her chest expand. Nobody had ever complimented her body, and she'd always felt frumpy around the stick-thin women she knew.

Marion announced, "It's perfect for the camera. She can't wear anything too fussy. And an outfit which is too bold or sexy would annoy the other women. But they might be filming outside, so we need a short jacket or cardigan."

The elegant shop assistant produced a matching green bolero style jacket, which she held up for Dotty to slide her arms into.

"And shoes," considered Marion. "Flats, or a slight heel. They need to be comfortable, as she'll be on her feet all weekend."

Dotty slipped on a pair of pale green suede loafers with a half-inch heel. They had a cushion insole and felt snug.

"Walk around," commanded Marion.

Dotty complied but stopped at the far end of the small clothes shop, in front of a freestanding, full-length mirror. Now she really didn't recognise the stylish woman staring back at her.

"We'll take two sets," instructed Marion, "as she needs the same clothes for filming on Saturday and Sunday."

Dotty swung round. "I can barely afford one outfit, but certainly not two." She'd been ignoring the eye watering price tag she'd noted when she'd put the dress on.

Marion waved a credit card. "Don't worry, you're on expenses, and I bet yours will still be the cheapest outfit on the set."

"But the most attractive," drawled the shop assistant.

Marion sighed. "Youth will always win that contest."

# CHAPTER FIVE

After the initial excitement of discovering she'd be working at the filming of *The Antique Tour* at the weekend, Dotty settled down for the rest of the week to organise the May furniture, antiques and collectables auction.

The stone storeroom across the gravel yard from the auction house, which had originally stored sacks of flour when the antiques centre was a mill, was already half-full of furniture.

Norman Climpson was assisting two removal men unload the final delivery of the week from a white transit van, parked in front of the double doors, halfway down the large auction room.

Norman supported one end of a blue upholstered sofa as a removal man pushed it out of the van, jumped down and between them they carried it a few metres before lowering it to floor, next to two matching armchairs.

A second removal man placed two circular side tables on the bare concrete floor.

"Mahogany side tables, round," muttered Dotty as she checked the list attached to the clipboard she held. Finding the items, she ticked them off. She glanced around the empty auction room, which appeared forlorn and almost shabby, but she knew it would be transformed prior to the auction.

Once the furniture and larger items being sold were arranged, and the room was dressed with fresh flowers and strategically placed lighting, it would entice and excite visitors.

"That's it," grunted one of the removal men as he checked a large black watch on his hairy wrist. He held out a delivery note, which Dotty dutifully signed and returned to him. As the removal men slammed the rear doors of their white van shut, Dotty surveyed the mismatch of household furniture.

As if echoing her thoughts, Norman Climpson ran a hand through his sandy hair and commented, "Not much for a lifetime's collection. It almost makes me glad that I have so little, just a few photos and mementoes."

"But you also have your tools, and what about your fishing equipment?" enquired Dotty.

Norman waved her comments away with his hand. "I expect they'll end up on the tip, as I doubt they'll be worthwhile selling at auction. A car boot sale, perhaps," he mused.

"Of course, there are also the Duke's medals, but I'll donate them to a military museum soon. They're too much of a liability for me to keep and people should know how brave the Duke was."

"And your father," Dotty reminded. She placed her clipboard on the arm of a blue upholstered armchair and picked up the company camera.

"Let's photograph everything, and then I'll write brief descriptions while you carry what you can across to the storeroom. Will you need my help with the sofa?"

"If you don't mind," replied Norman. "It's not heavy, just bulky."

"I'm afraid that'll have to wait," called David Rook in a clear, authoritative voice as he strode towards them from the direction of the office.

"Dorothy, Georgina and I are meeting the television crew at Charbury Castle Hotel, and I think it would be beneficial for you to join us. You can acclimatise yourself with the layout before tomorrow's filming."

Dotty looked down at her pale blue skirt, smeared with dust and what looked like a rust stain from helping unload a delivery of garden ornaments and equipment earlier.

She licked her finger and rubbed at the skirt, but that only made the mark more obvious. Biting her lip, she followed David out of the auction room.

"Have you ever visited Charbury Castle Hotel?" asked David as he manoeuvred his silver vintage Mercedes out of Akemans' yard and onto the narrow road.

Dotty shook her head.

"It's located on the far side of Cirencester and has a long and colourful history. Built in early Tudor times, it became a royal palace and there is a story that Henry VIII stayed there with his new Queen, Anne Boleyn, after their secret marriage.

"Unfortunately, the main part of the castle burnt down in the nineteenth century and was left in ruins until a rich London financier rebuilt it as a family home. I believe it became a hotel after the war, sometime in the 1950s. It's been upgraded and remodelled several times since then and is a very luxurious place to stay. Marion and her friends like to visit the spa."

David joined the main dual carriageway between Swindon and Cheltenham and pushed his foot down on the accelerator, but after only a few miles, he slowed down and indicated left.

Their pace was slower on the narrow winding roads, but a breathtaking landscape stretched out before them.

Rolling green fields of spring grass were dotted with sheep and horses, and separated by a crisscross of hedges. Deciduous trees, rejuvenated with spring leaves, seemed to be cascading down hillsides or nestled in hollows.

The road followed the contours along the side of a hill with wonderful views of the countryside below them. As the terrain flattened out, David turned into a tarmac drive.

On either side, the wide grass verges were neatly mown and ancient oak trees stood solidly guarding the approach to the hotel.

Dotty glanced to her left and watched a farmer loading his sheep into a covered trailer. A sheepdog dashed from side to side behind the small flock, driving them forward and preventing any individuals from breaking away from the group.

"I understand that field will be used as a car park for the public on Saturday," David said, breaking into her thoughts. "Here we are, Charbury Castle Hotel."

The building in front of them was impressive, with a wide stone frontage, broken up by small mullioned windows, and a large round turret at the right-hand corner.

David turned left and parked in one of six spaces marked 'Visitors'. As Dotty crossed the tarmac to the front door, she looked up and noted the defensive rampart running along the top of the building, like a row of square teeth.

She followed David through the revolving entrance door into a large reception area and once again her eyes were drawn upwards following a central circular staircase which spiralled up to a glass domed roof.

She heard David say, "Good afternoon. We're looking for the television crew."

A neatly dressed receptionist, with short dark hair and a professional smile, replied, "They are in the bar. Would you like me to take you to them?"

"Just point me in the right direction," David responded with a smile and turned to his left, in the direction indicated by the receptionist.

The only people in the bar area were sitting in a rough circle around three square tables which had been pushed together.

A dark-haired man with streaks of grey running through his flowing locks stood up. He wore a pair of dark jeans with a yellow shirt and green floral cravat. He held out a hand to David and enthused, "It's great to see you. How was your recent trip?"

"Most satisfying," replied David, shaking the proffered hand, "and let me introduce Dorothy, who is helping you this weekend."

Dotty clasped her hands in front of her and looked down at the water jug and tumblers arranged on one of the tables in the centre of the group. She really wished she'd worn something more presentable.

"Dorothy, this is Max, the show's producer."

As Dotty glanced up, she noted Max's disapproval at her appearance and fought the urge to flee.

"Dorothy has been working in the auction house today, moving and cataloguing items. I'm afraid we received some rather old and dirty garden equipment." David looked across at Dotty and smiled. "But Marion told me you look charming in the dress you chose together in Cirencester."

Max's shoulders dropped, and he smiled in relief. He turned to David and enquired, "Is George joining us?"

A young woman on the far side of the group stood up. She wore black cargo pants and a cropped top with 'Value this!' written across it. Her strawberry-blonde hair was tied up in a knot on top of her head.

"Hey, how are you, Dorothy? I'm Mel, and you'll be working with me." Mel's voice had the vowelly tones of an Australian accent.

"Please, call me Dotty."

"Why don't you two grab a pew and wait for George while we finish off," suggested Max.

David led Dotty to an empty table close to the production team.

"I think that's everything for Saturday." Max addressed his crew. "Moving on to Sunday. Mel, have you found somewhere indoors to film, as the forecast is for rain?"

"Yeah, there's the room they call the library on the second floor. Not sure why as there are only a few bookcases, but it spans the front of the hotel. They use it for events and that sort of thing. Anyway, with its carved stone pillars and vaulted ceiling, it's an ideal location to shoot Sunday's detailed evaluations of the most interesting items the public brought along on Saturday."

"Good," agreed Max, nodding his head. "And is the room secure? Can we store the items there overnight?"

"I think so. And my room is close to one of the entrance doors. In fact, I think you, me and all the experts are sleeping on that floor."

One of the crew members muttered, "I wonder what Madam Zenobia will think about slumming it on the second floor with you lot?"

# CHAPTER SIX

George Carey-Boyd swept into the bar area at Charbury Castle Hotel, gushing an apology, "Max, so sorry. I was held up valuing the estate of the late Sir Reginald Adams."

Max stood and George strode across and air-kissed him on both cheeks. In a breathless tone, she asked, "What have I missed?"

"George, how lovely to see you." He stood back and held her at arm's length, assessing the bright red trouser suit she wore with poise and self-confidence. He turned to his crew.

"I think that's everything for now. I'll show George around and run through her script. David, would you like to join us?"

Dotty wondered if Max was being polite or if he was seeking reinforcements, as she suspected George's self-assurance would evaporate once nerves got the better of her.

She knew George would be professional when the cameras started rolling, just as she was when an auction started, but she was always a nervous wreck before a sale, shouting and snapping at everyone. Only David was able to calm her down.

"Dotty, come and meet the Carols," suggested Mel.

Puzzled, Dotty joined Mel and five middle-aged women, one of whom stepped forward and held out her hand for Dotty to shake. "I'm Carol, and this is Carol-Ann, Caroline, Carrie and the other Carol."

All five women smiled warmly at Dotty, who couldn't help asking, "And what is the name of the lady I'm standing in for this weekend?"

"Anthea, but she's happy being part of the Carols." Whichever 'Carol' had spoken tilted her head to one side.

Mel explained, "Dotty, your role tomorrow is to direct people to the relevant expert to evaluate whatever they've brought with them. It might be easiest to walk through it. The forecast is for a clear, sunny day, so we're setting up outside."

Mel led Dotty and the Carols out of the bar, through a side door, and across the tarmac drive which ran around the side of the hotel, into the grounds.

Dotty glanced to her right and admired the wide herbaceous borders, which stretched away to a gate in a brick wall, which she presumed was the entrance to a walled garden. She hoped she'd have the chance to look around it at some point during the weekend.

Mature trees were dotted around the grounds and the white and purple pyramidal flowers of the horse chestnut trees resembled candles nestling amongst the bright green leaves.

"One of these tents," announced Mel, indicating towards two small, white marquees erected beside the drive, "is for the furniture, which will be unloaded directly into it, or carried across from the visitor parking spaces at the front of the hotel. In the other, we'll put those items shortlisted for Sunday's evaluation."

Mel continued into the grounds. "Over there," she pointed to a white gazebo erected next to a flowering cherry tree, "is the sculptures area. I reckon the blossom will make an awesome backdrop for Zenobia. And that gazebo is for paintings and pictures."

She pointed to a gazebo erected beside a stone fountain.

"Will the water be turned on?" asked one of the Carols.

"I hope so," replied Mel.

"Then we'd better move paintings and pictures. We don't want the fountain to damage any of them. Why not put jewellery there?"

"Good idea," agreed Mel, and wrote something on the clipboard she was carrying. She looked up.

"Let's move paintings and pictures to the entrance of the rose garden. The natural arch of the hedge will provide a beauty of a backdrop, and we'll put miscellaneous artefacts in front of the stone mausoleum."

The other Carols nodded their heads in approval. One of them asked, "Where is the entrance?"

"Let me show you." They walked across the grounds towards a black, metal-railed fence which surrounded the field where the farmer had been loading sheep. Walking around another white marquee, Dotty noticed a metal pedestrian gate set in the fence.

"All the public, except those who have bulky furniture, are parking in this field." Mel turned to Dotty. "People will queue up in the gateway and enter one at a time. Either I, or one of the Carols, will greet them and direct them to the relevant receptionist. Let me see."

She lifted up a sheet of paper on her clipboard and said, "I've put you down for jewellery to start with. Your expert is Jennifer Boyle."

"She's lovely," one of the Carols remarked.

Mel strode across and stood with her back to the gate. "Imagine I'm a member of the public and I've brought a diamond necklace to be valued." She held out her hand. "I'll be greeted by me," she waved her hand up and down, "and directed to you." Mel walked towards Dotty. "You'll ask me how my journey was, or what I've brought with me as you guide me around the back of the tent, along this gravel path, to the stone fountain."

The Carols followed Dotty and Mel. They all stopped by a white gazebo with 'The Antique Tour' printed on the front in gold lettering.

Mel continued, "At this point there will be a table with a stack of A5 sized numbered cards. Take the top one, give it to me and ask me to fill out the form on the back with my name, contact details and brief description of the item. A diamond necklace, in this case.

"The number does two things. It makes it clear who is next in line, and it is handed to the expert who writes notes on the back. If the item is to be considered for Sunday's detailed evaluation, the expert will ask me to take the card and my diamond necklace to the holding tent next to the furniture tent. Does that make sense?"

Dotty wasn't entirely sure it did, but she understood her role, which was simply to take people to the tent and give them a number.

"If there's a long queue, or someone needs the loo or a cup of tea, they can leave their number on one of the chairs inside the gazebo to hold their place."

"That's right," agreed another Carol.

"Ok, ladies. Any more questions?" asked Mel.

One of the Carols asked, "Is it true Gilmore Chapman is the paintings and pictures expert? He's rather dishy."

The Carols giggled and Dotty felt her face flush.

# CHAPTER SEVEN

"You're early, Miss," said a grey-haired man wearing a high-visibility jacket on Saturday morning. "Public parking is through that gate."

"I'm with the crew," replied Dotty, hoping she looked more professional than she felt. She wore a pair of jeans, which Marion had persuaded her to buy in the boutique in Cirencester, in spite of their price tag of £79.99, and one of her husband's pink shirts, tied in a knot at her waist.

"Your name?" asked the man, consulting a clipboard.

"Dorothy Sayers."

"Like the author," stated the man, grinning.

"Just like the author." She smiled. She'd ignored such comments in the past, having never read one of Dorothy L. Sayers' detective novels, but Gilly Wimsey had given her a couple to read while she recovered from her head injury the previous autumn.

Now she was rather chuffed to be associated with the author, who she knew also liked cats.

"Here you are." He made a ticking motion on his clipboard. "Follow the sign for deliveries around the back of the house."

Dotty did as directed and grinned as she drove her little Skoda Fabia along the impressive tree-lined drive. She parked at the rear of the hotel and noted that David's car was absent, although George's black Volvo 4x4 was parked at an angle and occupied two spaces.

She noticed a side door and entered the hotel. A young couple and a family were eating breakfast in the restaurant area, but she turned away from them, weaving her way between armchairs, sofas and occasional tables to the front reception area.

Even before she reached it, she recognised the angry, raised voice of Serena De Rossi. "Madam expects the first-floor suite, to which she is accustomed to. Not a room on the second floor with the television staff."

'Madam' was sitting in an armchair on the edge of the reception area, looking bored.

"I assure you, we've given her the largest room on the second floor. The suite is occupied by a honeymoon couple tonight. Besides, all the other experts, including Gilmore Chapman, have rooms on the second floor."

Zenobia Richardson looked up at the mention of Gilmore's name. "Serena," she called, "there's no need to make a fuss. Just get the keys. I need to change, as I must look my best for the public." She stood and waved a hand airily.

"Yes, madam," replied Serena contritely, taking the two keys the receptionist had placed on the counter.

Dotty approached the reception desk and whispered, "Dotty Sayers. You should have a room reserved for me."

"Yes, Mrs Sayers. Here you are. Take the elevator to the second floor." She lowered her voice and whispered, "You're on the far side of the staircase, well away from our celebrity diva and her assistant."

Dotty smiled uncertainly and took her key.

She opened the door of her room and remained rooted to the spot. The large bed was covered in a soft purple throw, which matched the decadent floor-to-ceiling curtains. Purple was a royal colour and she certainly felt as if she was being treated like royalty.

She stepped inside and hung her dress bag in the wardrobe.

The vintage chrome alarm clock showed a quarter past nine. She was expected to meet Mel and the Carols at nine-forty five downstairs, which meant she had time for a shower in the huge walk-in one in her ensuite bathroom.

After her shower, Dotty sat on the tapestry stool at a wooden dressing table and dried her hair. She'd bought a new round hairbrush so she could curl the ends of her bob inwards and she was pleased with the result as she admired herself in the mirror.

She contemplated blusher, but it was only likely to smear during the day. Instead, she curled her lashes with a mascara wand. Now for the dress.

She fastened it around her waist but was still worried that it would open too far and expose the top of her leg, or something more. Just in case there was such a mishap, she'd bought new cream underwear.

Slipping into her green suede loafers and shrugging on her bolero jacket, she took one final turn in front of the mirror. She was impressed, but doubted anyone else would be.

As she stepped out of her room, she had the urge to walk down the ornate wooden circular staircase. She placed her hand on the smooth wooden bannister and looked down, catching her breath. The staircase spiralled below her in decreasing circles, reminding her of a whorl inside a seashell.

Gripping the bannister, she stepped forward on the red patterned carpet. She slowed her pace as she turned the last bend to face the reception area and heard the buzz of excited voices. The Carols were already assembled and three of them giggled as they spoke to a dark-haired man who had his back to her. One of the Carols looked up and smiled at her in a motherly fashion.

The dark-haired man turned with an expression of polite interest on his face and locked eyes with her. His face lit up, and he smiled broadly as Dotty felt the heat rise in her cheeks. Why had she decided to make such a public entrance when she could have used the elevator?

She carefully picked her way down the final steps, conscious of everyone watching her, and stopped in front of Gilmore Chapman.

"Beauty," called Mel in her Australian twang and the group turned to face her as she stepped out of the elevator and approached them.

"Everyone's here. Hiya, Gilmore. Do you have everything you need?"

"Just about," he replied, and Dotty wondered if she imagined his eyes resting on her. Maybe she should have worn blusher to conceal the redness that continued to colour her cheeks.

"Follow me, ladies." Mel turned towards the bar area and the Carols moved forward en masse.

Dotty felt a restraining hand on her shoulder, and she looked back at Gilmore.

"You've brightened up my morning. Will you join me for a drink later, when our work is done?"

"Sure," she stammered before dashing to catch up with her group.

As they filed out of the side door of the hotel, one of the Carols commented, "Someone's caught Gilmore's eye." Her eyes twinkled as she looked across at Dotty.

"Just keep out of Zenobia Richardson's way," another one warned. "I saw the way she eyed him up earlier."

# CHAPTER EIGHT

A s Dotty followed Mel across the hotel grounds, enjoying the warmth of the soft May sunshine, she felt excited about the day ahead, but also rather nervous.

She heard someone shout, "Oh, this is no good," and turned to see George Carey-Boyd standing in front of the hotel entrance, surrounded by cameras and the television crew.

David Rook stepped forward and placed his hands on her shoulders. Dotty wasn't sure what he said, but George nodded, and smiled awkwardly. David returned to the group and George picked up her microphone and smiled at the cameras.

Beside Dotty, one of the Carols remarked, "Nerves. But it doesn't matter if she or any of us makes a mistake in front of the cameras. It can be edited out or reshot. The only thing the film crew can't do is repair an item which one of us drops or damages. And it does happen."

Dotty didn't feel particularly reassured by her comments.

They approached the gazebo beside the cherry tree covered in an abundance of pink blossoms and Dotty breathed in the delicate vanilla, almost rose scent. She loved spring and the promise of new life.

"Madam cannot stand here all day by that tree. She will sneeze." As if to make her point, Serena De Rossi turned away from Max, the producer, and sneezed violently.

Max shook his mane of dark hair with its distinguished silver streaks. "Would Madam prefer to be dampened by the fountain or scared by the ghosts at the mausoleum?"

Serena turned back, making the sign of the cross across her chest. She looked around and demanded, "What about over there?"

"The entrance to the rose garden," considered Max. "She's not allergic to roses, is she?"

"No," snapped Serena, crossing her arms.

"Oh, very well." Max indicated towards a crew member, who was placing a wooden table in the gazebo.

One of the Carols shook her head and remarked, "I don't know why the powers that be insist on a celebrity expert for each show. They cause Max more headaches than all the other valuers put together."

"The word I have issue with is expert," a male voice with a slight lisp remarked.

"Casper," cried one of the Carols.

"Hello, sweetie. Like the outfit. Very fetching."

The Carol giggled.

Casper had spiky brown hair and a single square diamond earring, but Dotty's attention was drawn to the bright red tartan waistcoat he wore.

He must have noticed her inspecting it as he stepped towards her and introduced himself. "A new face, and a lovely one at that. I'm Casper Dupré, the furniture expert. And you are?"

"Dotty,"

"Oh, I hope not. We have enough mayhem on this show as it is," Casper guffawed, and the Carols joined in.

"Casper," growled Mel.

Dotty felt comfortable in his presence and emboldened, she asked, "What do you mean, you have trouble with the word 'expert'?"

"Zenobia Richardson has an amazing voice, or should I say, had an amazing voice. She's a bit past it now. So instead, she thinks she can waltz onto shows like this claiming to be an expert in sculptures, when it's taken the rest of us years of learning and experience to gain our status. I doubt she knows her Henry Moores from her Frederic Remingtons."

"Don't be so catty, Casper," admonished Mel.

Casper sighed. "I guess I should find my place. That'll be my tent, I suppose, by the driveway? No cherry blossom backdrop for me."

"You know you have to be close to the road for furniture deliveries," Mel said in an exasperated tone.

"Very well," he remarked as he sloped away.

Mel consulted her watch and urged, "We must get on, the gates open in twenty minutes."

They joined the gravel path and Dotty glanced to her right, to the stone fountain beside another gazebo. The fountain water had been turned on and it cascaded down over the two raised bowls into the stone pond beneath them.

She watched it, mesmerised, until she felt a soft tug on her sleeve and turned to face one of the Carols.

As they approached the entrance tent, she became aware of a steady stream of cars slowly bumping across the grassy field in front of them.

She caught a movement out of the corner of her eye and looked over at the drive as a grey pickup truck drove along with a lumpy black tarpaulin covering whatever treasures it carried.

Two of the crew were making final checks on the entrance tent, hammering in pegs, and making sure the banner on the front was straight. A man in a high-visibility jacket directed the vehicles in the field to park in a neat row in front of him. Dotty wondered how many people would come, and if the field would be large enough for all their vehicles.

As people emerged from their cars, they removed cardboard boxes, plastic bags and cloth-wrapped bundles. A small queue formed behind the entrance gate and Dotty thought she recognised the rich brown-skinned young man, third in line.

Bread popped into her mind. Of course, he, or someone very similar, had been loitering in the street in Cirencester, looking into the bakery window, when she and Marion were searching for an outfit for today.

Mel came across to Dotty and said, "If you stand here, at the end of the tent, I'll direct anyone with jewellery to you, and then you can escort them to the tent beside the fountain." She turned and addressed the Carols. "Are you all ready?"

The ladies formed a line across the tent facing the entrance gate and field. One of them smoothed down her navy skirt and another turned to Dotty and smiled.

Dotty took a deep breath as Mel opened the black metal gate, and announced, "One at a time, please. And don't push. We've time to see you all."

First through the gate was an elderly lady with curly white hair, leaning on a walking stick. "It was my mother's, you see. That's why I want to learn more about it." She rested her weight on her walking stick, removed the cloth bag hanging from her arm and passed it to Mel.

Mel lifted out a paper bundle, which she unwrapped to reveal a figurine of a dancing lady. She turned to one of the Carols, who stepped forward and took the small statue from her. "Would you like to follow me?" she said to the elderly lady.

The two women left and Dotty heard the older woman chastise, "You be careful with that. It might be valuable."

A gentleman in a navy blazer and what Dotty thought was a regimental tie stepped forward carrying a picture-shaped bundle, covered in bubble wrap.

Another of the Carols stepped forward without the need for Mel to signal her, and said, "A picture? Follow me."

The young man, with rich-brown skin, stepped through the gate and Mel asked, "What have you brought?"

"Nothing, I just want to meet Zenobia Richardson."

"I'm afraid only people with sculptures or statues can see her today."

"But …"

"No buts mate. Can't you see we're flat out here? Come back if you have something to value." Mel blocked the gateway and the young man was forced to turn round. Dotty felt sorry for him as he walked dejectedly away to a small red Honda car.

Mel looked up at a tall, dark-haired lady wearing large, round sunglasses. The woman removed a green leather case from her oversized black handbag, undid the clasp, and opened it.

Dotty wondered if she expected Mel to admire or praise it, but instead Mel turned and indicated towards Dotty.

"Would you like to come with me?" said Dotty to the lady and led her around the back of the tent and along the gravel path towards the stone fountain. She looked back at the woman and asked politely, "What have you brought to be valued?"

"Nothing of interest to you," snapped the woman.

Dotty shivered and looked up as a cloud covered the sun. Trying to ignore the dampening effect of the woman's rudeness, she glanced towards the front of the hotel where several vehicles were parked in the visitors' spaces, including the pickup truck she'd seen earlier.

The tarpaulin lay on the ground and the tailgate had been lowered. A man wearing a maroon top leaned in and pulled a table towards him.

Dotty reached the white gazebo beside the fountain. She took a number from a pile on the table and handed it to the dark-haired woman, saying politely, "Please write your name and contact details on the back, and a brief description of the item being valued."

"Can't you do that?" demanded the woman, seating herself in the front row of chairs.

"Sorry, I have other visitors to escort." She clenched her hands into fists to keep herself calm but couldn't help smiling when the woman's mouth dropped open as she turned away.

She found a young woman in her twenties, wearing jeans and a white shirt, waiting for her at the entrance tent, so she retraced her steps to the gazebo and handed her a number.

She was about to return to the entrance tent when a pleasant-looking woman, wearing a bold orange tunic and matching long velvet jacket, approached her.

She reminded Dotty of Aunt Beanie and she even held back her long grey hair with an orange headscarf.

"Darling, you must be Dotty, my helper. How delightful. I'm Jennifer and I think we're going to have lots of fun today." She winked and looked towards the gazebo by the cherry blossom tree where Gilmore Chapman was arranging a series of pictures on artists' easels.

Dotty looked down at her hands, which she clasped in front of her.

Jennifer said, "Now run along and find masses of wonderful pieces for me to value. Who knows what gems we might unearth?"

# CHAPTER NINE

The next time Dotty returned to the gazebo, Jennifer, the grey-haired jewellery expert, was examining the contents of a green leather case while the dark-haired lady, who had not removed her sunglasses, stood imperiously beside her.

"I'm very sorry, but these aren't real rubies," apologised Jennifer.

"But they must be. This necklace has been in my family for centuries. We know it was given to my distant relative by a member of Louis XIII's court."

"Then I suspect at some stage the real necklace was copied, perhaps to raise funds. It's an excellent copy, but not worth more than £500."

"Really," snapped the woman as she grabbed the case from Jennifer and strode back down the gravel path.

Jennifer joined Dotty and said, "Oh dear, I don't think my first client approved of my evaluation." She lowered her voice and confided, "I think the reason she's so disappointed is that she wanted to sell it herself."

Next time Dotty returned to Jennifer's gazebo, a camera crew was filming. Jennifer held up a bright red and green necklace. The young woman wearing jeans and a white shirt grinned with delight as Jennifer exclaimed, "It's wonderful. A Christian Dior Tutti-fruiti necklace."

"It was my grandmother's, and she bought it at a local jumble sale. I remember her wearing it, but I haven't dared as it's so intricate."

Jennifer explained, "Christian Dior was the first designer to create jewellery especially for a particular outfit or collection. See how these stones are arranged. They're like bunches of grapes, and the white ones could represent oranges or peaches."

Jennifer turned the necklace round and peered at it more closely as she moved the stones around in her hand. Her face fell.

"I'm afraid some of the stones are missing, which reduces its value considerably."

She looked up at the young woman and said, in an apologetic tone, "At auction today, I would expect it to fetch in the region of £600 to £800. If it was complete, the value would be double that, and if it was in the original case, with the earrings which were made to match it, you would be looking at closer to £5,000."

"£5,000? I would never feel able to wear it," declared the woman, "and even though £800 is a lot of money, I think Granny would prefer me to wear it, rather than hide it away in a drawer."

Smiling, the young woman thanked Jennifer and took back her necklace. The television crew stopped filming as Jennifer spotted Dotty.

"Well, that's a relief," she confided. "Not many people are happy with me valuing their jewellery at considerably less than it could be worth."

"I think I understand her relief," replied Dotty. "She can wear it now without feeling any guilt. And she can still feel special wearing a necklace designed by Christian Dior." Dotty smiled appreciatively.

"Well, when you put it like that."

Jennifer and Dotty returned to their respective posts. In the entrance tent, Mel was holding an interesting looking bronze sculpture of a blindfolded woman holding up a pair of old-fashioned balancing scales.

The muscular man in front of her, who wore a tight fitting polo shirt, had an expectant expression.

"Definitely sculptures," commented Mel and the man was led away by one of the Carols.

Dotty guided a mother and daughter towards Jennifer's tent. They each carried a plastic bag bulging with costume jewellery and Dotty didn't envy Jennifer sorting through it to see if there was anything of value.

At the jewellery tent, a gold necklace with large gold discs had been hung on a green velvet covered display board.

"Extraordinary," mused Jennifer. "I feel it should be exhibited in a museum rather than out here, in the grounds of a country hotel. What can you tell me about it?"

"My husband's father was a keen traveller, and he returned with this from one of his trips to the Middle East. I've always been intrigued by the detailing on the disks."

"Yes, the granulated rosettes," agreed Jennifer.

"But I don't know anything else about it."

Jennifer took a deep breath and squared her shoulders. "If it was a genuine Babylonian necklace, from around 600 BC, it would be extremely valuable, but I think it's more likely to be a nineteenth-century copy."

Slightly deflated, Dotty left the jewellery area. Instead of walking back to the entrance tent via the gravel path, she walked across the grass to the gazebo beside the cherry tree. She stopped to watch Gilmore as he talked animatedly to a gentleman about a picture on an easel which depicted a large ship, probably a military one, at sea.

"And this shows us ..." Gilmore looked up at Dotty and faltered. He caught her eye, smiled, and returned his attention to the man beside him.

Dotty stepped lightly back to the entrance tent, and did a double take. The young man with rich-brown skin was back, and he held a small marble bust of a veiled lady.

Mel said something to him and turned towards Dotty. "Do you mind showing this gentleman to Zenobia's tent? Carrie is taking a break."

As Dotty led the young man towards the entrance to the rose garden, she asked, "Where did you find that?"

"I bought it."

She didn't think he was being deliberately abrupt as he appeared distracted and she noted a bead of perspiration on his forehead. At the gazebo she handed him a number and said,

"Please write your contact details on the back, together with a brief description of the item you've brought to be valued."

She wasn't sure he had heard her as he was staring intently at Zenobia Richardson.

Zenobia was walking around a plinth, examining the bronze sculpture displayed upon it.

"Quite exquisite. Lady Justice, also known as Blind Justice or Scales of Justice. See how her eyes are covered with a blindfold so she cannot see the person being judged? It ensures she does not fall prey to prejudice or corruption."

The bald-headed muscular man, who Dotty remembered presenting the sculpture to Mel, wore a smug expression, which was strange.

Other members of the public were usually delighted when their objects were praised or valued highly, and some could barely contain their emotions. So why was this man so calm?

"Am I next?" asked the young man beside her.

She turned back to him. "I'm afraid not. You'll have to wait for your turn. All these people," she indicated towards the men, women and some children, sitting on chairs inside the gazebo, "are before you."

The young man's shoulders slumped as he took a seat.

Zenobia's voice was rising in volume and pitch. "If this is genuine, which it certainly could be, I'd value it in the several millions, even tens of millions of pounds."

Many of those sitting in the gazebo who had been listening intently jumped to their feet and clapped. The television camera panned across them, capturing the excitement of the discovery.

Elsewhere on the grounds, people stopped and looked towards them.

# CHAPTER TEN

I t had taken Dotty several minutes to register the enormity of Zenobia's words and she was still staring at the bronze statue, displayed on the plinth, when she heard David Rook say, "That's what all the fuss is about."

She turned to him and asked, "How can it be worth so much? It's so ... small."

"Needless to say, if it is from the Roman period, then it is a couple of thousand years old, but age isn't everything. Scarcity is the dominant factor. The Greeks and the Romans valued art and created numerous bronze statues and sculptures, but most of them have been melted down."

David was interrupted by one of the Carols who said, in a breathless voice, "Dotty, there you are. I've been looking for you. Mel says it's your turn for a break. Can you be back at the entrance tent at two?"

"Excellent," responded David. "I'm also on a break. Shall we?" He indicated with his arm to a path leading away from the rose garden. "Drinks and a buffet lunch have been set up for the crew in a tent towards the back of the hotel."

As they wandered across the grounds, Dotty watched the activity around the various gazebos.

All was quiet and orderly at Jennifer's jewellery tent, beside the fountain, and Gilmore was discussing a landscape painting, resting on an easel, with an elderly couple outside his gazebo beside the rose garden.

As they approached the furniture tent, two men wearing maroon polo shirts carried in a large grandfather clock. Dotty shivered.

"Are you all right?" asked David.

"I have an aversion to grandfather clocks. Bad memories."

"Understandable," muttered David.

"So, returning to the subject of sculptures. Age is not the major factor in considering their value. Scarcity is, as well as perceived quality and the notoriety or fame of the sculptor. Artists more famous for their paintings like Picasso, Matisse and Degas, have had their sculptures sell for millions."

They stopped to watch Casper, the furniture expert, and David chuckled, "Just like Casper to wear a bright red tartan waistcoat. He hates being upstaged, especially by someone like Zenobia Richardson, who I'm sure he doesn't consider a real expert."

Casper was inspecting a mahogany table.

"He said as much earlier," Dotty confirmed as Casper began his evaluation.

"We have here an Irish silver table, dating back to George II, so around 1740. It's very attractive with this raised moulded edge, and beneath it this charming floral frieze design."

"There's going to be a but," whispered David.

"But what I'm most surprised about is its condition, which is excellent. Irish fires were notoriously peaty and furniture like this is usually blackened from the soot."

A debonair middle-aged man laughed, "It was rather dirty when I bought it so I had it stripped down and restored to its original splendour."

Casper tilted his head to one side and said in a disappointed voice, "What a shame."

The debonair man braced himself. "What do you mean?"

"The soot, and the wear and tear are part of the character of a piece like this. In its original state, it would be likely to make, at auction, between £8,000 and £12,000. But now it's been restored, it's unlikely to fetch more than £3,000."

The debonair man was speechless, but his eyes bulged and his cheeks reddened.

"Time for lunch," announced David, and he guided Dotty behind the furniture tent and along the tarmac drive to another marquee, near the entrance to the walled garden.

They helped themselves to wilted sandwiches and sausage rolls which, when Dotty bit into one, seemed to be all roll and no sausage. But she was very grateful for a cup of tea.

"That's better," remarked David. "It's nice to sit down for five minutes. I find these events fascinating, but they are draining. A few minutes' peace is just what I need."

"Peace, don't be ridiculous," broke in Casper. "All you need is a stiff drink. What would you two like? My round."

"Too early for me, Casper," responded David.

Dotty picked up her teacup. "I'm happy with this, thank you."

"Suit yourselves."

Casper sashayed away but returned only a few minutes later with a glass of what smelt to Dotty like whisky. He sat down at their table, raised his glass and pronounced, "Chin chin."

He took a large mouthful, savouring the flavour, and looked from Dotty to David. "So, can you believe our celebrity sculpture expert has unearthed a priceless treasure? Who would have believed it?"

"Do you think it's genuine?" asked David in a sceptical tone.

"I don't see why not. Unlike that forgery which was only discovered after Gilmore's auction house sold it for millions, the clothing and details appear authentic on this bronze. I can't wait to inspect it later. But what gems have you two discovered?"

David sat up and his eyes shone. "An elderly lady, rather a character actually, brought me a late nineteenth century rhinoceros horn side-saddle whip, with an engraved gilt-brass handle. She was absolutely delighted with my valuation of £1,000 to £1,500.

"Said she rode with the local hunt with it for fifty years." He turned to Dotty, "And what about you, my dear? You were there when Zenobia announced her valuation of the statue, but has anything else caught your eye?"

"I've been escorting people to the jewellery tent most of the time. There was an unusual gold necklace with large gold disks. Babylonian, I think Jennifer said, but she thought it a modern replica rather than the real thing."

"I wonder," mused David.

"Righty-ho," announced Casper, jumping to his feet. "No rest for the wicked," and he strutted out of the refreshment tent.

# CHAPTER ELEVEN

Dotty and the other Carols searched the grounds for any loitering members of the public early on Saturday evening and escorted them to the car park.

"I think that's everyone," announced Mel. "Good on ya for today. It's been flat out. There's one last job left."

"I love this bit, even though I'm a bag of nerves and worry I'll drop something," enthused one of the Carols.

"That's right. We need to move all the items short-listed for tomorrow's detailed evaluations to the library on the second floor."

"That sounds a long way. Isn't there anywhere to store them on the ground floor?" suggested another Carol.

"No. Besides, we can keep an eye on them as we're all sleeping on the second floor, and we won't have to move them in the morning as we're filming in the library."

The group made their way up the gravel path and across the grass to the two tents beside the drive. Two men wearing maroon polo shirts, with Vintage Removals embroidered on them, approached Mel and said, "We've moved the clock, desk and chair upstairs as instructed. Is that all?"

"Yes, thank you," Mel replied before leading the Carols to the second tent, which Dotty hadn't been in, and announcing, "Come in."

Dotty thought the words 'open sesame' would have been more appropriate, as the treasures inside the tent made her think of Ali Baba's cave, but something was missing.

"Where's the statue?" she asked, her chest tightening. Had someone stolen it? And if so, would she and the Carols be blamed?

"Max took it upstairs himself, so he and the other experts could examine it more closely."

"You mean they don't trust Zenobia's opinion," someone called out, and the Carols sniggered.

Mel's eye narrowed. "This could be a very important discovery and the show needs to verify the statue is authentic before announcing it on TV."

Suitably chastised, the Carols each picked up an item to carry to the library. Dotty was surprised to see the gold Babylonian necklace hanging on a green velvet display board and she wondered if Jennifer had changed her mind, and decided it was an original and not a modern replica.

She carefully picked it up and carried it inside.

The library extended the entire width of the hotel and was part of the original castle, with small mullioned windows facing the front drive, and carved stone columns and a stone vaulted ceiling.

As Mel had said the previous day, there were only three bookshelves located at one end, but the curved seats wrapped around the interior of the circular turret near them looked very inviting. She would happily find a book and curl up in there to read it.

"Over here, Dotty," called Mel.

Dotty made sure the necklace's display board stood securely on the white-clothed table. Beside it there was an attractive circular art deco ring.

Mel saw her looking at it and confided, "There's a wonderfully romantic story accompanying that ring, and it's valuable too."

Dotty looked at Mel with surprise. She hadn't taken her for the romantic type.

Further along the table, the Carols placed a gilt-topped whip, which was probably the one David had enthused about earlier, a box which contained five Dinky toy racing cars, and a mahogany novelty sewing box in the shape of a piano.

They had to make a second trip to bring up the remaining items which included two large paintings, one a portrait, and the other an unattractive arrangement of dead pheasants and fruit on a table, and a series of five collages which looked as if they had been created from newspaper and magazine cuttings.

"Let's call it a day, ladies," declared Mel. "We'll meet downstairs in the restaurant for supper at seven thirty. In the meantime, if anyone fancies a cold one, I'm heading to the bar."

"Good idea, darling. Are you paying?" called Crispin as he walked into the library, followed by the other experts.

Max was at the back and he skirted the group, carrying the bronze sculpture of Lady Justice, which he placed on a plinth, already positioned in the centre of the room.

Stepping back to admire it, he pronounced, "Perfect." Turning to Mel, he said, "I'll join you. The excitement of this statue has created quite a thirst."

Dotty kneaded her hands in front of her. Would it be rude not to join the others in the bar? As well as the large walk-in shower, her ensuite bathroom had a luxurious bath with jets. Lying in it would be like having her own personal hot tub.

"You look happy."

Dotty looked up into Gilmore Chapman's eyes and blushed guiltily.

"Sorry, I was envisaging a relaxing bath." As she said it, her feet began to ache. "I've been on my feet all day. What about you? Are you going for a drink?"

"I ought to, unless I receive a better offer." He raised his eyebrows.

Dotty bit her lip.

Gilmore placed his hand on her back and guided her out of the library. "I tell you what. Why don't you meet me downstairs in the bar at seven? That way you can enjoy your bath and then I can enjoy your company, without the rest of the crew."

Dotty wondered what to wear. She hadn't counted on needing a separate outfit for supper and didn't want to wear the dress she'd worn during the day, as it was sweaty and had a mark on the bottom.

But she didn't want to risk spilling soup or a drink on the one she was wearing tomorrow.

That left her new jeans. Would she be too casual? She searched around in her green canvas overnight bag and found a cream linen top.

She had been attracted by the red and yellow flowers, embroidered down the front and across the top of the sleeves, as it hung on a rail in one of the vintage clothes concessions, in Akemans antiques centre.

As she removed it from her bag, she became aware of shouting outside her room. Quickly, she pulled the top over her head and dashed to her door, opening it and looking out.

Raised female voices emanated from the room on the far side of the open staircase. Was that Zenobia Richardson's room?

The door opened and Serena De Rossi stalked out, her elegant face the same colour as her fiery hair. "That's it. I'm leaving."

Leaving for good, or just for tonight, wondered Dotty.

Serena turned and caught her watching. "Yes. What do you want?" She spun on her heels and walked deliberately down the staircase, her back straight and her head held high.

Dotty looked around, but nobody else seemed to have heard the altercation. She returned to her room and slipped on her green suede shoes. They felt tight and the top of her little toe rubbed against the suede.

Hopefully, she could slip them off during supper without causing offence.

She decided against following Serena down the staircase and took the more discreet elevator to the ground floor.

Gilmore was already seated at a corner table in the bar. He stood and smiled at her and she thought how relaxed he looked in his pale yellow, opened-necked shirt.

He asked, "What would you like to drink?"

# CHAPTER TWELVE

D otty and Gilmore Chapman walked into the hotel restaurant. The red carpet that covered the central staircase extended through the reception area into the dining room.

Matching full-length curtains appeared at intervals along the two external walls and tables covered in white cloths, set for two or four people, were dispersed around the room.

In one corner, a mother and father were attempting to engage their three teenage children whose heads were bent over their electronic devices. They only lifted them when two waitresses approached and placed large round plates before them. An aroma of rich, pungent roast meat tingled Dotty's nostrils.

"Roast venison," observed Gilmore.

"A little too rich for my taste," commented David as he joined them, wearing a navy blazer and blue-checked shirt. "But I understand wood pigeon is one of the restaurant's specialities."

He looked around the grand room. "I'm pleased they've kept some of the previous owner's paintings. What do you think, Gilmore?"

David and Gilmore strode across to examine a large painting of a landscape in an ornate gilt frame. Dotty followed them, but stopped beside a table set for fourteen.

They were soon joined by other crew members.

"Sweetie, you were marvellous today. Such a shame you can't be a regular," enthused Jennifer, the jewellery expert, who was resplendent in a lush green velvet coat, which reached down to the floor, and her silver hair shone in the light cast by fan-shaped art deco wall lights.

Dotty was starting to feel considerably underdressed until Mel walked in, wearing a pair of fawn cargo pants and a black T-shirt with 'Do Not Touch the Artwork' printed on it.

"Like the T-shirt, Mel," remarked Max, who had followed her into the dining room. He had cultivated his producer image well and tonight he was dressed entirely in black, which somehow enhanced his thick mane of dark hair with its silver streaks.

He looked around the group and observed, "So we're waiting for the Carols, Crispin, Zenobia, and her assistant Serena."

Zenobia clearly liked to make an entrance as she swept into the dining room wearing a full length, midnight-blue satin skirt with a matching sequin top. "So sorry to keep you all waiting. Unfortunately, Serena can't join us tonight."

"Is she ill?" enquired Mel.

"Nothing she won't recover from by the morning."

Serena had looked far from ill when Dotty had last seen her.

"Oh, dear, that makes thirteen," worried Max.

"Fabulous," cried Casper as he approached them, his arm around a bald-headed man whose pectoral muscles strained against his white T-shirt. "There's room for Emery. He's the owner of the bronze statue and is staying in the hotel tonight to keep an eye on his treasure."

"Delighted," responded Max. "I'm sure the television company can stretch towards buying dinner for the owner of the star of our show."

At that moment, the gaggle of Carols appeared giggling. "Oh, Casper, do introduce us to your handsome friend."

Emery bowed his head as Casper introduced him.

Dotty sympathised with Emery as she usually clammed up in the company of others and hoped nobody would notice her.

The Carols swept Casper and Emery to the far end of the table, and Max stood behind the chair at the head of the table.

Gilmore pulled out the chair on Max's left and looked enquiringly at Dotty.

"Always such a gentleman, Gilmore," enthused Zenobia as she stepped in front of the chair, waiting for him to push it forward. "And you'll join me?" She tapped the empty seat beside her.

Mel was already sitting on the other side of Max, opposite Zenobia, so David stood behind the chair to her right and said, "Dotty," indicating the empty chair next to him.

Jennifer completed the table, sitting beside Gilmore, opposite Dotty.

"Are you a vegetarian?" she asked, but before Dotty had time to reply, she continued, "Well, even if you're not, I recommend the spinach and ricotta cannelloni. It's rich and creamy, and fabulous when accompanied by a rocket salad with cherry tomatoes."

"Of course, the pasta in England can't touch the dishes served in Italy. I remember ..." but Zenobia was interrupted by Max, who called, "Waiter."

The waiter approached and Max instructed, "Two bottles of champagne, no, make it Prosecco if we're in an Italian mood."

Zenobia bridled. "There's nothing wrong with champagne."

"Except the cost," whispered David to Dotty. "And Zenobia's rather partial to champagne, and if she starts with it, she insists on drinking it for the entire meal. That was quick thinking on Max's part."

Gilmore looked across at Dotty and said, "I'm told the seafood dishes are very good."

Dotty glanced down at her leather-bound menu and turned the page to 'Main Course'. There were salmon and smoked haddock fishcakes, served with a chive herb sauce, a soft boiled egg and watercress, or tempura prawns with a sweet chilli sauce served with grilled asparagus.

"What do you recommend for me?" demanded Zenobia, batting her eyelashes at Gilmore. "For an experienced woman of the world?"

Gilmore, who was in the process of sipping a glass of recently poured Prosecco, choked. "Sorry, must be the bubbles."

He looked across at Dotty again and asked, "Anything take your fancy?"

At the other end of the table, Casper guffawed. He downed his glass of Prosecco and held it up to the waiter to refill. "I'm sure she does, you old goat."

Zenobia tapped Gilmore's arm. "Leave the child be. She's only staff."

There was a collective gasp from the Carols, followed by tutting and one of them remarked," At least her best days are ahead of her."

Zenobia ignored the jibe but David, who had been discussing the opening of a new art gallery in New York with Mel and Max, drawled, "Zenobia, we are all staff under the definition of the word, as we are employed by the television company and you, my dear, are paid more than the rest of us."

Casper, who was half-way through his second glass of Prosecco, called, "Anyway, we all know how you treat your staff."

Zenobia closed her eyes, pinched her lips, and looked away from him.

A white-jacketed waiter approached and, with his pen poised over his pad, asked, "Are you ready to order?"

Zenobia picked up her menu and, without waiting for anyone else, declared, "For starter, the seared scallops with truffle beurre blanc, followed by the lobster Thermidor."

Dotty looked down at her menu. She hadn't realised they would be ordering a starter. She turned back the pages in her menu. The scallops were by far the most expensive item.

She glanced further down and noticed the duck liver mandarin parfait, accompanied by orange chutney and toasted brioche. She made her own chicken liver pate, but this sounded far more exotic, so she decided to try it.

After they'd ordered, the volume of conversation around the table increased. Dotty chatted to Jennifer across the table, fascinated by the countries she'd visited to increase her knowledge of jewellery as she searched for unique pieces.

Gilmore had joined the discussion about art museums with David, Max and Mel.

Dotty looked across at Zenobia, whose shoulders sagged, and she seemed to have shrunk into her chair.

Knowing how lonely it felt to be ignored, Dotty asked, "Zenobia, have you ever visited Venice? I'd love to stay there and explore the canals and admire the architecture."

"Mia Cara, visit? Why I lived there for three glorious years singing in La Fenice, and at outdoor venues during the balmy summer evenings."

"And you were brilliant," added David. "I was fortunate to hear you sing Tosca."

Zenobia smiled graciously. The waiter arrived with their starters and there was an outburst of laughter from the far end of the table where Crispin had his arm around Emery.

"Crispin's taken rather a liking to our sculpture owner," commented Max.

"Looks to me like they're on a date," added Mel.

Zenobia glanced down the table. "It does rather." She wore a thoughtful expression.

"Tuck in, before it gets cold," chided Jennifer.

Dotty turned to the Carol beside her, who she discovered was actually called Carrie, and they chatted contentedly about filming other episodes of the show and the amusing incidents Carrie had witnessed.

Every so often, Dotty glanced across at Zenobia, who had become increasingly withdrawn. She kept glancing down the table at Casper, who was entertaining the other Carols and Emery.

But when, after their dessert plates had been cleared away, Max called for the waiter to bring the port, she rallied.

Turning to Gilmore she said, "I was interested in those collages you chose. They're not your usual style."

"No, they're not, but there's an interesting story behind them."

As Gilmore enthusiastically regaled Zenobia, David turned to Dotty and said, "You look exhausted. Do you want to go up to your room?"

"Thank you, but I'll wait until everyone else leaves. I don't want to break up the party."

After the port had been passed around the table, in a clockwise direction at Gilmore's insistence, and consumed, Max rose. "I'm going to the bar if anyone wants to join me for a nightcap."

The Carols immediately pushed back their chairs. "Not missing this chance, not if Max is paying."

Zenobia purred to Gilmore, "I've a fully stocked drinks cabinet in my room. Why don't you join me and tell me all about the portrait you've reserved for tomorrow's filming?"

Dotty pushed back her own chair and Gilmore looked up at her, his forehead wrinkling.

"Well, I ..." he began.

"I won't take no for an answer," asserted Zenobia. "Come on."

Dotty turned to David and said, "I'll turn in now. I presume tomorrow will be another long day?"

"There'll be less for you to do, but it will involve plenty of hanging around as the film crew manoeuvre themselves for the close-up shots."

Close-up shots. "Where's George? Isn't she staying at the hotel?"

"No, she went home."

Jennifer came and stood beside David. "Thankfully. One diva is quite enough. Come on, David, let me buy you a drink. I want to hear all about your recent trip."

As they left the dining room, Dotty heard David say, "George isn't that bad."

"She's better when you're around. But she'll be that nervous about tomorrow, and Casper winds her up terribly."

Dotty left the restaurant and thought of the luxurious bed in her room. She was looking forward to a good night's sleep.

# CHAPTER THIRTEEN

Dotty's bedroom was at the end of the corridor, next to one of two doors leading into the library. She remembered the bookcases and carefully opened the library door.

Switching on a light for her section of the long room, she glanced over to the collection of antiques, which were illuminated by dim moonlight from the small mullioned windows.

She stepped inside the circular turret, whose curtainless window looked out over the shadowy hotel grounds.

Was someone out there? Did something move beside one of the trees? But as she continued to stare, everything remained still. She was just being silly, but even so, she shivered and returned to the bookshelves.

Tilting her head so she could read the titles on the spines, she found a book entitled *The History of Charbury Castle*. She plucked it from the shelf and returned to her room, remembering to switch off the library light.

A light still shone under Zenobia's door, on the opposite side of the large, open staircase, beside the second library door. Was Gilmore still there? She heard a deep murmur, followed by Zenobia's laugh. Clearly he was.

Surprised by a pulling sensation in her gut, she reprimanded herself. Gilmore was a distinguished art expert who wouldn't be seriously interested in someone like her. Besides, he was probably married.

As she entered her room, she wondered why she hadn't asked him about his family, but then their conversation had always remained on a professional level.

Dotty undressed and, as she climbed between the crisp sheet and plush duvet, she squirmed with delight. She turned on the bedside light, leaned against the plump pillows and opened the book from the library. The opening chapters detailed the construction of the original castle and she read quickly until she came to a section entitled 'Ghosts of Charbury'.

She was wondering whether to read it when she heard a creaking on the other side of her door and, as she glanced over, a shadow fell across the gap at the bottom. Who or what was outside?

After a minute, although it seemed far longer as she was holding her breath, the shadow moved and light once again seeped into her room. Two women laughed loudly.

She realised her pulse was racing. Was it from anticipation or fright? Unsure, she decided to skip the ghost section of the book and instead read about the gardens.

She must have dropped off as she woke with a start and found the bedside light still on, and the book she had been reading open on the floor. Climbing out of bed, she bent to pick it up when she heard a scraping noise. She froze.

It sounded as if it had come from outside the hotel. Glancing across at the full-length purple curtains pulled across her window, she climbed back into bed, turned off the bedside light and pulled the duvet over her head.

When she woke again, the light under her bedroom door was dim and the hotel appeared still and quiet. Wondering what had woken her this time, she climbed out of bed and tip-toed to the bedroom door.

Opening it, she looked down the shadowy corridor and thought she caught the movement of a door closing. Then all was still.

Glancing across the open staircase, a dim light seeped under Zenobia's door, but a much brighter light shone out below the adjacent library door.

As she watched, the library door opened, and Dotty pulled back, closing her door until only an inch-wide gap remained. "Goodnight," she heard a man's deep voice murmur and as she slowly opened the door again, she saw a figure walk steadily down the gloomy corridor. Was it David? If so, what had he been doing in the library and who else was in there?

Still wondering, Dotty returned to her bed, hoping there would be no more night-time disturbances.

Dotty rubbed her eyes with the back of her hand. Disoriented, she looked around and remembered she was not in her cottage at Meadowbank Farm, but in a room at Charbury Castle Hotel. Daylight seeped around the edges of the thick purple curtains.

What time was it? Had she slept in? And what had woken her?

She heard someone call, "What's happened? Did someone scream?"

Someone else shouted, "Go back to bed. It's only quarter to six."

Dotty sat up, feeling more awake. She knew she wouldn't go back to sleep now, but she could hardly get up and wander around the hotel. It was too early. She pulled back the curtains and looked up at the stormy skies and down at the ground, which glistened with recent rainfall.

Turning back to the room, she spotted the kettle and sachets of tea and coffee. As the kettle boiled, she searched for milk. She'd expected small sealed plastic pots of UHT milk, but to her delight, she discovered a fridge, hidden behind a door in the desk and inside it a jug of fresh milk.

She took her tea back to bed and returned to the 'Ghosts of Charbury' section of the book she'd borrowed from the library.

Over the past two hundred years, there had been several sightings of a ghostly woman at the bottom of the circular staircase. Although the original staircase had been destroyed in the fire, along with most of the castle, the London businessman who rebuilt Charbury insisted the new staircase should replicate the original one.

The ghost was thought to be that of Lady Violet Waltham who, at the tender age of sixteen, had married the Duke of Waltham, a man in his forties renowned for his violent temper, especially after a few drinks.

Lady Violet fell in love with Robert Loughborough, the son of one of the Duke's friends, the two having met when Robert and his family stayed at Charbury. Robert arranged for Violet to run away with him, but the night she tried to leave, the Duke had been playing a late night game of cards and he caught her leaving her room, fully dressed.

Robert was waiting in the hall, and when he heard the Duke's shouts, he rushed up the staircase to rescue Violet. A terrible fight ensued with both men trying to grab Violet, who was caught between them. Nobody seemed to know exactly what happened, but Violet fell over the balustrade and hit the stone floor below, where she died.

Dotty put the book down, both fascinated and appalled. Perhaps reading the chapter on ghosts had not been a good idea this morning. She padded into the bathroom and turned the shower on.

After her shower she dried herself and, although it was only quarter to seven, she slipped on the second wrap-around dress and tied a neat bow at her waist. What time did breakfast start?

She sat down at the dressing table and, repeating the actions of the previous morning, carefully dried and brushed her hair into its neat bob. As she turned the hairdryer off, she heard a hammering on her door.

"Dotty, are you in there?"

It sounded like Gilmore, but his voice was strained and high-pitched.

"Come in. The door's open and I'm dressed." Well, nearly. Her bolero jacket hung on a hanger from the open wardrobe door and she wasn't sure where her green suede shoes were. She pivoted round on the tapestry stool to face the door as it opened.

"You're all right," gasped Gilmore breathlessly. He wore a long sleeve navy-blue t-shirt and red and blue checked pyjama bottoms. His feet were bare.

Dotty wrinkled her brow. "Of course, I'm all right."

David appeared, fully dressed with a pale blue shirt, silver tie and charcoal grey waistcoat. "Dotty's safe and sound?"

"Yes," replied Gilmore.

"Will someone tell me what's going on?" insisted Dotty.

"Didn't the receptionist call you? A woman's body's been discovered at the bottom of the staircase," explained David.

"But she wouldn't tell us whose," added Gilmore. "Just that we have to remain on the second floor until the police arrive, and breakfast will be served in the library."

"Lady Violet," breathed Dotty.

"Who?" enquired Gilmore.

Dotty shook herself. "Sorry, I was reading a book about the history of Charbury, and the ghost of Lady Violet Waltham, who died after falling over the bannister of the central staircase."

David and Gilmore exchanged glances.

David said, "I don't think this is a ghost, or a body from the past."

"Zenobia," shouted a woman with an Australian twang. "Where is Zenobia?"

Gilmore and David both turned towards Dotty's open door. Barefooted, and still holding her new hairbrush, Dotty followed them.

She watched Max enter Zenobia's room but return a minute later. He looked across at David, Gilmore and Dotty and shook his head. "She's not there, and her bed's not been slept in."

# CHAPTER FOURTEEN

Dotty, the other crew members of *The Antique Tour* television show, and Emery, the owner of the bronze statue of Lady Justice, gathered together in the library at Charbury Castle Hotel.

The hotel had brought up two tables and laid a buffet breakfast out on one, and tea, coffee, and fruit juices on the other.

"Any chance of a Bloody Mary?" Crispin muttered to a waiter, who placed a flask on one of the tables and positioned a plastic sign with 'hot water' in front of it.

"I'll see what I can do."

"Bring a jug then, I'm sure I'm not the only one who needs a pick-me-up." Crispin surveyed the room, but nobody responded.

Dotty poured herself a cup of tea, picked up a croissant, which she placed in a paper napkin, and carried them both to one of several chairs arranged along the outer wall.

Max was pacing the room between the two entrance doors, and Mel was examining the antiques. David, Gilmore and Jennifer huddled close together, their heads bowed.

The Carols had pulled their chairs into a circle and, after raiding the buffet, they sat silently eating pastries and bowls of fruit salad.

"David," a female voice shouted.

The room fell silent.

"Max," the voice called again.

Dotty stood up and looked out of the mullioned window beside her.

George Carey-Boyd stood at the front of the hotel, wearing a raincoat and looking up at her. George waved, but a uniformed police officer strode over to her.

Dotty did not catch what he said but he indicated to the visitors' parking area where other figures huddled under stripy umbrellas.

The policeman turned away and George looked up at Dotty and pointed towards the side of the hotel, away from the area where the television show had been filmed the previous day.

Dotty made her way along the library to the room in the turret. She found the window partially open, so she pushed it wider and looked down at George.

George shouted, "What's happening? Why are the police here? They won't let me come up." The hood of her raincoat slipped back to reveal her blonde hair.

Dotty called back. "There's been an accident. A woman's body has been found and we're all confined to the second floor. All except Zenobia. We can't find her. Is she down there?"

David joined Dotty in the turret room and asked, "Who are you shouting at?"

"It's George. The police won't let her in."

Dotty stood back to allow David access to the window.

"Georgina. You mustn't stand out there like that. You'll get soaked."

"What about the filming?"

"It won't happen at the moment. Neither you nor the film crew are allowed up here."

Dotty looked around the compact room. She felt like a princess locked in a tower. She looked out of the window, over David's shoulder, as a metallic grey Mercedes appeared and stopped next to George.

Dotty groaned as the bulky figure of Inspector Evans emerged, a dark windcheater jacket falling open over his habitual brown suit.

Dotty hadn't realised how thin the hair on top of his head was, but it was clear from this angle that he combed it over in an attempt to hide his bald patch.

"Mrs Carey-Boyd," his deep melodic Welsh voice easily carried up to the turret window. "I'm not being funny, but why are you standing out in the rain shouting up at your colleagues?

That receptionist of yours is not Rapunzel. She won't be dangling her hair out of the window for you to climb up."

Dotty straightened up. How had the inspector known she was up here?

"Just a minute, Sergeant," called the inspector and, intrigued, Dotty leaned back down and looked out of the window.

She hoped her friend Constable Varma would forgive her for not sending a card to congratulate her on her promotion. The constable had cancelled last month's theatre trip as she had been revising for her sergeant's exams.

The engine stopped, but instead of a female figure emerging from the car, a dark-haired, dark-suited man appeared.

"Sergeant, what do you make of this?" called Inspector Evans, indicating to the ground at the base of the turret.

Dotty felt a thickness in her throat. Constable Varma hadn't been promoted, and she hadn't been there to console her. What sort of friend was she?

"What is it?" asked George in an authoritative tone as she joined the policemen at the bottom of the tower.

"It looks like footprints, from a pair of trainers," replied the sergeant.

"Young man. The locals round here, particularly those who work at a certain antiques centre," Inspector Evans looked up at the open window and Dotty blushed, "have a habit of interfering with police investigations. I'd appreciate it if you didn't give them information, I would."

The inspector turned away from his sergeant and faced George, who crossed her arms over her chest. "At least members of my staff solve crimes," she deliberately slowed down to articulate the last two words. "What's your excuse?"

Dotty was not sure if she'd actually heard the inspector growl, but George lowered her arms and stepped back. She muttered, "Anyway, when can I join the television crew?"

"What television crew?" asked the inspector, looking wildly around him.

"The one that's staying here to film an edition of *The Antique Tour*. Have you locked them in the tower as well?"

Dotty heard one of the Carols cry, "An ambulance."

She left David in the turret and returned to the library, joining other members of the crew as they gathered around the mullioned windows.

She found a space next to Jennifer, who she wasn't sure was dressed or still wearing her night attire, as she wore a flowing grey silk kimono, with large bold prints of tulips, over a green silk top.

Beside her, Mel wore a black fleece with 'The Antique Tour', printed on the back in gold lettering.

Peering down, she watched the lemon yellow roof of an ambulance reverse towards the hotel entrance. Two crew members climbed out wearing moss green uniforms and disappeared from view.

They soon returned, climbed back into the ambulance and reversed it down the drive and around the side of the hotel towards the walled garden.

"Where are they going?" asked Jennifer.

"They can't get a stretcher through the revolving door, so they must be using the side entrance by the bar," replied Mel.

Dotty helped herself to another cup of tea, having abandoned her first cup when she went to the turret to talk to George.

"Good idea," said David as he joined her. "I need a coffee, even if it is a dreadful hotel brew."

"What is George going to do?" asked Dotty.

"After the police left, I suggested she try the door by the dining room. At least inside the hotel she can dry off and wait in some comfort for us to be released."

The library door opened and the sergeant who had accompanied Inspector Evans entered.

All conversation stopped and everyone turned to face him as a Carol cooed, "Oh, he's dishy."

His cheeks reddening, the sergeant cleared his throat and announced, "The inspector apologises for keeping you waiting."

"Quite right, so he should, keeping us shut up in here," complained Casper. Then he grinned and added, "He's no idea what mischief we might get up to." He gave the sergeant a flirtatious look.

Gilmore approached the young sergeant and Dotty heard him ask, "Is it possible to return to my room to shower, shave and change? I'd rather not meet your inspector still dressed in my pyjamas."

The sergeant pulled at the sleeve of his jacket and looked around the room at the expectant faces. He pushed his shoulders back and lifted his chin. "Ladies and gentlemen, if you would like to return to your rooms to change, I suggest you go now."

One of the Carols jumped up and dashed towards the door. "After all that tea, I need the bathroom."

"Ah, here's the waiter with my Bloody Mary. Who's going to join me?" asked Crispin.

The rest of the crew ignored him as they scrambled for the exit. Finally, the library doors closed, leaving Crispin and Emery sipping Bloody Marys as they wandered between the antiques still displayed in the room.

The sergeant looked rather perplexed and Dotty, who was pleased she had already dressed for the day, wondered what Inspector Evans would have to say when he learnt that the crew had been allowed to leave.

Timidly she walked towards the sergeant and asked, "Would you like a tea or coffee while you wait?"

He focused on her, looked her up and down, and smiled. "Thank you. That's exactly what I need. Strong and black, please."

She walked across to the drinks table. Was it her imagination, or was he staring at her? Never mind, this was her chance to find out more about the body downstairs.

She returned and handed the sergeant a cup, as he stared at Crispin and Emery. She opened her mouth to speak, but he asked, "Who is that couple?"

"They're not a couple," laughed Dotty.

The sergeant raised his eyebrows sceptically.

"No, Crispin is the furniture expert for the show and Emery, well I guess you can call him the star of the show, although Zenobia might disagree."

"Why?"

"He brought that bronze sculpture they're looking at now to be evaluated yesterday and Zenobia valued it in the millions."

"What?" cried the sergeant, splashing coffee on his jacket. "For that?"

"It's old, Roman in fact, so very rare." Dotty decided this was the time to ask about the body.

"Is it true a woman was found dead this morning at the bottom of the staircase?"

"Yes, a hotel cleaner found her when she started her morning shift." The sergeant dabbed his jacket with a tissue.

"And do you know how she died?" Dotty asked in an innocent voice.

"There was a pool of blood around her head, but we'll have to wait for a post-mortem for more details."

"Poor woman," Dotty shook her head. "I wonder who she was? Her family must be devastated."

"Oh, she didn't have any family, at least none that we are aware of?"

"How can you be so sure?"

"When someone famous dies, it's easy to discover almost everything about their life with a quick search on the internet. And I'm pretty sure Zenobia Richardson was all alone."

# CHAPTER FIFTEEN

"Sergeant Onion, have you found a room for us to conduct our interviews?"

"Onion?" repeated Dotty, staring at the sergeant.

The young sergeant rolled his eyes. "Unwin."

Dotty turned to the inspector and smiled impishly. "Sergeant Unwin," she carefully enunciated his name, "was asking if you could use my room as it's closest to the library, apart from Zenobia's, but you won't be allowing anyone in there."

"And why is that?" The inspector narrowed his eyes.

Dotty faltered, gulped and replied, in a slightly higher pitch, "Because she's missing. None of us have seen her this morning."

The inspector peered at her and then shook his head. "All right, show me your room."

"Just a minute. I'll remove my things." Dotty scampered out of the library as she heard Inspector Evans declare, "I'm not being funny, but all our suspects have vanished, they have."

Suspects, thought Dotty as she brushed her teeth and returned her toiletries to her spongebag. So the inspector did think the death was suspicious.

When Dotty returned to the library most of the crew were back. She carefully folded her dress carrier over the back of a chair and placed her green canvas bag on the floor. She handed the keys to the sergeant and said, "All yours."

He raised his eyebrows and grinned.

Dotty blushed.

Max asked, in a loud clear voice, "Inspector, please can you tell us what is going on? We've a full day's filming to complete, but we can't start without the crew, George Carey-Boyd or Zenobia."

The inspector cleared his throat. "I regret to inform you that Zenobia Richardson's body was found this morning ..."

There was a collective gasp from the Carols and one of them cried, "Zenobia, but that's not possible."

"I'm afraid it is, and as this case will be highly scrutinised, and will receive a great deal of media attention, I shall start by interviewing each of you in turn. There will be no film crews or any outsiders on the second floor until my men have conducted a thorough search.

"It goes without saying that Zenobia's room is out of bounds. From now on, if you wish to return to your rooms, the sergeant or one of my men will accompany you."

"But what about the statue?" cried Crispin. "We can't just leave it here?"

"Why not Mr ..."

"Dupré, Crispin Dupré. Furniture expert on *The Antique Tour*." Crispin tightened the cord of his white waffle hotel dressing gown.

"Well, Mr Dupré. With this police presence, I can't think of a more secure location for it to be at the moment, I can't."

"I suppose not," grumbled Crispin and turned back to Emery.

"If you'd like to get dressed, Mr Dupré, my sergeant will accompany you back to your room."

Crispin pivoted around and ran his eyes over the young sergeant. "Now there's an offer I can't refuse."

As they left, Inspector Evans eyed the remaining occupants of the library and asked, "Who's in charge of this mob?"

"I am." Max stepped forward and ran a hand through his mane of hair.

"Follow me."

Dotty poured her third cup of tea, hoping she'd get a chance to sit quietly and finish this one. Picking up the *History of Charbury Castle*, which she'd brought with her, she settled down at a table near the bookshelves.

Opening the book, she skipped over the ghosts section and found the one about the fire. She was just about to read it when David sat down opposite her.

His naturally dark skin tone was tinged with grey and his large dark eyes were watchful, their usual playfulness having vanished.

"I can't believe Zenobia is dead. She was very much alive when I last saw her, although she was worried."

"About what?"

"That statue, and about making a fool of herself on television by announcing in front of millions of viewers that it was worth a fortune, only for someone to discover weeks or months later that it was a fake, like the one sold through Gilmore's auction house."

Dotty closed her book and pushed it to one side. "I heard someone mention that. What happened?"

"The art and sculptures department valued a sculpture of a Roman goddess at £2,000,000. But two bidders fought hard and pushed the bidding to over £12,000,000. Gilmore thought that was the end of it, but a telephone bidder entered the foray and pushed the price up to £21,000,000. It was a record for such a statuette and clearly everyone was delighted."

David sipped his coffee and winced. "Several months later, rumours started to circulate that it was a forgery, an excellent one, but still not a genuine Roman sculpture. Analysis of the composition of the statuette had already been taken, so the creative process wasn't the cause of such doubt."

David paused and looked up as Gilmore entered the library.

"What was?" asked Dotty, fascinated.

"The composition. The robe was considered not to be a style the people of the day wore, as it was far shorter, and the face was devoid of expression."

Dotty frowned. "And those are reasons to denounce it as a fake?"

"They were enough to cause doubt about the statue's authenticity. Some, including the original valuer at Gilmore's auction house, stand by the original finding, and still treat it as the real thing."

The door nearest their table opened and Max walked in. His face was pale and his jaw was clenched.

The inspector followed and boomed, "Gilmore Chapman."

Dotty and David sat silently in the library after Gilmore was called for questioning. David appeared deep in thought, and Dotty didn't want to disturb him.

The door at the far end of the library opened and a figure wearing a blue hazmat suit shuffled in. They removed their blue latex gloves and pulled the hood of their suit down.

Dotty recognised Constable Varma's dark hair gathered into a bun at the nape of her neck and as she turned, her large oval eyes found Dotty's.

She scuttled over, the plastic of her suit making a swishing sound as she moved, and exclaimed, "Dotty, what are you doing here?"

The noise seemed to break David's trance, and he looked up and said dully, "Good morning, Constable. Although, it's not, of course."

"Mr Rook," replied Constable Varma in a calmer voice.

"Constable Varma, Keya." Dotty felt uncomfortable using the constable's Christian name, but she wanted to speak on a personal level, "I'm so sorry about your sergeant's exams, and not getting your promotion."

"Oh, I passed my exams." The constable grinned. "They weren't that difficult, and I should have taken them ages ago."

"But I thought you'd be working for Inspector Evans?"

"No, the rumours were true. They parachuted in a fast tracker from Bristol. Still, he's rather attractive, don't you think?"

Dotty pressed her lips together but didn't respond.

Constable Varma's eyes brightened, "Besides, I'm thinking of applying for a sergeant's position in the new Rural, Heritage and Wildlife Unit, which my current role will be absorbed into."

Dotty smiled in relief and said, "That's great. You certainly have the experience, and knowledge of the local communities."

The constable straightened up. "Talking about heritage, I've been sent to search the area around the items which were supposed to be filmed today."

"Be careful. Some of them are hugely valuable," warned David.

"Oh, no." The constable's shoulders sagged. "That's why the others were laughing when I left the dead lady's room. They know how clumsy I am." She looked around. "First, I need a glass of water. Wearing this thing is so hot and sweaty."

"What about a cup of tea?" Dotty's cup sat on the table, partially drunk.

"That would be lovely, but I don't have time."

Dotty took another sip of her tepid tea and watched Constable Varma down a glass of water, then replace her hood and gloves and shuffle from left to right across the far end of the room. Her head was bent as she stared at the floor. Dotty jumped up. If the constable carried on, she would crash straight into the easels supporting Gilmore's chosen paintings and collages.

She dashed across and grabbed Constable Varma's arm.

"What?" The constable jumped.

"Sorry, I didn't mean to frighten you, but you were about to knock over that painting." The constable turned towards the portrait of a woman and stepped closer to Dotty. "She's scary."

"And probably valuable. Let me help search around the antiques. What are we looking for?"

"Anything and everything. I bag it and we'll check it all back at the station, or in the incident room here. Anything of particular interest will be sent to the forensics lab for fingerprints and that sort of thing."

Dotty began her search around the plinth of the bronze statue and her eyes scanned across to a grey upholstered dining chair, placed opposite the statue. There was something resting against the chair leg. "Keya," she called, "I think I've found something."

Constable Varma knelt down, opened a transparent forensic bag and in it she placed a small black notebook and pencil.

# CHAPTER SIXTEEN

D otty was still kneeling by the empty chair, which faced the statue of Lady Justice, when she felt a rush of air as the library door nearest her opened.

She looked up as Sergeant Unwin entered and coloured as she realised he wasn't staring at her face. She stood up quickly and pulled at her dress.

The sergeant, who wore blue latex gloves and carried a laptop, averted his gaze and turned to survey the other occupants of the room.

He asked, "Does anyone know Miss Richardson's password?"

Mel, who had been subdued all morning and was slumped on another grey upholstered dining chair, answered in a flat tone, "You'll have to ask her assistant, Serena De Rossi."

"And where will I find her?"

Mel shrugged. "I don't know. She didn't join us for supper last night."

Dotty gulped and said, faintly, "Excuse me."

"Yes." The dark-haired sergeant turned back to her and raised his eyebrows.

Nervously, Dotty continued, "Zenobia and Serena had a row last night."

"When?"

"Before supper. I was changing when I heard raised voices. I opened my bedroom door and realised they were coming from the room on the opposite side of the staircase, Zenobia's room. As I watched, Serena stormed out and declared, 'I'm leaving' before marching down the stairs."

"And what time was that?"

"Just before seven o'clock. I left my room shortly afterwards and took the elevator downstairs and went to the bar."

Gilmore strode across and Dotty felt his hand on her shoulder. "I can confirm that. Dotty met me for a drink, but I didn't see Serena."

The young sergeant pressed his lips into a thin line as he looked from Dotty to Gilmore.

"The penny drops," proclaimed Casper. "There wasn't a room for Emery when he first asked. But we were having a little tipple in my room when a nice lady from reception called and told us they'd had a cancellation, and if he still wanted to stay, they'd prepare his room while we were having supper."

The sergeant's level gaze turned back to Dotty, and he asked, "Did you hear what they were arguing about?"

Dotty shook her head.

"They were always having rows," dismissed Casper. "What do you expect when you employ a fiery Italian as your assistant," he added cattily.

Inspector Evans' burly figured appeared in the far library doorway.

"Development?" he asked instinctively.

"Yes, Sir." The young sergeant approached him and continued, "Zenobia Richardson's assistant, Serena De Rossi, is unaccounted for. And she was overheard having an argument with the victim, early yesterday evening."

"Then why are you still standing here? You need to find her, you do."

"Yes, Sir."

"Crispin Dupré," called the inspector.

"How exciting. It's my turn." As Crispin approached the inspector, he asked, "You don't bite, do you?"

Inspector Evans growled, and Crispin giggled and followed him out of the room.

"Come and sit down," whispered Gilmore to Dotty, and he led her back to the table beside the bookshelves. Dotty's half-drunk cup of tea sat forlornly on the table.

"I haven't apologised for abandoning you last night and accompanying Zenobia to her room for a drink."

Dotty smiled and replied, "You don't need to apologise." She paused before asking, "How was Zenobia?"

Gilmore sat back. "She dropped her diva act as soon as we entered her room and began quizzing me about the controversial Roman statuette my auction house sold last year."

Dotty nodded. "David told me about that, but what did it have to do with Zenobia?"

"As I expect David also said, my colleague stands by his original evaluation but, because he does, some in the art world are now questioning his judgement. And he's a renowned expert in his field.

"As Casper enjoyed pointing out, Zenobia hadn't established herself as a professional valuer. If she made the wrong evaluation on television, it would ruin her reputation and her career. She damaged plenty of other careers in her singing days, so she was all too aware of the consequences."

"What did you tell her?"

"I tried to reassure her, but sculptures are not my area of expertise and I know there are some incredible forgeries out there. She wouldn't be the first expert to be duped."

Dotty tilted her head to one side and remarked. "I'm starting to feel sorry for her. I thought she was only on the show for her celebrity status, but from what you've told me, she was approaching her work in a professional manner."

"I only stayed for one drink as she began tapping away on her laptop, the one the sergeant was carrying. She said she needed to find out more about Roman sculptures, so I used it as my excuse to leave."

"When was that?"

"Not late, about half past ten. There was still a light on in your room."

Dotty stared at Gilmore. "How do you know?"

Gilmore looked sheepish but was saved from answering by the arrival of David Rook.

As David pulled out a chair and sat down, Dotty wondered if it was Gilmore's shadow she'd seen beneath her door, and if so, was she relieved or disappointed he hadn't knocked?

Gilmore turned to David and said, "We were discussing whether I was the last to see Zenobia last night."

David smiled solemnly. "You're off the hook there. I believe I have that honour."

"You do?" Dotty narrowed her eyes at David.

"I had trouble sleeping last night, so I wandered down to the library to, well that doesn't matter, but Zenobia was sitting in that chair," David indicated towards the empty dining chair, opposite the statue, where Dotty had found the small notebook.

"She was reading something on her laptop and when I asked what she was doing, she told me 'research' so I said goodnight and returned to my room."

"So it was you I saw leave the library last night, and the person you spoke to was Zenobia," declared Dotty.

"You saw me? Excellent, I may need your corroboration for the police."

Dotty mused, "So Zenobia was last seen in the library, not her bedroom."

# CHAPTER SEVENTEEN

David Rook, Gilmore Chapman and Dotty sat silently at their table beside the bookcases in the library at Charbury Castle Hotel.

"How much longer is this going to take?" asked one of the Carols in a weary voice.

"At this rate, we'll still be filming tomorrow," moaned Mel.

Between the two library doors, Max paced up and down, speaking into his mobile phone.

Suddenly, there was a cry. It sounded like Constable Varma. Dotty jumped up and looked around.

Constable Varma, still wearing a hazmat suit, was examining the small room inside the turret. Dotty rushed across to join her and asked, "What have you found?"

The constable pointed towards the bottom of the metal window frame on which a piece of denim material was snagged.

She asked, "Can you take a photo with your phone, and send it to me later? Otherwise I'll have to strip off my gloves and my hands are horrible and sweaty and I've nothing to wipe them on."

"Of course." Dotty took several photographs from different angles. When she'd finished, Constable Varma carefully pulled the material away from the window frame and held it up. There was a double row of orange stitching running across it.

"Part of a pocket from a pair of jeans," suggested Dotty, staring at it.

"But how did it get here?" asked Constable Varma. "Do you think someone sat against the window frame and caught their trousers on it?"

"I'm not sure." Dotty glanced around and something else caught her eye. "What's that under the bench beside the window?"

Constable Varma bent down and, with her spare hand, she felt around under the padded bench. "Got it," she gasped. Withdrawing her hand, she held up a key attached to a plastic tag.

Dotty bent down and read out loud, 'The Hollies 3'. The light from the library dimmed, and she felt a presence behind her. Straightening up, she turned towards Inspector Evans, who stepped to one side and indicated for her to leave the turret room.

Bowing her head, she left Constable Varma and their discovery, but instead of returning to the table where Gilmore and David still sat, she examined the contents of the bookshelf closest to the turret entrance.

Sergeant Unwin entered the library and Dotty thought the wide knot of his tie hung a little lower, and was that a sheen of sweat on his forehead?

"Ah, there you are, Sergeant. Have you located Miss De Rossi yet?" asked the inspector.

The sergeant squared his shoulders and replied, "She checked out of the hotel yesterday evening, at seven o'clock, and hasn't been seen since."

"You shall have to widen your search then, but while you're here, is there a room in this hotel called 'The Hollies'?"

Constable Varma must have placed the key in a forensic bag as the inspector held a transparent bag in front of the sergeant's face.

"Not that I'm aware of, Sir, and as you know, the keys for the bedrooms here are attached to large metal plates."

The inspector drew his eyebrows together. "If you could just check."

The inspector turned his back on Sergeant Unwin and Dotty heard Constable Varma explain, "It was caught here, inspector."

The inspector opened the window and the delicate-pink flowers of a climbing clematis, with four large petals arranged in a cross shape, were blown against the side of the window frame.

He looked down as if examining the side of the turret or the abundance of clematis blooms. Drawing his head back inside, he called, "One minute, sergeant."

Sergeant Unwin had reached the library door and, when his name was called, his back and shoulders tensed, and he hesitated before turning around and re-tracing his steps.

"You're a sporting man. Could you climb up the ladder trellis to this window?" asked Inspector Evans.

"Not in this suit," replied the young sergeant, stepping back.

"I don't mean now. But if you were, say, wearing jeans and a pair of trainers. Would it be possible to use the trellis to climb up the side of the turret?"

The inspector stepped back, and it was Sergeant Unwin's turn to lean out of the window and examine the outside of the turret.

He stuck his hand out and appeared to be pulling at something. When he pulled his hand back inside, he held a broken piece of the trellis.

"That looks recently broken, it does," observed the inspector. "So, could you do it? Could you climb up the turret?"

The sergeant nodded. "I reckon I could, but what would be the point if the window was closed?"

Inspector Evans rocked back on his heels. "Good point. Was this window fastened when you first inspected it, Constable Varma?"

"Yes, Sir."

Dotty heard an 'oh' sound behind her and turned round. Everyone in the room, apart from Casper and Emery, who were deep in discussion beside the bronze sculpture, had drawn closer to the turret as they listened to the police discussion.

The Carols stood, rather than sat, in a circle, which was inching closer to Dotty, and Max, Mel and Jennifer were standing beside Gilmore and David's table, beside the bookcase.

David cleared his throat and announced, "Inspector, that may be my doing. I closed and fastened the window after speaking to you and

George earlier. I can't swear it was secured when I opened it."

"You didn't open it," disclosed Dotty. She turned back to the inspector. "I pushed it open, when I first spoke to George, and the window wasn't closed."

"An intruder," cried one of the Carols.

"That's a relief," declared Max. "I thought if Zenobia's death was suspicious, one of us would be blamed. But if someone climbed in through that window, it sheds an entirely different light on the matter. Anyone could be involved. A deranged fan, for instance."

"I'm not being funny, but why would anyone risk climbing up the side of the turret on the off chance that the window was unfastened?"

The inspector crossed his arms. "No, if they did, it was because they knew they could gain entry, and in that case, the window could have been left open by an accomplice."

"It wasn't me," said one of the Carols defensively.

"I've always dreamed of a handsome stranger climbing into my bedroom window," admitted another.

"To rescue you?" asked the first.

"Oh, no." They all burst into laughter, which eased the tension in the room.

"Inspector," said Max, walking towards the turret. "If your forensic person has finished their inspection, do you think we can start filming? We've lost several hours, but if we start now, we should complete it today."

Casper joined the group and asked, "But who's going to value the statue?"

"Can't you, Casper?" replied Mel, stretching her arms into the air.

"Not me, sweetie, I can't do it."

"I will," volunteered David, although he sounded less than enthusiastic. "But I shall be very cautious and I won't be throwing out a huge valuation."

# CHAPTER EIGHTEEN

"So, how did David manage the tricky valuation of the bronze sculpture?" asked Aunt Beanie on Sunday evening.

She, Norman and Dotty were sitting at the antique pine table in the kitchen at Meadowbank Farm. Uncle Cliff was also sitting on a pine dining chair, which had been turned towards a small television set positioned on top of a bookcase.

He appeared very content watching the weekly, late afternoon programme about farming and the British countryside.

Norman used a flat metal bottle opener to prise the cap off his bottle of Wiltshire Gold beer. He tipped the brown bottle and dark liquid slowly ran down the inside of his pint glass until he sighed with satisfaction.

Picking the glass up, he took a swig before wiping foam off the small beard he'd grown recently. "That's better."

Dotty was fascinated by Norman's ritual.

Earl Grey uncurled himself from his place between the bottom of the Aga range cooker and Agatha, his Berkshire pig companion. He padded across the terracotta tiled kitchen floor and jumped onto Dotty's lap.

"Hello, boy. Did you miss me?" Dotty asked.

Earl Grey returned to a sleeping position.

Aunt Beanie put down her glass of ruby-red homemade damson gin and repeated, "So tell me, what did David say about the sculpture?"

Dotty stroked Earl Grey's soft warm fur and replied, "He was very complimentary, emphasising its attributes and fine detailing."

"Yes, but what value did he give it?" asked the older woman impatiently.

Dotty looked across the table at Aunt Beanie. "He said it would fetch in the region of £5,000 to £10,000 at auction, but if it could be authenticated, and was of Roman origin, the value would increase significantly, and it could fetch several million."

"Which is a conservative estimate, if you look at the top end of today's sculpture market," noted Aunt Beanie. "I wish I'd had the chance to see it."

Dotty said eagerly, "But you will, if you don't mind travelling to London," Dotty said eagerly. "Casper, who has become very friendly with Emery, the sculpture's owner, has offered to display it in his gallery."

"I bet he has." Aunt Beanie raised her eyebrows and her glass of damson gin.

After a minute or so of silence, Aunt Beanie asked, "Did Gilmore have anything to say on the matter?"

"No, he maintained a distance from the whole proceedings. But I found his evaluation of a collection of collages, made from strips of newspaper and magazines, fascinating."

Aunt Beanie sipped her gin before commenting dryly, "Not his usual area. No portraits of long dead people or an assortment of still-life objects?"

"He had some of those as well," admitted Dotty, observing Aunt Beanie. There were untapped depths to the older woman's knowledge and experience.

Norman, whose pint glass was half empty, observed, "So an interesting weekend despite the tragedy."

Aunt Beanie sighed. "And I was onto a good thing giving private tours around Windrush Hall, but I suppose the house and its contents will be sold again, if she has no heirs. Great business for Akemans, don't you think?"

"I suppose it is, but it's rather morbid," confessed Dotty. "The auction house makes most of its money from dead people."

"Death and taxes," announced Norman, standing up and walking across to the fridge.

Dotty's mobile phone rang, and she read the caller ID before she answered. "Hello David, do you have any news?"

"About what in particular?" he replied.

"Zenobia Richardson's death. I thought the police would have discovered how she died by now."

"If they have, they haven't told me. After you left, I watched Jennifer value the gold necklace with the disks and then I took my leave. The reason I'm calling, and apologies for disturbing your Sunday evening, is that George has just spoken to the executors of Zenobia's estate.

"There are a few irregularities with the will and they want us over at Windrush Hall first thing tomorrow morning, to start documenting the contents. I have copies of the catalogue from the Duke's sale which should make the job easier. So don't go into the office tomorrow. I'll collect you from the farm at half-past eight."

"But what about this month's auction? I still have to photograph and prepare descriptions for items from last week, and there will be more deliveries tomorrow."

"Don't worry, Marion has agreed to take care of that. And George kept Monday and Tuesday clear so she could recover from the weekend. They'll sort out the auction between them. This is a sizeable job, and very prestigious.

"The solicitor who's handling the will is driving down from London and will meet us tomorrow morning. And he'd also like Norman there so he can discuss the upkeep and ongoing maintenance of the estate, so can you tell him I'll also give him a lift, and drop you both back at Akemans later?"

Dotty put her phone back on the table, looked across at Aunt Beanie and said, "You were right. I'm going with David tomorrow morning to begin an inventory of Windrush Hall."

She turned to Norman, who had poured his second pint of beer while Dotty was on the phone. "And he wants you to come with us. We're meeting a London solicitor who needs your advice about the upkeep of Windrush Hall."

Norman drew his eyebrows together, and replied, "But surely they'll sell it as soon as they can."

Aunt Beanie reasoned, "There'll still be probate, although that should be a simple process if there are no fighting relatives."

Uncle Cliff became restless and Aunt Beanie glanced towards the TV. *"The Antiques Tour* is on next. Shall we all watch it?"

She settled Uncle Cliff and sorted out the volume so they could all hear as the programme started.

Dotty considered David's telephone call. "David did say there were some irregularities with Zenobia Richardson's will."

Aunt Beanie sat back down. "Typical. Even in death she still wants to be the centre of attention."

# CHAPTER NINETEEN

David navigated the narrow Cotswold lanes with expertise in his vintage silver Mercedes.

Dotty felt guilty sitting in the front passenger seat, but Norman had insisted on squeezing himself into the narrow back seat, where he now sat with his legs angled across the footwell.

Fresh green leaves were unfurling on the oak trees and, as they drove across the top of a ridge, Dotty noticed the carpet of yellow rapeseed flowers spreading out into the distance.

Sunday's clouds had cleared, and she leaned back, feeling the warming rays of sunshine on her face.

They turned off the road and drove between the familiar stone columns at the entrance to Windrush Hall.

Norman swivelled round as far as he could in his cramped position to observe his old stone cottage.

"It appears to be occupied," observed David. Pretty floral curtains hung in the nearest window and there was a vase of wild flowers, including yellow cowslips and bluebells on the windowsill.

"Good, I'd hate to see the old place empty and falling into disrepair," replied Norman, with a note of nostalgia in his voice.

They drove down the sweeping drive and drew up by the stone steps which led up to the front door of the Georgian country house. A dark red Fiat 500 was already parked there.

Serena De Rossi appeared in the open doorway and carefully walked down, one step at a time, carrying a large cardboard box.

As Dotty helped Norman out of the rear of David's car, Serena pushed the box onto the back seat of the Fiat.

David strolled across, looked over Serena's shoulder and observed dryly, "Removing Zenobia's things?"

Serena flung her head back and cried, "These are not madam's. They belong to the fan club of which I am chairperson."

Dotty joined Serena, who had moved to the rear of the Fiat. The boot was open and filled with suitcases and holdalls, and something glinted from a partially open cloth bag.

Serena must have noticed her scrutiny as she pulled the ends of the bag together and yelled, "Mine," before slamming the boot shut.

Intrigued by Serena's behaviour, Dotty asked, in a quiet voice, "Are you leaving?"

"Yes." Serena crossed her arms and lifted her chin.

Dotty continued, "But surely you'll help sort things out. There must be paperwork and computer files that only you know how to access."

"Madam make it clear on Saturday that she not appreciate all I do." Serena uncrossed her arms and held them up to the sky in an imploring manner and shouted, "I give up my career to help her. I good singer. But look how she repay me."

"How?" asked Dotty.

Serena dropped her arms to her side, looked down at the gravel drive and answered in a resigned tone, "That not matter now."

Dotty felt a fluttering of sympathy for this fiery Italian woman, who was probably very lonely. What did she have to show for a life dedicated to 'madam'?

Dotty continued, "Is that why you and madam were arguing on Saturday evening, at the hotel?"

Serena looked up with watery eyes. "Yes, I tell her if that what she thinks I go. And I do."

Dotty pressed on. "So, where did you stay on Saturday night?"

"I come home to my little cottage. My dear, sweet home."

Dotty glanced across at Norman, who nodded his understanding. David stood slightly apart, observing the conversation.

Serena declared, "But now I leave that too. I finish here. Goodbye." Before any of them could stop her, she jumped into her car and drove away.

Dotty, Norman and David watched her speed up the drive.

David asked, "Do you think she was upset about Zenobia's death?"

"I'm not sure. She appeared more concerned with her own future, but I guess that's understandable. She's given up the best part of her life for Zenobia."

"I'm going to have a wander round," announced Norman and he strode away, around the corner of the house.

"I wonder what she meant by 'look at how she repay me'," mused David.

"I don't know, but I'm sure the police will want to speak to her. Should I call them?"

David tugged his ear. "It might be best. Why not speak to Constable Varma? That way, it can be unofficial, just a friend calling with information."

"Good idea."

"While you do that, I'll take a tour of the house." David turned and climbed the stone steps to the front door.

Dotty returned to David's car. She removed the wicker basket she'd brought and rooted about under her laptop and the paperwork David had given her from the previous auction at the house, and found her mobile phone.

"Hi, Keya," she said brightly when the constable answered her call.

"No. I don't have an update," Constable Varma responded stiffly.

"Is Inspector Evans with you?"

"That's right, madam."

"Can you go somewhere else? I've something to tell you and I wondered if we could trade information."

"I'm not sure about that. Hold on."

Dotty waited, and she heard a door open and footsteps cross a vinyl floor. She had visited the police station back in November, when Norman had been taken in for questioning.

"OK, I'm outside. Sorry about that, but you know what the inspector's like, and he hates you and me discussing current cases. Maybe he thinks we'll crack them before he does. Anyway, what did you want to tell me?"

Dotty took a deep breath and said, "First, tell me how Zenobia Richardson died."

There was a pause. Then Constable Varma admitted, "I suppose everyone will know soon, since the inspector's getting ready for a press conference this afternoon. It's put him in a foul mood. Anyway, Miss Richardson broke her neck and died instantly."

"That's a relief," remarked Dotty, "So it was an accident."

"Not necessarily," Constable Varma replied hesitantly.

Dotty thought she understood. "Zenobia fell down the stairs, didn't she?" Just like the supposed ghost, Lady Violet Waltham. "Do you think she was pushed?"

"We don't know, but from the angle of the body we know she did not fall down the steps, but through the centre of the open staircase."

Exactly like Lady Violet.

"So what information do you have for me?" asked Constable Varma.

"I've just seen Serena De Rossi, and I wondered if you are still looking for her?"

"Sergeant Unwin's on his way to Windrush Hall as we speak. I think he was relieved to get away from the inspector. Maybe it was a blessing I didn't get that job."

"But you're still working for the inspector. Actually, I'm at Windrush Hall, so I expect I'll see the sergeant soon, but I'm not sure if Serena is at her cottage, at the entrance to the drive, or if she left. Her car was loaded up."

"Constable." Dotty heard the deep baritone voice of Inspector Evans.

"I have to go. Thanks for the info and speak later." Dotty was about to finish the call when Constable Varma added, "And watch yourself with Sergeant Unwin. I saw the way he looked at you yesterday."

Dotty ended the call, feeling the heat rise in her cheeks. She looked down at her husband's old blue shirt, which she'd tied at the front, over her trusty long denim skirt.

Maybe it was time to invest in some new work clothes. After all, she was earning a steady income, her bills were not huge, and she also had her army widow's pension.

David stood on top of the stone steps and called, "Dorothy."

Time to get to work.

# CHAPTER TWENTY

Dotty climbed up the stone steps to the entrance of Windrush Hall.

"Good morning, ma'am. It's nice to see you back," greeted Benson, the elderly butler she'd worked with on her previous visit. He still wore his black and grey livery uniform, despite the passing of his mistress.

"Thank you, although I wish it was in more pleasant circumstances. How is Françoise?"

Benson bowed his head. "I'm afraid she is terribly upset and has taken to her bed. There is no fresh bread today, but I can offer you scones or the cakes she baked over the weekend."

How wonderful. "That sounds lovely, but perhaps later. I ought to do some work first."

"Very good, ma'am." Benson turned and walked through the dining room towards the kitchen.

"You two are on good terms," remarked David.

"I helped out in the kitchen when I came with Aunt Beanie for the private performance and tour of the house. He and his wife, Françoise, who is the cook, were very kind, and sent me away with some tasty leftovers which Aunt Beanie, Norman and I enjoyed for our supper."

"Are there any other staff?"

"I believe there is a maid, but I didn't meet her as she was ill. Where shall we start?"

David looked around and replied, "In the dining room. It looked relatively unchanged from when the Duke lived here. We'll check the paintings against the list I gave you from the previous sale."

They worked quickly through the paintings and discovered that the ornaments on the bow-fronted mahogany sideboard had also belonged to the Duke, and had been moved to the dining room from other places in the house.

Benson appeared carrying a tray which held a cafetière of fresh coffee, hot water, a variety of tea bags, milk, cups, and homemade shortbread biscuits.

Dotty nibbled on a biscuit as David poured himself a cup of coffee and declared, "I think we're finished in here. We'll tackle the drawing room next."

Dotty carried her cup of tea into the peacock blue drawing room she admired so much.

David said, "I must admit, Zenobia had impeccable taste," reflected David. "This room is a delight and pays homage to the original decoration. But I wasn't expecting this collection of ceramics. Somehow, it's not in keeping with the rest of the house."

He sipped his coffee and smiled in appreciation.

"Benson told me it's Zenobia's private collection, which she started when her singing career began."

"Some interesting pieces, although that bright pink leprechaun is rather gaudy. For the purposes of this valuation, I'll lump them all together with an estimate for the collection as a whole. What else do we have?" He surveyed the room.

As Dotty and David finished their inventory of items in the drawing room, they heard the front door open.

Sergeant Unwin appeared in the drawing room doorway and remarked, "I see you're quick off the mark. The owner's body is barely cold and you swoop straight in."

David turned to face the sergeant. His salt and pepper moustache twitched and his large dark eyes became cold. "We are not scavengers, prowling round a carcass. The executors asked us to undertake the valuation as soon as possible, as I understand there are some irregularities with the will."

The sergeant pulled at the large knot of his shiny green tie and replied, in a contrite voice, "I have also been asked to meet the solicitor this morning."

He turned to Dotty and his brow furrowed. "Dotty, is it? You were at the hotel yesterday with the film crew."

"That's right," she replied brightly, but rather than the appreciative glances she'd received the previous day, the sergeant wrinkled his nose and turned on his heels.

She glanced across at the gilt mirror hanging over the fireplace, and realised that instead of yesterday's sleek locks, she'd scraped her hair back and fastened it into a small knot on top of her head. That, and her old, unshapely clothes, were a far cry from yesterday's elegant outfit.

She really should buy some new clothes but she wasn't sure she could afford another shopping trip with Marion. Maybe she should ask Keya to go with her.

And Sergeant Unwin? Well, if he couldn't see past her outer appearance, he wasn't worth bothering about.

Unperturbed by his snub, she followed him out of the room and called, "Sergeant, are you looking for Serena De Rossi?"

He turned and replied, "I was, as a matter of fact."

"She was loading up her car when we arrived and sped off up the drive. She's been living in the cottage by the stone entrance gates, but I'm not sure if she's there any longer."

The sergeant shook his head. "I stopped by the cottage and it's locked up."

"Was there any sign of her red Fiat?"

Again, the sergeant shook his head. "She must have made a run for it. I'll contact Inspector Evans."

"If I may?" murmured Dotty.

"Yes."

"I wouldn't speak to Inspector Evans, not before a major press conference."

"How do you know about that?"

She ignored his question and continued, "If I were you, I'd call Constable Varma."

"You would. Actually, that's not a bad idea. Excuse me."

As Sergeant Unwin walked out of the entrance hall and stood at the top of the stone steps, speaking into his phone, Dotty observed a large black car crawling down the drive.

David must have noticed it from the drawing room window as he stepped into the entrance hall and remarked, "The solicitor."

He was correct. A portly, bald-headed man climbed out of the back of the car, wearing a navy pinstriped suit. His red cheeks were flushed as he climbed onto the top step and remarked, "Nice place Zenobia has here, but I don't know why it has to be so far from London."

Ignoring Dotty, he thrust his hand towards David. "Charles Willoughby, Zenobia's solicitor, and I've been appointed to represent the executors of her estate."

"David Rook, from Akemans Antiques."

Sergeant Unwin finished his call and turned to the solicitor. He also held out his hand and said, 'Sergeant Unwin. I believe you requested a police presence today."

"Most irregular I know. But first, shall we go inside? It's rather chilly standing out here. If you don't mind, I'll get straight down to business, as I have to be back in the City by three for a senior partners' meeting."

As David led them through to the dining room, Charles Willoughby turned to Dotty and instructed, "Fetch me a coffee, fresh, none of that instant rubbish and whatever my colleagues would like."

Dotty looked at David, who nodded discreetly, so she continued into the kitchen as the men sat down.

Mario, Zenobia's British Blue cat, was standing on the worktop and he meowed as Dotty entered. Benson looked up from the paper he was reading, in which Dotty noted a large black-and-white photograph of Zenobia.

"Mario's been crying for his mistress all weekend," Benson reported. "I swear he knows something has happened to her."

Dotty stroked Mario as she said, "The solicitor's arrived from London and is asking for coffee."

Benson stood up. "Very well, ma'am. And don't take any notice of Mr Willoughby. He likes ordering others around. You should have seen Serena's reaction when he asked her to sort out tea on his last visit.

"Her cheeks were the same colour as her hair, but he simply ignored her, which only made matters worse. If I hadn't gone to the music room to enquire if madam needed anything, they'd have remained thirsty."

Dotty returned to the dining room and sat down in a spare chair next to David.

"Does she need to be here? What I have to say is confidential." Charles Willoughby made it sound as if Dotty was a bug on the end of his bulbous, broken-veined nose.

"Dorothy is my assistant, and will be handling the sale."

"Yes, well," fussed the solicitor as he shuffled papers.

He glanced around. "I'm glad to see that Italian assistant of Zenobia's is not here, but that's hardly a surprise. What about the staff?"

David turned to Dotty, who tried to sound more confident than she felt. "Benson is making coffee in the kitchen and his wife is very upset about her mistress's death, and is in bed. I don't know about the maid."

Benson entered from the kitchen carrying another silver tray with a fresh cafetière of coffee. There was also a plate of assorted cakes, which he placed in front of Charles Willoughby.

The solicitor eyed them eagerly and plucked a slice of Bakewell tart from the plate, as he used his free hand to turn a page.

Benson poured coffee for the solicitor and turned to leave when Charles Willoughby instructed, without looking up, "Stay, Benson. What I have to say affects you."

Those around the table waited in silence while the solicitor finished his Bakewell tart.

"As some of you already know," the solicitor began, "there are a few irregularities with Zenobia's last will and testament. This," he held up a piece of paper on which Dotty noticed 'Charbury Castle Hotel' written across the top, "is an amendment which I received after her death."

Benson gasped.

"Quite so. It is dated 20<sup>th</sup> May, which was Saturday, and the courier collected it from the hotel at 7.39 in the evening. I visited the hotel before coming here, and can confirm that the signatures on it are those of the evening receptionist and one of the hotel waiters. While it is unusual, it is still legally binding."

Dotty had never been to a will reading before. Ian Puck, the welfare officer, had dealt with Al's will after he died and he'd left everything to her, as his wife. She wondered what changes Zenobia had made.

"The smaller monetary endowments, mostly to theatres and arts charities are unchanged, but the bulk of her estate no longer passes to her assistant, Serena De Rossi, instead ..." The solicitor stopped and glanced around the room, "it is left in trust to her cat, Mario."

David's eyes bulged and Sergeant Unwin tried, but failed, to contain a snort of laughter.

Poor Benson, who had refused to take a seat, grabbed the back of a chair and leaned against it.

Charles Willoughby looked across at him and continued, "My faithful Benson and Françoise are to remain at Windrush Hall to cater to the needs of Mario, and then there are details about your pay and annual increases.

"On the event of Mario's death, and then she lists a number of small gifts, including something for Benson, to remember her by, but the bulk of her estate will pass to her beloved La Fenice theatre in Venice."

# CHAPTER TWENTY-ONE

Those gathered in the dining room at Windrush Hall appeared stunned by the terms of Zenobia Richardson's will.

Benson coughed. "Excuse me, Sir, please can you explain that to me again?"

"Certainly." The solicitor examined the plate of cakes in front of him and removed a gooey-looking chocolate brownie.

"Your employment, and that of your wife, is to be extended at Windrush Hall, which should come as a relief to you." He greedily bit into the brownie, scattering crumbs across the polished mahogany dining table.

"I was hoping for a pension settlement, Sir. Neither my wife nor I are getting any younger."

The solicitor slowly finished his brownie and replied, "There's no mention of a pension or cash settlement in Zenobia's will, even on Mario's passing."

"Oh dear." Benson looked dejected as he leaned heavily against the back of the chair.

"How hard can it be, looking after a cat?" exclaimed Charles Willoughby.

"This house must take a lot of cleaning," broke in Dotty, feeling sorry for the elderly butler and his generous wife.

The solicitor narrowed his eyes at Dotty. "The maid can do that. What's her name?"

"Esme, but she left last week," replied Benson forlornly.

Dotty wondered why Esme had left. Had she also had a falling out with her employer and did she also have a motive to harm her?

"Not to worry, there's enough money in the estate to pay for a cleaner and gardener. Talking of which, is the Duke's old groundsman here?"

David, who had kept quiet during the proceedings, sat up and replied, "Norman Climpson. I think you'll find him outside."

"Good chap, is he?"

"Excellent. We've employed him at Akemans as our porter."

For the first time, the solicitor lost his composure, and appeared flustered. "Oh dear, I was hoping to employ him to oversee the grounds here."

The solicitor slurped his coffee. "Anyway, I don't think it's realistic to expect the building work to continue. This house has been an expensive project, and I'm only sorry Zenobia didn't get the chance to enjoy it."

Dotty wondered what building work he was referring to. The house appeared complete, and she understood that landscaping the garden had been Zenobia's final project, and that was finished. She'd like to visit it, if she had got a chance.

The solicitor stood, and the others followed his lead.

"If you'll excuse me, I need to tell my wife what has happened." Benson shuffled away into the kitchen.

Dotty cautiously approached Charles Willoughby as he returned his papers to his black leather briefcase. "Excuse me, but I was wondering about Zenobia's fan club."

The solicitor paused briefly and frowned. "Of course," he considered. "That's not part of her estate. It is a separate entity run by Serena De Rossi on behalf of Zenobia."

"So what will happen to it now?"

"I expect its numbers will swell. Death makes artists more distinguished, even heroic."

"And who will benefit from that?"

"The fan club itself, and Serena De Rossi."

Charles Willoughby snapped his briefcase shut and addressed David. "Shall we find your man?"

He was about to leave the table when he stopped, leant over and removed a piece of millionaire's shortbread from the plate of cakes.

David led Charles Willoughby outside, leaving Sergeant Unwin and Dotty in the dining room. The sergeant looked uncomfortable as he tightened the knot of his shiny green tie.

Dotty sensed an opportunity and asked, "Do you think changing the terms of the will gives Serena De Rossi a reason to kill her employer? After all, she wouldn't know Zenobia made the changes on Saturday night and sent them by courier to London."

The sergeant narrowed his eyes as he stared at her, and Dotty dropped her gaze to the polished table. "How do you know she was killed?"

Dotty hid her hand behind her back and crossed her fingers as she replied in an innocent voice, "I didn't. I was just surmising that if Zenobia's death was not an accident, then her changing her will, and cutting Serena off from a fortune, was a pretty solid motive."

The sergeant's forehead wrinkled. "If Miss Richardson's death happened to be suspicious, then, yes, Miss De Rossi would be a suspect. Now, if you'll excuse me, I need to return to the station."

Dotty placed the solicitor's half-empty cup of coffee on the silver tea tray, together with the depleted plate of cakes. Should she return them to the kitchen or leave them to Benson?

She really wanted to see the garden. Picking up a piece of flapjack, she wandered through the hall into the music room.

It was flooded with light from what she now realised were patio windows in the circular alcove at the front of the room, where Zenobia had performed on her last visit.

She pushed open the doors and followed the gravel path into the new gardens.

The neat beds were delineated by small box hedges and the green mounds of lavender which lined the path would provide a pleasant perfume when they flowered in a month or so.

She continued down the path into a second garden area which contrasted with the first as the neat lines gave way to curves and the borders were packed full of flowers and bushes, each with a designated colour scheme.

She bent down to examine the delicate heads of a cluster of pink snapdragons.

As she did, she heard Benson's voice. "We have no choice, my dear, but to stay on."

"But what about my operation? Zenobia said she would pay for it," replied a lady's voice with a French accent, presumably Françoise.

"We'll have to take our chances with the local health service and see if we can get you on a waiting list."

"But how long will that take?"

"I'm afraid I've no idea."

Dotty stood up and strode quickly along the path towards the house.

Halfway back, she turned around and observed Benson and Françoise sitting on a wooden bench, on the lawn beside the formal gardens.

They were looking across at the woods where bushes of purple and dark pink rhododendrons added splashes of colour.

"There you are, Dorothy," called David Rook. "It's time to get you and Norman back. I'll finish the inventory and valuations tomorrow."

Dotty glanced back at the elderly couple as they sat with their arms wrapped around each other and smiled. It would be nice to have someone else's love and support.

# CHAPTER TWENTY-TWO

As Marion and George were progressing well with the catalogue for the upcoming auction, Gilly Wimsey took the opportunity to ask Dotty to help her in the antiques centre.

In addition to the vast open plan floor space on the ground floor, the conversion of the old mill building had created two upper floors.

The second floor was empty, as was the first, apart from a storeroom and Gilly's office.

The ground floor space was the retail area of the antiques centre and it was divided into booths, some of which were run by Gilly, but most were licensed to individuals who sold a variety of antiques, collectables and bric-a-brac.

Gilly and Dotty stood in front of a stall towards the rear of the building, where a thin layer of dust covered the contents and a vase of dead flowers stood forlornly on an empty table.

Gilly pushed her orange-framed glasses up her nose and said, "It's a shame Mrs Wade couldn't make this work. Such a lovely idea, but her prices were too high."

Gilly picked up a green metal tray decorated with hand-painted flowers, which made Dotty think of canal longboats, and turned it over. "She was charging £100 for this when it's really only worth £30. Pretty though, like everything else."

The whole stall had a floral theme. From trays arranged along a shelf, to a collection of biscuit and cake tins, and a delicate tea set on a grimy linen table cloth near the front.

"What shall I do with everything?" asked Dotty.

"I'll help you. We'll start by giving everything a thorough dusting. Then we'll see which items I have space to sell on my stalls now, and everything else can either be packed up to display later, when I have room, or thrown away."

"That's rather a waste," remarked Dotty.

They turned and walked towards the cleaner's cupboard.

Dotty continued, "I visited a reclamation yard in Scotland once, which also handled house clearances. They had a display cupboard in which everything displayed was £1. I picked up a pretty green and white serving dish. It has a crack on the bottom, but nobody ever notices."

They paused at the bottom of the wide open metal staircase and Gilly looked up it to the first floor.

"There's so much empty space up there, but before I can let it to stallholders, I need to prove customers will climb the stairs. A bargain section is a great idea. And much better than being charged by the local council to throw things away.

"And I hate the way the men at the recycling centre look at me, and rummage around in the boxes and tell me what I can and cannot chuck away."

She opened the cleaner's cupboard and removed a couple of yellow cotton dusters.

Dotty picked up a bucket and sponge. "I think some items will need more than a dust."

Gilly turned to Dotty. "You could take on that project. And I could give you items which I haven't sold and you can charge what you want and keep the profits. It'll be your own little business. The only condition is that you have to get rid of anything you can't sell. As I said, I hate going to the recycling centre."

Dotty considered the proposition and looked up the stairs to the first floor. Gilly was right. There was plenty of room, and as she learnt more about the things people bought, she could join Constable Varma at car boot sales or bid for lots at the auctions.

There were often boxes of household or kitchen items which nobody wanted, which sold for only £10 or £20.

"It's certainly tempting. But what if you give me items I don't like? Can I give them back?"

Gilly pressed her lips together as she pondered the question.

"Of course you can. That's only fair, but it has to be immediately, before you put them out on your stall."

"And do you have any spare shelves and tables I could use to display things on?"

"Take what you need from Mrs Wade's stall, and anything else you find in the storeroom that we're not using. You'll need to encourage people up the stairs. Perhaps you should design some signs, nothing garish but along the lines of 'More discounts upstairs', or 'Sale'."

Gilly grinned. "People can't resist a bargain."

Excited, Dotty filled her bucket with water and returned to Mrs Wade's stall.

On Wednesday morning, Dotty and Norman arrived early at the antiques centre and walked to Mrs Wade's old stall, at the rear of the room.

"So, what do you need me to do?" Norman asked.

"First, we need to move these shelves and tables upstairs, and then the boxes marked with a 'D'. Those with an 'S' we'll put in the storeroom across the yard, if there's space amongst the auction lots, and the rest Gilly is putting out on her stalls.

Rather than dismantle the long shelving unit on which the trays had been displayed, Dotty and Norman man-handled it up the metal staircase to the first floor.

"Are you certain this is where you want it?" asked Norman, after Dotty had changed her mind several times and they had dragged it back and forth across the wooden floor.

"I think so. It's so hard. I've never done anything like this before."

"Start small, or people will be distracted and spend too much time walking about, rather than concentrating on the objects for sale," advised Norman.

"You're right. And the front of the stall should be welcoming and face the top of the staircase. The shelving unit does a good job marking the rear boundary. Now for everything else."

As they descended the staircase, Dotty felt her phone vibrate in her pocket and as she stepped off the bottom step, she fished it out and said, "Hello."

"Hi Dotty, it's Keya. Are you free for an early lunch today? I'm attending a Parish Council meeting in Eastington this morning, so I thought I'd drive back to Cirencester via Coln Akeman."

"Yes, I'm free. It'll be nice to catch up," replied Dotty, thinking she could also find out if the police had discovered exactly how Zenobia Richardson died.

"I'll see you at The Axeman at twelve thirty."

The Axeman was an attractive Cotswold stone pub in the centre of Coln Akeman, a village less than a mile from the antiques centre. As Dotty drove along the street towards it, she noted tables and chairs arranged outside the nearby shops and houses.

Constable Varma was already sitting at a table outside The Axeman, and she waved as Dotty passed and turned left, parking at the rear of the pub.

As she followed the footpath back to the Main Street, Dotty regarded the dark green leaves of the Virginia creeper spreading across the side wall of The Axeman. When she'd first visited, in the autumn, the leaves were a stunning array of yellow, orange and reds.

She greeted Constable Varma. 'Hi, I wasn't expecting us to sit outside, but it's actually rather warm in the sun." She pushed up the sleeves of her cardigan and glanced at the post office next door, which was adorned in Union Jack bunting. "What's going on?"

"Morris dancers," exclaimed Constable Varma in delight. "I know they're an old British tradition, but I've never seen them before."

"Neither have I," replied Dotty, absorbing the constable's enthusiasm. "Can I get you a drink?"

"Orange juice and lemonade please, and can you make it a pint? I suddenly feel thirsty sitting out in the sun."

Dotty bought their drinks at the bar inside, ordering a bitter lemon for herself, and as she emerged through the front door, she looked across at the village green.

It was a wedge shape, with a lane and houses running down each side to the point where it met the path that ran alongside the River Coln. The village was partly named after the river, which ran parallel with the main street.

Men dressed in white outfits were climbing out of a minibus parked next to the green.

As she placed their drinks on a circular pub table, Dotty noticed an elderly couple carry plates of food out of their house, three doors down, and settle themselves on a wooden bench, facing the green.

She picked up the menu, which consisted of a single sheet of paper, as Constable Varma asked, "Did you watch Inspector Evans' press conference on Monday?"

"No, but Aunt Beanie has been following the case and giving me regular updates. I understand the reporters were annoyed that the inspector refused to confirm if Zenobia's death was accidental or if someone else was involved."

"It could still be accidental even if someone else was involved, and," Constable Varma leaned forward and lowered her voice, "we think there was." She sat up. "But don't tell anyone."

"Have you found out who?"

"Possibly. We think we've identified the mystery intruder."

"Did someone really climb up to the turret window?" Dotty picked up her glass.

"The inspector thinks so. Sergeant Unwin didn't find a hotel called The Hollies and no bed and breakfasts have rooms with that name. So guess who had to search the internet? Do you have you any idea how many people rent out properties, even single rooms, in their houses? It's creepy. Just think who could be staying."

"A murderer," suggested Dotty dryly.

A group of young mums with toddlers and babies in pushchairs arranged themselves noisily at another table outside the pub.

Constable Varma continued, "After searching online, I spent the rest of yesterday on the phone. Eventually I spoke to a woman who's converted her outbuildings into small suites she's called The Hollies. And one of them was occupied by a young man on Saturday night, who arrived back late and woke her up.

"He said he'd lost his key. She thought he was drunk and had been in a fight as his jeans were ripped and he had a fresh scratch across his cheek. Also, next morning she noticed his muddy trainers outside his room."

"Who was he?"

Constable Varma removed her notebook from her trouser pocket. "He gave his name as Felix Jefferson, and he was in his mid-twenties with deep copper-coloured skin."

Dotty drew her eyebrows together as she considered the woman's description.

"What? Do you know him?" asked Constable Varma.

"I'm not sure, but a man fitting that description kept turning up whenever Zenobia was around. I first saw him loitering outside a clothes shop in Cirencester, and then he arrived at *The Antique Tour* without anything to value. Mel sent him away, but he returned several hours later carrying a marble bust."

"That sounds odd. It's not as if you go to your local garden centre and buy one of those."

"It depends on the garden centre," mused Dotty. Where had he found the statue? And why was he hanging around Zenobia?

Constable Varma picked up her menu as a middle-aged couple sat down at the table next to them. "Shall we order?"

As Dotty felt comfortable and warm sitting outside in the sun, she chose a chicken, mango and bacon salad.

"That sounds good," agreed Constable Varma, "I'll have the same, but without the chicken and bacon." She stood up, bumping clumsily against the table behind her. 'Oh, toda." She apologised to an elderly couple at the table and headed inside the pub to order.

Across on the green, several of the morris dancers appeared to be fighting each other with wooden battens. She thought morris dancing was an uplifting display.

Constable Varma sat back down and asked, "What did you do to Sergeant Unwin? He hasn't mentioned you once since his visit to Windrush Hall."

Dotty smiled. "I think he liked the dressed-up Dotty with expensive clothes and perfectly coiffured hair. Not the regular one with her hair tied up in a knot, wearing an old skirt and her deceased husband's shirt."

Constable Varma giggled.

"Although," hesitated Dotty, "it would be nice to buy some new clothes. My denim skirt and Al's shirts aren't really appropriate for the work at Akemans, especially since I'm visiting some smart houses with David Rook. But I'm not sure where to go."

"Cheltenham," declared Constable Varma. "I'd like to look round myself, but I better wait until payday at the end of the month. Talking of work, can you look through my application form for the sergeant's job with the Rural, Heritage and Wildlife Unit?"

As Constable Varma handed Dotty the papers, she heard accordion music.

The Morris dancers had added red or blue sashes to their white outfits and they all wore straw hats decorated with fresh flowers. The wooden battens were not weapons, but part of the dance routine.

The men formed two rows facing each other and began to skip, jump and turn in time to the music. The wooden battens made hollow sounds as the men tapped the ends on the floor and then against one another's battens.

Some of them wore strings of bells wrapped around their calves, which jingled as they moved.

Only in England, Dotty thought contentedly.

# CHAPTER TWENTY-THREE

The previous porter at Akemans, before Norman, had delivered auction catalogues to the shops and post offices in the surrounding towns and villages, but Dotty had willingly taken over the task.

She enjoyed exploring the Cotswolds and was even making friends with some of the shopkeepers and regular customers who awaited her arrival.

She delivered the majority of brochures on Friday, but on Saturday mornings, she made her rounds of the villages closest to Coln Akeman.

It was a damp, drizzly Saturday, and she was relieved that her last stop was the post office in her hometown, Fairford. She parked in the small car park at the top of High Street, beside the open parkland of Fairford Park and Farmor's School.

The River Coln flowed peacefully nearby.

It was always a race against time to reach the Post Office before closing time, but today she had half an hour to spare. She handed brochures to the customers waiting in line and left a stack on the usual shelf inside the shop.

Waving to the two women behind the counter, she pulled the hood of her raincoat up and stepped outside.

"Dotty, there you are," called Aunt Beanie. She was standing on the pavement at the entrance to a three-storey stone building which housed the parish offices and community centre.

Dotty joined her and asked, "How was your church meeting? Are you on better terms with the vicar?"

"I've served my penance," replied Aunt Beanie airily as she linked arms with Dotty and walked with her back to the car park.

The drive home took only a minute once they'd crossed the stone bridge over the River Coln.

"I'm so pleased the contractors have put cows in the meadow fields," acknowledged Aunt Beanie. "Cliff always used to keep cows in those fields when he was well enough to run the farm."

A large black Daimler passed them, heading towards Fairford. The elderly driver was hunched over the wheel.

"That looked like Zenobia Richardson's butler, Benson," remarked Aunt Beanie, swivelling around in her seat to watch the retreating car. "I wonder where he's been?"

As they parked in the yard at Meadowbank Farm, Norman appeared and when they climbed out of Dotty's car he asked, "Have you seen Benson?"

"So it was him," replied Aunt Beanie. "He was driving a large black car into Fairford. Why are you holding a scythe? It looks as if you're auditioning for the part of grim reaper."

Norman looked put out as he replied, "Benson asked if I had one he could borrow, to cut back weeds from the wood which are encroaching onto the lawn at Windrush Hall. He said he didn't trust strimmers."

"Has Benson added gardening to his job description?" asked Aunt Beanie.

"There isn't much butlering to do for a cat, or cooking for that matter. Benson and Françoise are happy to take on some of the everyday gardening jobs which I've agreed to oversee, and I'm allowed to hire people for trickier jobs, and those that require brute strength."

"Well, good for you all," commented Auntie Beanie as she passed Norman and went inside the farmhouse.

"I think it's a great idea," agreed Dotty as she locked her car and walked towards her front door.

"Come round for lunch, Dotty," invited Norman. "Benson brought a cool box full of food for us. Most generous."

Inside the main bedroom of her cottage, which looked out over Aunt Beanie's garden and the meadow to the River Coln, Dotty peeled off her damp clothes and changed into her jeans and a cosy jumper.

"Earl Grey," she called. He had been asleep on her bed when she left this morning.

There was no sign of her furry cat, and she presumed he was in the farmhouse with his friend, Agatha.

She entered the farmhouse kitchen but was surprised to find the black Berkshire pig alone, stretched out along the bottom of the Aga range cooker. "Have you seen Earl Grey?"

Norman was removing clingfilm from paper plates piled with slices of quiche, homemade scones and individual pies.

"He was here not long ago, sleeping next to Agatha. In fact, I expected to find him on the table when I returned, as he was sniffing around Benson's cool box. Does he like pies?"

"You know Earl Grey. He isn't fussy and will try most things."

Norman looked at her sympathetically. "Let's have lunch, and if he hasn't appeared when we've finished, I'll help you look for him. I'm sure he hasn't gone far. He hates the rain."

# CHAPTER TWENTY-FOUR

Dotty padded into Aunt Beanie's farmhouse kitchen on Sunday morning wearing Al's faded blue towelling dressing gown over her floral nightdress.

Uncle Cliff was already positioned in an armchair by the French windows in the conservatory area at the end of the kitchen, wearing a pair of headphones.

Aunt Beanie bustled in and enquired, "Sleep well?"

Dotty shook her head of crumpled hair and replied, "No, I couldn't stop thinking about Earl Grey stuck down a hole. I swear I heard his pitiful meow during the night." She laid her forearms and her head on the pine table.

She heard Aunt Beanie lift one of the heavy metal lids on the Aga and place the kettle on a hotplate to boil.

In a sympathetic tone, Aunt Beanie said, "Norman was up and about early looking for him. The rain has stopped, for now, but it's still very windy."

Dotty thought that would be worse for Earl Grey. All the frightening noises wind could make and, if he was trapped in an outbuilding, they'd be unlikely to hear his meows and he'd probably be huddled in a corner with fright.

And what if he was hungry? Or thirsty? Or cold? Or all of those things? She groaned as Aunt Beanie placed a cup on the table and she smelt a mint fragrance.

"I bought some Twinnings Morning Blend tea to try," commented Aunt Beanie. "It certainly has a reviving smell."

Dotty lifted her head and inhaled the sharp, fresh aroma, and reached for the cup. As she took her first sip, the kitchen door opened and

Norman appeared, carrying a rolled up bundle of newspapers. He moved his flat tweed cap and placed it on the side of the Aga. "It's a bit blustery out there."

"Did you find Earl Grey?" asked Dotty but she already knew the answer.

Norman exchanged a clenched smile with Aunt Beanie and came to sit at the table with Dotty.

"I'm afraid not. I searched the outbuildings again, calling for him, but there was no response. I also asked in the Co-op in town this morning but they hadn't heard anything about a stray cat. They would be happy for you to put up a poster behind the counter if you'd like to."

"And I'm sure the Post Office would let you put one in their window tomorrow."

Tomorrow, thought Dotty. Would Earl Grey survive until tomorrow?

Aunt Beanie placed a mug of coffee in front of Norman and joined them at the table.

Norman grunted his approval as he unwrapped the bundle and removed the main section of The

Mail on Sunday. As he spread it on the table, he noted, "The government is in trouble again."

"Nothing new there," responded Aunt Beanie as she extracted the 'You' magazine from the remaining sections of the newspaper.

Silence fell over the kitchen and Dotty stared over Uncle Cliff's head at the garden beyond. The morning light was dull and grey and the blossom from the apple tree twirled as it was whisked away from the tree branches.

As if it wanted to deepen her melancholy mood, rain splattered against the full-height conservatory windows.

"Now this is interesting," remarked Aunt Beanie, pulling the magazine closer to her. "A priceless statue of Lady Justice, discovered at a recent filming of *The Antique Tour*, is going on display at Carlow Gallery in Cork Street, in London's West End, before being auctioned at Gainfords."

She looked up. "If Gilmore's auction house has agreed to sell it, after last year's controversy over that Roman sculpture, they must have found someone important to authenticate it."

She looked at Dotty and announced, "We should go."

Norman looked up. "Go where?"

"To the see the exhibition."

"But it's in London." Norman sounded alarmed.

"Yes, it's not like it's St Petersburg in Russia. You can catch a train from Kemble direct to Paddington station."

"Personally," mused Norman, "I'd rather go to St Petersburg. Always fancied visiting the Hermitage Museum."

"Oh yes," agreed Aunt Beanie. "And the Shuvalov Palace, where the Fabergé Museum is housed, is supposed to be beautiful. But I digress." She turned to Dotty. "What do you think about a trip to London?"

"The auction's this week," Dotty replied dully. At least she'd be busy and have less time to worry about Earl Grey.

"Of course it is. Anything special in the catalogue?"

"Not really, the usual house clearance items. Tables, chairs and boxes of crockery, glasses and odds and ends."

"We could go on Friday, after the auction," Aunt Beanie suggested, "and ask Constable Varma to join us. I'm sure she needs a break from Inspector Evans."

"She's probably working, and I don't think she can afford a trip to London."

"Nonsense. I'll pay. It'll be my treat for coming with me. I'm excited just thinking about it."

Dotty smiled weakly. It was hard not to be infected by the older woman's enthusiasm.

"This is interesting," noted Norman. "Felix Jefferson, 26, has been taken to Cirencester police station in connection with the death of Zenobia Richardson. The police have not revealed details about his link to the famous opera singer, who tragically died last weekend."

Aunt Beanie turned the page of her magazine and gasped.

"What is it?" asked Norman, without looking up.

"A double page article about Zenobia's assistant, Serena De Rossi, accompanied by a large glossy photo of her in an unnecessarily revealing pose. And it's titled, 'How Zenobia Richardson couldn't live without me'. What poppycock."

But Aunt Beanie read on. "Zenobia was so distraught when I told her I was leaving to pursue my own singing career, which I stopped when she begged me to become her personal assistant, that she threw herself down the stairs." Aunt Beanie wrinkled her nose. "Shameful behaviour."

"And I doubt Inspect Evans will be happy about it," remarked Norman.

"Certainly not," agreed Aunt Beanie. "But it's utter rot. I heard her sing once at the London Opera House and she would never have made a soprano, she didn't have the range. If it hadn't been for Zenobia, she'd have eked out a living singing in the chorus."

"Still," considered Norman, "It's good publicity if she does want to sing again."

Dotty thought about the last time she had seen Serena, at Windrush Hall and said, "And it's good news for Zenobia's fan club, which Serena runs."

She looked at Aunt Beanie and continued, "When I went with you to Windrush Hall for the private tour, I remember her setting up a display of Zenobia's opera singing merchandise, and David and I witnessed her loading it into her car before she left."

Aunt Beanie looked down at the magazine and read, "I miss her dearly, and if you do too, why not join her fan club for a special introductory price of £29.99. You'll also have the chance to buy her exclusive *Best of CD* for £10.99 plus postage and packaging."

"Disgraceful," cried Aunt Beanie, throwing the magazine across the table.

# CHAPTER TWENTY-FIVE

D otty woke early the following Friday, and after a quick shower, she stood in her bedroom wearing only a towel, trying to decide if she would wear her wrap dress or her jeans with a nice top to London.

She peeked through the curtains and saw the sun had risen into a cloudless sky. Wrap dress it was.

The week had been busy, and the auction a success and thankfully uneventful. She'd been surprised by the number of in-person bidders on Thursday, as there were no star attractions, but it had been a miserable wet day.

She glanced at the bottom of her bed, still expecting Earl Grey to be curled up on it, and her stomach ached.

There had been no sign of him on the farm and although a couple of people had called her, after she'd printed and put up 'Lost' posters around Fairford, they had been false alarms.

One lady just wanted rid of a litter of unwanted kittens which were sweet as they rolled about and fought on her living room carpet, but they weren't her large cuddly, Earl Grey.

"Are you ready?" called Aunt Beanie from below. "Norman's starting the Land Rover."

Aunt Beanie and Dotty squeezed into the front passenger seats of the farm's Land Rover Defender and Norman manoeuvred the long gear stick and drove out of the farmyard.

Avoiding the morning rush hour traffic on the main Swindon to Cheltenham road, they followed the country lanes to the lakes of Cotswold Water Park.

"I remember when these were limestone quarries," reflected Norman.

"They've done a good job turning them into nature reserves and recreation areas," agreed Aunt Beanie.

"Reckon those houses they built beside the lakes are worth a bit."

"They will be now that silly planning rule has been removed, where owners had to vacate for one month a year. Nobody ever did, and it's far better for local businesses to have permanent occupiers, rather than Londoners using the houses as holiday homes, although I know some still do."

Kemble was a small rural station with a single-storey, Victorian stone ticket office. As Norman drove up to the front of the building Dotty spotted David and Marion Rook waiting outside.

David had thought the trip a marvellous idea, and he'd persuaded Marion and Gilly to join them.

George had a parent-teacher meeting in the afternoon so she was staying behind at the auction house and helping Norman pack up and dispatch items from the previous day's auction.

"Excellent," declared David, "You're in good time."

A small, white Mini Metro police car, with orange stripes running down each side, drove into the car park beside the station building.

"And that will be Constable Varma, so we're only waiting for Gilly," said David in a satisfied tone.

"I do hope she's on time," remarked Marion.

"Have a good day, and let me know what time your train is due in this afternoon, and I'll come and pick you up." Norman climbed into the Land Rover which spluttered into life and he drove away.

"Isn't this exciting?" exclaimed Constable Varma as she joined them. She wore a deep-green tunic over baggy black trousers.

"Do you all have your tickets?" asked David.

The women removed pieces of paper from a range of handbags. Dotty and Constable Varma had both chosen discreet bags which they wore across their bodies. Dotty had heard stories about pick pockets and handbag snatchers in London, so she wanted to be careful.

Aunt Beanie hadn't taken such precautions and carried a large, blue and white striped straw basket.

David looked impatiently at his watch and tapped his foot. "We'll give Gilly two more minutes and then we'll have to go through to platform 1 to wait for our train."

They chattered for a bit but there was still no sign of Gilly.

"Come on, everyone," instructed David, and they passed through the ticket barrier onto the station platform and joined a smattering of other people, mostly men wearing business suits, waiting for the London train.

Although on the main line between London and Wales, the small station was attractive and had retained its original features.

There were only two platforms, linked by a covered wooden footbridge, and above each were ornate wooden canopies edged with wooden dagger shaped moulding. Dotty wondered if this was the Victorian version of bunting.

David turned to the group. "A trick of mine is to sit in the restaurant car and have breakfast, and stay there all the way to London. The train becomes very crowded after Reading."

Dotty heard a crackle along the overhead electric lines.

"Here it comes. Everyone stand back." David held his arms out and stepped back a pace.

As the smart pine-green GWR train pulled into the station, Gilly rushed onto the platform. Her glasses were askew, and she was sweating.

"So sorry I'm late. Peter was away half the night attending to a patient who'd suffered a stroke, and we both slept through this morning's alarm." She took a deep breath as the train doors swished open and they climbed aboard.

The restaurant car was half full, but they found two tables, one set for four people and the other for two, across the aisle from each other. Marion sat down at the smaller table, so Constable Varma and Dotty slid across the double seats to the window of the larger table, where they were joined by Aunt Beanie and Gilly.

Gilly sat back and closed her eyes.

"Isn't this fun, and breakfast too," enthused Aunt Beanie.

Constable Varma was studying the menu and shaking her head.

"This'll be my treat ladies. I've just been paid for the private tour I conducted around Windrush Hall. Very lucrative, and such a shame there won't be any more."

"Thank you," gushed Constable Varma, perking up.

"A pleasure, constable."

"Please, everyone, call me, Keya. Constable Varma is so formal and besides," she giggled, "I'm working undercover today."

"How did you manage that?" Aunt Beanie raised her eyebrows.

"I persuaded Inspector Evans we needed to check out the sculpture, as there's been a lot of fuss about it in the newspapers. I told him you never know who you might bump into at these events. Actually, I think he was distracted searching about gardens on the internet. He just grunted his approval."

Dotty watched two waiters, further along the carriage, serve a table of four women who also appeared excited about the day ahead. They toasted each other with glasses of champagne before the waiters served them breakfast.

Dotty was surprised and amazed at the waiters' skill as they placed each breakfast item on the ladies' plates. She would have expected the chef to load up the plates in the kitchen and the waiters to carry them through to the restaurant car.

The train banked as it swept around a corner, but the waiters appeared unperturbed and carried on serving.

One of the waiters lifted his head and Dotty noticed a scar running across his deep, copper coloured cheek.

He quickly bowed his head and continued serving, but Dotty thought she'd seen a spark of recognition in his eyes.

The second waiter approached their table and took their orders. Everyone ordered a full English breakfast apart from Keya who chose eggs Florentine.

Aunt Beanie regaled them with stories about previous trips to London, and Dotty enjoyed the party atmosphere, while continuing to watch the waiter.

"Excuse me," she said, and Aunt Beanie shuffled out of her seat to allow Dotty to pass. Dotty made her way down the carriage to the kitchen area where the waiter was wrapping knives and forks in white cotton napkins.

Summoning her strength and courage, she asked, "Isn't it time we were introduced? I presume you are Felix Jefferson."

The waiter reached for another napkin.

With a note of awe in her voice, Dotty asked, "Did you really climb up the clematis trellis on the side of the turret at Charbury Castle Hotel?"

Felix glanced at Dotty and smiled nervously before continuing with his work.

"It was very brave," pressed Dotty.

"Not really. The trellis was like a ladder and easy enough to climb." It had been covered in a thick layer of clematis leaves and flowers, so Dotty doubted it had been as simple as Felix made out.

"But why take the risk when you had no idea if you could get in through the top window?"

"It wasn't a risk. I'd unfastened the turret window in the afternoon. I overheard the Australian lady say all the short-listed items, to be filmed on Sunday, would be kept overnight on the second floor, and security wouldn't be an issue as the crew were sleeping on the same floor.

Someone joked, 'Even Zenobia', and she said yes."

"Come on, Felix, take the plates. We're ready to serve," admonished the chef, through the open kitchen hatch.

"This is your food, miss."

On an impulse, Dotty asked, "When does your shift finish?"

"When we pull into Paddington station. Why?"

"Then why not join us? We're going to an exhibition which is displaying the bronze statue from that weekend. The one that could be worth millions of pounds."

"Felix," called the chef.

"Excuse me." Felix picked up a pile of plates and carried them down to Dotty's group's tables, where he carefully placed one in front of everyone except Keya.

He returned, and the chef handed him a plate with two poached eggs sitting on spinach-covered English muffins. A white jug held a rich yellow sauce.

"Please, miss. I need to work."

"Will you join us when we reach Paddington?"

Felix signed. "I suppose so, but I don't know about any exhibition."

Dotty and her friends ate their breakfasts enthusiastically, and they were finishing their second cups of tea and coffee when the guard announced over the tannoy, "Next station, London Paddington. This train terminates at London Paddington."

# CHAPTER TWENTY-SIX

Marion and David gathered their belongings together and led Gilly, Aunt Beanie, Keya and Dotty off the train.

Dotty hesitated beside the restaurant car door closest to the front of the train.

"I'm not sure we'll all fit into one taxi," declared David.

"Taxi," repeated Aunt Beanie. "Much quicker and cheaper to take the underground. The Bakerloo line goes directly to Oxford Circus, and it's less than ten minutes' walk to Cork Street from there."

The other waiter, who'd been serving the people in the restaurant carriage, climbed down from the train.

"Is Felix coming?" asked Dotty.

"He's just getting his coat."

Aunt Beanie and David were still arguing about the best mode of transport as Felix stepped down onto the platform.

"Ready?" she asked.

"I'll come with you as far as the tube station. You can ask me what you want on the way."

"I'm going by tube," insisted Aunt Beanie. "As you said, there isn't enough room in a taxi for all of us."

"I'll come too," added Dotty quickly, "And so will Keya, won't you?" She looked round at her friend, who shrugged her shoulders.

"That's settled," announced Aunt Beanie. "Race you," and she set off down the platform with such speed that Dotty, Keya and Felix had to run to catch her up.

As they slowed to a walk, Dotty said, "This is Felix."

Keya looked at him and screwed up her eyes. "Hang on, I know you. Sergeant Unwin brought you in for questioning. You climbed the turret at Charbury Castle Hotel."

"That was very daring of you," remarked Aunt Beanie, hoisting her straw basket further up her arm.

Felix stopped. "You didn't tell me the police were with you."

"Keya's not really police," replied Dotty brightly. Out of the corner of her eye, she saw her friend frown. "Well, she is, but she's the nice, understanding side of the force. Anyway, it's her day off."

Dotty hid her hand behind her back and crossed her fingers.

"Look, we only want to find out what happened when you climbed into the library at the hotel. If Inspector Evans thinks you're involved, he'll tease away at you like a terrier and you won't have any peace. It's far better to let us help you discover the truth," Dotty reasoned.

"Come on," insisted Aunt Beanie.

They set off again at a jog towards Paddington underground station.

"What ticket do I buy?" asked Keya.

"If you don't have an Oyster card, just use your credit card," instructed Aunt Beanie, removing a blue card from her wallet.

"Hold the card against the yellow pad on the right of the barrier and do the same at Oxford Circus when you leave." Aunt Beanie marched across to a row of metal gates, held her card against the pad and the gate flicked open, allowing her through.

Gingerly, Dotty followed her lead and Felix was relaxed as he also used a blue plastic card to open the gates. There was a cry behind them as Keya rushed through the gates before they closed on her.

"Dangerous place, London," she remarked.

The platform was only a third full and the monitor above it told them they had one minute to wait until the first train, which terminated at a place called Elephant and Castle. Dotty felt a rush of air and then a squat white train with red doors and a blue undercarriage pulled into the station with a whoosh.

They climbed aboard and found a pair of double seats facing each other. Dotty decide to start at the beginning and asked, "How did you know Zenobia Richardson?"

Felix replied, "We met when I sang alongside her at the National Theatre."

"Wow, you're an opera singer." Dotty raised her voice as the noise increased along with the train's speed.

"I'm a blues singer, but I was asked to sing a supporting role in a new opera, and it was great fun. I'd only performed in nightclubs and small venues before, so to stand on stage in front of nearly twelve hundred people, it was exhilarating."

As they pulled into Marylebone Station, Felix's eyes flashed with energy until a shadow passed across them. "But Zenobia Richardson didn't like someone else gaining attention, nor did she like to be turned down."

"What do you mean?" asked Keya.

"I think I know," nodded Aunt Beanie sagely. "A young, virile man like yourself. Zenobia wouldn't be able to help herself. But she wasn't your type, was she?"

Felix's cheeks shone, and he looked down at the floor.

The train stopped at Baker Street and lots of people disembarked while others got on. A teenager wearing a large pair of black headphones, which didn't entirely hide the rhythmic bass sound of the music he was listening to, sat across the aisle from them.

As the train moved away from the station, Felix whispered, "You're right. I'm gay, but because I refused her advances, she started blaming me when things went wrong, and then she accused me of assaulting her.

"It was a complete lie, but who do you think they believed? An established star or new black singer? I was dismissed from the show and I haven't been able to get a part in a show since."

"So why have you been hanging around Zenobia?" asked Dotty.

"I'm fed up of scratching a living as a waiter and only being given the odd slot to sing at nightclubs. The stage was fun, and I know I have the talent to perform, if only someone will give me a chance."

"So why hang around Zenobia?" repeated Dotty.

"She ruined my life, but I thought if I apologised, she would lift whatever invisible embargo she had preventing me from landing a singing role. But I could never get close. That talentless assistant always spotted me and sent me away."

"So, what happened on Saturday evening?" asked Keya.

"This is Oxford Circus," a voice announced. "Change here for the Central and Victoria lines."

Dotty, Keya and Aunt Beanie stood up.

"Aren't you coming?" enquired Dotty.

Felix consulted his watch. "I suppose I might as well."

Aunt Beanie led them through the maze of corridors and out onto Regent Street. Dotty was taken aback by the imposing five and six-storey stone buildings and the sheer number of people who pushed passed them. And the noise. Black taxis honked and the shoes of crowds of people slapped the stone pavement as they walked. She watched the red London buses slowly moving along the road.

As Aunt Beanie marched ahead, Keya and Dotty stared at the passing window displays of world renowned clothing brands.

"Can we go in here?" cried Keya as a line of red canopies, protruding from a stone building, revealed they were outside the famous Hamleys toy shop.

"Not now," replied Aunt Beanie as she skirted a group of animated children. "This way," she instructed, and they followed her as she crossed one lane of Regent Street, stopped on the central reservation for a gap in the slow-moving traffic, and crossed the second lane.

They turned into a quiet, elegant side street with cars parked outside expensive looking restaurants.

Dotty walked alongside Felix and asked, "So, what did happen on Saturday night?"

"Despite buying a marble bust at the Antiques Centre in Cirencester, I wasn't able to speak to Zenobia properly during her valuation. When I heard she was staying at the hotel, I asked for a room but none were available.

"Instead, I looked on the internet and found somewhere to stay nearby. Then I looked for a way to speak to her on her own, without the possessive presence of her assistant. I hoped it would be in the bar or restaurant, but just in case, I made a back-up plan."

"To climb up the side of the hotel and break in through the turret window," remarked Keya.

"I wasn't breaking in."

"How did you know which room was Zenobia's?" Dotty asked, wanting to keep the conversation casual.

"While I was hanging around the hotel lobby, the receptionist was called away and I was able to look on her screen."

"So your plan was to climb up the tower, into the library, and knock on her door. What if she was asleep or refused to open it?" Keya frowned.

He shrugged. "I would have waited. Slept in the corridor outside her room if necessary. I wasn't leaving until I spoke to her."

Dotty turned to him and asked, "And did you?"

# CHAPTER TWENTY-SEVEN

Aunt Beanie certainly knew her way around London's smart West End. She turned left onto Saville Row, famous for its men's outfitters, and Dotty glanced into the windows of elegant shops displaying tweed and wool suits.

Then they turned right and entered Clifford Street, with large Georgian townhouse-style buildings and a scattering of restaurants and specialist shops at ground floor level.

"Here we are, Cork Street," announced Aunt Beanie.

As they entered a tarpaulin-covered tunnel that protected them from the construction works on the building above, Dotty repeated, "Did you speak to Zenobia?"

"Yes," admitted Felix. "When I pushed open the turret window, I heard a man's voice call 'goodnight' and a door close. It was awkward climbing through the window and as I twisted around, I caught my jeans on the ledge as I tumbled to the floor. It was not the discreet entrance I had been hoping for."

He grinned sheepishly.

"I had no idea who was in the library until I heard Zenobia shout out, 'Who's there?'. This was the opportunity I'd been waiting for, but I hesitated. Zenobia called out again, so I stood up, brushed myself down and walked as confidently as I could into the room."

"What was Zenobia doing?" asked Dotty.

"It was strange. She was sitting on a chair facing a sculpture, presumably the one we've come to see today, with her laptop, and a notebook and pencil beside the chair."

Dotty turned to Keya. "That must be the notebook we found. And have the police accessed her laptop?"

"Yes, but there wasn't anything incriminating or exciting. Her last internet searches were all about the history of bronze sculptures and that sort of thing."

"A draw," declared Aunt Beanie.

Dotty, Keya and Felix came to a halt beside some black railings, outside a Georgian brick building with a glass shop front.

Gilly, Marion and David stepped out of a black cab, which had just pulled to a stop beside the kerb.

"I hope you had a pleasant journey," said David.

Dotty felt flushed and a little dishevelled after her march through the West End.

"Isn't London a fascinating place?" enthused Gilly, smiling widely.

"Shall we?" David pushed open a black panelled door and they entered Carlow Gallery.

It was surprisingly light inside. The room occupied the full width of the building and extended back at least twenty metres. The walls were painted white but were not stark and cold but warm, perhaps as a result of the mellow wooden floor and lines of overhead lighting. Pictures and paintings hung on the walls while statues, sculptures and other collectables were displayed on plinths or inside glass boxes, placed around the gallery.

A crowd of people were gathered at the far end.

Casper Dupré held his arms out in greeting and called, "It's the country set. Welcome to my humble abode."

"Thank you, Casper," replied David. "You know my wife, Marion, and this is Gilly Wimsey, a colleague at Akemans Antiques, and Bernadette Devereux, who founded the company."

Casper shook hands with each of them as Keya commented, "I'd forgotten Aunt Beanie set up and ran Akemans."

"I think she misses being involved in the antiques world," replied Dotty.

A dark-haired man wearing a waistcoat over a striped shirt and pair of jeans turned towards Dotty and smiled. It was Gilmore, but before Dotty could approach him, David called, "Gilmore, thank you for coming this morning." The two men moved further into the gallery.

Dotty spotted a table of refreshments to her left. "Let's grab a drink and see if we can finish our discussion."

She, Keya and Felix stood in a corner holding glasses of orange juice and water.

"To recap," began Dotty, "you climbed into the library through the turret window and heard a man leaving the room. I think that was David. You found Zenobia alone, studying the sculpture.

"I know, from discussions with David and Gilmore, that she was worried about making a fool of herself, or even worse, jeopardising her career if she made the wrong valuation on Sunday. That must be why she was researching it. So what happened next?"

"She didn't even recognise me." Felix bowed his head.

"She'd ruined my career, but it meant so little to her. It rather knocked my confidence, and I clammed up, but she kept badgering me, asking what I wanted. Eventually I snapped and cried, 'I want my life back'. That surprised her." Felix smiled, but it did not reach his eyes.

"I explained who I was and how my career was in ruins, all because she had me sacked from the show at the National. She waved her hands airily and told me to keep trying, and if I had talent, I'd land another role.

"Then she told me to go away, but I refused. I said I wasn't going anywhere until she lifted the curse which was stopping me getting parts, and I sat down.

"She huffed and puffed and eventually said, 'all right, I can't concentrate with you staring at me. If I write you a note, will that do? Marcel is auditioning singers for a new show at the Soho Theatre. Take it along to him and see if you get a part. But if you don't, stop blaming me for your woes'."

"And did you?" asked Keya, wide eyed.

"The first round of auditions was last week, when you had me banged up in your police station."

Keya bit her lip.

"But there are auditions for the minor parts this afternoon, and the theatre is near here, which is why I'm happy to hang around here, with you lot this morning, rather than go home."

Dotty smiled. "That's really exciting, and well done. And what happened after Zenobia gave you the note?"

"My nerves got the better of me. I stammered my thanks and ran down the staircase and out of the side door, by the bar. There were still people drinking in there, so they, or the barman, should have seen me leave."

"I'll make sure we check," agreed Keya.

# CHAPTER TWENTY-EIGHT

The crowd at the far end of the gallery dispersed and Dotty saw the bronze of Lady Justice illuminated in a glass case.

"Shall we view the sculpture?" asked Dotty. "It is the reason we came."

Still cradling their soft drinks, Dotty, Keya and Felix navigated around other visitors and works of art and approached the centrepiece of the exhibition.

It appeared far more impressive on display in the gallery, rather than in the hotel garden or library, and Dotty marvelled at the detailing of the folds of the figure's gown and the scales she carried, which contrasted with her smooth skin. The effect was captivating.

"I can understand what all the fuss is about," Felix commented as he slowly walked around the glass case, studying the sculpture from all angles.

"But it's all rusty." Keya sounded disappointed.

Aunt Beanie must have overheard her. "Wouldn't you be if you were two thousand years old? Bronze is an alloy created by melting copper and tin. As the years pass, the copper oxidizes with the air and deteriorates.

"Sculptures were finished by hand painting a protective layer, called a patina, but over time it wears down and the copper turns red, like her arm, or green as it is on her sword and around the base."

"So it really is from Roman times." Keya was staring at the sculpture with her mouth hanging open.

"That's what the experts say." Aunt Beanie pressed her lips together.

A distinguished-looking gentleman approached, wearing a well-cut charcoal grey suit which accentuated his presence while disguising his slight paunch.

He asked, "What does your nose tell you about this treasure, Bernadette? It's certainly the talk of the town."

"Chief Inspector," exclaimed Aunt Beanie. "It's not so much my nose as my gut, but since you're here, I expect you have the same misgivings."

"It's plain inspector at the moment, and has been since the Gloucestershire Antiques and Antiquities division closed down. You left at the right time. It was criminal closing the office with a number of cases still unsolved, especially those we'd been working on for several years.

"As for this sculpture, it's certainly unusual for a priceless antique to surface without anyone knowing about it. But it does happen." He smiled thinly.

"Like looted treasure reappearing in Iraqi museums?" Aunt Beanie remarked.

"I see you haven't let that one go. Rumours continued after you left the division, but we could never pin any of them down."

Aunt Beanie's mouth twitched.

"I'm not saying you were wrong, but we didn't have the resources to pursue it."

The inspector turned to Dotty, Keya and Felix. Dotty had been listening to the conversation with interest while Keya and Felix whispered together on the far side of the display cabinet.

"This is my young friend, and lodger, Dotty, who works at Akemans."

"Pleased to meet you." The man held out his hand for her to shake and smiled warmly.

"And this is another friend, Constable Varma, or Keya as she's told us to call her today." Aunt Beanie lowered her voice. "She's working undercover."

Felix's face darkened as Keya sidled away from him.

"Really, that's most interesting," mused the inspector.

"It is?" Aunt Beanie drew her eyebrows together.

Dotty grabbed Felix's arm as he stalked past her. She whispered, "It was the only way Keya could afford the trip to London."

Felix scowled.

"I've received an application from a Constable Varma for a sergeant's position in the new Rural, Heritage and Wildlife Unit, which I will be heading up for Gloucestershire Police."

"You're returning to the area?" Aunt Beanie grinned.

"And I hope to reopen some of those unsolved cases." He pressed his finger to the side of his nose. "But that's just between you and me." He turned to Keya and said, "So young lady, why do you want to join the new unit?"

Keya hesitated, and Dotty nudged her gently in the back and whispered. "Go on, this is your chance."

"It will be fun, and interesting," she said stiltedly, and gave Dotty an imploring look.

Dotty nodded her encouragement.

"And I love working with the local people and businesses in the Cotswolds and it's such a wonderful area and I know I can help protect and support it."

"As you do now," added Aunt Beanie.

"Well said, constable. Keep up the good work and you may find the position yours. Bernadette, if I may?" He indicated towards an empty area at the rear of the gallery, and the two of them moved away.

"So you are on duty today," Felix spat.

Keya sighed. "I'm always on duty to some extent. And as Dotty said, now I know the full story, I can look for witnesses who were in the bar and saw you leave, well before Miss Richardson's body was found."

"If you say so." Felix appeared only partially appeased.

Keya turned back to the statue and said, "The information on the back of the case says that there is a reserve on the statue of £500,000. Is that like a price?"

"A minimum price," explained Dotty.

"But I could buy a house for that, and a car, and a new wardrobe and holiday in the sun."

"You're talking about a different world," explained Felix. "For rich people, buying a car is like me buying a new pair of trainers. And I don't think it's because they like the sculpture.

"The person who buys this claims the bragging rights for outbidding everyone else. I've seen people like that in some of the clubs I've performed in, and I used to benefit when they gave me a £50 or £100 tip. Now that's a good gig to have. Shame I lost so many of them."

"But if you get a new part in a show," suggested Dotty.

"If." Felix looked dejected.

"The sculpture's owner is a lucky man," said Keya.

"Yes," Dotty agreed. She looked back along the gallery and spotted Emery and Casper being greeted by a fashionably dressed couple, who Dotty recognised as actors from a recent Sunday evening television drama.

"And it isn't doing Casper and his gallery any harm, either." She watched as the fashionable couple moved away, and Casper wrapped his arm around Emery's thickset waist. Emery wore a polo shirt, but it still strained against his muscled torso.

"And it looks as if he and Emery have developed a close relationship since the weekend at Charbury Castle Hotel," she added.

Felix stood beside Dotty and followed her gaze. "I know Casper Dupré. Is he the owner of this place? He's a regular at one of the clubs I play in, and if you mean his partner, the bald-headed man wearing the tight fitting shirt, then they've been an item since Christmas."

Dotty turned to him, wide-eyed. "But at the filming of *The Antique Tour*, they made out they'd only just met. And how do you know how long they've been together?"

"From that club I mentioned. It was one of the few who supported me after the theatre fiasco, and I sing there three or four times a month. I did some extra gigs over Christmas and New Year and I remember those two meeting.

"The bald guy came in with other overly muscular friends and they caused a bit of trouble. The manager was about to throw them out, but Casper intervened and calmed the situation down. I've seen them together several times since then."

Dotty felt her stomach tighten. "Then why did they pretend not to know each other?"

# CHAPTER TWENTY-NINE

Dotty, Keya and Felix moved away from the bronze sculpture of Lady Justice as the fashionable actor couple moved towards it and were immediately accosted by three student-age girls holding out mobile phones.

The couple fixed smiles on their faces as they became the focus of selfie photos. Dotty wasn't sure which was the bigger attraction, the sculpture or the couple.

Felix looked at his watch. "I better go and find somewhere quiet to prepare for my audition."

Dotty placed a hand on his arm. "Good luck. Do you have Zenobia's letter?"

Gilly joined them as Felix unfolded a piece of paper ripped from a notebook. "I hope they believe Zenobia wrote it."

Gilly leaned over and looked at the note. "Don't give that away. It could be worth something now she's dead."

Felix wrinkled his forehead as he refolded the note.

"And we'll come and see you in the show, won't we, Keya?" encouraged Dotty.

"Of course. I'd love to see a West End show."

"So would I," agreed Gilly, "But for now I'd like to visit Ralph Lauren's flagship store. It's supposed to be an exhibition in itself. And there's an interesting life-size statue of a horse and rider on the pavement in front of it."

They waved Felix goodbye and joined Aunt Beanie, Marion and David.

David said, "I've booked a table at The Grill at The Dorchester at one-thirty."

"Inspector Ringrose is taking me to another exhibition," announced Aunt Beanie.

"And we're going to look round the shops, aren't we girls?" enthused Gilly.

As they poured out of the gallery, Dotty heard David call, "Don't be late for lunch."

"We really must go," said Dotty in an exasperated tone. "It's a fifteen-minute walk to The Dorchester Hotel. Google maps say it's on Park Lane."

"That sounds smart," said Keya, but her attention was on the bright floral skirt displayed on the mannequin in front of her. She lifted up the soft material and let go, watching it float back into place.

The Polo Ralph Lauren store occupied a prominent corner position, and Dotty had noted one street was New Bond Street. Inside, it was divided into rooms, each with a distinct theme. Her favourite was devoted to classic menswear.

The walls were covered with wooden panelling and the leather furniture and butler's trays, with bottles of water for thirsty customers, enhanced the effect of a gentleman's club.

A billiard table had been placed in the centre of the room, covered with a violet coloured felt cloth which supported a large silver trophy holding several orchid plants with white blooms.

A display of menswear, including brown brogue shoes and a leather overnight bag, was neatly arranged upon it and she imagined a younger, more glamorous version of Benson, Zenobia's butler, laying it out.

She was now in the women's section with Gilly and Keya.

"What wonderful flowers," exclaimed Gilly as she stepped behind two mannequins. One was wearing a pretty blue and white floral dress and the other white trousers and a blue and white striped boating style top. Behind them, a table held a huge display of blue hydrangeas and delphiniums, and white lilies and roses.

"It is, but it's time to leave," insisted Dotty. "I've looked up the restaurant we're going to, and it has a Michelin star. I don't know about you two, but I've never eaten at such a place, and I don't want to be late."

Gilly and Keya finally left the shop with Dotty, who followed the map on her phone as she led them up new New Bond Street to Bruton Street, around the top of Berkeley Square and along Hill Street, which appeared to be a mix of offices and upmarket period houses and flats.

When the imposing Dorchester Hotel came into view, she stopped to take a breather. The concave concrete front of the hotel didn't face onto Park Lane but instead looked down it, with a private drop off area and small garden in front of the entrance.

The architecture of the building, including the iron railings across the front balconies, was an art deco style and this, together with two rows of red cyclamen above the entrance, captivated Dotty.

A smiling doorman dressed in a green uniform, complete with a black top hat and bow tie, directed them to the Bar and Grill. Dotty spotted an ornate gilt clock on the wall. They were only five minutes late.

The restaurant was much smaller than Dotty had expected. David was seated at the head of a table set for seven people, and beside him were Aunt Beanie and Gilmore. Dotty counted only twelve other tables, seating two to four people, although most of the bar seats which, unlike bar stools, had backs to them, were also occupied.

The art deco theme continued through the geometric-shaped wooden floor tiles, and the patterns on the mirrored wall and ornate ceiling. The overall colour scheme was cream, gold and brown. It felt extremely opulent.

Marion appeared and took the seat next to Gilmore as the others sat down.

"I need a drink after that dash across Mayfair," exclaimed Gilly, removing her navy cardigan and fanning her flushed face with her hand.

David announced, "Gilmore has kindly ordered a bottle of champagne, and don't worry about the cost, constable - sorry Keya - the company is paying."

Gilly grinned, and whispered to Dotty and Keya, "Even though George will be furious when she finds out we've been here."

As well as chilled champagne, the waiter bought each of them a small plate of delicacies which he said were, "Compliments of the chef. I present lightly smoked trout mousse, a skewer of sea bream and a blini of salmon eggs."

Dotty leaned towards Keya and asked, "Can you eat this?"

Keya looked slightly queasy. "I do eat fish, but I'm not sure about the salmon eggs."

"If you don't want them," interjected Aunt Beanie, "Pass them along. They're far tastier than caviar."

Dotty savoured the champagne, her delicious food and the ambiance of the restaurant.

She was still lost in her own world when Aunt Beanie elbowed her in the side. "Stop daydreaming and answer Gilmore's question."

Dotty felt the heat rush to her cheeks as she stammered, "What question?"

Gilmore smiled. "I was only interested to know what you thought of the sculpture today?"

"It looks very impressive, displayed in its case, in the gallery. The light enhanced all the details."

"Who's going to buy it for half a million pounds?" asked Keya, a note of doubt in her voice.

"If it's the real deal, a rich Arab sultan or Russian oligarch, most likely," replied Gilmore.

Dotty heard Keya mutter, "Money to burn," under her breath.

She looked from Gilmore to David to Aunt Beanie and said, "If it is the real deal, which is literally the million dollar question, how can its authenticity be either proved, or disproved?"

David sat back and replied, "Shall we order before embarking on that discussion?"

Dotty chose Cornish crab tart for her starter and pork with black pudding stuffed cabbage, which sounded intriguing, as her main course.

"Wonderful to see such a great use of British ingredients," enthused Aunt Beanie.

When the waiter had taken all their orders and departed, David began, "There are a number of so-called tests, although most are easier to undertake with modern sculptures, where someone uses a real statuette to create a mould, from which a replica is cast. Nobody has seen a sculpture exactly like the one on display, so it must be an original."

David sipped his champagne, so Gilmore continued. "Next, we look at the detailing. Replicas are often poorly defined but the chasing work, which is done when the bronze cast is cooling, is detailed and precise on this sculpture. And there is a lot of detailing. It took a skilled craftsman to finish it."

David took up the explanation. "But the most difficult element to replicate is the wearing down of the patina which was painted on the sculpture to prevent it corroding. You noticed the green and red tints?"

"I pointed them out to her," interrupted Aunt Beanie.

"The Lady Justice is well preserved, but as expected, some of the patina has worn down. It's extremely difficult to fake that as it depends on the handling, atmosphere and, of course, the passage of time."

"But is it possible?" asked Dotty.

The waiter returned and placed their starters on the table.

David held his hands together as if praying and replied, "I believe so."

# CHAPTER THIRTY

On Tuesday morning, Norman drove himself and Dotty to Akemans Antiques in the farm's Land Rover Defender.

The red battery warning light had flashed on Dotty's Skoda Fabia dashboard on Saturday morning as she was returning from the supermarket. Norman told her it meant the battery had a fault and was not charging, and might need replacing.

He helped her start her car on Monday morning and picked her up from the garage at Coln Akeman. She was still waiting for an update on what work needed doing.

She spent the morning finishing paperwork from the previous week's auction.

A mahogany corner cabinet still needed collecting and two sets of dining tables and chairs, an assortment of table lamps and a collection of kitchen paraphernalia needed returning to the store to be re-presented at the following month's auction.

George stalked into the office and said, "I've just had Marion on the phone asking if we need her this week. David left on a last-minute trip abroad and she only has a round of golf and a tennis match in the diary. I've agreed and thought it would be a good opportunity for you to help Gilly sort out the antiques centre.

"I know she gave it a good airing the other week, but can you persuade her to call the contract cleaners? There are layers of dust on the walls and the floor is filthy."

Dotty was happy to help in the antiques centre and leave the organising and delivery of the first Lots for next month's auction to Marion.

George spun round in the doorway to the auction room and added, "And Gilly tells me you are setting up a bargain stall on the first floor. Take the leftover boxes of assorted kitchen items. There's no point putting them in next month's sale as they'll be lucky to reach £20, and they take up a lot of space."

Dotty closed her computer and followed George into the auction room where Norman greeted her.

"George has told me to take these boxes to your stall on the first floor of the antiques centre," he said. "Is that right?"

"That's what she's just told me." Dotty considered the contents of the boxes and her enthusiasm grew. In one she noted a slow cooker, a set of green table mats and a large ceramic bread bin. And they were now hers, to sell on her very own stall.

She picked up the box and carried it through to the antiques centre.

At the top of the metal staircase, she came to an abrupt halt. Clearly, Gilly wasn't the only one with unwanted items to get rid of. In the middle of the space Dotty had marked out for her stall there were at least twenty cardboard boxes and an assortment of lamps, vases and bowls had been left on the rear shelving unit.

Was this going to be more work than she had anticipated? And where should she start?

Norman grunted as he manhandled a pine table to the top of the stairs. He dropped it to the floor and said, "George has donated this. She said there's no point trying to sell it next month as we have a have an assortment of tables from a house clearance."

"Can you put it over there?" Dotty pointed to a circular oak table with a large burn mark in the centre. "I need somewhere to unpack all these."

Norman looked around and grinned. "That'll keep you busy for the rest of the day."

He was right. Dotty unpacked the boxes and as she did, she was able to separate the contents into groups. All the trays she displayed on shelves next to the wall, beside the floral ones from Mrs Wade's stall. Beneath them were a collection of glasses and above them jugs and mugs.

There was another shelf for baking related items, one for crockery and another for an assortment of ornaments. She arranged the costume jewellery and knick-knacks on the pine table, covered with one of Mrs Wade's tablecloths, which she'd washed and ironed at home.

She found an embroidered circular linen table mat in one of the boxes from the auction, which neatly covered the burn mark on the oak table.

On it, she placed a large porcelain vase decorated with images of peacocks. She swivelled it around so the chip on the lip faced away from the stairs.

Gilly opened the door to her office and spotting Dotty, walked over to her stall. "I hate paperwork," she declared, "but I still have a stack of invoices to send out and bills to pay." She surveyed the stall area. "Wow, how much did I give you?"

"It's not all yours. I think the other stall holders heard of the new venture and George gave me some unwanted items from the last auction."

"What are you doing with this vase? It has a chip in it."

"I know, but it's large and attractive. I thought I'd take a tip from the Ralph Lauren store we visited and fill it with fresh flowers. They'll brighten the place up and their fragrance will hide some of the fustiness."

Norman climbed the stairs, wearing his flat cap. "Are you ready to go, Dotty? I've got that appointment with Zenobia Richardson's solicitor at Windrush Park at four thirty."

"Is that OK?" Dotty looked at Gilly.

"Of course it is. I'll see you tomorrow."

Norman ground the gears and manhandled the long gearstick as the old Land Rover chugged along the narrow Cotswold lanes until they turned off the road and drove between the stone pillars which marked the entrance to Windrush Hall.

A large black car was already parked in front of the house, so Dotty and Norman climbed the stone steps to the front door. Inside, they spotted Benson in the dining room, serving Charles Willoughby coffee from a cafetière.

"Come, come," said the solicitor, impatiently, "I have to get back to London this evening."

"I'll pop through to the kitchen to see Françoise," Dotty told Norman, but as she moved towards it, Benson stepped into her path.

"I'm afraid it's rather a mess in there," he disclosed. "Françoise would be mortified if you saw it, but let me tell her you're here."

"And Mario?"

Benson paled.

"Is he OK? He seemed very upset about his mistress's death last time I was here."

Benson inhaled and replied, "He still misses her and is not quite himself at the moment."

Benson turned away and as he opened the kitchen door, she heard a mournful 'meow'.

She turned back to the dining room and noted several piles of papers arranged in front of Charles Willoughby, on the polished mahogany dining table. He looked up at Norman and said, "I need to resolve which of Zenobia's projects have been completed and which are still ongoing."

Benson returned and whispered to Dotty, "Françoise will be with us in a few minutes."

"First, has the summer house been completed?" asked the solicitor.

Norman looked at Benson who replied, "What summer house, Sir?"

"The ones these plans are for." He unfolded an architect's drawing of a building resembling a Greek temple.

"I'm not aware of any summer house, sir."

The solicitor mumbled something Dotty did not catch and lifted the top sheet from another pile. "What about the cedar wood garage and storeroom?"

Benson shook his head. "The Daimler is parked in the stone barn, which I believe the Duke converted for such a purpose."

"He did," confirmed Norman.

Charles Willoughby muttered something else to himself and picked up a sheet from a third pile. "Surely the greenhouse has been built."

"Not the new one, Sir. The mistress was planning to, but she couldn't decide where to put it or how large it should be. We were discussing options the week before she died."

"But she'd already had these plans drawn up." The solicitor waved the paper.

"I'm sorry, Sir," said Benson, apologetically. 'But she hadn't finalised the design, and I know she hadn't had any plans drawn up."

Charles Willoughby sat back and placed his arms on the table. "I don't understand. I was given a list of proposed works and I sent money over so drawings and costings could be prepared."

He lifted his hand to indicate the papers in front of him. "And when I'd received those, I sent money for the building work." He looked at Benson and wrinkled his brow. "So, where is the money? And why has this work not been done?"

"It is the first I have heard of any of this, Sir." Benson maintained eye contact with the solicitor.

Françoise bustled into the room wearing her yellow-tinted glasses and carrying a silver tray. "There we are, mes chéris, warm scones straight out of the oven with my raspberry jam and some fresh cream."

Dotty's stomach gurgled and Norman stared intently at the plate as his smile grew.

"Never mind scones," cried the solicitor. "Where is the money?"

Françoise yelped, and the tray clattered to the stone floor.

Norman pulled a handkerchief, or it could have been a rag, out of his pocket and began mopping jam as it spilled out onto the fine Turkish rug beneath the mahogany dining table.

"Really, Sir," beseeched Benson. "We know nothing about any building work, nor any money for it. Maybe you should ask Serena."

"I've tried to, but she's surprisingly elusive at the moment."

"Did you speak to Miss Richardson directly about these projects?" asked Dotty in a timid voice.

"No, I always dealt with Serena."

The colour drained from Charles Willoughby's face.

Françoise scuttled back to the kitchen, her face flushed, and the scones, cream and jam, scattered around her tray.

Norman turned towards the solicitor and remarked, "I think you've been taken for a ride."

# CHAPTER THIRTY-ONE

D otty returned to Meadowbank Farm on Wednesday evening in her Skoda Fabia. The garage at Coln Akeman had replaced the battery for £150, which Norman told her was reasonable.

She wandered through to the kitchen of the main farmhouse and Agatha, the Berkshire pig and Earl Grey's friend, trotted across to greet her.

Agatha's body was covered with wiry black hair and she had white legs, which resembled socks, and a broad white stripe down the centre of her nose and around her snout, which she lifted enquiringly up to Dotty.

Her erect ears listened as Dotty squatted down, stroked her and said consolingly, "You're missing Earl Grey too, aren't you?" In response, Agatha snuggled up to Dotty.

Uncle Cliff was seated in his customary chair in the conservatory section of the kitchen, wearing his headphones.

Aunt Beanie and Norman strode into the kitchen together. Aunt Beanie tucked stray strands of grey hair under her brown headscarf as she said, "I'm pleased that five-bar gate finally arrived since you've worked so hard repairing and painting the walls in the shed. Are you still interested in buying a cow?"

"I am and that's why I wanted to fit the gate today. Some Jerseys are being sold at Thursday's livestock market, at Driffield."

Dotty looked up and asked, "Where's that?"

"Just off the main dual carriageway, between the Cotswold Water Park and Cirencester," replied Aunt Beanie, before turning back to Norman and asking, "But how do you know one good cow from another?"

"I don't, which is why I hoped you'd come with me. I've already spoken to Mrs Todd, and she's free that day to sit with Cliff, until her late afternoon bingo."

"Why not," declared Aunt Beanie. "It'll be fun visiting the market again, but I think we'll take Cliff with us. He might enjoy the trip. At one time, he visited the old market in Cirencester every week to catch up with friends and keep abreast of local farming news."

There was a knock on the kitchen door.

"Are we expecting company?" asked Norman.

Aunt Beanie shook her head as Dotty straightened up and went to open the door.

"Hiya," beamed Keya, as Dotty felt comfortable referring to her since she wasn't wearing her uniform. "I hope I'm not disturbing you."

"No, you're not. Come in."

Keya walked past Dotty carrying a purple plastic folder.

Aunt Beanie lifted the lid on the Aga hot plate and placed the black metal kettle on it.

"Excuse me," said Norman and he left the kitchen

"Take a seat, constable," instructed Aunt Beanie. "I want to hear all about Serena De Rossi. But first, Dotty, what shall we have for supper? And you'll join us?" She looked across at Keya.

"Why don't I cook a risotto?" Dotty suggested. "I can use the leftovers from Sunday's roast, but keep the chicken separate. She turned to Keya. Is that OK? A vegetarian risotto."

"It sounds fabulous. I'd only have toast or a ready meal if I ate when I got back home tonight."

Aunt Beanie made tea as Dotty removed ingredients from the fridge. "Do you mind if I use the rest of the white wine?"

"Help yourself. I've already put another bottle in there in case we want a glass later."

Aunt Beanie placed a cup of tea in front of Keya and sat down. Lifting up her own cup, she asked, "So, is the news correct? Has Serena been arrested for Zenobia Richardson's death?"

Keya sipped her tea. "Not exactly. She's been arrested for embezzlement."

"Which is what exactly?" asked Dotty as she thinly sliced shallots.

"A form of stealing, but worse because the person who steals knows and is trusted by the victim. As you found out, Serena told the lawyer she needed money for building works, which Miss Richardson had asked her to organise. But that was a lie. She made up the building work and instead of doing it, stole the money."

"It was quite a scheme," declared Aunt Beanie. "Dotty told me she'd had architects' plans drawn up and proper costings."

"She was clever, but so is the lawyer. But he hates visiting the countryside, and she knew that. She doubted he'd check the work had been done, at any rate, not until she'd left with all the money."

The pan hissed as Dotty added chopped shallots to melted butter and stirred them. She asked, "So she was planning to leave?"

"It looks like it. Her cottage is pretty bare and there are no pictures or ornaments. I think she'd already packed and moved them, but she won't tell us where."

Dotty added carnaroli rice to the pan and stirred it to coat it with the buttery mixture. "Do you think that's what the row was about on Saturday evening at the hotel?"

"Sergeant Unwin's not sure. He thinks Miss Richardson found out Serena was stealing, but not from her directly, but from her fan club. He's investigating that angle at the moment."

"From the article I read in the Sunday papers, she's been milking Zenobia's death," noted Aunt Beanie. "She certainly benefitted from it. But does the inspector think she caused it?"

Dotty slowly added hot bouillon stock from a small pan, simmering on the side of the hot plate, and stirred the rice mixture.

"The inspector's problem, as he keeps reminding us, is a complete lack of evidence that anyone else was involved in Miss Richardson's death. She definitely went over the side of the bannister and fell down the middle of the staircase, but was it an accident? Or was she pushed, or worse still ..."

"Committed suicide?" announced Aunt Beanie in a sceptical voice. "I can't believe that. I don't believe it."

"Neither does the inspector." Keya's head and shoulders sagged. "But it's hard to think that she accidentally fell over the bannister. And nobody saw her drinking excessively."

"Someone pushed her. It's the only explanation." declared Aunt Beanie.

"But who?"

"Serena de Rossi. Realising that her embezzlement was about to be uncovered, she sneaked back into the hotel, somehow managed to entice Zenobia into the corridor and pushed her over the bannister."

Dotty stirred another ladle of stock into the risotto and then returned to the kitchen counter and started grating parmesan cheese. "Would Serena have been strong enough?" she mused. "And surely someone would have heard her arguing with Zenobia."

"I know that's Sergeant Unwin's concern, but how else could she have died? And Serena certainly has a fiery Italian temper. I wouldn't put anything past her," Keya remarked.

There was silence and Dotty returned to the pan, stirring another ladle of stock into the plumped up rice which was developing nicely into a rich creamy consistency.

"It's a conundrum," agreed Aunt Beanie, dully.

There was another silence.

Dotty added chopped asparagus, peas and spinach to the risotto and half of the grated parmesan cheese.

Keya reached for the purple plastic wallet she'd brought with her and said, in a hesitant voice, "I've been given an interview for the sergeant's job in the new Rural, Heritage and Wildlife Unit."

"That's excellent news," approved Aunt Beanie, smiling.

"And I wondered if you could help me with my interview technique and what I should say. You know Inspector Ringrose, and he's heading up the panel."

Keya opened her plastic wallet and she and Aunt Beanie started discussing the types of questions she was likely to face and how she should answer clearly and concisely, and keep to the truth and not embellish it.

"You've developed an excellent relationship with people in this community, and in the other Cotswold villages. That's a valuable asset, which you need to highlight," instructed Aunt Beanie.

Norman appeared with damp hair and a flushed face, and Dotty presumed he'd had a bath. He laid the table and helped Uncle Cliff to his chair at the dining table, from where he could watch the television.

Norman turned it on and Serena De Rossi appeared, speaking to the press. She denied any involvement with Zenobia's death, but her eyes flashed and she shouted angrily at a reporter who'd asked her if she felt the need to steal from Zenobia's fan club because of her own lack of talent.

Norman commented, "Hell certainly has no fury like a woman scorned."

# CHAPTER THIRTY-TWO

On Friday afternoon, Dotty was considering calling it a day when David Rook walked into the office and asked, "Is George about? Gilmore and I found a community of brilliant new artists in north-eastern Spain, and we thought an exhibition of their work in the auction room would be good for business, for all of us."

Dotty shook her head. "Sorry, she left early to collect her kids from school. But tell me all about these artists." Dotty sat back in her chair, happy to have an excuse not to work.

"It's a fantastic initiative which we discovered on our trip. The inhabitants of a remote hillside town, which has seen its economy and population dwindle over the last fifty years, set up a project to attract young, impoverished artists. There are plenty of old buildings, which have been patched up for accommodation, studios and exhibition space.

"Last year they held their first festival of art which included work by the residents, new and old. It was wonderful to see how bringing creative talent to the town has unleashed the inner artistry of the original residents. A group of elderly women have returned to the traditional method of making bright, elaborately patterned fans, which they sell through boutiques in Madrid."

"What a fascinating trip," mused Dotty wistfully, "and it sounds as if you both enjoyed yourselves."

A shadow fell across David's face and his large, dark eyes became watchful.

"Visiting that town was both the high and low point of our trip. We'd been told about a talented sculpture artist working there, and from examining his metal sculpture art, depicting animals and nature, it was clear he could have created the Lady Justice statue, including the intricate chasing details."

Dotty sat up. "So that was the reason you and Gilmore took a last-minute trip. You were on the trail of the sculpture?"

The door from the antique centre opened.

David sighed. "When you've been in the business as long as Gilmore and I have, you rely increasingly on gut instinct and ours was telling us there was something not quite right with that sculpture, but neither of us could say why we thought that, nor could we prove anything."

"I couldn't agree with you more," confirmed Aunt Beanie. "I sometimes felt like one of those old-fashioned tracker dogs, the ones with the floppy ears."

"Bloodhounds," suggested David.

"Yes, those are the ones. I felt like one of those when I visited a sale or exhibition where counterfeit work was suspected." She turned to David and said, "And I have the same feeling as you about that sculpture. Don't get me wrong, the artistry is fabulous, but statues like that don't just turn up in people's attics. Well they do, but it's exceedingly rare."

Dotty returned her attention to David and asked, "So, what happened?"

"We found the young artist, and he became wary the minute we asked about bronze sculptures, and denied having worked with the material. But Gilmore rummaged amongst the things in his studio, while I talked to him about his work, and discovered a wax statue of Lady Justice, and a mould. It was clear from the work he had on display that it was not his usual subject, but he claimed it was for a future piece he was considering."

"But why would he have made the sculpture? And how did it find its way to the filming of *The Antique Tour* in the Cotswolds?"

"That's what we failed to find out. Gilmore called a police contact in Madrid and they took the young man in for questioning. Hopefully he'll see the error of his ways and tell us who commissioned him to do the work, but he's not forced to. We can't definitively link him to the sculpture, even though Gilmore and I are both convinced he created it. Such a waste of talent." David pressed his lips together.

Dotty examined Aunt Beanie for the first time and wrinkled her forehead. "Why are you dressed in overalls?" she asked.

"Norman and I are collecting Buttercup."

"Who?"

"The Jersey cow he bought at the auction yesterday. I've hooked up the old trailer to the Defender and Mrs Todd is looking after Cliff."

"One more thing, Dorothy," interrupted David.

She turned her attention back to him.

"The sculpture is being auctioned tomorrow, and I wondered if you'd like to join me on a trip to London? Marion has a ladies' doubles tennis match over in Winchcombe."

"What a fabulous idea," declared Aunt Beanie, "I'd love to come, and Norman will be at home sorting out Buttercup so he can keep an eye on Cliff."

David's jaw clenched, but then he turned to Aunt Beanie and smiled, although it didn't quite reach his eyes, and replied, "I'd be delighted to accompany both you ladies, but it'll be an early start. Can I pick you up from Meadowbank Farm at seven tomorrow morning?"

"We'll be ready. Ah, here's Norman."

Norman appeared from the auction room and placed his flat tweed cap on his head. "Dotty, I've locked the storeroom and the double doors in the auction room, so that's me finished for the day."

"Join us for supper," called Aunt Beanie as she left the office, "I found some salmon in the 'must use today' section in the Co-op."

David stepped closer and said, "I must be on my way as well, Dorothy. I'll see you tomorrow."

The office felt empty as Dotty switched off her computer. She was washing up dirty coffee cups, which someone had left in the sink, when she heard the door to the antiques centre open.

"Hiya," called Constable Varma. "I'm on my way to a village show meeting in Aldsworth, but I just had to stop by and tell you the news."

"A village show meeting on a Friday evening?" remarked Dotty as she rinsed the cups.

"Yes, two of the committee members weekly commute to London, and they've asked me to join them and give my views on security. I don't mind. I enjoy being involved in village events, and it's not as if I have anything else to do."

Dotty stared at the back wall of the office, above the sink. She had promised to visit the theatre or cinema with her friend, but other things kept cropping up. Next week should be quieter.

"Anyway," declared Constable Varma, excitedly, "I have to tell you that Inspector Evans has charged Serena De Rossi with the manslaughter of Zenobia Richardson."

Dotty spun round and exclaimed, "No way."

"Oh, yes," grinned Constable Varma. "Sergeant Unwin argued that there was no evidence that it was premeditated murder, so Inspector Evans agreed to run with his theory that Serena and Miss Richardson had another argument, and in a fit of Italian rage, Serena shoved Miss Richardson over the balustrade."

"Serena did have a motive," mused Dotty.

"Yes, she admitted that Miss Richardson told her she would be cut out of her will, although Serena appeared really surprised when she was told she had been the main beneficiary in it. And she doesn't have an alibi. She's sticking with her story that she drove back to her cottage, at the entrance to Windrush Hall, and spent the night there."

"Can Benson or Françoise confirm her story?"

"No, they didn't see her. I interviewed them again today and sneezed all the way through from that furry cat. It was creepy how much like yours it is."

Dotty sniffed and screwed up her eyes.

"What's the matter?" cried Constable Varma.

"Earl Grey is missing."

# CHAPTER THIRTY-THREE

On Saturday morning, David collected Aunt Beanie and Dotty up from Meadowbank Farm at seven o'clock in the morning, as promised.

Aunt Beanie had eaten a slice of toast, but Dotty could only face a cup of tea. Still, she was excited about another trip to London and the prospect of an auction at Gainfords, one of the top auction houses in the country, if not the world.

She wore her wrap-around dress, while Aunt Beanie had chosen a bright patchwork tunic-style top over black leggings. She placed a blue padded picnic bag in her blue and white striped straw basket and covered it with a red shawl.

The drive along the M4 motorway to London was uneventful and Dotty daydreamed as Aunt Beanie, sitting in the front passenger seat, chatted away to David.

When David announced, "Knightsbridge," she stared in fascination at Harrods department store. It was a large, pink-brick, six-storey gothic style building and was well branded with its name in gold letters over the entrance doors and on the green canopies above the shop windows.

David parked in an underground car park beneath Hyde Park and hailed a taxi directing the driver to "Gainfords, St James."

Dotty realised today was going to be all about grandeur and elegance. They alighted in front of a neo-classical building built of white stone with a columned entrance, more suited to a country house than a London business premises.

At street level, black metal planters filled with dwarf conifers and pink snapdragons rested on ledges below long casement windows.

"Ladies, after you," indicated David towards the door, opened by a red-liveried doorman.

Inside, the building was just as impressive, with high, moulded ceilings and large, open rooms.

David suggested, "Why don't you two have a look around while I find Gilmore? The sale starts in half an hour, in the auction room on the first floor."

Dotty kept her distance from the exhibits, fearing that she'd break or damage them, but Aunt Beanie wandered slowly alongside a claret-painted wall, examining various sized paintings, hung in guilt frames.

"A Stubbs," she cried in delight at a picture of a horse.

They climbed an oak staircase with elegantly carved wooden balusters to the first floor, where a reception area had been set up for the auction. "Are you here for the sale?" asked a pretty woman in her twenties, her dark hair tied neatly back in a ponytail.

"We are, although more as observers than bidders. We're friends of Gilmore's."

The woman smiled and handed them both glossy brochures with the bronze statue of Lady Justice on the front.

"The smaller items are being exhibited in the two rooms to your left, and the auction will take place in the room behind me. If you'd like to bid for anything, please let me know and I'll register you."

The first item which caught Dotty's eye was the necklace with the gold disks which she'd seen Jennifer discuss at *The Antique Tour*.

"Additional item, Lot 15," read Aunt Beanie. "Nineteenth century replica of a Babylonian necklace with gold disks with granulated rosettes."

"It's beautiful," mouthed Dotty.

"It certainly is." But Aunt Beanie pressed her lips together before muttering, "Nineteenth century replica."

The sculpture of Lady Justice stood proudly on a Roman column-style plinth in the centre of the next room, surrounded by gaping onlookers. A burly security guard was positioned beside the door, leading back to the reception area, with his hands clasped in front of him. Clearly, they were taking no chances with the centrepiece of the auction.

David appeared in the doorway and caught Dotty's eye. He indicated for her to join him and when she did, he said hurriedly, "I suggest you and Bernadette take your seats, and I would be grateful if you can save one for me. I'll join you shortly."

The taupe-coloured walls of the auction room gave it a modern feeling and the two chandeliers which hung from the ceiling felt out of place.

A bank of desks formed a row along the left wall, each with a computer screen and several telephones. Behind the auctioneer's rostrum, a large screen hung down, with 'Gainfords' displayed on it, and beside it was a large television screen.

"They show the current bid in several different currencies on that screen," explained Aunt Beanie.

More people entered the room, so they moved forward between rows of black upholstered chairs and chose seats half-way down the room, leaving the one beside the aisle empty for David. Aunt Beanie placed her blue and white straw basket on it.

Young men and women filed in and took their places at the row of desks. Some of them placed headphones, with mouth pieces, over their heads. It was all very professional.

A lady wearing a red jacket arrived at the rostrum and stood behind it while her two female assistants sat down beside her.

She glanced over Dotty's head and said, "Two minutes, ladies and gentlemen." Her voice was amplified, and Dotty spotted a small microphone pinned to the lapel of her jacket.

The screen behind the female auctioneer changed to display Lot 1, "A Josef Hoffman armchair'. David stood in the aisle and Aunt Beanie removed her basket so he could sit down. His cheeks were red and glistening, and his eyes darted warily around the room.

Dotty was surprised by his appearance, as he usually appeared calm and collected, but her attention was drawn to the auctioneer who'd stepped behind her rostrum.

"Isn't this exciting?" whispered Aunt Beanie, mirroring her own thoughts. It certainly was. Dotty opened her catalogue and looked up the opening Lot. The armchair was valued at £3,000 to £5,000.

The bidding began slowly, with two of the young people behind the desks at the side of the room dominating the auctioneer's attention.

A lady in the room, seated in front of Dotty, joined the bidding when it reached £2,500 and the price rose quickly to the top end of the estimated value. At £4,800, the lady in front of Dotty shook her head, and the auctioneer looked around.

Dotty was about to look up the next Lot when the auctioneer called, "New bidder," and the price increased again. Dotty thought there were three bidders, someone in the room to her right and two telephone bidders, and they pushed the price to over £11,000.

The person to her right stopped, and it became a battle of the telephone bidders. Finally, a young man with spiky blond hair shook his head. The armchair sold for £13,750.

"If every Lot exceeds its valuation by that much, we're in for a thrilling day," grinned Aunt Beanie.

As the auctioneer called sold on Lot 13, David stood up and muttered, "Excuse me."

"Do you think he's OK?" asked Dotty.

"I think he and Gilmore are up to something," disclosed Aunt Beanie, as the bidding for Lot 14 got under way.

Dotty was more interested in Lot 15, the replica Babylonian gold necklace

"A reserve of £200 to £400," scoffed Aunt Beanie. "That's barely the value of the gold if it was melted down."

There was a murmur around the auction room as the auctioneer announced, "Lot 15, a nineteenth century gold necklace in the Babylonian style. Who'll start me at £250? 250? 200?"

"I've a good mind to bid for it myself," said Aunt Beanie irritably, and she crossed her arms.

"£100. We have a bid of £100."

The phones remained silent and the young men and women at the row of desks sat back, looking relieved to have a break from the frenetic biding of previous Lots.

The bidding limped slowly on until the auctioneer finally called, "Sold," at a price of £250. She peered over Dotty's head and said, "Bidder 78. Thank you. Lot 16 …"

"Really," proclaimed Aunt Beanie and the woman in front of her turned around with a pinched expression and uttered, "Hush."

"That was one of the more blatant forms of auction rigging I've seen. Someone clearly put the word out not to bid for that necklace."

"It still made its estimate," noted Dotty.

"Barely," spat Aunt Beanie.

Dotty was enjoying herself. She wondered what other surprises the auction had in store.

# CHAPTER THIRTY-FOUR

"Ladies and gentlemen, that is the end of the first section of the auction, so we'll take a fifteen minute break. Refreshments have been provided in the reception area," the auctioneer concluded, before turning away from the rostrum at the front of Gainfords auction room.

Aunt Beanie turned the page in her catalogue. "Next up is the artwork, and then the sale of Lady Justice. But now I need a cup of tea, and perhaps something stronger after all that excitement."

She smiled mischievously at Dotty, picked up her blue and white stripped basket and stood up. Dotty followed her out of the auction room to the reception area on the first floor landing.

She stood by the oak bannister, which formed a rectangular shape around the open top of the staircase, in the centre of the room. It reminded her of the one at Charbury Castle Hotel and she shivered and looked behind her, but nobody was there.

Further away, by the refreshment table, Aunt Beanie was laughing with a gentleman Dotty recognised as Inspector Ringrose. She continued to look round and spotted Emery standing on his own beside the entrance to the room where the sculpture was on display.

He glanced nervously inside, then across to the refreshment table and then the entrance to the auction room in a series of short, jerky movements.

He pulled at the collar of the white, short-sleeved shirt he wore which strained across his muscular chest. Dotty suddenly felt sorry for him. This was an exciting day, but he looked completely out of place amongst the well-dressed patrons and established members of the antique community.

She picked up Aunt Beanie's wicker basket and walked around the central staircase.

"Hello. I'm not sure you'll remember me, but we had supper together when *The Antique Tour* was at Charbury Castle Hotel."

Emery wrinkled his forehead, so Dotty pressed on.

"It's exciting being here today, but rather daunting with all these distinguished people," confided Dotty.

Emery rubbed the back of his neck. "It's not my sort of thing, but Casper insisted I come and show my face."

Aunt Beanie joined them as Emery was speaking, carrying two cups of tea. She looked at his pale face and said, "I could fetch you a cup of tea, but I suspect you'd prefer something a little stronger."

She handed Dotty both cups and bent over her basket, which Dotty had placed on the floor. Unzipping the blue canvas picnic bag, she furtively removed a bottle containing a deep, claret coloured liquid, which she poured into two plastic glasses.

She stood up and passed one to Emery as she declared, "This should put some colour back in your cheeks, my home-made damson gin." She took a large swig from her own glass and added, "That's better."

Emery cautiously sniffed his glass before taking a tentative sip. He must have enjoyed it as he gulped down the rest of the gin.

"You look perkier already." Aunt Beanie finished her gin and returned the two empty glasses to the canvas picnic bag.

"Thank you," said Emery. "I needed that." He turned to Dotty, and confided, "I hope I wasn't rude before, but you're right, this is a different world and I feel completely out of place."

"But isn't it an exciting one?" Aunt Beanie's eyes glowed. "Most of the Lots so far have exceeded their estimates. You must be very excited about the sale of your sculpture."

Emery looked down at the floor.

Dotty gave Aunt Beanie her cup of tea and said, "Do you mind me asking how it came to you? Was it a family heirloom?"

Emery looked up and smiled for the first time. "My family doesn't have things like that."

"So, where did you find it?" Dotty pressed.

"That's exactly what I did. Find it. In the attic of a flat I moved into in Islington. I wanted to create access to a roof terrace and when I was pulling away boarding, I found some boxes of what I thought were rubbish, which someone had stored in the attic and forgotten about."

"But it wasn't all rubbish?" Dotty suggested.

"Most of it was. Some chipped figurines of shepherdesses, and a wooden mantle clock missing the minute hand, and what I thought was an old metal sculpture."

"It was an old metal sculpture, but a valuable one," said Dotty in an encouraging tone.

"Exactly. It intrigued me, so after I'd cleaned off all the dust, I decided to get it valued, but not at one of the shops around me. I didn't trust them. I saw an advert for *The Antique Tour* and thought that would be somewhere I'd get a fair and honest opinion of the sculpture."

Emery relaxed as he told his story. "And when Zenobia Richardson said it could be worth millions of pounds, I couldn't believe it."

"And I guess neither could Casper?"

"No, he was delighted for me."

"I bet he was," remarked Aunt Beanie.

Dotty asked in an innocent voice, "Did you know Casper before the filming of *The Antique Tour*?"

A young man walked up the stairs and turned his head towards them. It was Felix, the turret-climbing, singing waiter.

"No," replied Emery, whose eyes darted towards the staircase and he coughed, "Excuse me," and rushed inside the room displaying the sculpture.

"What spooked him?" asked Aunt Beanie as her gaze followed Emery's retreating back.

"Morning," grinned Felix. "I hoped you'd be here. What about your police friend?"

"She's working this morning. And not undercover but back at Cirencester police station."

"Then you'll have to pass on my good news."

Aunt Beanie focused on Felix. "And what's that?"

"I have a part in the musical I auditioned for. It's only in the chorus, but I've also been asked to understudy for the leading man."

"More excitement and good news. I think this calls for some more of my damson gin in celebration."

Felix's eyes bulged. "It's a bit early for me, thank you."

"Never mind." Aunt Beanie looked longingly at the basket, while she sipped her cup of tea.

"So, will you come and watch me? You did promise."

"Of course we will, young man," cried Aunt Beanie. "I'm beginning to enjoy our trips to London. And we should make a night of it, Dotty. Go out for supper in Covent Garden, and maybe even stay over."

"I'm not sure about that, but I'd love to see the show, and so would Keya."

Just then, a man called, "Ladies and gentlemen. Please return to your seats. The auction is about to resume."

Dotty whispered to Felix, "Are you certain Emery, the owner of the sculpture, and Casper Dupré have known each other for a while?"

"Of course I am. I did an extra gig at the club on Christmas Eve, and I remember them cheering Christmas Day in with champagne."

Aunt Beanie picked up her basket and asked, "Are you both coming?"

# CHAPTER THIRTY-FIVE

David was already seated at the end of a row in Gainfords auction room and he stood up to allow Dotty, Felix and Aunt Beanie to take the three empty seats beside him.

The auctioneer called, "A George Stubbs painting of a chestnut racehorse, with a spaniel, in a landscape setting. Who'll start the bidding at £100,000?"

A young woman, wearing large black-framed glasses, sitting at one of the row of desks at the side of the room, raised her hand.

Dotty sat back as the bidding rose to £200,000 and beyond.

"Any advance on £305,000. Final warning, at £305,000." The auctioneer looked around the room, before announcing, "Sold."

There was a discreet ringing sound and David stood up and walked towards the back of the auction room.

On impulse, Dotty jumped up and followed him. She'd been thinking over her earlier conversations with Emery and Felix and she wanted to discuss them with David, but as she left the auction room, she realised he was speaking into his phone.

He finished his call as she tentatively approached and, lifting his chin, revealed, "That was the Spanish police. The young artist finally opened up and admitted he was commissioned by an Englishman to make a one-off bronze sculpture of Lady Justice."

"Did he say who the man was?"

"No. Only that he was paid cash and posted the sculpture, hidden inside a wooden clock, to an address in Islington, London."

Islington. Emery lived in a flat in Islington.

"Dorothy, what is it?"

"I spoke to Emery earlier. He was very nervous. But he told me he found the sculpture in a box in the attic of his flat in Islington."

"That sounds too much of a coincidence. If only we could find his address and give it to the Spanish police. They might be able to persuade the artist to confirm if that is where he sent it."

Dotty brightened. "Keya, Constable Varma should still be at work." She checked her watch. It was 11.30 am.

She found her phone and called her friend.

Keya immediately answered the call and asked breathlessly, "Has the sculpture been sold?"

"Not yet. But I'm with David and he's doing some research into the sculpture's history. He's also in discussions with the Spanish police."

"Why are the Spanish police involved?"

"It's a long story. But could you do me a favour and find out where Emery lives in Islington?"

"The owner of the sculpture? What's his surname?"

Dotty looked up at David and asked, "What's Emery's full name?"

David opened the auction catalogue, which had been tucked under his arm and flicked through it. "The sculpture is in the ownership of Emery Brown."

"Emery Brown," repeated Dotty into her phone.

"Brown is a common name, but Emery isn't. If he's registered on the electoral role, that will be the quickest way to find him. Just a minute." She put Dotty on hold.

David and Dotty waited in silence.

"Any advance on £12,100,000?" asked the amplified voice of the auctioneer.

Once again, David consulted his auction catalogue. "That will be the Leonardo Da Vinci sketch. Incredible detail, despite being only four inches square."

"Sorry, Dotty, I have to go, but my colleague will look for the address. Can she text it to you?"

"Of course. Thank you." She ended the call and reported, "Someone at the police station is looking for the address, and they'll send it to me if they find it. Out of interest, do you know how much the Spanish artist was paid for the sculpture?"

"I do. $3,000, which is a lot of money for him. I hope he continues his career, despite this incident, as he obviously has talent." David raised his eyes to the ceiling and pinched his lips together.

"There was something else," admitted Dotty.

David was silent for a few moments and then turned his attention back to her. "Yes?"

"The young man who climbed up the side of the turret at the hotel."

David's eyebrows rose.

"I'll explain later," Dotty said hastily. "Anyway, he sings in nightclubs and is adamant that Emery and Casper Dupré knew each other as long ago as Christmas Eve. He told me he saw them together."

"O what a tangled web we weave, when first we practise to deceive!" quoted David. He smiled at Dotty and explained, "From Marmion, written by Sir Walter Scott in 1808, but just as applicable today, don't you think?"

Dotty's phone pinged. "It's Emery's address in Islington."

David took out his own phone, and when his call was answered said, "Hola, puedo hablar con el Inspector Perez?"

He gave the inspector Emery's address.

"What now?" asked Dotty, when David finished his call.

"We need to update Gilmore. He'll be standing at the back of the auction room. Let me see if I can find him."

Dotty waited, looking around the elegant landing, where several small groups of people talked in hushed tones. There was a reverence surrounding the auction, almost like it was a spiritual gathering. Perhaps it was to the more ardent collectors.

David and Gilmore returned, but stood a little distance away from Dotty. David spoke for a length of time, after which she thought Gilmore asked him questions. They both turned and approached Dotty.

"My apologies," said David, "but I needed to update Gilmore."

On just the sculpture, wondered Dotty. But what else could it be?

Gilmore wore a serious expression as he remarked, "So we now know the young Spanish artist was commissioned to make a sculpture of Lady Justice, which he sent to an address in Islington. Emery Brown lives in Islington and was friendly with Casper Dupré before the sculpture was presented to Zenobia Richardson, at *The Antique Tour*. But why take a forged sculpture to such a public event?"

"Emery said he didn't trust his local antique shops," replied Dotty.

David pulled at his chin. "He may well have distrusted them. Any dealer or antique shop owner would be extremely sceptical about the legitimacy of an ancient sculpture. They would want to know its history and would have asked him for evidence of provenance. But a television show, in front of a live audience, where treasures which have been hidden under people's mattresses are periodically discovered, that would be a far more favourable setting."

Gilmore nodded. "Casper was dismissive of Zenobia's expertise, but if she, because of her inexperience, or desire to play up to the crowd, declared it genuine and worth millions, and that was aired to the whole country, then who would question its authenticity or its provenance?"

Dotty considered their statements. "So this was no accident. It was planned, and Emery and Casper were in it together?"

David and Gilmore exchanged glances, before David said, "It looks that way. Casper would have the knowledge and contacts, but he needed someone unknown in the antiques world. So, was Emery part of the scam, or an innocent party?"

Dotty noted a sheen on Gilmore's cheeks. "I'm not sure. But I know what I have to do now."

Dotty and David looked at him.

"Stop the auction."

# CHAPTER THIRTY-SIX

The auctioneer stood behind the rostrum, wearing her red jacket. One of her assistants handed her a note and her face fell as she read it.

Dotty stood in the doorway of the auction room and watched, while David and Gilmore spoke in hushed tones, behind her, next to the reception desk.

"Ladies and gentlemen, that concludes the sale of artwork." She paused and looked around the room. "But I am afraid the bronze sculpture of Lady Justice has been withdrawn from today's auction."

There were gasps, and someone shouted, "Why?"

The auctioneer waited for the room to settle before continuing. "I don't have any more information, but I suggest we take an hour's break for lunch before we continue with the auction."

Aunt Beanie turned and made eye contact with Dotty, who pressed her lips together in disappointment.

Casper Dupré pushed Dotty out of the way as he stormed out of the auction room. "What's the meaning of this?" he screamed at Gilmore and David.

Gilmore squared his shoulders and replied, "Let's not make a scene, Casper. Come to my office and we'll discuss it in private."

"Why should I? This is a public auction. And the sculpture is a valuable treasure. The public has a right to see it."

As people left the auction room, engaged in animated conversations, Dotty moved across to stand by the central staircase. She was soon joined by Aunt Beanie and Felix.

"What …" began Aunt Beanie.

"Shh," whispered Dotty.

Casper had his hand up and was straining to look around the growing crowd in the entrance area.

"Emery," he called. "Come here."

A few people stopped to watch Emery reluctantly cross the reception area, but most filed down the wooden staircase.

Dotty and Aunt Beanie edged closer to David, Gilmore and Casper as Emery joined them, keeping his eyes on the polished oak floor.

David stated, in an exasperated tone, "But it's not a valuable treasure. It's a Spanish forgery. An excellent one, but a far cry from a 2,000-year-old Roman masterpiece."

Dotty was certain Casper blanched at the mention of a Spanish forgery, but he regained his composure quickly and demanded, "Emery. Tell them. Tell them how you found it in your attic."

Aunt Beanie handed Emery a glass of damson gin, and said, "I think you might need this."

Emery still refused to look any of them in the eye as he sipped his drink.

Casper's voice became a menacing hiss. "I said tell them."

Emery finished his gin and handed the glass back to Aunt Beanie. He looked up at her and said, "Thank you."

"Are you ready now?" she asked.

"I think so." Emery took a step back and turned to look at Casper. "Casper, this has gone on long enough. A few thousand pounds to do up my flat would have been great, but millions? It's all got out of hand."

"Emery," growled Casper. "You wanted to be on *The Antique Tour*."

"You're right, I did. People like me don't usually get the chance to be on TV. I thought it would be fun. And I did think I'd enjoy duping the snotty people in the antique industry, but I've realised they're not all filled with self-importance."

He looked from Dotty to Aunt Beanie, who had refilled his glass.

He took large a gulp of the dark liquid, and continued, "If I'd known the venture would lead to a woman's death, I'd never have agreed to it."

Casper sprang at Emery, knocking the glass from his hand and grabbed him by the throat, yelling, "Not another word."

Emery seemed surprised when Casper attacked him, but he soon recovered and prised Casper's fingers away from his throat. He held Casper tightly by both wrists and seemed immune to the kicks and yells thrown in his direction.

"Enough," bellowed David.

It was the first time Dotty had heard him raise his voice, and she gulped as she looked at his eyes, which were dark and menacing.

"Take him to Gilmore's office while we decide what to do. Gilmore, please lead the way."

Gilmore and Emery, leading Casper who continued to struggle and twist around in his grip, walked down a corridor behind the reception desk.

David turned to Dotty, Aunt Beanie and Felix and smiled, but it did not reach his eyes, which had returned to their usual watchful state. "Why don't you three go downstairs and see if there is any lunch left?"

They did as instructed and walked silently down the oak staircase. It was clear from the loud chatter and occasional laugh which room lunch was being served in.

They entered a gallery with taupe painted walls on which modern art paintings hung. People were congregating around a table on the left-hand side of the room.

"There's a free table. I'll grab it while you two get some lunch," suggested Felix.

Aunt Beanie and Dotty weaved between tables of chattering diners to the buffet table, around which a few people still lingered.

"It looks like the children's clothes stall after a village jumble sale," exclaimed Aunt Beanie as they stared at empty white plates and a couple of limp ham sandwiches.

A waiter appeared carrying a full plate of sandwiches and finger food and those people lurking around the buffet table moved swiftly towards him, but not quickly enough. Aunt Beanie intercepted the waiter, grabbed the plate from him and said, "That's very kind of you." She dodged around the other diners, back to the table which Felix had secured.

"Are auctions always this exciting?" asked Felix as he picked up a sausage roll.

"They have their moments," replied Aunt Beanie, examining the sandwiches. She picked up a small brown roll filled with egg mayonnaise.

"I have seen two rival bidders fight over a portrait of a naked lady, but it turned out one of them was married to the subject and the other was her spurned lover." She bit into her sandwich.

Aunt Beanie turned to Felix and asked, "So, tell me about this play you're in?"

Dotty listened contentedly to Aunt Beanie and Felix as she slowly ate her lunch.

"Ow, what was that for?" Felix had elbowed her in the side.

"Sorry, but isn't that your police friend looking around the door?"

Dotty looked across the room at Constable Varma, who waved and mouthed, "Hiya."

"Excuse me," muttered Dotty, and she left the table to join Constable Varma. "How did you get here so quickly? You were in Cirencester when I spoke to you a couple of hours ago."

"More like an hour and a half," giggled Constable Varma. She indicated towards Sergeant Unwin, who was speaking to the red-jacketed auctioneer.

"The sergeant put his blue light on and I don't think his speed dipped below a hundred until we hit the outskirts of London." She lowered her voice. "He loved it. You know, boys and their fast cars."

"Constable," declared Sergeant Unwin, making Dotty jump. His eyes gazed swiftly over her as he said, in an appreciative tone, "and it's Miss?"

"Dotty, but you already know that," she replied impatiently. "I was about to ask Constable Varma, why you are both here?"

He smiled in a self-satisfied manner and crossed his arms. "You and your friends are not the only ones interested in the Lady Justice sculpture. I've been speaking to a colleague who joined Interpol and we've been comparing notes.

"He'd heard a rumour about a promising sculpture artist in Spain, so when I overheard Constable Varma ask a caller about the Spanish police, naturally I was very interested. She told me about the request for an address in Islington and I realised the action was in London, not Cirencester, so we jumped in the car and here we are."

"Where is the inspector?" asked Dotty, realising she had not heard his deep baritone voice.

Constable Varma smiled broadly and replied, "He's at the Chelsea Flower Show with his mum. He was very proud to have secured tickets."

"There's no need to bother him," declared Sergeant Unwin.

"Sergeant." The red-jacketed auctioneer strode towards them. "Gilmore Chapman would like to see you in his office."

Constable Varma made to follow, but the sergeant stopped, turned round and asked, "Is your radio on?"

She nodded.

"Stay down here with …" he paused and smiled at Dotty, "Dotty, and I'll call through when I need you."

He climbed up the wooden staircase, following the auctioneer.

Dotty followed him with her eyes and asked, "How will Inspector Evans react to his new sergeant taking over the case?"

"He was adamant that he wasn't to be bothered this weekend, but he'll be furious we've come to London." She shrugged her shoulder.

"But Sergeant Unwin's ambitious, and he'll get big brownie points if he solves this case. Just as long as I don't have to tell the inspector." She turned to Dotty wide-eyed and asked, "So, what's been happening here?"

"Gilmore withdrew the sculpture from today's auction."

Constable Varma gasped, "No way."

"Come and join Aunt Beanie. And Felix is here. He can tell you his news."

# CHAPTER THIRTY-SEVEN

"That's fantastic," exclaimed Constable Varma, when Felix told her he had a part in the musical he'd auditioned for. "We'll definitely come and watch, won't we, Dotty?"

"Don't forget me," added Aunt Beanie.

Constable Varma nodded. "Of course. So, tell me what happened when the sculpture was removed from the auction. How did the customers react?" She picked up an egg roll.

"They were delighted by the drama," declared Aunt Beanie.

"But Casper was furious," reported Dotty. "He flew into a rage and attacked Emery."

"That was brave of him. I'd have thought Emery could crush him with one hand."

Felix added, "I thought he would after Casper grabbed him round the throat."

"It's never dull being with you lot." Constable Varma's radio crackled into life. She held it to her ear and listened. "Roger. Out." She jumped up and blurted, "I've got to go. Catch you all later."

She ran out of the room, ramming her hat on her head as she did so, and knocking into a waiter who was handing out drinks from a metal tray to a table of diners.

They jumped up and cried out as the drinks spilled across the table.

Aunt Beanie's eyes gleamed. "What are you waiting for? We don't want to miss the action."

Felix checked his watch. "I've a shift at three." He looked from Aunt Beanie to Dotty, and asked, "Do either of you have a pen and paper?"

Aunt Beanie produced a pen from her basket, together with the auction catalogue. "You can write on the back of this."

Felix wrote something on the inside of the back cover and when he finished, he turned it towards Dotty.

"That's my phone number. Let me know how this turns out and when you want to watch the show. I might even get hold of some free tickets for the dress rehearsal."

As Felix left the room, Aunt Beanie stood up and hoisted her straw basket up her arm. "Come on. Let's see what's happening upstairs."

They climbed the wooden staircase but halted at the top. Sergeant Unwin was trying to restrain an angry Casper, whose arms and legs were flailing as he fought to free himself from the sergeant's grasp.

Constable Varma danced from one foot to another beside Dotty, who wondered if her friend was guarding against Casper's escape.

Sergeant Unwin gasped, as he ducked a blow, "Casper Dupré, I'm arresting you on suspicion of murder. You have the right to remain silent but ..."

The rest of his words were lost as Casper screamed, "Get off me!"

Dotty whispered to Constable Varma. "What's happened? Did Casper admit to murdering Zenobia?"

"No." The constable shook her head. "But we can't arrest him for the sculpture, as it's outside our jurisdiction. But I told you, Sergeant Unwin is ambitious. This way he can take Casper back to Cirencester and try to unravel the case of the sculpture and the murder of Miss Richardson.

"With Inspector Evans away for the weekend, this is his big chance. Actually, I'm rather enjoying myself. The inspector always leaves me to deal with the dangerous suspects."

She looked round at Dotty, and grinned, "Or you."

"Do you understand?" shouted Sergeant Unwin.

"Yes," yelled Casper, but he finally wrenched his arm out of Sergeant Unwin's grasp and before anyone could stop him, he darted towards the staircase.

Aunt Beanie jumped out of the way but Dotty pushed both her arms forward and with her palms facing Casper cried, "No, you don't."

Casper didn't slow down and as he drew closer, she realised he was glistening with sweat and his eyes were haunted, like those of a trapped wild animal.

He charged straight at her and, grabbing hold of her outstretched hands, hurled himself over the top of her.

Dotty felt herself falling backwards and gasped as her head struck something hard. She toppled over again and slid down the stairs feet first, on her front. At the bottom, she slid across the floor until her feet smacked into something and she came to a halt.

Gasping for air, she closed her eyes. She regained the feeling in her arms and legs as they began to throb, but that was blotted out by the pain in her head, which started at her temple and cut through her right eye.

She became aware of shouts and screams and then a pounding which was not inside her head but against it. It was people running down the wooden staircase.

Someone shouted, "Stop him."

Dotty thought she heard Gilmore's voice ask, "Dotty, can you hear me?"

And then Sergeant Unwin said, "We should call an ambulance."

"Out of the way, let her breathe," ordered Aunt Beanie.

Dotty felt someone squat down beside her and push a hand under her left one. Aunt Beanie's voice was calm but authoritative as she said, "Dotty, if you can hear me, squeeze my hand."

Slowly, Dotty moved her left hand and gently squeezed.

"Good girl. Now lie still."

Aunt Beanie turned away and called, "Keya, my basket."

Dotty gingerly pushed herself up into a sitting position, but her head began to spin and she thought she'd be sick. Something soft was draped around her shoulders and pulled across her front.

Aunt Beanie whispered, "That's better, not so revealing. But she shouldn't have moved. Not until qualified medics had examined you."

Dotty remembered she was wearing her wrap dress, and she tried to pull the two pieces of material together across her legs, but Aunt Beanie murmured, "It's OK. Nothing's showing. It's the top that's ripped."

Dotty closed her eyes and tried to hug herself, but her right arm ached.

She heard David ask, "Is she alright? That was most reckless."

"But she stopped Casper escaping," replied Sergeant Unwin. He moved away from Dotty and she heard him say, "Thank you. Don't I know you?"

"This is Felix, who climbed the turret," explained Constable Varma.

Dotty thought Felix had left for the audition and she hoped he wouldn't miss it.

"I've no idea what you're doing here," responded Sergeant Unwin brusquely, "but we'll take Casper now. Besides, he looks dead on his feet."

Dotty opened her eyes and looked towards the entrance door as Felix handed a sorry-looking Casper to Constable Varma.

"He needs to see a doctor," called Aunt Beanie.

Dotty felt something smooth against her lips.

"Drink this," encouraged Aunt Beanie, and this time, Dotty did.

"Don't worry, he will," replied Sergeant Unwin. "Mr Brown?"

As Dotty sipped the thick, smooth damson gin, she looked up at Emery, who was staring down at her.

He muttered in a haunted voice, "Just like Zenobia Richardson."

# CHAPTER THIRTY-EIGHT

Dotty woke up on Sunday morning with her whole body aching. She lay on her back and stared at the ceiling.

She lay like that for some time and thought about the events of the previous day. It would be a shame if the Lady Justice sculpture turned out to be a forgery, but she was glad that Casper wouldn't benefit from it.

But had he and Emery been involved in Zenobia Richardson's death? Emery seemed to know something about it.

"Oh good, you're awake," declared Aunt Beanie.

Dotty slowly swivelled her head and looked across at Aunt Beanie, who placed a cup on her bedside table. "English Breakfast tea to wake you up, and an ibuprofen on the side for the aches and pains. How are you feeling?"

"Sore." Dotty pushed herself up into a sitting position.

"You will be. You've bruises up your legs, your right arm, and across the top of your back. And there may be more, but at least that gash on the side of your head is not deep, although it may leave a scar."

Dotty reached up and touched her face, above the right eye, but winced with the pain.

"You could stay in bed all day, but I think it would be more beneficial to get some fresh air and exercise. Norman is driving across to Windrush Hall this morning, so why don't you go with him? It's a lovely sunny day and you can wander around the new garden."

Dotty reached for her cup of tea, and said uncertainly, "I'm not sure. Maybe I should just stay here."

"Rubbish. You can't mope around all day. You'll feel much better after a shower. Come on, up you get."

Dotty hadn't the energy to argue.

"OK. Give me half an hour to sort myself out."

"I'll cook you a bacon sandwich while you get dressed."

Dotty showered and changed. The wrap-around dress she'd worn the previous day lay in a crumpled ball on the floor. The rip across the front was unrepairable, but at least she had a second, identical dress. But she wouldn't wear it today.

She reached for her new jeans and winced as she pulled them on.

Dotty and Norman climbed the front steps at Windrush Hall, and Benson opened the door for them.

"How are you?" asked Norman as Benson led them through to the dining room.

"We're all well, Sir."

"I've told you, please don't call me sir. It's Norman, and I've worked here most of my life."

"Let me fetch the drinks, and Françoise has been cooking something special for you to try." Benson disappeared into the kitchen.

He reappeared a moment later, but as he did, there was a cry from Françoise. "No. The door."

Dotty glanced at Norman, who shrugged.

Benson was rooted to the spot at the entrance to the dining room, holding a silver tray, and looking at something on the floor.

The next moment, Dotty was aware of a flash of movement and she staggered backwards as a heavy, furry weight landed on her shoulder.

"What on earth?" exclaimed Norman. "Well, I never. I've only seen one cat perform that trick."

Françoise appeared next to her husband, wearing her yellow-tinted glasses, and wringing her hands and crying, "Je suis désolée."

Norman looked at the cat sitting serenely on Dotty's shoulder and then across to Benson and Françoise, and asked, "What's going on?"

Benson stepped forward and placed the tray on the dining table. "Please sit down."

Dotty removed the cat from her shoulder and screwed up her face against the pain in her arm. The cat refused to be put on the floor, so she sat down and cradled it in her lap.

Françoise snuffled into a white lace handkerchief while Benson poured teas and coffees. He pushed a plate towards Norman and Dotty and said, "Pâté en croute. Earl Grey's favourite."

"Earl Grey," blurted Dotty, looking down at the grey, British blue cat curled up on her lap.

"I thought as much," remarked Norman as he leaned forward and took a slice of the pâté. "After you've apologised to Dotty, I think you should explain."

"Ma chéri, I really am sorry, but we were desperate," cried Françoise, before hiding her face in her handkerchief.

Benson placed a hand on his wife's arm and murmured, "Don't worry, we'll work something out."

He turned back to Norman and Dotty and declared, "Look at us. We're too old to find new jobs. We don't have pensions and Zenobia said she would see us right, but she hasn't. All we'll get is a small gift."

Françoise wailed, "My eyes."

"She also promised to pay for Françoise's eye surgery, but again, she didn't. We can't afford to pay for private treatment and now there is a long waiting list for the operation on the National Health Service. So you see, we were desperate to keep our jobs, even if they were only looking after Mario."

Benson stopped and reached across for his wife's hand.

"So what happened?" asked Norman.

"Mario disappeared. I am not sure if he was pining after his mistress, or if someone took him, but he vanished. We knew that if the solicitor visited and he wasn't here, we would have to leave."

"But why take Earl Grey?" asked Dotty.

"We knew he was the old Duke's cat, Zenobia told us, and he looked like Mario, and knew Windrush Hall. He seemed like the perfect solution to our problem."

"So Mario hasn't returned?"

Benson shook his head. "I've walked the grounds on many occasions, but there is no sign of him."

"I take it that coming to see me and asking for a scythe was a ruse to get near Earl Grey?"

Benson dropped his eyes to the table and replied, "I'm sorry for deceiving you."

"I didn't know how we could get Earl Grey, but Françoise sent me with a cool box of food when I came to see you. I couldn't believe it when you took me into the kitchen and the cat was curled up by the Aga.

"When you left to find the scythe, I took a chance, grabbed Earl Grey and pushed him inside the empty cool box. That's why I ran off without saying goodbye. I didn't want you to hear him meowing."

"I thought he was stuck down a hole," stammered Dotty.

"I didn't mean to upset you. We just didn't know what else to do."

Norman looked at Earl Grey and reached for another piece of pâté en croute. "At least he doesn't seem to have suffered too much."

"Oh no, we gave him only the best food, just like Mario."

Dotty scratched Earl Grey under the chin and asked, "Have you been spoilt?"

In reply, he looked across the top of the table, jumped up and pattered across to the plate of pâté slices. Using his paw, he dragged a piece off the plate and began eating it.

Dotty smiled.

"See how much he likes my food?" cried Françoise, also smiling. "I would like to make him a regular supply, if I could." She dropped her hands into her lap and looked down at them.

"What will you do now?" asked Dotty.

Françoise sniffled and Benson wrapped his arm around her as he replied, "Inform Mr Willoughby that Mario has disappeared and prepare to leave Windrush Hall."

# CHAPTER THIRTY-NINE

"I always park in the lido car park as it's close to the hospital, but cheaper than parking there, and we can leave the car and walk into Cheltenham town centre," said Keya.

She had readily agreed to accompany Dotty to a check-up at Cheltenham Hospital on Tuesday morning, and also suggested it would be the perfect opportunity to do some shopping, especially as she had been paid the day before.

"Straight over the mini roundabout," she instructed Dotty. "You must be so relieved that Earl Grey is home."

"I am, and so is Agatha."

"The piglet?"

"She's more than that now, although not as large as some pigs, but she still insists on lying across the front of the Aga. Earl Grey curls up on top of her. It's very sweet."

"And he's none the worse for his experience?"

"I think he thought of it as a holiday and he was thoroughly spoilt, and now has a liking for pate. But I do feel sorry for Benson and Françoise. It must be awful being old and having nothing to show for a lifetime of hard work. I'm not sure how they'll manage."

"Straight on at this junction and then take the next left," advised Keya. "And what about Windrush Hall?"

"David was supposed to be meeting the solicitor there today, but he's disappeared on one of his trips, so George is going instead. I guess we'll be organising another sale."

"Sounds good for business."

"I suppose so," agreed Dotty, "but I hope whoever buys it appreciates the work Zenobia did, restoring the house and creating the new garden."

"Here we are. Park over there if you can find a space." Keya pointed to the far left-hand corner of the tarmacked parking area.

An hour later, they walked down the front steps of the main building of Cheltenham Hospital, between two double-height stone columns.

Keya stopped and looked around. "Why don't we start in Montpellier? It's more expensive than the town centre but has some lovely boutiques, and if we don't find anything there, we can walk into town."

They crossed the road and turned right, strolling past the lush playing fields and impressive gothic stone buildings of Cheltenham College.

"I'm not sure whether the doctor was pleased to see you or not," grinned Keya.

"I suppose he's right, though. I do only have one head and I can't keep damaging it. Remind me not to stand in the way of crazy criminals in the future. I should have realised that there were plenty of people on the ground floor who could have stopped Casper, including Felix."

"But the doctor didn't think you'd done yourself any serious harm, did he?"

"No, but as Aunt Beanie told me, I'll have an interesting scar above my right eye."

"War wounds," proclaimed Keya.

They walked on past an old art deco style cinema, which had been converted into an upmarket restaurant, and then Dotty stopped to read a blackboard outside a hair salon. 'Special offer. Full and Half-head Highlights'. "What do you think?" she asked Keya.

"Don't do it just because it's a special offer. What if they turn your hair green?"

Dotty laughed. "I don't think they will, but the hairdresser in Cirencester said highlights would lift my hair. After all, it is rather a dull, mousy-blonde." She cried, "Come on. Let's do it."

At two o'clock, Dotty and Keya stood outside the wide-columned frontage of The Ivy Montpellier Brasserie.

"What do you think?" asked Dotty. "Do you know if they serve tasty vegetarian dishes?"

"They have a separate menu," confirmed Keya. "I came here once for my aunt's birthday, but it's rather pricey."

"I'm feeling extravagant today." Dotty held up both hands from which hung six boutique shopping bags, and Keya carried another two for her containing shoes and a new pair of knee-high suede boots.

"I've already spent a small fortune, so what is lunch for two going to matter? Besides, I need to repay you for sitting at the hairdressers with me for two hours, traipsing around the shops and helping me decide what to buy."

"If you insist," giggled Keya and they pushed open the restaurant door walking through an intimate, but full, dining area with huge vases of pink roses and white and purple delphiniums arranged on the window sills.

Dotty gasped as they walked into the next room, which was a light, airy dining space beneath a glass domed roof. "What was this building?" she asked.

"The Montpellier Spa, Madam," replied a solemn waiter, as if her reaction was to be expected. "A table for two?"

"Yes, please."

They were seated at the edge of the circular room beneath a large wall fresco of a racehorse, beside an oversized potted palm.

"I didn't expect to find this," said Dotty in a voice of wonder. "It's very Mediterranean."

"I think you did very well with your shopping," observed Keya, as they piled bags onto a spare chair. "I wish I was brave enough to wear some of the summer dresses you chose, but they do show off every lump and bump."

"You don't have any lumps or bumps. You're as thin as a rake."

"Exactly. Your curvy figure looked wonderful in them."

Dotty blushed. "I suppose since I exposed myself in Gainfords, when I ripped my dress, I'm a little less self-conscious about wearing more revealing clothes."

"And you like the admiring glances you receive from certain policemen and antiques experts." Keya grinned.

Dotty blushed and looked down, concentrating on the menu. "I think I might join you with the vegetarian dishes. I like the look of the twice-baked cheese soufflé followed by the wild mushroom and truffle linguine."

Two men wearing business suits walked past their table and as Dotty glanced up one of them caught her eye and raised an eyebrow. She felt a fluttering in her stomach and heat in her cheeks.

Keya commented, "You're gathering admirers by the minute. It must be the new haircut, and that low-cut blouse you're wearing."

Dotty did feel like a new woman and she was actually enjoying the attention, where previously she would have shrunk away from it.

She smiled at her friend and said, "Let's order."

# CHAPTER FORTY

A t four-thirty on Thursday afternoon, Dotty was considering packing up for the day.

She'd spent most of it at Windrush Hall, where she'd been updating the previous sales catalogue in preparation for an auction at the hall in two weeks' time.

There was a lot of work to do in a short amount of time, but the solicitor had wanted it dealt with quickly.

The phone rang on her desk and she picked it up, answering, "Akemans Antiques. Can I help you?"

"Dotty, it's me, Keya. I wasn't sure I'd catch you, but are you free for a drink at The Axeman before you head home?"

"Sure, whenever you're ready. It's a lovely evening to sit out and I've had a busy day."

"And can you ask Gilly, and Norman? Is David back from his trip? And what about Marion?"

"David is still away. I'm not sure when he'll be back, and Marion hasn't been in all week."

"Never mind. Do you think Aunt Beanie would like to come?"

"I can call and ask her, but it will depend on Uncle Cliff."

Dotty wandered into the antiques centre and glanced up the stairs. She hadn't made any progress with the bargain stall as there hadn't been time this week, and now she had to organise the sale at Windrush Hall.

She'd put aside some time once that was finished, and she did want to start her own venture.

Gilly descended the metal staircase and smiled. "I still hardly recognise the new you, but it's very fetching." She reached the bottom step and halted. "It's as if you're growing up." She placed a hand on Dotty's arm. "But please remember to continue being kind and considerate to others, even as you grow in confidence and become more independent."

Slightly taken aback, Dotty stammered, "Constable Varma, Keya, called and asked if we'd like to join her at The Axeman."

Gilly checked her watch. "Five o'clock already. Where has the day gone? I can come for a quick drink, but then I have to collect the kids from their tennis lesson."

Keya was already sitting outside The Axeman pub, wearing the attractive green tunic top she'd worn on their first trip to London. Seated at the head of the table was Inspector Evans in his trademark brown suit and Sergeant Unwin was lifting a second table, which he placed next to the first one.

As he moved a chair he looked up at Dotty and smiled. "I like the hair. It suits you."

Dotty squeezed past Inspector Evans and sat down beside Keya, who grabbed her hand and whispered, "See, they'll all be after you now."

But was that because she had a new haircut and fashionable clothes? Sergeant Unwin hadn't thought much of her when she was plain Dotty.

"Inspector Evans," greeted Aunt Beanie, and she sat down next to him, opposite Keya. "Tell me all about your trip to the Chelsea Flower show. I bet your mum loved it."

"Cracking," replied the inspector, and he and Aunt Beanie started discussing roses.

Norman walked around the corner and leaned on the back of a chair at the end of the table. "What's the celebration?" he asked.

Constable Varma stood up and smiled at the group. "My promotion to sergeant, and my new position in the Rural, Heritage and Wildlife Unit under Inspector Ringrose."

"Congratulations," cried Aunt Beanie. She looked across at Norman. "I think this calls for a round of drinks. Put them on my tab."

"What have I missed?" asked a breathless Gilly, as she pushed her orange-rimmed glasses up her nose.

'Constable Varma will soon be Sergeant Varma," explained Dotty.

"That's great, but does it mean you're leaving us?"

"Not at all," replied Keya. "Actually, our division will be working more closely with rural businesses like yourselves."

Aunt Beanie addressed Inspector Evans. "And talking of police work, do you have an update on Zenobia's death and the Lady Justice statue?"

"I'll let Sergeant Onion tell you all about that. After all, he's the clever so-and-so who cracked the case, he is."

"I get by with a little help from my friends," sang Aunt Beanie, as if to herself.

Sergeant Unwin - Dotty loved how Inspector Evans referred to him as 'Onion' - had the decency to blush.

"Once we confronted Casper Dupré with Emery Brown's side of the story, he caved in and admitted he commissioned the sculpture after a trip to Spain searching for new artwork to sell in his gallery. But as Emery told us, they hadn't expected the sculpture to be so good and Casper got greedy.

"Rents in the West End are rising and his gallery is struggling. He saw exhibiting and selling the sculpture as a way to keep his business afloat. He admitted it was the controversy over a sculpture which previously sold for a huge price at Gainfords, which sparked the idea for his plan."

Norman carried a bottle of rosé wine and a pint of beer out of the pub, and he was followed by the barman carrying an orange and lemonade, and three wine glasses. Norman placed the beer in front of the inspector and disappeared back inside.

"Casper and Emery had become good friends after meeting in a London nightclub at Christmastime. So when Casper was asked to be an expert on *The Antique Tour*, and realised Zenobia was to be the sculpture expert on the same programme, he persuaded Emery to bring the sculpture along to be evaluated. If he could persuade Zenobia to tell the nation, on a popular Sunday night TV show, that the statue was worth a small fortune, he could use it to pull the crowds into his gallery and sell it to raise much-needed capital."

"So, is there a link between the statue and Zenobia's death?" asked Dotty.

Sergeant Unwin looked at her. "I think you realised some time ago that there was."

Had she? Once she met Felix, she realised he hadn't hurt Zenobia, but she'd still been uncertain about Serena De Rossi, until she realised Serena was playing a different game. Everything had kept leading back to the sculpture.

"Casper realised Zenobia was doubting the provenance of the sculpture. He was buoyed up by alcohol and insisted on finding Zenobia, intending to persuade her that the sculpture was genuine. Emery tried to stop him, but Casper marched off and found Zenobia sitting in the library."

Norman placed a pint of beer in front of Sergeant Unwin and sat down next to him.

Gilly poured wine into the three glasses and pushed one towards Aunt Beanie and another to Dotty, and Keya picked up the glass of orange and lemonade.

The sergeant continued, "At first Emery said the discussion was amicable as Zenobia expressed her doubts and asked for Casper's opinion. She listened but then told them she would be saying it was an exquisite piece which, if its provenance could be verified, would be worth millions, but in her opinion it was an excellent copy worth between £3,000 and £5,000."

"She was spot on," declared Aunt Beanie. "Well done her."

"She may have been right, but that comment led to her death. Emery told us Casper became increasingly worked up as he tried to reason with Zenobia, but she had made up her mind up and said she was going to bed. Casper followed her out into the corridor. Emery heard raised voices and as he opened the library door, he watched Casper push Zenobia over the balustrade."

"And I thought Emery was the muscle man," commented Keya.

"More of a gentle giant," declared Aunt Beanie. "But we witnessed Casper's temper at Gainfords, didn't we, Dotty?"

Dotty nodded, but her thoughts were for poor Emery. "Have you offered Emery any counselling? I think, from some of the comments he made, that he's tormented by Zenobia's death. And probably more so if Casper persuaded him to hide the truth. I guess Casper told him they were both at fault and if Casper went down, he would drag Emery with him."

"That's a good point," agreed Keya. "I'll see what I can do."

Gilly put down her wine glass and asked, "Has Casper admitted to killing Zenobia Richardson?"

"No, he hasn't," Inspector Evans remarked and picked up his half-drunk pint of beer.

"I doubt he will," added Sergeant Unwin, "But I also believe Emery Brown was not responsible for Zenobia Richardson's death."

"And what about Serena De Rossi?" asked Norman. "How is she involved?"

"Greedy little so-and-so, that one," growled Inspector Evans.

"We've charged her with embezzlement. The money she stole from the Zenobia Richardson's fan club will be returned but we're still looking for the money she stole directly from Zenobia for so-called building work."

"It'll be a shame if Zenobia's fan club dies with her," mused Aunt Beanie.

"Oh, it won't," disclosed Sergeant Unwin. "Mr and Mrs Benson are taking over its management."

"Benson and Françoise," exclaimed Dotty. "That's great news."

# CHAPTER FORTY-ONE

A week later, Dotty returned to Meadowbank Farm to find Inspector Ringrose sitting at the pine kitchen table playing cards with Uncle Cliff.

"Isn't it great?" enthused Aunt Beanie. "Although Cliff can't remember what happened yesterday, he suddenly announced he wanted to play rummy. Inspector Ringrose and I had to look it up on the internet and remind ourselves of the rules, but Cliff knew them."

"How are you feeling, young lady, after your tumble at Gainfords?"

Self-consciously, Dotty touched the scab above her right eye as she replied, "I'm OK. My bruises are disappearing."

"I'm glad to hear it. It was a brave but reckless thing you did. Reminds me of someone else I know." He turned towards Aunt Beanie.

"I haven't prevented criminals escaping by throwing myself down staircases."

"Perhaps not, but I remember other incidences when you behaved impetuously and saved a rare item or thwarted a criminal gang."

"I'm not sure about that," but Dotty caught a gleam of pride in Aunt Beanie's eyes.

"Which reminds me, did you see the latest treasure to be returned to the Bagdad Museum of Antiquities?" asked Inspector Ringrose.

Aunt Beanie narrowed her eyes and replied, "No."

"A necklace of gold disks with granulated rosettes from the Babylonian Empire."

"I knew it was real," exclaimed Aunt Beanie, "So why did Gainfords describe it as a replica, and why was nobody bidding for it at the auction?"

"I don't know, but that's the sort of thing you can find out if you join my team."

"Aunt Beanie! Are you going to work in the Rural, Heritage and Wildlife Unit?" asked Dotty. "What a fantastic idea."

"I've asked her to join us as a consultant. That way, she can choose the crimes she wants to pursue. And the people." Inspector Ringrose placed a hand on Dotty's arm.

"A friendly word of warning. As you're drawn into the antiques world, just be careful who you trust."

Aunt Beanie and Inspector Ringrose exchanged a meaningful glance.

It was a glorious June day as Dotty welcomed guests to Windrush Hall for the sale of its contents. The auction was being held in a marquee on the back lawn beside Zenobia's new garden, which was full of colour.

The lavender bushes along the central path swelled with fragrant flowers and the borders exploded with pink peonies, brightly coloured lupins and the full blooms of heritage roses.

Despite it being early summer, and the previous auction at Windrush Hall having been at Christmastime, she still felt a sense of déjà vu.

"What a lovely dress, Dotty," complimented Françoise as she placed a plate of miniature cinnamon rolls on the refreshment table beside Dotty. They must have been taken straight from the oven, as Dotty could smell the rich butter pastry and the sharp, sweet smell of cinnamon.

"And how is Earl Grey?" asked Françoise.

"He's very well, except for his habit of believing he should eat with us in the evening. He even jumps onto the table and sits by my place, which I know irritates Norman. And how does Benson feel about selling Zenobia's collection of figurines and porcelain?"

"Conflicted. Mr Willoughby made out that Zenobia had only left us a small gift, not her entire collection. Benson would have preferred to keep it, but where would we put everything?

I doubt the pieces will make very much, but Benson has promised that if we raise enough money, I can have my eye operation. That means I'll be able to find a job in a cafe or something and supplement our salaries from running Zenobia's fan club. So we're much better off than we expected."

She stepped closer to Dotty. "But I am pleased he decided to keep the statuette of the black cat holding a bunch of flowers, which started Zenobia's collection."

Dotty greeted more guests and, when the auction started, she seated herself at a desk, at the back of the marquee, and began entering sales information and winning bidders into Akemans' auction computer system.

She looked up when George announced, "Lot 36, a 1950s pink leprechaun cookie jar. Who'll start me at £100?"

"£100 on the internet. 120, 150, 200."

The price rose to £2,700 without anyone in the room having a chance to bid. George did a good job of hiding her surprise. "I have £2,700 on AuctionRoom.com. Any advance on 2,700?"

Aunt Beanie stuck her hand up. "2,900 on the telephone." David Rook had still not returned from his trip and Aunt Beanie and one of George's friends were manning the phones for the auction.

The bidding rose slowly.

"£3,600. Final call." George looked round the room. "Sold."

"I can't believe it," cried Françoise behind Dotty. "That will pay for my operation."

Dotty didn't like to tell them that a commission of twenty-three per cent would be deducted from the sale price, but hopefully, other items from Zenobia's collection would also sell well. None of them had expected such a price for a small, brightly coloured cookie jar.

She watched Benson hug his wife and then turned back to the auction as George declared, "Lot 37, a Lladro figurine of a flamenco dancer. We've had a lot of interest in this gorgeous piece of porcelain with its intricately detailed, vivid red dress. I shall start the bidding at £5,200."

"Oh, mon dieu!" cried Françoise.

Aunt Beanie was busy on the phone again and this time her client was the winning bidder, paying £7,300 for the piece.

"I didn't realise Zenobia had such a fascinating collection," remarked Gilmore.

Dotty looked up quickly. "Hi," she stuttered, "I thought you were away with David."

"No, I returned last week, but he had additional work to attend to." He paused to examine her. "I see you've had your hair done. It suits you. When are you next coming to London? I'd like to buy you dinner."

Will Dotty's increasing confidence boost her standing at work … and in love? Find out in book 3, *Bidding for Revenge*.

Stolen antiques. An unexplained death. Can an amateur sleuth tell a fake from the real deal and solve a curio of a murder?

Or buy Bidding For Revenge from Amazon or VictoriaTait.com

Would you like to know how Dotty obtained her job at Akemans and solved a murder? Find out in the FREE prequel, *Hour is Come,* when you sign up to my newsletter for updates.

A dead husband. A hidden body. Can an inexperienced amateur sleuth save herself and identify a killer in the stroke of time?

**Hour is Come is FREE to download at**
www.bookfunnel.victoriatait.com/hs6uypfw34

Would you like to know what happened to Mario, Zenobia Richardson's cat?

Click the QR Code or visit
www.VictoriaTait.com/2022/06/11/marios-journey/

If you enjoyed this book, please tell someone you know. And for those people you don't know, leave a review to help them decide whether or not to read it.

Leave a review on the site you purchased from. For Amazon you can hold your phone over the QR Code

For more information visit VictoriaTait.com

# ROBERT MUCHAMORE'S
# ROBIN HOOD

## JET SKIS, SWAMPS & SMUGGLERS

First published in Great Britain in 2021 by
HOT KEY BOOKS
80–81 Wimpole St, London W1G 9RE
Owned by Bonnier Books
Sveavägen 56, Stockholm, Sweden
www.hotkeybooks.com

A CIP catalogue record for this book is available from the British Library.

ISBN: 978-1-4714-0949-3
*Also available as an ebook and in audio*

1

Typeset by DataConnection Ltd
Printed and bound in Great Britain by Clays Ltd, Elcograf S.p.A.

Hot Key Books is an imprint of Bonnier Books UK
www.bonnierbooks.co.uk

# ROBIN HOOD

# THE STORY SO FAR . . .

**It is a troubled time in Sherwood Forest . . .**

Evil gangster **Guy Gisborne** has the declining industrial town of Locksley under his thumb, controlling everything, from petty drug deals to police and judges.

He works in an uneasy alliance with the Sheriff of Nottingham, **Marjorie Kovacevic**.

The ambitious Sheriff likes to portray herself as a successful businesswoman and get-tough politician, who locks up criminals and cracks down on immigration. But deep in Sherwood Forest, Sheriff Marjorie has a private army of guards who deal brutally with anyone who gets in her way.

**But good folks are fighting back!**

For more than a decade, **Emma** and **Will Scarlock** have fought to protect the thousands of vulnerable people who live in Sherwood Forest. From their base inside an abandoned outlet mall, their team provides shelter, healthcare and food to anyone who needs it.

**And a new hero is rising . . .**

When **Ardagh Hood** spoke out about corruption in Locksley, Guy Gisborne had him framed by crooked cops and sentenced to three years in prison.

Nobody expected his thirteen-year-old son **Robin Hood** to fight back, but so far Robin has shot Gisborne in the plums with an arrow, staged a daring robbery to raise money for Forest People and helped sabotage a big-game hunt at Sherwood Castle Resort.

**Now Robin is in danger!**

With Robin's name graffitied on thousands of walls, and videos of his actions watched by millions, Sheriff Marjorie fears Robin could spark a rebellion and destroy her political ambitions.

So she's agreed to help Gisborne hunt Robin down, using a posse of former special forces soldiers.

# PART I

# 1. DINO BULLCALF

The rooftop market at the abandoned Sherwood Designer Outlets was a bustling social gathering for the rebels, runaways and refugees who lived in Sherwood Forest. Traders travelled overnight, emerging from dense forest dragging their wares in nylon bags and backpacks as they crossed the mall's weed-strewn car parks.

A bunch of stalls in the centre of the market sold hot food. Harsh sunlight hit Dino Bullcalf's bald head as he strode between them, catching whiffs of shish kebab, curry, baby back ribs and stale cooking fat.

Bullcalf had been a judo champion, an elite Italian army paratrooper and most recently a man with a reputation for finding people who didn't want to be found. But at seventy-six years old his haggard face made it easy to ignore a frame that could run 5K without breaking sweat and bench-press more than most men half his age.

One of Bullcalf's tattooed hands held a cardboard coffee cup. After swallowing the last mouthful he shuffled

3

into a gap between two stalls and bumped a woman energetically sweeping dropped food under her burrito stand.

'You've come the wrong way, fella!' the woman said cheerfully, as she pointed the old man back to the customer side.

Bullcalf acted doddery and confused. 'So hot today!' he said breathlessly, with a Neapolitan accent that hadn't faded in the forty years since he'd fled Italy. 'I hate litter, but I can't see a bin.'

'Gimme,' the woman said, reaching out to take the cup.

As she turned away and flipped the cup into a bin under her stall, Bullcalf deftly pulled a plastic-wrapped packet from his trouser pocket. The outside had pads of double-sided tape, while the inside contained finely ground aluminium powder and a delicate glass vial filled with green fluid.

Without opening the packet, Bullcalf crushed the vial, enabling the liquid to start mixing with the powder. Then he reached under the burrito stand and felt the contents start to fizz as he stuck the package to the bright red gas cylinder that fuelled the grill.

In a few minutes, the chemical reaction inside the plastic bag would reach a critical temperature, making the aluminium powder explode in a white flash. This would fracture the metal cylinder and ignite the pressurised gas inside. If things went to plan, the resulting bang would be loud enough to distract the market's heavily armed security guards.

'*Grazie*, my dear!' Bullcalf told the burrito chef once she'd binned his coffee cup.

'No problem,' she answered cheerfully.

Once he was away from the food stalls, Bullcalf dropped the doddery act and walked fast. The other four members of the posse Guy Gisborne had hired to capture Robin Hood were standing near the edge of the mall's flat roof.

Hughes, Denton and Zev were tough-looking blokes who'd done time in the army and knew their stuff. The fourth – and the man Gisborne had put in charge – was Venables. He had buzz-cut red hair, a round freckled face and he irritated Bullcalf every time he opened his mouth.

Venables had convinced Guy Gisborne that he could put together an elite squad to track down Robin Hood. He'd even talked the notoriously tight gangster into paying thirty thousand up front for expenses.

But when Bullcalf asked around he'd discovered that his new boss was all talk. Venables had no experience tracking people down, the military exploits he boasted about were bogus and he was wanted by the police in Capital City for a series of armed robberies targeting wealthy pensioners and charity fundraisers.

'Still alive, grandad?' Venables carped as he slapped Bullcalf on the back and checked the time on his gigantic diver's watch.

'We need to move fast when that cylinder blows,' Bullcalf said curtly. 'Is everyone set?'

'I've tied off the ropes,' Zev answered. 'Denton is gonna whack the nearest security camera when the blast happens, so it'll look like the explosion knocked the camera out.'

'Good thinking,' Bullcalf said appreciatively.

Venables was supposed to be in charge and hated it when the three younger men showed Bullcalf respect.

'Do you need to sit down, old man?' Venables said.

*How many times can you make the old-guy joke?* Bullcalf thought to himself.

A younger Bullcalf would have ripped Venables's head off. But he'd grown patient with age and Venables was going to get what he deserved soon enough . . .

# 2. MAN ON THE INSIDE

Ninety seconds later, the gas bottle ruptured. The blast shook the entire mall roof as the flaming metal canister rocketed thirty metres into the air.

Market stalls toppled as traders and shoppers dived for cover. There were screams and objects clattering. The burrito chef looked back at her wrecked stand and realised she was only alive because she'd stepped away to flirt with the pit master on the barbecue stall.

After flying more than seventy metres, the spiralling, red-hot cylinder crashed into one of the mall's rooftop greenhouses. A quick-thinking gardener rushed to the scene, edging between jagged glass and smothering embers with shovelfuls of damp compost.

Although the rooftop market was open to anyone who handed over their weapons and passed through an airport-style scanner, the mall's interior was strictly residents only. Bullcalf was pleased to see a guard sprint towards the food stalls, while another helped a distraught old lady who'd been trampled by panicked shoppers.

'Move out!' Venables ordered enthusiastically.

Hughes, Zev, Bullcalf and Venables slid eight metres down a rope slung over the side of the mall roof. Their landing spot was a narrow ledge, formed by the top of the letters **ET** on an immense **SHERWOOD DESIGNER OUTLETS** sign.

The plastic signage was crusted with bird poop and creaked alarmingly under the weight of the four burly men. Venables was no fan of heights, and as he tried not to look at the concrete twenty-five metres below, Hughes used a crowbar to lever open a rusted metal access hatch.

Hughes squeezed through the opening and dropped into a narrow hallway. His boots made the only prints in the dust, suggesting he was the first to walk this route in years. Denton had stayed back to wreck the rooftop camera, so he came last and needed a tug from Zev to drag his stomach through.

'Denton ate all the pies!' Zev joked. 'Did anyone see us drop down?'

Denton shook his head as Venables turned a corner and reached a narrow metal door. It clanked, but after opening a few centimetres a padlock and chain snapped tight.

Venables fumed as he peered through the fist-sized gap. 'Mr Khan, are you there?'

Sneakers moved warily up metal steps on the other side of the door. 'It's me, Khan,' a man answered. 'Are you Venables?'

'Who else?' Venables spluttered. 'Father Christmas?'

Mr Khan coughed nervously. 'Mr Venables, you are going to get everything we agreed to. But I must protect myself. There are five of you, and if you killed me you wouldn't have to pay my ten thousand.'

Venables battered his palm against the door. 'Listen, dirtbag, a deal is a deal . . .'

Bullcalf set his hand on Venables's shoulder and warned him to stay cool.

Mr Khan's gold-ringed hand appeared briefly and flicked a folder filled with papers through the gap in the door. 'That's a map showing where Robin Hood is hiding,' he explained.

'I heard Robin got sent away from here,' Bullcalf said.

'He was away for a while,' Mr Khan said. 'But he had a couple of run-ins with bandits chasing the bounty on his head, so Will Scarlock decided Robin was safest back here. There's always a guard, but they stay outside the main door of Robin's new den, and that map shows how to access the room via a hatch at the rear.'

'If you're lying, you'd better pray we *all* get killed,' Venables warned.

'I have all my family here at the mall,' Khan said gently. 'I know better than to betray a powerful man like you.'

Venables was easily flattered and cracked a smile.

Bullcalf inspected the document pouch Khan had passed through. It contained a folded architectural plan of the mall. A route marked out in pink highlighter showed how to reach Robin Hood's hiding place and an escape route via the sewers.

'Give him the money,' Bullcalf whispered to Venables. 'It's not like we have a choice.'

Venables reluctantly passed a stuffed envelope through the crack in the door and they heard Khan tear it open and fan the notes.

'Satisfactory!' Khan said.

'Open up,' Venables demanded.

'It's a combination lock,' Mr Khan explained, calmer now he had his cash. 'Eight, seven, six, one, two, three.'

Bullcalf realised the combination lock was a smart move. If Mr Khan had opened the lock or handed over a key, the posse would be through the door in seconds. But it took Venables almost a minute to reach around the door and dial in six numbers, by which time Khan had vanished down the metal steps on the other side.

The five men were relieved as the lock clicked open and the chain clanked to the floor. Mr Khan had left a battered army kit bag on the landing and Venables looked chuffed as he unzipped it and checked the contents.

'Two guns, knives, ammo, tools and keys,' he said as he rummaged. 'I can taste Guy Gisborne's money!'

'Good stuff,' Bullcalf said, as the younger men behind him made happy noises. 'Let's go find Robin Hood.'

# 3. SHERWOOD SCREENS

Venables led the way across the mall, though he was puzzled until Bullcalf made him turn the map the right way up.

They were directly below Designer Outlets' roof, and after crossing a metal gantry that had a view down at the lighting and ventilation of a store that had once sold pricey suits, they jogged the length of a bare concrete hallway, went down four flights of steps and through a fire door propped open with a plastic chair.

Bullcalf's nose tingled from a musty smell as his boot squelched mildewed red carpet. A Rage Cola vending machine had been tipped over and trashed, while kids had drawn boobs and willies on the **COMING SOON** posters for fifteen-year-old movies.

'Sherwood Screens,' Denton read aloud, then felt hunger pangs as he passed an ad for a Quad Combo Deal – *Nachos, Popcorn, Hot Dog & Frozen Cola. JUST £12.99 . . .*

'My first-ever date, I took a girl to see *Blade: Trinity*,' Zev said fondly, as he spotted that movie's faded poster. 'I spilled Fanta in my lap and the girl said she wasn't walking home with a guy who looked like he'd wet himself.'

Denton and Hughes snorted with laughter. Bullcalf thought they were making too much noise, but before he could tell them to can it, he felt his phone vibrate. He answered in a whisper, as Venables located a door that led through a staff break room, then upstairs to the cinema's projection booth.

Bullcalf spoke softly into his phone. 'Mamma, what's the matter? OK, OK, calm down. Listen carefully . . . You can't find Cairo's food because he's not with you any more. You haven't had a cat for six years . . . I can't visit today because I'm working, but Andrea will call in on her way home . . .'

Venables rounded the top of the stairs into a gently curved room with four projectors along each side and two at the far end. Sherwood Screens closed before cinemas went digital, so old-skool mechanical film projectors pointed through slot windows into the cinema's eight auditoriums.

A hole in the roof brought sunlight and fresher air than downstairs, but there were heaps of fizzing wasps and a nest bulged from a ceiling vent.

'Wasps are the worst,' Denton said, as he swatted.

Venables jolted as a wasp buzzed close to his ear, while Bullcalf was still speaking to his mum.

'I have to go, Ma. *Stop* crying. You know I love you, but I'm far away at work. Put the TV on and do your breathing exercises until Andrea gets there.'

'Hard to believe your mother's still kicking,' Venables boomed as Bullcalf pocketed his phone. 'What is she – two hundred years old?'

Bullcalf wanted to punch Venables more than he'd ever wanted to punch anyone. But they had to stay focused.

'Keep the noise down,' Bullcalf warned as he flicked a wasp off his brow. 'Venables, what screen is Robin supposed to be in?'

'Five,' Venables said.

'Which one's five?' Zev asked.

Hughes had already noticed that the projectors were numbered. He stopped by number five and peered through the rectangular hole in front of the lens.

It was one of the smallest auditoriums and around half of the fifty seats had been stripped out. A huge electric fan was spinning and there was a double airbed and a tent in the open space. Archery targets had been pinned to the cinema screen, and there were so many holes in some spots that parts of the screen were in tatters.

'Bullseye,' Hughes whispered.

Bullcalf and Venables knocked skulls as they rushed to peek through the little window.

'That's Robin's den all right,' Venables said happily.

'Can't see the kid though,' Bullcalf said.

Six eyes scanned the gloomy auditorium and Hughes spotted something first.

'Third row of seats, one from the aisle,' Hughes whispered. 'See?'

Venables and Bullcalf locked eyes on a mop of scruffy hair sticking above the seat line, silhouetted by bluish light from a laptop screen.

'No point sticking around,' Venables said keenly. 'Let's do this.'

'There's an access hatch down to the screen,' Hughes said, as he knelt in front of the projector and saw two bolts. 'Drop is two metres, maybe three.'

'I know what I'm doing, Hughes,' Venables said, tapping his map. 'What about you, Bullcalf? Can those old hips handle the drop?'

Zev got stung by a wasp and yelped as Bullcalf backed away from the projector.

'Hips work fine,' Bullcalf said acidly. 'But remember – your friend Khan told us there's a guard out front who might start shooting or run off and raise the alarm. I've got the second gun, so how about I head to the front of screen five and take out the guard?'

'Obviously,' Venables said, though he clearly hadn't thought of it. 'Do you need one of the others?'

Bullcalf shook his head. 'I can take one guard.'

Zev yelped again. 'Wasp up my trouser leg! Why am I the only one getting stung?'

'Stop whining, Zev,' Venables hissed.

'Venables, I'll text you when the guard is dealt with,' Bullcalf said. 'I'll be waiting to grab Robin if he runs for the exit.'

'Good luck,' Denton said, as Bullcalf headed out of the projection booth and started back down the stairs.

'Don't do anything stupid,' Bullcalf responded.

But when he got to the staff break room, Bullcalf didn't head for the front of screen five. He went back the way they came, through the fire door propped with a chair and upstairs towards the roof.

# 4. WASPS ARE GITS

Venables's phone pinged.

'Bullcalf?' Denton asked.

Venables nodded as he read the message. 'He's disabled the guard. Let's move.'

There was a grating sound as Denton opened a wooden panel at the base of screen five's projector. As he dropped into the last row of cinema seats, he watched the kid stand up and stride quickly with the laptop tucked under his arm.

By the time Venables landed, Denton had a bad feeling. When people hear an unexpected noise, they glance about to see where it came from. But the kid darted off like he was expecting something.

Hughes landed next.

'Bullcalf, we're in!' Venables shouted cheerfully.

'Zev, don't jump – it's a trap!' Hughes shouted.

Venables hadn't figured it out. 'What are you talking about?'

The boy dived through a grille beneath the cinema screen, and before Hughes could explain his suspicions to the others there was a clattering sound, followed by the deafening flash of a stun grenade.

The three men were deaf and blind as all the auditorium lights came on. Two women in body armour stormed through the main door as Will Scarlock and Mr Khan came through a fire exit at the side, wearing combat helmets and holding assault rifles.

'KHAAAAAN!' Venables raged.

A smart person might reason that that someone who'd betrayed him wouldn't have supplied a working gun. But Venables found out the hard way when he shot wildly into the grenade smoke and the exploding weapon blew the tips off of two fingers.

Denton gasped in horror as Venables's blood misted his face. An instant later the two women pointed their guns at point-blank range.

One shouted: 'Kneel or die! Hands in the air!'

'Now, turds!' the other one added.

As Mr Khan stepped behind and started fitting Venables, Hughes and Denton with plastic zip cuffs, Will peered through the hatch from the projector room and was surprised to hear masses of fizzing wasps.

'Sam, are you up there?'

Will's nineteen-year-old son, Sam Scarlock, sounded alarmed. 'Dad, there's a wasps' nest,' he shouted back. 'They went berserk when the grenade went off.'

'Have you been stung?'

'I'm staying well back,' Sam said. 'But we dragged one guy out. He's stung bad and not breathing right. We're gonna carry him straight to the clinic.'

'You be careful – wasps get nasty when the nest is threatened,' Will warned. 'What about the other guy?'

'It's just him,' Sam said.

Will thought of the five people he'd watched on surveillance footage from his command tent.

'I'm missing the dark-skinned dude and the old man,' he shouted up.

'The guy we carried out is black,' Sam answered.

'You're certain the old man's not up there?'

'I'm sure, Dad, and I'm outta here before these wasps get me.'

Will sighed as he turned to Mr Khan and the two women. 'The old guy went missing.'

He took his radio and called his head of security. 'Azeem, do you copy?'

'Yeah,' she answered, sounding stressed.

'I want a mall-wide security alert. Get everybody you can on search duty.'

'What's going on?' she asked. 'I'm on the roof with smouldering wreckage and a dozen injured.'

'We mounted a sting operation to catch the posse Gisborne sent after Robin,' Will explained. 'One of them got away. I'll send you his picture in a second . . . OWW!'

'What was that?'

'Wasp stung my wrist,' Will gasped.

'I'm your head of security,' Azeem said, aghast. 'How can you mount a sting operation without telling me?

'You had enough on your plate running the market,' Will explained.

'Are these the guys that blew up a gas cylinder?' Azeem asked.

'Khan agreed to meet them and lead them to Robin,' Will said sheepishly. 'We didn't anticipate they'd set off a bomb to cause a distraction.'

'It's a miracle nobody got killed,' Azeem said furiously.

'Look, Azeem, I'm sorry I didn't involve you in the plan. But let's find the fifth man now and you can tell me what an idiot I am later.'

Mr Khan interrupted. 'Will, Venables is spitting mad. But he moaned something about *Bullcalf* betraying them.'

Will nodded. 'Azeem, we think the guy we're looking for is called Bullcalf. His last known position was exiting the projector booth at the back of Sherwood Screens.'

'We're stretched thin up here,' Azeem sighed. 'But I'll get some people on it.'

PART II

# PART II

# 5. FINALLY, OUR HERO

While four-fifths of a posse got lured into a trap by Mr Khan and a ten-year-old in a wig, the real Robin Hood was a hundred and seventy kilometres away in the swampy Eastern Delta. More specifically, Robin was listening to deafeningly loud grime music, while hanging upside down from a chin-up bar doing stomach crunches.

'Forty-six, forty-seven . . .'

After fifty Robin pulled his torso up, grasping the bar and letting his legs drop. The sweat running down his bare chest changed direction and he had to dangle from one arm to swipe at the drips trickling off his brow into his eyes.

Muscle-ups came next. The brutal exercise started with a chin-up, then you had to keep pushing until your whole torso was above the bar with your arms straight.

Robin hadn't been able to do muscle-ups when he arrived in the delta six weeks earlier, but the guy he was staying with, Diogo, had taught him the proper technique and, after working out most days, Robin's personal best was sixteen.

'Thirteen, fourteen . . .'

Robin tried to continue but his arms became jelly. His right hand slipped and he dropped off the bar, moaning loudly because he'd wanted to break his record.

The space Robin used for working out and practising archery was a roller-skating rink inside an abandoned holiday village. He rubbed aching shoulder muscles and caught his breath as he admired himself in a wall lined with tarnished bronze mirrors.

Robin needed a haircut, and the thirteen-year-old wished he was taller. The workouts had bulked his arms and chest, though his appetite for junk food meant he was some way off a six-pack.

After drinking from his water bottle and squirting the dregs over his head, Robin straightened up Diogo's dumbbells, gathered arrows he'd shot into targets at the far side of the rink, then switched off the music and headed out, with his bow in one hand and Diogo's boom box in the other.

Home was a few hundred metres' walk. Crickets chattered and sun toasted Robin's bare back as he passed the abandoned resort's kiddie playground and ducked through a rusted wire fence onto a sliver of gravelly beach littered with dumped air conditioners and fishing net.

Diogo called his battered wooden house The Station. At low tide you could reach the embankment on which it stood by crossing mushy sand, but Robin hated his Nikes getting flooded and reached The Station via a creaking wooden jetty.

The building's name came from its original use as an emergency lifeboat station. Diogo had bought it in wrecked condition, added an extra storey and turned it into an eccentric home a kilometre from his nearest neighbour.

'Anybody home?' Robin yelled.

The sliding door was locked, so he took a key from under a flowerpot, then stepped in and switched off Diogo's home-made security system by disconnecting a metal bulldog clip from a car battery.

Robin checked an orange 1970s-style wall clock and worried when he saw it was past three. His best friend, Marion, had gone out with Diogo on his boat before breakfast and they were normally back by lunchtime.

But Diogo was a smart guy, so Robin wasn't too worried as he rummaged in the fridge and scoffed egg salad and a giant turkey drumstick left from last night's dinner.

Next came a shower, which wasn't like in any normal house. First, the shower was a piece of copper pipe with a head made from a perforated beer can and was *outside* the building. Second, Diogo's solar water heating had a busted thermostat and ran dangerously hot when the sun came out.

Robin stuck with cold water, since he liked the idea of his skin remaining attached to his body. His phone rang as he hopped back inside, trailing drips and doing an alarming skid on the wooden floor as he answered. He hoped it was Marion, Diogo or maybe Robin's brother, Little John, but *Will Scarlock* was the name on-screen.

"Sup, boss?' Robin gasped.

'You OK?' Will asked, surprised by Robin's startled tone.

'Ran from the shower, almost sprawled on my face. Everything OK?'

Will laughed as Robin squatted on the arm of a cracked leather armchair.

'It's complicated . . .' Will began.

Robin put the phone on speaker and towelled his hair as Will told the whole story: how Mr Khan heard that Gisborne's posse was looking for an informant inside Designer Outlets. Then luring them to the mall on market day and isolating them in a remote location so they could be taken down without endangering shoppers.

'Who was my stand-in?' Robin asked.

'Marion's brother Matt. We gave him a fright wig from a Halloween costume.'

'My hair's not *that* scruffy,' Robin objected. 'Good on Matt for helping out though!'

'The bad news is, one guy got away,' Will said gravely. 'We got his escape on CCTV. He abseiled down from the roof and got swallowed by the forest before we'd even started searching for him.'

'Still,' Robin said brightly, 'five guys looking for me this morning, now there's only one.'

'Mr Khan was a Locksley cop before Gisborne's goons drummed him off the force for being honest,' Will explained. 'He used an old police contact to pull up the guy's record. His name is Dino Bullcalf and his only convictions are for speeding and driving without insurance, but his name crops up in several investigations into suspicious deaths, either because they were police informants, or they owed money to very bad people.'

Robin shivered. 'Sounds like the kind of guy you don't want coming after you.'

'Agreed,' Will agreed. 'But only Diogo, my wife and Marion's parents know where you are. I'll message Bullcalf's picture, so you know who to look out for.'

'What about the other guys you caught?' Robin asked.

'One's dead . . .'

'Dead?'

'Wasps,' Will explained. 'Unai took a look after it happened. He found a massive nest, going two metres deep into a ventilation shaft. Zev got stung dozens of times. By the time they got him down to the clinic his airway had closed up. There was nothing Dr Gladys could do.'

Robin winced. 'Nasty way to die . . .'

'I like to think I'm a caring person,' Will snorted, 'but forgive me if I lack sympathy for a man who tried to make money by capturing a kid so that a gangster could torture him.'

'Good point,' Robin said.

'Their leader – Venables – is wanted by cops in Capital City,' Will continued. 'Mr Khan is going to escort him down south and drop him at a police station. The other two don't pose much of a threat on their own, so we'll dump 'em up in bear country in their underwear.'

'You're *sure* they won't come after me?' Robin asked.

'They're soldiers, not leaders,' Will said. 'Bullcalf had his escape route set up, so he must have realised we were setting a trap. But instead of warning his comrades, he used us as an opportunity to get rid of them.'

'So this old fart's gonna try to find me and nab the whole bounty for himself?' Robin asked.

'Seems that way,' Will agreed. 'And Dino Bullcalf has spent most of his life tracking down people who don't want to be found, so we can't take the threat lightly.'

# 6. BUILT FOR SMUGGLING

Dried, deodorised and dressed in shorts, Robin still felt hungry as he padded down spiral steps from his little upstairs bedroom. As he crossed The Station's sloping ground floor, which was cluttered with books and retro furnishings, he remembered not to bash his toes on the wooden rails that had been put there to launch a lifeboat.

Fresh air hit as Robin rolled up a clattering garage door, opening the room to a sunny waterfront balcony with a sofa swing and gas barbecue. Although The Station jutted from a trashed beach with a dead holiday village behind, the view out over the delta was spectacular.

The Macondo River ran almost the entire width of the country. Starting at Lake Victoria and growing broader until it became the Eastern Delta. This marshland stretched to forty kilometres wide where it met the sea.

Vast reed beds were packed with wading birds and turtles, while the waterways formed more islands than you could count, from little mud embankments to Skegness Island, with its lavish homes and mega-yachts.

The central delta had shipping lanes deep enough for oil tankers, but The Station was on the southern bank, where shallow water trickled and, in the current hot weather, slimy algae bloomed on the surface.

Robin looked out from the balcony past the reeds at dazzling water stretching to the horizon, broken by the hazy outlines of a lush green island and the hulk of a pleasure boat that ran aground years earlier.

He had rinsed his sweaty workout gear while showering and he pegged socks and shorts to a line before flicking on the barbecue.

While the grill got hot, he grabbed a set of binoculars and wondered again where Marion and Diogo had got to. There was no sign of Diogo's boat, but he saw an anchored pleasure launch with people riding jet skis launched from its rear platform. Further out was the sinister grey outline of a prowler, a type of fast patrol boat used by the Customs & Immigration Service (CIS).

Robin took two burger patties from the fridge, along with cheese slices and some stale baps that he hoped would be OK if he toasted them. As his afternoon snack sputtered, Robin heard the buzz of a drone. It was impossible to patrol the delta's maze of islands and waterways by boat, so customs and police routinely used them for surveillance.

Robin guessed this drone had been launched from the CIS boat he'd spotted through the binoculars. But while the flight wasn't unusual, law-enforcement drones had powerful zoom lenses and facial recognition, so he edged around the barbecue so that it would only see his back.

The burgers were slightly charred when Robin flipped them, so he lowered the heat as the drone buzzed inland, skimming the holiday village. But as it flew back over The Station the sound seemed off, and Robin risked a backward glance. Drones fly fast and smooth, but this one was shuddering and Robin guessed it had clipped a bird or treetop.

After dropping low the drone jerked up a hundred metres, as if an automatic protection system had kicked in. Then it made a loud popping sound and plunged, trailing dense grey smoke. Robin couldn't see as it plummeted behind The Station, but he heard a crash beyond the treeline and dozens of spooked birds launched into the air.

Robin imagined something dramatic like the drone getting shot down, but with one eye on his burgers he picked up his phone and searched *exploding drone*. The first result took him to an article on how drones use lightweight but unstable lithium-polymer batteries which can fail dramatically. There was even a link to a video of a mid-air blast, with a popping sound matching what he'd just heard.

He flipped the burgers again and was pleased they hadn't burned on the lower heat. Then he put cheese slices on to melt and started toasting two halves of stale bap.

Robin had never used a barbecue before he'd arrived in the delta and was chuffed with his giant double cheeseburger as he stacked it up, then squashed it so all the parts stuck together. He hated the midges that fizzed about near the water, so he took the plate inside. But as Robin sat to eat, he heard Diogo's boat, *Water Rat*, puttering out of a gap between the reeds.

'Ahoy, matey!' a mud-caked Marion shouted, as Robin rushed back onto the balcony. 'Throw us a rope.'

Diogo's boat was as quirky as his home. *Water Rat* had triple outboard motors for speed, but if you lifted them out of the water there was also a huge fan that enabled its flat-bottomed hull to skim over water a few centimetres deep. It was finished in shades of grey that made it hard to see, and the only protection from the elements was a plastic windscreen and roll-up cloth roof.

As Robin threw Marion a rope, he saw chunks of jagged fibreglass where the side of the boat had scraped rocks, while the flat-bottomed hull was filled with plastic drums caked in mud.

'Did something go wrong?' Robin asked.

Marion looked down at her filthy clothes as she hopped onto the balcony. 'How'd you figure that out, genius?'

Diogo emerged from under the canvas roof as Robin tied *Water Rat* to one of the thick wooden pilings supporting the balcony. The Portuguese was a biker, though not a member of any gang. He was in his late thirties, with a shaggy black beard and fading tattoos stretched over a bodybuilder physique, though as a concession to life on water, he mostly wore waterproof trousers and rubber boots rather than denim and bike leathers.

'Hell of an afternoon!' Diogo told Robin as he stepped ashore, reeking of sweat and with his bottom half almost as muddy as Marion.

'Gotta pee,' Marion said, as she stripped muddy boots then raced inside.

'We had no bother picking the drums up,' Diogo said, continuing his explanation. 'But as we pulled away, one of those new CIS prowlers came at us. They're stealthy suckers. Cruise all day at thirty-five knots and they don't show on my radar until it's too late. I couldn't outrun a prowler over any distance, so we blasted through reeds to an inlet too shallow for them to chase.

'I thought they'd launch drones to search for us. So we jumped out, dragged *Water Rat* up onto an island and covered her with greenery. We were thigh deep in mud and the flies bit lumps out of us.'

'Then you waited?'

Diogo nodded. 'Nothing flew over. They must have got called away to something more important.'

'Or they didn't fancy chasing smugglers through mud,' Robin suggested.

Inside, Marion exited the toilet, and spoke happily. 'Great, I'm starving.'

Robin gasped as he looked indoors and saw her biting an enormous chunk out of his burger.

# 7. PILLS AND THRILLS

While Diogo hosed off muddy gear and cooked more burgers, Marion braved the outdoor shower and Robin carried the cargo out of the boat.

After lifting each filthy drum onto the balcony, he unscrewed waterproof seals and emptied out medical supplies like scalpel blades, bandage packs, dental amalgam and thick polythene bags filled with pills.

Diogo's contacts overseas would sail to the edge of the delta at night and dump goods in shallow water or on one of the unoccupied islands. The following morning, Diogo would take *Water Rat* out and bring the stuff back to shore.

Diogo worked only for himself and stuck to what he knew. Even if he'd wanted to make big bucks smuggling guns or the kinds of drugs people use to get high, he wouldn't have dared because those markets were controlled by powerful gangs.

But the government had made laws stopping people from getting medical treatment without swiping an up-to-date identity card. Since most Forest People were either refugees with no ID, or people on the run, a lot of people in Sherwood could only use illegal clinics and black-market medical supplies.

Marion kept her icy shower short and came down with straggly hair as Diogo plated up his batch of burgers and some corn cobs he'd thrown on too.

'After this, I'll hose out *Water Rat* and fix the crack where I banged her up,' he said, as the trio filled their faces at a wobbly outdoor table. 'Robin, now you have everything inside, I need you to start bagging pills.'

Robin sighed.

To save weight and space, most medicines were smuggled in bags containing thousands of loose tablets. Before being passed on to underground clinics and pharmacies in Sherwood Forest, they had to be split into smaller quantities and carefully labelled.

'Don't moan,' Diogo said, as he bit into his corn cob.

'I didn't say anything,' Robin answered defensively.

The sigh had been instinctive – hours printing labels and packing pills was brain numbing. But Robin admired what Diogo was doing. The biker took risks that could land him with serious jail time, and as most of the informal medical clinics had no money, he gave heaps of stuff away, or sold it for a minimal profit.

'Robin always moans,' Marion said, stirring it.

'I didn't say I *wouldn't* do it,' Robin said, before trying to turn the tables. 'Can Marion help?'

'I spent half the day hiding up to my tits in mud, while you sat around,' Marion snapped.

'I worked out,' Robin said. 'And I'd go out on the boat if Diogo let me.'

'We can't take risks,' Marion teased. 'You're the famous Robin Hood and you're in hiding.'

Diogo extravagantly flung his chewed-up corn cob over his shoulder, letting it splosh into the delta. 'It's cute the way you two lovebirds bicker!'

'We are *not* . . .' Marion said, shuddering.

'First comes love,' Diogo sang, putting on a ridiculous old-time crooner voice, 'then comes a marriage, then comes da baby, in a carriage . . .'

'Nope!' Robin said, shaking his head.

Diogo kept winding the thirteen-year-olds up. 'I expect you'll make me godfather when your triplets are born.'

'I'm trying to eat!' Marion said, making a face like she was going to spew.

Diogo wolfed the last quarter of his burger in one huge bite, then stood and noisily slapped his hairy belly.

'That's enough fun and games! I'll fix *Water Rat*. Robin, sort pills; Marion, wash plates, then you deserve a rest. Also . . .'

They looked up from the table as Diogo paused dramatically.

'I need you two to make yourselves scarce this evening, because Diogo has a date.'

Marion smiled. 'Seriously?'

'Never more so,' Diogo said.

'The one you had drinks with last week?' Robin asked. 'From online dating.'

'You said that date was a dud,' Marion added.

'I thought she was pretty great, and it seems she liked me more than I realised,' Diogo said proudly. 'I already spoke to Emma Scarlock. She's expecting you two at Boston Church Hall around half past seven. She says you can order pizza and stay overnight at her cottage.'

'Fine by me,' Robin agreed. 'Change of scene. Neo's got a PlayStation, and he's a laugh if he's around.'

'Leave those rubber boots of yours in the boat if you've got female company,' Marion warned. 'You can smell them from twenty paces. And use a nail brush to scrub the muck from under your nails.'

Diogo smiled. 'Marion, I was wooing ladies before you were born.'

Marion shot back, 'But if you'd had the benefit of my advice, you wouldn't still be single . . .'

# 8. DOUBLE CHOC MAGNUMS

It was after seven, but at this time of year it would stay light for hours.

Diogo had a workshop for his motorbikes, in a metal shed just off the littered beach. Marion had wheeled out and fuelled two mangled but powerful dirt bikes, being extra careful not to scrape Diogo's monstrous chromed Harley Davidson, or his collection of classic Japanese racing bikes.

'I've been waiting here like a lemon for ten minutes,' she complained, as Robin clambered through the holiday-village fence holding a tangle of metal and melted plastic. 'What the heck is that?'

'Police drone came down earlier,' Robin explained, as he closed in. 'I told you I was going to look for it. I had a rough idea where it crashed, but I had to walk further than I thought.'

Marion studied the wreckage as Robin put it inside the bike shed. 'It's junk,' she noted.

'Interesting junk,' Robin said. 'I want to see what tech these things pack. I might even be able to work out the frequencies they transmit on.'

'Such a geek.' Marion smiled fondly.

'Geek and proud,' Robin said. 'It's probably burnt out, but you never know. I like playing around with tech stuff and I've not got much on when you're out on *Water Rat* with Diogo.'

'Whatever.' Marion said, checking the time on her phone. 'I've filled both bikes with gas. Your helmet's hanging by the door. And I grabbed this for you on the way out of The Station.'

Robin looked baffled as she tossed him a rolled-up raincoat.

'Check the sky.'

'Good thinking,' Robin said, as he looked at a sunny evening in one direction, but ominous hammerhead clouds closing from across the water.

He stuffed the waterproof down his backpack and put on his helmet, by which time Marion had kick-started and buzzed away.

The only road leading from The Station to the rest of civilisation wound along the delta's southern edge for five kilometres. Cutting through the holiday village halved that distance, so after a few hundred metres Marion flung her bike left and sliced expertly through a gap in the wire fencing. She didn't slow down, but Robin was a less experienced rider and used his brakes.

By the time Robin was back up to speed, Marion was blasting over dry weeds between the lines of alpine-style chalets that once housed holidaying families. After a sharp turn they came to the empty bowl of a giant outdoor leisure pool.

They both juddered down steps at the shallow end, but as soon as Marion reached the deep end, she picked up speed, steered up a twisting waterslide, then launched her bike off the platform at the top. She made a jarring landing on her front wheel but kept upright.

Robin considered the stunt as the end of the pool closed in, but he twisted his brake and stopped with his front wheel at the base of the faded blue ramp. The fact was, he'd been riding dirt bikes for a few months, while Marion's dad was a biker who'd put her on two wheels as soon as she could walk.

After pushing backwards, Robin rode a circle of shame and exited the pool via the kiddies' paddling area. Marion waited with a smug expression, and Robin thought she looked ridiculously cool, sat astride the bike with sun catching her black helmet and hair trailing out down her back.

'That jump was internet-worthy,' Robin said, flipping up his visor as he pulled alongside.

'I assumed you'd ride along the edge,' Marion said. 'Almost gave me a heart attack when I thought you were gonna copy me.'

'Probably would have died,' Robin admitted.

Marion laughed. 'Stick to climbing and archery – and being a geek – and leave the bike stuff to me.'

Thunder rumbled over the delta behind them as she flipped her visor down and blasted off. They cut through more of the holiday village, passing through a derelict staff car park, then under the burnt-out shell of the central dome.

Sunshine Road led from the holiday park's main entrance to the edge of a little seafront village called Boston. There was never any traffic on this sand-blown road, which went nowhere except the dead resort, but their bikes had no plates or insurance so they couldn't risk being stopped by a cop on the much busier road leading to the coast.

Marion parked behind a boarded supermarket and souvenir shop and the pair felt spots of rain as they strolled briskly downhill to the seafront. Boston beach was large and clean and the tide was way out. The seafront strip had a fish-and-chip shop and an Indian restaurant and three local girls played soccer on the sand.

Marion and Robin bought chocolate-raspberry ice creams in a corner shop and were still eating them off sticks as they arrived at a grotty church hall, which was run by a religious group called the New Survivors.

A sixteen-year-old volunteer was mopping the floor as they stepped into a hall the size of a classroom.

'Hey, guys!' she said brightly. 'Haven't seen you for a while.'

'Hello, Bo,' Marion answered, enjoying the way this rhymed.

The New Survivors ran lunch and supper clubs for local seniors, and while the oldies had all gone home, the lingering smell of mashed-up food and pee reminded Robin of infant school.

Bo smiled at Robin. 'Didn't you buy a choc ice for *me*?'

Robin had only met Bo twice before, but she was gorgeous and he had a little crush.

'Shop's open,' he blurted. 'I'll go back and get you one if you like.'

'Just joking,' Bo said. 'What have you been up to? Spending time on your Uncle Diogo's boat?'

Bo only knew Robin and Marion by their cover story and the names on their fake ID cards: Ross and Mary Monto, a brother and sister spending summer with their Uncle Diogo while their parents went through a crummy divorce.

'I go out on the boat a lot,' Robin lied. 'And I've been bulking up, working out with Uncle Diogo's weights every day.'

Marion rolled her eyes, then had to stifle a laugh when Bo crushed Robin's ego with, 'Aren't you a bit little for lifting weights?

'Emma told me you two were coming,' Bo continued. 'But one of our spotters sighted some refugees and she had to rush off with Neo in the dinghy. She said to wait in her office at the back.'

Marion mocked Robin as they crossed the empty hall and moved out of Bo's earshot. 'Hey, Bo-Bo-kins! Do you want ice cream? Did I tell you I've been bulking up? Do you want to see my muscles?'

Robin couldn't think of a good comeback, but he noticed Marion's top was baggy behind the neck. He just had a tiny blob of ice cream left on his stick, so he moved fast, posting it down the back of Marion's shirt and laughing his arse off as she flew into the air and yelped.

# 9. VENGEANCE SHALL BE MINE

Emma Scarlock's office at the back of the church hall was barely big enough for a desk and a file cabinet. There was a small aerial and radio base station marked *Property of Customs and Immigration Service* on the desk and a detailed chart on one wall, showing islands and waterways along the southern side of the delta.

Robin studied the push pins sticking out of the map. Red ones marked places where a refugee boat had landed, while black pins showed spots where dead bodies had washed ashore. He jolted as Marion stepped in, buttoning her shirt, with a big wet patch on the back where she'd rinsed off the ice cream.

'You'd better be nervous,' Marion said, as she wagged her pointing finger. 'On my brothers' lives, I shall bring merciless vengeance!'

Robin smiled warily. 'You can't stand your brothers.'

'So, did Emma call or anything?' Marion asked, as she flopped into an office chair and thumped her boots on the desk.

'Nope,' Robin said. 'Just hope her emergency doesn't mean we're stuck in this boring office all night.'

'A lot of people die out there,' Marion said, as she studied the map.

'I counted twenty-six black pins,' Robin said sadly. 'And that map's nowhere near the whole delta.'

Marion got her phone out to mess around. Robin nosed in the filing cabinet, but a hole punch was as interesting as it got.

'Wonder how Diogo's hot date is going,' Robin said.

'Oooh, I forgot to show you his picture,' Marion said. 'I took it while you were searching for the drone.'

She turned her phone around and Robin laughed at a snap of Diogo. He'd smartened up drastically, with chinos, a linen shirt and his hair tied back.

Robin grinned. 'He almost looks civilised.'

'I even got him to trim his eyebrow gap.'

Robin zoomed the picture and laughed. 'That's so much better. It's usually like a hedge running across his whole face.'

A door slammed and there were vague shouts outside. Marion shot out of the seat as Bo yelled, 'Ross, Mary, come help!'

Robin and Marion dashed into the hall.

Bo stood in the middle of the shiny wooden floor. Stocky eighteen-year-old goth Neo Scarlock wore a wetsuit and held a shivering woman wrapped in a foil blanket. Neo's mum, Emma, had a bawling toddler in her arms and held the door as three more soggy refugees stepped in.

'Ross, grab the medical kit!' Neo shouted. 'Third drawer of the filing cabinet.'

As Robin charged back to the office, Marion set out stacking chairs for the three healthier arrivals to sit down, then found a kettle to make hot drinks.

'We need the dry clothes and towels from the storeroom,' Emma said, as she peeked outside before locking the main door.

'Did anyone see your boat come in?' Bo asked frantically. 'You know you're not supposed to bring arrivals here unless it's dark.'

'We had no choice,' Neo said. 'We found them stuck on an embankment, and the tide was already up to their chests. There's a storm closing and our dinghy was taking on water with seven people aboard. We'd never have made it to the main rescue centre.'

Robin realised the woman Neo had laid out on the floor was pregnant as he threw the medical kit over. Marion flung Robin a cushion and Bo raised the woman's head so he could slide it underneath.

'I think she'll be OK,' Neo said, as he opened the medical bag and clipped an oxygen monitor to the woman's fingertip. 'Just needs warming up.'

'The water out there's icy,' Bo agreed. 'Even in this weather.'

They couldn't understand anything the refugees were saying, so as Marion made drinks and Bo got towels and armfuls of dry clothes out of a storage room, Emma held up a laminated book with flags and words on the front page. When one of the refugees pointed to a crescent symbol, Emma flipped to a page written in Arabic.

The writing explained that the refugees had been picked up by an organisation called Delta Rescue. If they consented, they would be taken to the organisation's welcome centre, which was hidden in the eastern tip of Sherwood Forest. Once there, they would be examined by a doctor, allowed to rest for a few days and be given travel tickets, phone credit, food and anything else they needed for the next stage of their journey.

'Delta Rescue is good, I know!' the oldest of the refugees said, as the little boy dived into his lap. 'We know of you.'

'I'm glad you speak some English!' Emma said, speaking slow and making gestures. 'I know you are all tired, but this is a busy area. People who saw us bring you up the beach might call CIS. We need to find a car and get you out of here.'

'My uncle's taxi takes six,' Bo suggested.

Emma looked hopeful. 'We can trust him?'

'He'll want paying, but he'll keep his mouth shut,' Bo said. 'I'll buzz him now.'

Neo stood up from the floor holding the medical bag and spoke quietly to Emma. 'Mum, there's nobody on the beach with the dinghy, and we can't afford to lose another one.'

Emma nodded. 'Get it back in the water and clear out of here.'

'Called my uncle,' Bo said. 'He'll be here in five.'

'Good work,' Emma said. She pointed to a toilet door and reverted to her slow English. 'If any of you want to go, you need to go now.'

As Neo rushed back to the beach to launch the rescue dinghy before cops arrived, the hall became a frenzy. Refugees took turns using the toilet, Marion handed out drinks and found a bandage for a woman with a cut on her wrist, while Robin and Emma sorted towels and dry clothes.

'Taxi's arriving!' Bo shouted from the doorway.

Robin and a refugee helped the pregnant woman out to the taxi and the little kid threw a massive tantrum as they all piled in, tucking muddy backpacks between their legs as blobs of rain pelted the roof.

'Good luck,' Emma shouted, giving the driver a roll of cash, then slid the door shut.

Back inside, the hall felt quiet, with a puddled floor, half-drunk mugs and soggy clothes piled around the chairs.

'Kids. I'm sorry,' Emma told Robin and Marion as she took out a bunch of keys. 'I know this isn't pizza and PlayStation. But we've had more tip-offs about refugee sightings today than in the previous two weeks.'

'Why so many?' Robin asked, as he took the keys.

'Refugees in small boats wait for warm weather and calm seas,' Emma explained. 'You two better not stick around here in case the cops come looking, but you know the way to my cottage from here?'

'Sure.' Marion nodded.

'Did you see that big radio on my desk?' Emma asked. 'I'm supposed to be here monitoring that, but Neo's crewmate didn't show. With a storm brewing, we need all of our rescue boats ready to help any arrivals that get into trouble. Do you think you can take the radio with you? Listen to the CIS channels and log anything they say about boat positions and refugee sightings.'

'Happy to,' Robin said.

'Happy to be useful,' Marion agreed.

'I'm going to radio Neo and try to catch up with our boat,' Emma said, before turning urgently to Bo. 'Can you clean up the mess here? Then head up to meet these two at my place and you can run communications between our boats.'

Bo got a bucket and mop as Emma took a deep breath, then glanced about like she'd forgotten something. 'Kids, I am so sorry, but I have *got* to run.'

'Stay safe,' Marion said, as Emma ran out. 'And nothing to be sorry for.'

'If you order food, there's money in the kitchen, under the knife block,' Emma yelled back. 'Have a good night and stay out of trouble!'

# 10. THEY SEEM TO JUST VANISH

Robin pitied the drowned-rat delivery rider as he opened the door of Emma Scarlock's cottage.

'Keep the change!' he told her, as he handed over a twenty then kicked the door shut.

'Today we eat all the healthy foods!' Marion said cheerfully, as Robin carried two pizza boxes into a low-ceilinged living room with rustic beams and plates on the wall.

By fiddling with the aerial, Robin had got the stolen CIS radio working so they could monitor communications between prowler boats and their base.

Bo had arrived after cleaning up the church hall and they'd spent the last hour logging potential refugee sightings called in by Delta Rescue's network of lookouts. Their aim was to keep track of the organisation's four high-speed dinghies, so they could pick up refugees while avoiding the Customs and Immigration Service's better-equipped prowlers.

If CIS found refugees first, they'd be given a two-year prison sentence before being sent home. Robin and Marion had tipped the Delta Rescue boats off about several refugee sightings, but the five Emma and Neo brought to the church hall remained Delta Rescue's only success of the night.

'This is Prowler Nine, north of Conch Island,' a voice announced over the CIS radio, as Robin settled on a sofa and took a pizza slice. 'We've got an upturned boat, floating luggage and one body, female.'

'Roger that,' the CIS controller answered. 'Do you need assistance?'

'Negative,' the agent answered. 'Will recover body and seek SOL.'

Robin looked across to Bo. 'What's SOL?'

'Signs of life,' she said.

Marion sounded frustrated. 'Is it always this depressing?'

Bo sighed as she grabbed a slice of vegetarian and opened a diet cola. 'Delta Rescue used to have seven dinghies, and Customs and Immigration had boats like ours,' she explained. 'But two of ours got seized by cops and their new prowlers outmatch us.'

As they ate the pizza one of the dinghies radioed news of a minor success. A Delta Rescue volunteer lookout had spotted two refugees walking along a breakwater. They'd been taken aboard and were now on their way to the welcome centre.

The radios stayed quiet for a while, but as Robin came back from dumping pizza boxes in the recycling, a call went up saying that Prowler Four had boarded a fishing vessel.

'Smuggled goods, six or seven refugees,' the CIS captain said. 'Will escort vessel to Landing Dock Y for processing.'

Marion looked across the living room to Bo. 'Shall I message one of our boats?'

'No point,' Bo explained. 'There's nothing our little dinghies can do about a large boat that has already been boarded by a prowler. But I'll let Emma know. She likes to be kept up to date.'

Bo couldn't get through to Emma's radio, so she messaged her phone. When Emma called back a couple of minutes later, Bo got excited and kept saying stuff like *yes, OK* and *I'll get on that right away.*

Robin and Marion could only hear Bo's end of the conversation, so they were intrigued as she ended the call.

'Tonight just got interesting!' Bo announced while diving out of a rocking chair and shuffling on her knees to a glass-topped coffee table.

They didn't have a detailed chart like the one in Emma's office, so Bo found a roll of baking paper and drew a crude map with a Sharpie. The approximate locations of the four Delta Rescue dinghies were marked with lapel badges, refugee sightings were paperclips and penne pasta represented the last known position of CIS prowlers.

Bo checked a map on her phone before adding the approximate location of Landing Dock Y to the table map.

'None of our boats will get there,' she groaned as she thumped the table, making coins and badges rattle.

'What's the problem?' Marion asked as she and Robin knelt over the other side of the map.

'Emma and I were looking at government statistics on how many refugees are captured in this part of the delta,' Bo explained. 'The number of refugees in the stats is far lower than what we hear reported over their radio.'

'Maybe the numbers are wrong,' Marion suggested. 'Like, two boats report the same incident so you count people twice?'

Bo nodded. 'That's possible, but this is what made us suspicious.' She tapped Landing Dock Y on the map before clarifying. 'The government spent eighty million on a new Customs and Immigration headquarters with docks for all prowlers that work the southern half of the delta. It's got state-of-the-art facilities and detention cells for three hundred people. So why do boats still get sent to unload at Landing Dock Y?'

'What's at Dock Y?' Robin asked.

'It's a fishing wharf. There used to be a fish processing plant, but now there are just a couple of crab boats.'

'That makes no sense,' Robin said.

Marion thought about her smuggling trips with Diogo. 'Actually, an abandoned dock makes a lot of sense if you're a crooked immigration officer offloading gear.'

'If we can prove that CIS are corrupt, it would be an amazing boost for our campaign to have refugees treated with respect.' Bo said. 'But our nearest dinghy is fifteen kilometres from the wharf, and the storm means rough water and poor visibility, so they have to keep slow.'

'Can I see where it is?' Marion asked, as she reached for Bo's phone, which still had the delta map on screen.

Bo slid her phone across the table.

'Dock Y is only eight kilometres from here,' Marion said.

'I'm trying to think of someone who lives out that way,' Bo said.

'Me and Ross can go,' Marion said boldly.

Bo scoffed. 'It's over an hour's walk. The roads aren't lit, it's blasting with rain and you might be dealing with dangerous people.'

Robin sniffed adventure as he glanced at Marion. 'We've got our dirt bikes parked just outside the village.'

Marion nodded. 'We'd be there in fifteen minutes, twenty tops.'

'No offence,' Bo laughed, 'but you're just kids.'

'We are *just* kids,' Marion said. 'But we'd *just* be observing.'

'Let's see what Emma thinks,' Robin said, pulling out his phone.

Marion snatched it out of his hand. 'I'll speak to her,' she said. 'You're bound to say something dumb.'

# 11. JUST DO IT

'You and Robin are bright kids,' Emma told Marion. 'But the weather is atrocious and we've got no idea what you'll run into at Dock Y.'

Marion ended the call, took a big gulp, and lied. 'Emma says it's fine if we're careful.'

Bo's eyebrows crossed suspiciously. 'Emma Scarlock said *that*?'

Marion hoisted Robin off the couch and dragged him into the hallway.

'Get your shoes and bag,' she said urgently.

Robin whispered. 'Did Emma say yes?'

'Do you want to sit here on your butt doing nothing useful?' Marion hissed through gritted teeth, as she grabbed her crash helmet off the hallway carpet.

'I love it when you're bad!' Robin said, cracking a huge grin.

'I'm going to call Emma back,' Bo yelled from the living room. 'You two, wait! I need to see exactly what she wants you to do.'

But Robin and Marion were out of the front door. In Robin's case, with one shoelace undone and his waterproof jacket still rolled up in his backpack. His T-shirt and jeans were soaked after five steps and on the sixth his trainer sploshed a giant puddle.

'This rain is mental,' Robin said. 'Are you sure it's safe to ride?'

'Pah, drizzle!' Marion said, as a massive flash of lightning lit up the village. 'Stay with your girlfriend Bo if you're chicken!'

For better or worse, Robin was a thrill seeker. His whole body fizzed with excitement as they sprinted through the cobbled street in lashing rain. They could see that there was a cop car on the seafront by the church hall, so they cut along a back alleyway and scrambled over a hedge, before sprinting uphill towards the gravel lot where they'd parked their dirt bikes.

'I think we'll get there before the bad guys,' Marion said, as she checked directions on her phone. 'Prowler Four may be fast, but the boat they're escorting won't be.'

She glanced back as she straddled her bike, but Bo hadn't chased.

Robin had doubts as he put his helmet on. It was dark, his visor instantly fogged and the water streaking down the outside meant he could barely see to get on his bike, let alone ride it.

He felt scared as they set off and seriously considered pulling over as he rode with eyes locked on Marion's blurry rear light, far enough back to avoid spray off her back wheel.

They were on a main road that started at Boston seafront and threaded through woodland and a couple of tiny villages. After six kilometres and a soaking when a van coming the other way hit a massive puddle, they turned onto an unmarked, unlit, gravel track.

Robin watched in horror as Marion's front wheel pitched into a rut made by tractors regularly exiting a farm gate. She almost went head first over the handlebars, and Robin had to swerve to avoid her.

As the track merged into a stretch of concrete waterfront with the fishing wharf over to their left, Marion pulled off into tall grass.

'That got hairy!' she said, as she got off the bike and held out a palm to check the rain. 'At least it's slowing down.'

Robin felt shell-shocked as he pulled off his helmet, then looked down and saw that his jeans were a wet, chalky mess.

'You look like you're gonna puke!' Marion said, as they wheeled their bikes deeper into the weeds to hide them.

Marion was less sure of herself when she pulled out her phone. The three missed calls from Emma were to be expected, but she felt crummy when she saw a missed call from her mum and imagined her back at Designer Outlets, worrying.

'I predict a lot of people yelling at us tomorrow,' Robin said.

Marion pocketed her phone and tried to brush off the mum guilt. 'No point both of us copping blame. Bo heard me tell you that Emma said we could go. Just say you believed me.'

'They *always* blame both of us,' Robin said, then looked towards the wharf. 'At least you were right about us getting here before the boats.'

# 12. THE GREAT WHITE WHALE

They moved stealthily through the dark towards the wharf. Robin wished he had his bow. But he'd left it at The Station, because carrying made it easier for people to figure out who he was.

Luckily Robin never cleaned out his backpack, so besides the toothbrush and change of underwear for his night at Emma's cottage, he was carrying a multitool with a sharp blade that Marion had bought him for his birthday, and a small pair of binoculars that he used when he shot distant targets.

'Give us a peek through those,' Marion said.

The rain was now a fine mist, but they were both wet through as they squatted in swaying grass behind the metal-sided fish processing plant.

'Thoughts?' Marion asked, as she scanned the binoculars along the wharf, looking for movement.

'There's no obvious surveillance cameras. No lights, no people,' Robin said.

Marion nodded. 'Bo and Emma must be right. The only reason to dock here is if you don't want anyone seeing what you're up to.'

'What now?' Robin asked, as his phone pinged noisily.

Marion's head snapped around. 'Put that on silent, dumbo!'

'Thought I did,' Robin said, as he pulled his phone.

He had messages from Will and Emma Scarlock. The latest ping was a message that Neo had clearly typed in a rush.

**Robin, you're being a massive duck.**

**Go back to the collage before you get in tremble.**

'I can never remember if it's silent when the shush icon is lit up, or silent when it's grey,' Robin explained. 'But now I think about it, we should both put our phones into airplane mode. Those prowlers have surveillance tech, and I'll bet they can detect phone signals.'

'Good idea,' Marion said, as they both found airplane mode. 'Now I guess we find the best view and see what happens.'

'So itchy,' Robin moaned, peeling his shirt off his skin as he walked. 'Trousers, neck, armpits . . .'

'Wet clothes suck,' Marion agreed.

They rounded the side of the processing plant and kept low as they crossed a flat, windswept area that had been used to dump everything from tractor tyres to photocopiers.

A pigeon fluttering out of a hole in the metal building gave them a fright, but also a chance to peek inside. They saw nothing but silhouettes of a conveyor belt and stacks of crates that had once been used to pack fish.

At the waterfront, the pair got a proper look along the wharf. There were two small crab boats and a plastic-hulled pleasure boat that had flooded and tipped on its side. A manmade rock barrier reached into the water, protecting boats from strong tides, while a maze of disused piers and pontoons stretched across the waterfront.

Robin looked around. 'How about hiding in the tall reeds over there?'

'If you want your ankle bitten by a snake,' Marion scoffed. 'We'll get a better view from that building.'

Marion led as they jogged to a two-storey wooden structure at the edge of the wharf. The lower floor had been a workers' cafe, with a faded menu offering mugs of tea and fry-ups. The upper level was accessed by a set of external metal steps and had been the wharf's admin office.

The office door, windows and half the tin roof had been stripped, making it wet but easy to peek out.

'This is ideal,' Robin said, as he crossed the mildewed space, almost twisting his ankle where some floorboards were missing.

'It's not much of a jump from here,' Marion said, as she looked out of a small back window. 'And we're near our bikes if we need a quick getaway.'

Robin found an office chair with squeaky wheels and a missing back and rolled it so he could sit by the window. Marion propped herself against the edge of a desk, looking concerned as she stared at her phone screen.

'Did we do the right thing?' she asked.

Robin was scanning the water beyond the wharf through his binoculars and tried to laugh it off. 'Bit late now, Marion.'

'My mum worries about everything,' Marion sighed. 'She's always threatening to send me to live with my dad. What if she really does this time?'

'Your dad's OK.'

'For a day or two,' Marion said. 'But imagine living at that Brigands compound. With the fights and booze and . . .'

'Hush!' Robin said urgently as he spotted the mast of a boat sweeping above the reeds.

'Is it the prowler?' Marion asked, as she scrambled to the window.

'Too tall,' Robin said.

'Maybe it's just passing by.'

But a half-minute later the bow of a large white pleasure boat rumbled into the harbour. It was over twenty-five metres long, with three decks, but the hull was streaked with rust and several windows had been crudely replaced with wooden boards.

'Let's see,' Marion said.

Robin handed her the binoculars. Marion noticed that the boat's name had been covered up by hanging tyres and fishing nets over the side. The cruiser turned sharply as it used a bow thruster to dock, and this enabled Marion to check out a rough-looking bunch drinking beer on the rear deck. One burly woman in camouflage trousers was bossing everyone around and had a gun holstered over a loud shirt.

'No idea who they are,' Marion said, as Robin snapped pictures with his phone. 'But they're up to no good.'

# 13. LANDING DOCK Y

A few minutes after the cruiser docked, Robin and Marion watched a rust-streaked ocean trawler crawl into the wharf. It had a communist hammer-and-sickle symbol moulded into the belching funnel and people crammed on the open rear deck.

It was tailed by Prowler Four. The hi-tech CIS boat was only twelve metres long, but looked sinister, finished in grey radar-absorbing paint, with a double-barrelled cannon mounted above the sloping glass cockpit and twin jet engines that made it sound like a giant vacuum cleaner.

'Badass,' Robin whispered to Marion. 'I hear prowlers can hit fifty knots.'

Fenders on the captured fishing boat squashed as its hull hit the dockside with a clank. The thugs from the cruiser lined up along the shorefront holding guns and baseball bats as a tattooed Southeast Asian man leaped from the fishing boat and began tying up to a bollard.

'There's at least seventy refugees on there,' Marion said. 'They said *six* on the radio.'

Prowler Four didn't dock, but two CIS officers hopped from its rear deck onto one of the wharf's rotting pontoons and jogged to the shore.

Robin tried filming as the officers shook hands with the woman in the camouflage trousers from the white cruiser and tattoo guy from the fishing boat.

'Looks like they're best of friends,' Marion said, tutting and shaking her head.

'Wish I had a better phone,' Robin moaned. 'There's no zoom and the video's useless in the dark.'

Once the fishing boat was tied off at both ends, its metal gangway was lowered to the wharf. The first people off were two women with assault rifles around their necks, while the captain yelled orders in some foreign language over the boat's tinny public-address system.

'Japanese?' Robin guessed.

Marion shook her head. 'Refugees come from places a lot poorer than Japan.'

The women on deck started filing onto the wharf area in front of the processing shed. The only light came from inside the boats, but it was enough for Robin and Marion to see they were Southeast Asian, and none looked older than twenty.

'Line up!' the thugs yelled, as the women shuffled ashore.

A woman who tripped at the bottom of the gangplank got yanked to her feet by a man three times her size.

Another who stopped to ask a question got shoved hard in the back. When she spun around and tried again, the woman in camouflage trousers smashed a palm into her nose.

'Bloody hell!' Marion snarled, with bunched fists and furious eyes.

'Do as you're told, scum!' camouflage trousers roared. 'Mouths shut or we'll shut them for you!'

Robin counted seventy-four women down the gang-plank. There were also five little kids and a middle-aged couple with Louis Vuitton luggage trunks and nice clothes, who were treated to respectful bows and handshakes as they stepped ashore.

Robin's eye caught something flying off the back of the fishing boat.

'What was that?' Robin asked, not sure he'd seen it.

Marion shrugged. 'What was what?'

But someone aboard Prowler Four had seen it too, and the dark grey boat powered up a bank of searchlights, blazing the water behind the fishing boat.

'I think someone jumped in,' Robin explained.

A couple of members of the prowler crew stepped out on deck. One picked up a long-handled boathook used to pull people out of the water, but there was nothing to reach for.

'I hope they didn't drown,' Robin said, as he looked through the binoculars. 'But I can't see anyone swimming.'

Back on shore, the thugs ordered the women to march to the white cruiser. Before stepping aboard they were stripped of any luggage, made to empty their pockets into a plastic bin and then had their wrists bound with plastic cuffs.

A woman who protested as she tried to hold onto an inhaler got slapped, while the one who'd put up a fight on the gangplank boarded last with blood streaming from her nose.

'This is awful,' Marion said, wiping tears out of her eyes.

'I don't care how much trouble we're in,' Robin said determinedly. 'People need to see what's going on.'

The prowler crew had ended their search of the water, but as the thugs from the cruiser pulled in the ramp linking it to the shore, Prowler Four's searchlight swung towards Robin and Marion.

'Balls,' Robin gasped, diving for cover, assuming they'd been spotted.

But Marion peeked around the door and realised the light was aiming right of their building at someone sprinting powerfully towards the reed beds. She was dripping wet from her swim and had what looked like a bundle of pillows clutched to her chest.

'It's not us they're after!' Marion said, relieved.

Robin shielded his eyes as he peered out into dazzling light.

Two CIS officers leaped off the prowler to give chase, but the runaway was already a hundred metres ahead and the officers had to navigate the rickety pontoons to get ashore.

'We've got to help her!' Marion shouted, as she ran across the room and jumped out of the back window.

Robin's brain took a couple of seconds to catch up. He rolled as he landed in the weeds out back and followed Marion as they sprinted towards their bikes.

They blasted off without their helmets. Marion's skill enabled her to ride faster than Robin, throwing her bike down a tiny gap between two abandoned cars, while Robin circled out wide around all the debris.

The reeds were three metres tall and they couldn't see the runaway, but they could see the stiff grass parting as she ran, and she was properly fast.

'Jump on. I'll help you!' Marion shouted, as she drove parallel to the reed beds.

Robin was a long way back and saw two CIS officers. An overweight woman had stumbled to a breathless halt, but the other sprinted athletically with his gun in one hand. Since an escaped refugee threatened what was clearly a major people-smuggling operation, Robin didn't doubt that the charging officer would shoot to kill.

'I'll help you!' Marion screamed again, as her bike kept pace with the runaway.

Marion guessed the runaway didn't speak English, and since it was dark and she was running flat out, she'd have no idea that the two chasing bikes were on her side.

The speeding officer was gaining on the girl and hoped he could scare her into surrendering with a couple of wild shots. The runaway stumbled as her front foot sank into thick mud, and with deeper water ahead she scrambled from the reeds into the open ground ahead of Marion.

The runaway was blinded by the dirt bike's headlamp, but realised Marion was way too young to be a cop.

'Let me help you,' Marion pleaded, gesturing frantically as she stopped the bike. 'Get on, please!'

After a nervous glance around, the girl jumped on, the soggy foam pillows still strapped to her chest as she gripped Marion's waist. But Marion and the runaway made an easy target while they were stopped and Robin saw the CIS officer drop into a stable firing position.

Robin had never wanted his bow more, but without it the only way to stop Marion getting shot was to use his bike as a weapon. He gunned the throttle. The officer heard the bike come at him from the side but couldn't swing around in time to shoot.

Robin saw the imminent collision in slow motion. He knew he'd fly over the handlebars, and with no crash helmet, if his head hit a rock or some of the abandoned junk, it would probably crack his skull.

# 14. BLOOD AND BULLETS

The bike smashed into the bulky CIS officer with a dull thud. Robin got bucked into the air and flew upside down until he crashed into the tall reeds.

Sharp stems went up the back of Robin's shirt and speared painfully as he landed with a squelch. Mushy sand went in one ear and down his bum crack. This was a good thing because the cold focused his brain as the commander stumbled into the reeds after him, determined to aim his gun, even though he was dragging a broken ankle.

'Boy, you are dead meat!' the commander thundered as he closed in.

The only thing Robin had to hand were the binoculars around his neck. He threw them at the commander's shooting hand, which bought him enough time to roll out of the way.

Robin felt his trainers sink into mud as he stood, with the commander's face contorted in pain as he tried to shoot. The man was double Robin's weight, but Robin didn't want to give him room to aim so he lunged forward and clawed the officer's neck.

If the commander had been healthy, Robin would have been swatted away. But the bike had left the stocky officer with torn back muscles and a shattered ankle.

Robin's trainer got sucked off by the mud as he jumped on top of the commander. He used his left elbow to smash the commander hard under the chin, then both hands to snatch the gun and yank it free.

'Are you OK?' Marion shouted, as she peered into the reeds from a few metres away.

Robin grabbed reeds and got to his feet. He held the commander's gun in one hand and picked up his binoculars with the other, but when he looked back for his shoe it had vanished under puddle water and he realised there was no time to feel around in the dark.

Marion had circled back to the scene of the collision and as Robin stumbled out onto open ground, she picked up his bike and restarted the engine.

'Are you OK?' she asked. 'There's more CIS coming.'

'I'll live,' Robin answered.

The commander groaned from the reeds, barely conscious. Robin dripped mushy sand and was half deaf from water in his ear, but the soft ground had saved him and his only injuries were scratches and cuts.

'Can you ride?' Marion asked desperately.

'Think so,' Robin said, as he saw two running CIS officers, cut out by the searchlights from Prowler Four.

They were pretty far off, but before straddling his bike Robin aimed two wild shots, making them dive for cover. Then he tucked the gun into the back of his jeans and spun his rear wheel as he blasted off.

Marion's bike was parked a few metres in front, and as Robin passed it he saw the runaway and realised what had looked like pillows clutched to her chest was actually a float, made from two foam life preservers with a tiny human sandwiched between them.

'Where to?' Robin shouted, as Marion and her passengers caught up and cruised alongside.

'Main road, where else?' Marion said.

The sky flashed bright white from a flare launched off Prowler Four. Robin realised the bad guys had all arrived in boats. They had no vehicles to chase on land, but once the bikes hit the gravel track, they had a CIS drone on their tails.

Marion knew they stood no chance of shaking the drone on open ground, so when they reached the junction with the road back to Boston, she pulled off into the trees and came to a halt.

The drone hovered noisily overhead.

'That'll follow us back to Boston if we take the open road,' Marion said.

Robin nodded as he tilted his head to drain water out of his earhole. At the same time, the runaway unknotted some twine that held the floats together. She let them drop, exposing the baby strapped to her chest in a sling.

'Baby!' Marion said, in absolute shock. 'How did I not see a baby?'

'Calm down and think,' Robin urged. 'If I had my bow, I'd smash a drone that size. I've got that officer's gun, but no shooting skills.'

'Do you think we can lose that thing if we ride cross-country?' Marion asked.

'Might,' Robin said. 'But there's one drone and two of us. I'll stick on the main road and head towards Boston, you go the other way then cut across country. Hopefully the drone will follow me and I'll figure out a way to lose it.'

Marion didn't look convinced but had no better plan.

'There were cops sniffing around when we left Boston,' Marion said. 'The Station is nearer and I know every track around there.'

The runaway couldn't understand what Robin and Marion were discussing and looked confused. She also seemed wary of the baby hanging from her chest, which made Robin suspect she wasn't its mother.

'We're going to find somewhere safe,' Marion said slowly and clearly to the runaway. 'I might have to go across country, so hold on tight.'

'See you at The Station!' Robin said, as he restarted his bike.

As he rolled onto the road, Robin pulled the gun sticking out of his jeans. He couldn't be certain the drone would follow but hoped the pilot aboard Prowler Four would instinctively go after someone who attacked it.

As Robin rode into the open, he kept slow until the drone swung out from above the trees, then fired upwards before twisting the throttle. Aiming backwards at a black object in a black sky from a moving bike was hopeless, but Marion watched the drone zoom after Robin's bike, before spinning up her back wheel and heading in the opposite direction.

# 15. GETTING LUCKY

Diogo's bedroom on The Station's upper floor had a panoramic window with a view over the delta. A huge thunderclap exploded as rain streaked down the glass and his date, Napua, stepped into the room.

'Did you find the good towel?' Diogo asked anxiously. 'My niece and nephew are staying for summer holidays, and you know . . . Kids are slobs.'

'This *is* an amazing spot to watch a storm,' Napua said, smiling as she stepped up to the window. 'I thought it was a line to get me up to your bedroom.'

Diogo laughed. 'Can't you tell I'm a gentleman?'

He couldn't believe how great the date was going. Napua had picked every scrap off the bones of the rack of lamb he'd cooked, said the cassata cake he'd bought from an Italian deli was the best she'd ever tasted and laughed at all of his jokes.

'I've met a few guys since I started online dating,' Napua said. 'A supermarket manager, a stock-control accountant. Boring cars, boring houses, and ex-wives. A smuggler with a house on the beach is refreshing.'

Diogo felt uneasy. 'Who says I'm a smuggler?'

Napua gave a naughty-girl smirk as a gust of wind sent rain pelting against the window. 'I grew up in the delta, Diogo. Boats like *Water Rat* are for smuggling or taking tourists to see turtles. And I don't see many tourists around here.'

'Smart *and* beautiful,' Diogo said cheesily as he moved in close. 'May I?'

Napua tilted her head and they started kissing. Then she took Diogo's wrist and stepped backwards.

'I was on my feet all day at work,' she said, giving a teasing smile. 'Why don't we move to the bed?'

As Diogo let Napua lead him towards the bed, a key turned in the front door. He hoped his brain was playing tricks, but the distinctive sound was followed by hurried footsteps and clattering water pipes as someone ran the kitchen tap.

'Expecting a guest?' Napua asked, slightly annoyed.

'Stay right there,' Diogo said.

He snatched a cricket bat from under the bed before charging down the spiral stairs. Robin stood at the sink, peeling his wet, bloody shirt over his head.

'Why, God? Why?' Diogo pleaded, as he flicked a light on and threw down the bat.

When he saw the state Robin was in he changed from furious to worried. One shoe missing, jeans ripped, mud everywhere and his back smeared with blood.

'What happened?' Diogo asked. 'Did you come off the bike? Why isn't Marion with you?'

'I crashed your bike,' Robin admitted. 'Marion's not here with the baby? I thought she'd get here before me.'

'What baby?' Diogo spluttered. 'And what do you mean, you crashed my bike?'

'I was being chased by a drone,' Robin said, as he took the gun from the back of his jeans and placed it on the counter next to a stack of dirty dishes. 'I got lucky. The rain started lashing, and drones can't fly in that kind of weather. But then I caught a massive skid coming back through the holiday village. Ripped my jeans is all, but the bike's light smashed. I couldn't get it restarted and walked the last couple of kilometres with one shoe.'

*Drones, crashes, babies, guns* . . . Every word out of Robin made questions pop into Diogo's head. His eyebrows shot up as he inspected the gun.

'This is a police weapon,' he said, raising the muzzle to his nose and sniffing gunpowder. 'And it's been used.'

'CIS actually,' Robin said. 'Officer tried to kill me. Are there bits of reed stuck in my back? It didn't hurt at first, but now the adrenaline's worn off, it's agony.'

'You had a loaded gun down the back of your trousers when you crashed my bike?' Diogo asked furiously, as he clicked on the safety. 'You're lucky you didn't shoot your dick off.'

Diogo heard feet on the stairs. He looked back to Napua, coming down with her shoes hooked over her fingers.

'What happened?' she gasped when she saw Robin's back.

'My nephew, Ross,' Diogo said.

'Poor little guy,' Napua said, as she glowered at Diogo. 'You need to deal with those wounds before you yell at him!'

'I . . .' Diogo spluttered, unable to believe he'd gone from having a woman on his bed to having her scowl at him in under three minutes.

'I learned first aid when I worked as an airline steward,' Napua said. 'Do you have medical supplies? Like tweezers and disinfectant? He may need a couple of stitches.'

'Got plenty of medical supplies,' Diogo said, as he stomped across the room.

He took a bottle of antiseptic and three sterile tweezer packs out of a box. He almost banged them down by the sink, but realised he'd blow his chance with Napua if he didn't calm down.

'Maybe if Ross sits at the dining table . . .' Diogo said. 'I'll get the lamp from my desk so we can see better.'

Napua told Robin to take off his filthy jeans and socks, leaving him sat at the dining table in soggy undershorts with blood soaked into the waistband.

'I've got syringes and local anaesthetic if you need to numb it off,' Diogo said. 'Who wants a drink?'

'Glass of water would be amazing,' Robin said, as he switched his phone out of airplane mode, hoping for a message from Marion. But the only new ones were from Marion's mum Indio.

'I'm lost,' Diogo said, as he gave Robin water, then cracked a beer for himself. 'Can you go back to the beginning and explain what's been going on?'

'He needs to sit still while I'm doing his splinters,' Napua said. 'Leave the kid alone for two minutes! Now, Ross, lean forward. There's a couple of big ones and it's going to sting, OK?'

Robin's filthy hands gripped the edge of the dining table and tears welled as Napua tweezered a five-centimetre splinter out of his shoulder blade. Diogo decided to call Emma and try getting some sense out of her.

But as he scrolled down his contacts list, Diogo saw a headlamp flash through the frosted glass in the front door. When he opened the door Marion and a young woman with an infant charged through the rain across the jetty between the beach and The Station.

'Diogo, it won't stop screaming,' Marion gasped, water dripping out of her hair as she ran inside. 'Do you have any idea how to work a baby?'

# 16. THE BEARD GRABBER

Robin went to clean up so his wounds didn't get infected. The good news was that Diogo's solar water system was less likely to strip skin after sundown, the bad was that showering outside in a thunderstorm was weird, and the shampoo stung when it found the cuts on his back.

'Doing OK in there?' Napua asked sympathetically, from the other side of the shower's wooden privacy screen.

'Ain't dead yet,' Robin answered.

'I've left your towel and some tracksuit bottoms inside the door.'

Once the soap ran away, the hot water was soothing. Robin took his time because he'd heard Emma and Neo arrive in their Delta Rescue dinghy. He didn't feel like facing them, and briefly considered a bonkers plan to climb up to the roof and sneak through his bedroom window.

But Napua was waiting to dress his wounds, and as Robin reached for the towel, he could already feel a fresh trickle of blood.

'Hello,' Robin said meekly as he stepped back inside, avoiding eye contact with Emma and Neo.

Everyone was so busy that Robin barely got noticed as he sat sideways in a dining chair so that Napua could stick on two dressings that she'd already cut to shape.

Diogo, Neo and the baby stood in the kitchen area down by the balcony. The big biker was childless, but he'd looked after baby sisters from his dad's second marriage so he wasn't out of his depth.

He'd calmed the tiny dark-haired boy by giving him sips of water, then he'd sat him in the sink to wash his filthy body and folded his best dish towel into a nappy to reduce the risk of getting peed on.

Emma and Neo had brought feeding bottles and infant formula, and now Diogo stood by the sink, trying to stop the little guy from yanking his beard, while Neo read instructions on how to mix and heat the powdered feed.

'He knows you're making his food,' Marion said, from the opposite end of the open-plan space. 'Look at his little arms waggling!'

While Diogo and Neo dealt with the baby, Marion, Emma and the runaway sat on floor cushions.

The runaway spoke a little English, and once Marion plugged the girl's battered smartphone in to charge, she used an Indonesian–English translation app to help tell her story.

Marion got a pen and paper and had written two pages of notes before Robin came back from his shower.

The runaway was fifteen years old. She was from Jambi in Indonesia and her name was Srihari. She'd left home with her brother after they were promised well-paid work in a garment factory, but after a few days in a crowded dorm all the men were dragged out by thugs and forced to sign contracts for work on a remote construction site.

The women left behind were loaded onto a large freighter. They were at sea for a month, with little food and a crew that beat anyone who complained. They'd been transferred to the smaller fishing boat for the last two days of their journey.

Srihari had made friends with the baby's mother during the journey. The boy's name was Bejo and he was seven months old. But other women warned Bejo's mum that her baby would be taken away and sold to rich people for adoption when they arrived at their destination.

At this point in the story, Srihari opened her phone's photo gallery to a selfie she'd taken a couple of years earlier. She was dressed in an orange swimming cap and had five medals around her neck.

Marion was amazed as Srihari explained how they had used two life vests and part of a cushion to make a floating crib. Then Srihari dived off the boat with Bejo and swam expertly to the wharf while the baby stayed dry.

Emma Scarlock had a lump in her throat as she caught up on Srihari's story by reading Marion's notes.

'You and Bejo are safe with us,' Emma assured Srihari, as she rubbed the girl's arm. 'You are so brave. I've brought fresh clothes and personal items for you. We'll take you to a place where you can rest and get seen by a doctor.'

'And we'll try to find where they've taken Bejo's mum,' Marion added.

Srihari nodded, though she hadn't understood everything.

Marion cracked up laughing as she looked across the room and saw Bejo guzzling his formula in Diogo's arms, while still keen to pull out his beard. The laughter evaporated as her phone vibrated with *Mum* on the screen.

Marion had been putting off replying, but knew Indio would keep calling.

'Hello, Ma,' Marion said warily.

'Emma told me you're safe, thank God!' Indio blurted.

'I'm good,' Marion agreed. 'Robin's a bit battered.'

'I am *so* mad at you two,' Indio snapped. 'You both sat in Will Scarlock's office and *swore* to me that you would never run off again. You used to be the sensible one, Marion. Now you give me more sleepless nights than all your brothers combined!'

'Mum, it was important,' Marion said determinedly. 'Did Emma tell you we've got video of this whole corrupt Customs and Immigration thing? And we rescued a girl and a tiny baby.'

Indio ignored this. 'Maybe you and Robin need to be kept apart.'

'Stop blaming Robin,' Marion said. 'I've got my own brain.'

Robin glanced around in shock, because Napua was in the room and they were supposed to be Ross and Mary in front of outsiders.

'I know you both mean well. But I . . .' Indio tailed off and gave a big sigh. 'Do you know what, Marion? I am so tired right now, I don't know what I think . . .'

'Mum, I *am* sorry that I made you worry,' Marion said. 'But I saw some horrible things at that wharf. We took a risk, but if we hadn't, we'd never have found out about those poor women. I'll take whatever punishment you dish out. But I'm not sorry for what I did.'

'You just turned thirteen!' Indio said tearfully. 'It's too young.'

Hearing her mum cry made Marion well up and they ended up sobbing at each other.

'Let me speak to her for a second,' Emma said softly, as she took Marion's phone away. 'It's 2 a.m. and you're a mess. Get ready for bed. Everything else can wait until tomorrow.'

Marion wasn't sure how her mum would react to Emma taking the phone away, but she felt bad for upsetting her family, dumb for blurting Robin's name, sick of being in itchy wet clothes and too tired to fight anyone.

As she ran upstairs to get clean clothes and a towel, Napua looked at Robin.

'It doesn't matter that she said it,' Napua told him. 'I figured you were Robin Hood when I got the tracksuit pants from your room.'

'Seriously?' Robin asked.

'Archery gear, books about hacking computers and I read an article when they sent your dad to prison, so I recognised him in the picture beside your bed.'

Neo stepped up close to Napua and sounded serious. 'Robin is in serious danger if Guy Gisborne finds out where he is.'

'Just spent an hour patching this kid up,' Napua pointed out. 'I'll have wasted the effort if I snitch on him.'

Robin smirked and gave Napua a fist bump.

'Also, I'm a blackjack dealer at Stone's Casino on Skegness Island,' Napua continued, sounding sour. 'Last time I saw Guy Gisborne, the creep spent all night ogling my chest, won six thousand at my table, but left me with a lousy ten-buck tip . . .'

# PART III

# 17. OLD MA BULLCALF

Dino Bullcalf slid a bowl of sausage rigatoni onto a serving table and wheeled it up to his mother's high-backed armchair. She'd lost most of her hearing, so the gardening show on TV was at max volume.

'What's this?' the ninety-seven-year-old asked, squinting and pushing glasses up her nose.

'It's from last night,' Bullcalf shouted over the TV. 'I warmed it up in the microwave.'

His mother tutted and turned away.

'Doctor said you lost another two kilos! Take a mouthful and make me happy.'

As his mother's trembling hand grabbed a spoon, Bullcalf felt his phone vibrate in his trouser pocket.

'Let me take this call,' he said as he strode into the kitchen, away from the blasting TV. 'I'll bring you a nice glass of lemonade, but eat some pasta first.'

Bullcalf didn't recognise the number on his phone.

'Dino?' the woman on the other end said.

'Who is this?' Bullcalf spat back. 'If you're from Hampden Life Insurance, I told you to stop calling.'

'I wasn't sure if this was still your number,' the woman said. 'It's Alison Smith.'

Bullcalf scratched his bald dome. 'Refresh my memory, sweetheart.'

'I'm the tech at Extant Labs. I ran DNA samples for you a few years back. You were seeking a man who kidnapped a drug dealer.'

'Alison, of course!' Bullcalf said, his tone warming. 'I'm sorry, I hear a lot of names.'

'It was four years ago,' Alison said. 'I'm not that memorable.'

Bullcalf laughed as he glanced into the living room and was delighted to see his mother tucking into the pasta.

'I'm told you're looking for a young man on behalf of Guy Gisborne,' Alison continued. 'A kid who's fond of shooting arrows . . .'

'I might be,' Bullcalf said cautiously.

'How's that working out?'

Bullcalf sounded irritated. 'I'm stood in my ma's kitchen, so not exactly hot on the kid's trail.'

'I've got information,' Alison said. 'But I'm risking my job, so it's got to be five thousand up front.'

'Five grand is a lot.'

'So is the bounty Gisborne put on Robin Hood,' Alison replied sharply.

'What will the money buy me?'

'We had a guy from CIS turn up in reception,' Alison persisted. 'He brought two items in for DNA testing.'

Bullcalf sounded suspicious. 'CIS have their own forensics. Why use a private lab?'

Alison laughed. 'He paid cash and said he didn't want paperwork.'

Bullcalf gave a sly laugh. 'Must be more crooks working for CIS than in Pelican Island prison.'

'It was two beat-up motocross helmets. I found traces of DNA from nine individuals who'd worn the helmets at various times. I ran samples against the national crime database. Only one matched a suspect. *Robin Hood – wanted by Locksley Police Department for attempted murder, armed robbery, computer hacking, common theft, resisting arrest, destruction of police property and causing a riot.*'

'Is it a decent sample of DNA?' Bullcalf asked.

'I found Hood's hair and saliva, along with fresh skin flakes,' Alison answered. 'The helmet was found ten days ago, and I'd say that's when he last wore it.'

'Do CIS know?' Bullcalf asked.

'The match has gone no further than my desk. The items came in CIS evidence bags, with tags showing the location where they were found and the name of the officer who bagged them.'

'CIS won't find out you made a DNA match with Robin Hood?'

'Not unless you want them to.'

Bullcalf smiled as he took a pen out of a kitchen drawer. 'I think we have a deal, Alison. Give me your bank details and I'll make the transfer straight away.'

# 18. PUNISHMENT SMORGASBORD

Robin and Marion had rescued Bejo and Srihari and unearthed a sophisticated people-smuggling operation, but the grown-ups still felt the pair had to be punished for lying and running off.

Everyone agreed both kids would have all electronics taken away and be grounded at The Station for one week. Indio cut off Marion's allowance for the rest of the summer and Diogo took away their dirt-bike privileges and made Robin pay for his lost helmet and the headlamp he broke when he crashed.

Finally, once their grounding was over, Emma suggested she could keep Robin and Marion out of mischief for a while by making them go to the church hall in Boston and sort out a room full of clothes and junk that people had donated to Delta Rescue.

Rain pelted the hall's metal roof as Robin stumbled over mounds of bags, holding up a child's tricycle with a wheel missing.

'What joker would donate this?' he complained, as he sent it clattering onto the trash pile.

'I know,' Marion said, catching a nose full of mothballs as she ripped open a bin liner filled with clothes. 'Most of this stuff should have gone straight to recycling.'

'Probably people who don't like refugees,' Robin suggested.

'Like my dad,' Marion said. 'When I told him about Bejo and Srihari, he grunted and said, *Just what we need, more bloody immigrants.*'

'He's the leader of a motorbike gang,' Robin pointed out. 'They're not exactly renowned for tolerance.'

'True.' Marion sighed. 'When I pointed out that if you gave citizenship to *every* refugee living in Sherwood Forest, they wouldn't even fill half of the empty houses in Locksley, Dad said I'd spent too much time listening to my mother's *tree-hugging hippy-dippy crap* and had no idea what I was talking about.'

The next bag Robin opened strained from the weight of books. They were of no use to Delta Rescue, but they were in decent condition so he put them in a pile that would be taken to a charity shop. When he burrowed deeper, he was pleased to find half-decent clothes. Some still had labels and would be ideal for newly arrived refugees.

'Holy macaroni!' Marion blurted dramatically. 'This must be worth a fortune!'

Robin turned excitedly as Marion gawped into a tatty backpack. 'What is it?'

'Antique clock – it's absolutely stunning.'

Robin stumbled over junk, but when he looked into the backpack, he saw a tangle of socks and bras.

'Sack whack!' Marion yelled, as she slapped Robin between the legs.

'Oww, you psycho!' Robin said, moaning as he crashed backwards into a mound of black donation bags, cupping his balls. 'What was that for?'

'I told you I'd get you back . . .'

'What are you on about?'

'Last time we were here, you dropped ice cream down my back.'

Robin gasped. 'That was two weeks ago.'

Marion beamed. 'I didn't say *when* I'd get you back.'

'Not funny,' Robin protested.

As he stumbled to his feet, coughing, they heard tense voices in the main hall. Marion opened a door to peek out and saw a uniformed cop glowering at a woman dressed in a green polo shirt and chef's apron.

'I know you nutters are helping refugees in here,' the cop said cockily.

'I'm making lunch for the pensioners' club,' the woman answered. 'You're extremely welcome to look around our hall.'

Robin and Marion kept watching as a lad with masses of ginger hair in a net came from the kitchen holding a pamphlet.

'Officer,' he began cheerfully, 'have you considered your relationship with God? Would you like to read good news from the Church of New Survivors?'

'Get away,' the officer snapped, wagging his finger. 'I'm letting you religious weirdos know we've got our eye on this place.'

'You're welcome to join our club,' the chef said. 'Some of my ladies dance after lunch, and they'd love a little waltz with a man in uniform.'

The calmer the chef stayed, the more wound up the cop got.

'You're all nutters,' the officer said. 'What about the end of the world, eh? Wasn't it supposed to have happened already?'

He turned and stumbled out of the hall.

Marion grinned at Robin. 'You don't see that every day.'

'That cop was drunk, right?' Robin asked.

'Nothing to worry about,' the chef told the pair as he stepped towards them. 'Just our weekly dose of police harassment.'

'I picked up one of those New Survivor pamphlets,' Robin told Marion, once the chef was gone and they'd resumed their sorting. 'They're weird as. Stuff about building an ark to save humanity, and the world ending in a nuclear war.'

Marion nodded. 'They've got a giant underground compound in Sherwood Forest, out west, close to Lake Victoria. There are rumours that they pick up people in the forest and brainwash them.'

'Seriously?' Robin said. 'I'll google that later.'

'The New Survivors I've met seem harmless though,' Marion said. 'Pensioners' lunch club, mother-and-toddler group, stuff like that. And Delta Rescue is always broke. They donate to the refugee welcome centre and let Emma use this room and the office for free.'

'Sounds all right,' Robin said, then sighed as he turned away from the door and saw that they'd sorted through twenty bags in an hour but had three hundred more to go.

# 19. PRESIDENT MARJORIE

The chef offered Robin and Marion a free lunch with the pensioners, but after a week of being grounded they craved the outdoors and got lunch from Boston's seafront fish-and-chip shop.

As their food sizzled in the deep fryer, Marion rolled a coin along the glass countertop and half-watched the wall-mounted TV.

'Hey, there's your big brother,' she whispered.

Robin glanced up from his phone.

The TV was showing the one o'clock news headlines. Robin's sixteen-year-old half-brother John lived with his mother, Sheriff Marjorie. The volume was muted, but there was a clip of John and Sheriff Marjorie looking respectable as they strode through a rose garden at Sherwood Castle.

The scrolling news ticker read:

MARJORIE KOVACEVIC CONFIRMS INTENTION TO
STAND AS CANDIDATE IN NEXT PRESIDENTIAL

ELECTION — WILL STEP DOWN AS SHERIFF OF
NOTTINGHAM NEXT YEAR AFTER SIXTEEN YEARS
IN OFFICE . . .

'President Marjorie,' Robin moaned. 'Just what the country needs.'

It had stopped raining, so the pair headed out of the shop and sat with feet dangling off the sea wall, watching waves and dog walkers as they ate.

'I still can't believe you found that set of false teeth,' Marion said, as she flung a chip down onto the sand so the gulls could fight over it.

Robin grinned. 'Yeah, I should put them on Diogo's pillow or something.'

Marion laughed. 'You have *got* to do that!'

'Diogo is so loved up with Napua right now, he probably wouldn't notice.'

Marion nodded as she tossed another chip for the gulls. 'At least you're not in the next room. All that stands between my bed and their sex life is a thin partition.'

Robin laughed so hard he inhaled fish flakes and wound up in a coughing fit.

'Old people shagging is gross,' he said cheerfully. 'But I'm glad Diogo's found someone. He's a decent bloke and he seems lonely.'

As Marion nodded, a black Labrador started barking and straining on its leash. Robin looked up and realised it had been triggered by a police surveillance drone skimming across the waterfront.

'I've been waiting for one of those,' he said, as he put his chip packet on the wall and dived into his backpack.

Marion looked baffled as Robin pulled a contraption out of his bag. It was a circuit board taped into the bottom of a plastic sandwich box, with a bunch of soldered wires and a battery pack hanging loose.

'Making bombs now?' she asked, as he fumbled around trying to slot in a battery.

'Remember that police drone I recovered?' Robin answered. 'And the one that chased our bikes?'

Robin's electronics skills hadn't extended to fitting an on/off switch, so his contraption came alive when the battery went in.

The instant the connection was made, the speeding drone's motors cut out. After a silent dive, it clipped the top of a wave and its propeller arms broke off as it bounced like a skimming stone before sinking.

'Was that you?' Marion gasped.

'Yep.' Robin said, looking pleased with himself as he removed the battery and dropped the gadget back in his bag before anyone saw.

'How?' Marion whispered.

'I wasn't even sure it would work,' Robin said, as he broke off a big piece of fish.

'You made it last week?'

Robin nodded. 'When you were out on the boat with Diogo, I read everything I could find about sabotaging drones.'

'Emma brought our phones and laptops back *yesterday*,' Marion said.

Robin grinned. 'Diogo's laptop password is `Di0g0`. He basically deserved to be hacked . . .'

'In non-geek language, how does it work?'

'Military drones are hardened,' Robin explained. 'They use multiple radio frequencies and special tech so their signals can't be blocked. But that police drone I found was a regular photography drone fitted with extra sensors.

'I found the instructions on how to make a jamming circuit using the transmitter from the crashed drone. It locks onto the drone's control signal. If you're close enough, it blocks the signal coming from the drone pilot and . . .'

'Ka-boom!' Marion said.

Robin nodded and smirked.

'One thing I don't get, Robin,' Marion said, stroking her chin thoughtfully.

'What?'

'How is it you're smart enough to figure out something like that, but your socks never match, you drop toothpaste all over the sink *every* night and half the time you forget to put on deodorant?'

'Eccentric genius?' Robin suggested, as he tipped the tiny chips from the bottom of the packet in his mouth, then took an experimental sniff under his arm.

# 20. AFTERNOON SULK

Emma Scarlock was in her tiny office when Robin and Marion got back from the seafront. Just after three she came to the storage room to check up.

'Decent day's work!' Emma said, as she eyed a room with bags still stacked up one side, but neat piles of clothes, toys and other random stuff on the other. 'You might get finished if you put in a good shift tomorrow.'

'It'll be Robin on his own tomorrow,' Marion said. 'I'm out on *Water Rat* with Diogo, delivering supplies.'

Robin groaned, but cheered up when Emma said they should go. 'I checked the weather,' she explained. 'They're forecasting big storms in an hour, so you two'd better head straight home.'

The days when they could zip from Boston to The Station on motorbikes felt golden as Marion and Robin headed outside to a beaten-up pedal bike with a squeaky back wheel and Christmas tinsel woven through the basket on the front.

'My turn to drive,' Robin said, as Marion took off the bike lock.

'Nah,' Marion said, as she waggled her club foot. 'It's my bike.'

Robin shook his head and tutted. He'd seen Marion hike twenty kilometres of Sherwood Forest with no problem, but when Diogo confiscated the motorbikes she claimed she couldn't walk far with her club foot and guilt-tripped him into finding her a bike.

'You know what?' Robin said irritably. 'I'd rather walk.'

They'd spent most of the day in the same room. Marion had sack-whacked him, made him pay for lunch because her allowance was cut off, told him she was off doing something more exciting the next day, and now she wanted him to be propped on the back of the saddle for an uncomfortable ride home.

Marion was Robin's best friend, but you can have too much of anyone and she was getting on his nerves.

'What's wrong?' Marion asked. 'You can pedal if it's *that* important to you . . .'

'I'll run,' Robin said cutting her off. 'I need the exercise.'

'Why are you so grumpy all of a sudden?' she asked.

She got no answer, so she rolled her eyes and pedalled for home.

Robin liked running fast because it tires you out and you don't think about stuff when you're knackered. But he started a slow walk with his shoulders hunched and felt moody.

He thought about stopping to buy an ice cream but couldn't be bothered. He thought about Marion being annoying, about how crummy it was that his dirt bike had been confiscated. When he reached the edge of Boston and started walking down Sunshine Road to cut through the holiday village, he thought about seeing his brother on TV earlier. They used to bicker all the time, but Robin missed Little John. He also missed hanging with his schoolfriend Alan Adale and most of all he missed his dad.

Robin went blurry-eyed as his thoughts went further back, remembering his mum. He imagined an alternative life where she was still alive. She wasn't from Locksley like his dad, so they probably would have moved somewhere else before any trouble started.

Someone as smart as his dad could have got a good job working for a tech company in the capital. He imagined a nice house with an indoor shower and a washing machine that worked. He'd go to regular school. And his mum would . . .

Robin stopped walking and hurt all over.

He was six when his mum died and he realised he only knew things a little kid knows about someone. When he tried to think about the kind of music his mum liked, or what job she'd have done in his imaginary life, or the type of gift she'd have liked for her birthday, he had no clue.

The rain Emma warned about began as Robin entered the holiday village. It started with raspberry-sized splats, then erupted into a deluge that blew into his face.

He could have sheltered under the awning of an alpine chalet, but he was already soaked so he kept up his sulky walk and found himself wondering which version of Robin Hood he'd be if he had the choice: Robin the hero, who robbed cash machines and started riots. Or the imaginary Robin with a cosy posh house and school, homework and all that regular kid stuff.

He cheered up when he realised how boring that would be.

Then, since nobody was around to hear, Robin howled like a lunatic, pounded his chest and set off in a flat-out sprint towards The Station with the rain driving into his face.

# 21. RISING DAMP

Robin was breathless as he stepped inside The Station. The shutter that opened onto the balcony was wide open and stuff was blowing everywhere.

'Extra hands!' Diogo yelled urgently from the far end of the room. 'Come help.'

Robin left a trail of drips as he crossed the sloping floor. As he ran the narrow jetty between the beach and the embankment on which The Station was built, he'd noticed the water was high. But he hadn't realised it was enough to be lapping over the balcony and into the kitchen.

'High tide and all this rain washing downriver,' Diogo explained, as he used a power saw on a wooden sheet. 'If I don't get this barrier up the water will get into the electrics.'

At that moment Marion came through the front door, straining as she pushed a wheelbarrow full of gritty sand she'd shovelled off the beach.

'Hold them open,' she said, as she threw Robin a roll of garden sacks.

Robin held the first sack open while Marion shovelled in sand, but Robin was fitter so he took over shovelling duty for the next two. Then they ran back across the jetty for more sand.

When they came back a blast of wind had blown water into the lowest part of the sloping floor and Diogo was kneeling on the balcony. The board he'd cut made a half-metre high barrier and he was getting soaked by the spray hitting the balcony as he bashed nails to fix it in place.

'Water is heavy,' Diogo explained. 'The board needs reinforcement, so put the first sandbag against the middle and build outwards.'

When Napua arrived forty minutes later, Diogo had waterproofed the wooden barrier using urethane foam designed for emergency boat repairs, while Robin and Marion had worked themselves into a sandy, straggly-haired mess wheeling barrows from the beach and making a knee-height sandbag wall.

'You missed all the fun!' Diogo said, giving Napua a kiss as she put bags of groceries on the dining table.

'Will that hold?' Napua asked, poking her head over the barricade to see the balcony beyond lapping with ankle-deep water.

'It better,' Robin said, as he crashed backwards onto a floor cushion. 'I've never been so knackered in my life.'

'High tide just passed,' Diogo said, as he read the time on his microwave. 'We'll be OK tonight. But I'll have to get to a hardware store so I can make a proper slot-in barrier.'

'I thought I'd do a chicken tagine with almond couscous, then strawberries and cream,' Napua said, as she unpacked groceries.

'Perfect,' Diogo said, then kissed her again.

'I had the radio on while I was driving here,' Napua said. 'Weather lady said it's the first time in six years that the Macondo River is deep enough to navigate a boat the whole way from Lake Victoria to the mouth of the delta.'

'Water level is way up at Designer Outlets too,' Marion said. 'Last time I spoke to my mums, there was deep water in the southern end of the mall. Instead of wading across, anyone coming to the market from the south has to use a raft, or divert over the bridge, way upstream.'

'Food will take an hour,' Napua said, making a clanking noise as she pulled a cast-iron casserole dish out of a messy cupboard.

'You two sand monsters had better scrub up,' Diogo said, while mopping grit and sawdust. 'But no faffing – I need one too.'

The outdoor shower was even weirder than usual, with waves washing over the side balcony and sploshing Robin's feet. It was warm despite the rain, so he came down shirtless after towelling off in his bedroom.

Marion had showered first and was chatting to her little brothers Matt and Otto on her laptop, while Diogo was outside in the shower, noisily warbling traditional fado music in his native Portuguese.

'That chicken smells fantastic,' Robin told Napua. 'Do you want the table laid or anything? Because Marion's just lazing about on her useless butt.'

Robin grinned as Marion gave him the finger. She'd annoyed him earlier, but emergency sand shovelling had reminded him that they made a great team.

'You two are awful to each other!' Napua said, shaking her head. 'Did you see Emma at the church hall today?'

'Briefly,' Robin said.

'Did she say anything more about those poor women?'

'She mentioned that Srihari was OK.'

'And showed us a cute picture of Bejo in a bubble bath,' Marion added, as she closed her laptop.

'But are they investigating what happened to the rest of them?' Napua asked as she chopped spring onions.

'I'm sure they'll try,' Robin answered. 'But Delta Rescue run four boats and a welcome centre for refugees. They're not some big organisation with detectives who go round searching for people.'

Napua nodded. 'Emma said the video clips on your phone were too grainy to prove anything conclusively. But I've lived in the delta all my life and the only place you see big pleasure boats like the one that took those women away is the harbour on Skegness Island.'

Marion nodded in agreement. 'When I'm out with Diogo, we see massive boats like container ships and tankers in the central channel. But for pleasure boats, that was easily the biggest I've seen.'

The conversation was halted as the side door that led from the shower crashed open.

'Damned wind blew my towel away!' Diogo said, as he charged in, cupping his privates.

Marion laughed and Robin mucked about shielding her eyes as Diogo ran naked up the spiral stairs.

'So much body hair!' Robin laughed.

'Chewbacca!' Napua yelled, making Robin and Marion laugh even more.

'I heard that!' Diogo shouted down.

'Maybe now you'll build an indoor shower!' Napua shouted back. 'And fix the bloody thermostat while you're at it.'

After Diogo's comic interlude, Napua returned to her thoughts on the boat.

'I asked the concierge at the casino I work at,' Napua said. 'He knows boats because he organises trips for guests. He said big pleasure cruisers get bought by people who are incredibly rich. But they always want the latest model, so they get sold on to companies that rent them out, for parties, fishing trips, stuff like that.'

'Using someone else's boat would make sense,' Robin agreed. 'I mean, I've never seen a heist movie where the bad guys rob the bank in their own car.'

Napua nodded as she scraped shallots and garlic into a sizzling pan.

'My thoughts exactly,' Napua said. 'My concierge friend said there are a few hire boats of that size on Skegness. I would guess if you strolled around the island with your eyes peeled, you might well find the boat you're looking for.'

'That's a great idea,' Robin said brightly. 'The cruiser had its name covered up, but I took photos and I'd recognise it for sure.'

Marion seemed less certain. 'But where does that get us?' she asked. 'Finding a boat doesn't tell us where it took a bunch of people two weeks ago.'

'But it's a lead,' Robin said. 'If we find the boat, maybe we watch it and discover that the bad guys use it regularly. Maybe we can track where it goes, or someone on the crew will give us info if we slip them some money.'

'I smell delicious chicken,' Diogo said suspiciously, as he came downstairs in shorts and one of the smart shirts he wore when Napua was around. 'But I also smell trouble.'

'I guess it's worth going up there to try,' Marion said. 'Reuniting little Bejo with his mum would be the best thing ever.'

'I'll call Emma to see what she thinks,' Robin said, taking his phone out eagerly. 'If she lets us go tomorrow, I might get out of sorting the rest of that junk at the church hall.'

# 22. NEO-SKEGNESS

Emma liked Napua's idea of someone taking a look around Skegness Island to try and identify the cruiser. She was less keen on Robin and Marion getting into more mischief, so Marion stuck to delivering medical supplies with Diogo, while Robin took a forty-minute taxi ride with Emma's eighteen-year-old son, Neo.

While Sherwood Forest and most of the delta had suffered economic decline, Skegness Island, and particularly the three-kilometre stretch of seafront known as South Strip, was still a popular hangout for the kinds of people who flew first class and paid two hundred bucks for lunch.

Besides hundreds of yachts packing the harbour, the island had five-star hotels, golf courses, the provincial branch of Capital City's biggest modern art gallery, casinos, upscale nightclubs and the best seafood restaurants in the country.

The waterfront was pedestrianised, so the taxi dropped Robin and Neo at the back of the five-star Durley Grange resort. To fit with the upscale crowd, Robin had slicked back his tangled hair and wore chino shorts and his only designer-brand polo shirt with Diogo's best sunglasses hooked over the front pocket.

Neo was a goth, and he'd kept his spiky dyed hair and piercings but went for similar rich-kid-on-holiday clothes to Robin.

It was holiday season, so they passed through a restaurant with people eating a late breakfast, then crossed the hotel's grand lobby and exited through revolving doors into a sunny courtyard filled with the sound of crashing water from giant fountains.

Neo had picked the Durley Grange as their drop-off point because it was at one end of strip. Their search seemed daunting as they exited the courtyard and got a clear view along the harbour at more than a thousand moored boats.

But by the time their eyes had adjusted to the sunlight reflecting off the water, the hunt felt less overwhelming because few boats were anything like the one they were looking for.

The Durley Grange and a couple of its near neighbours were the finest hotels on the island, and the boats in their moorings were the toys of billionaires, protected by guards with assault rifles. As they walked down South Strip, things got less stratospheric, with lots of smaller yachts and pleasure boats.

Neo spotted a well-known soccer player signing an autograph for two young lads, and Robin was tempted by a super-fancy gelato shop until he saw that a single scoop cost nine bucks.

'Not for riff-raff like us,' Neo joked.

The centre of South Strip was a hectic stretch of beach. Jet skis buzzed about and tourists queued for fan boats that would take them out into the swampland to see the giant turtles and water-bird colonies.

After a quick stop to buy croissants, plus coffee for Neo and a milkshake for Robin, the pair felt they were onto something when they reached the end of the beach, and another set of moorings. The vibe here was more street, with skateboarding teens, traders with fake designer gear spread over the pavement and garish signs offering boats for hire.

They walked onto the gently swaying dock's main walkway to give a couple of larger boats a closer look.

'You boys wanna fish?' a young woman in tight shorts and **CHEAP DAY TRIPS** printed across her chest asked as she stepped in front of Neo. 'I can do a whole package. Hundred and twenty – that includes two beers each and no sneaky extras for bait or to clean your catch.'

Another woman hopped off a boat on the other side of the floating harbour. 'I can do a nicer boat than her for the same price.'

'Three beers each!' Cheap Day Trips said, then turned to the other woman and snarled, 'I see these handsome boys first. Keep showing me disrespect and I'll punch your mouth.'

'We're not looking to go fishing today,' Neo said politely, trying to get past.

'How can you not want fishing?' she asked, blocking Neo's path. 'Look at this sun. This water is beautiful.'

'Do I get beer?' Robin asked.

The woman looked excited now Robin had shown interest, but Neo gave Robin's shirt a *let's get away from this nutter* tug.

'I put the beer on the boat and we not gonna watch who drinks it, little man. Hundred and twenty. Such a great deal! What do you boys say?'

'We're looking for a big boat for my brother's eighteenth birthday,' Robin said, to Neo's surprise. 'Like, all of his friends, in a few weeks' time.'

The woman clapped, then pointed at the biggest boat in the harbour. '*Old King Henry* will do a buzzing party. I know the owner – I'll get you an amazing price. Can I get your number?'

'How many people will that take?' Robin asked.

'Seventy, eighty . . .' she answered. 'And I can spice tings up, if you know what I mean. If you want girls or reefer. Got all the best DJs in my contact list. It will be the night of your young lives.'

Neo cottoned on to what Robin was doing. 'Is there anything bigger,' Neo asked. 'Like a hundred . . . hundred and twenty-five people?'

The woman thought for a second. 'The only bigger boat on this harbour is *Swamp King*. She went out well early with a corporate party, but it'll be back soon. The only other one that big is *Cottontail*. It don't dock here, but it's owned by a pal of mine. Can I get a phone number, because I can make calls and get you a massive deal? Where are you boys staying by the way?'

'Durley Grange,' Neo said.

'Oh, you be rich boys!' the woman said, cracking an ear-piercing laugh as she pulled a business card out of her tiny shorts. 'This is me, Starlet McGill. Don't go behind my back to anyone else, because I swear all best deals go through me!'

'Thank you, Starlet,' Neo said, trying not to smirk as he pocketed the business card and started walking away.

She followed them. 'I don't mean to pester, but how about that mobile number?'

Neo was lost for words so Robin stepped in.

'Our dad's bodyguard says we should never give it out,' he said. 'But thank you, Starlet.'

Robin and Neo cracked up laughing as they finally broke free.

'That girl was full on!' Neo laughed, shaking his head in disbelief. 'What was that about our dad's bodyguard? You're so random!'

'It popped into my head,' Robin said, smirking. 'Where did she say the really big boat docked?'

'*Swamp King*,' Neo said, pointing. 'Right ahead.'

There was nothing to see but an empty berth with a flapping vinyl sign tied to a locked barrier. The sign had a picture of a pristine white boat, with a web address.

'Is that it?' Neo asked.

'Looks the right shape,' Robin said. 'But way newer.'

'Everything looks better in the ad,' Neo pointed out.

Robin wondered if he could find a different picture online, so he pulled his phone and searched *Swamp King Skegness Island*.

The top result was from a local news website with the headline:

**Party Boat Owners Slapped with Record Fine – Rat Droppings & Dead Kitten Found Onboard**

He clicked the link and saw a large tatty boat, with yellowed paint, boarded windows and cylindrical life raft containers crusted with bird poop.

Robin looked up at Neo and cracked a smile. 'We've found it.'

# 23. STRIP ARCHERY

Prices at this end of South Strip were more suited to the boys' budget. Neo found a seafood restaurant that had great online reviews and a view over the harbour, so they'd see when *Swamp King* returned to the dock.

Robin and Neo both had teen-boy appetites so they ordered a seafood platter with a massive bowl of chips on the side. As they waited for the food at their balcony table, Robin's eye was drawn to a patch close to the beach that had been a car park before South Strip got pedestrianised.

The cracked blacktop had food stands, a sprawling go-kart track and the storage shed for a jet-ski hire company, but the newest and busiest attraction was filled with kids doing archery.

'**Now Open, South Strip Archery – Have fun and learn to shoot like Robin Hood**,' Neo said, reading the sign aloud.

'I'm outraged,' Robin joked, glancing around to make sure nobody was within earshot. 'They should pay me royalties!'

They didn't have an angle to see the shooting lanes inside, but there was a steady stream of parents dropping off kids for parties and lessons, and Robin saw several leaving by the gift shop with chic mothers carrying plastic bags stuffed with bows, targets and fancy arrows.

'Looks like they're coining it,' Neo said, as a waiter gave Robin his Rage Cola and asked for ID before letting Neo have his beer.

'Rich brats,' Robin complained, as the waiter headed away. 'That kid getting in the taxi with his dad has a better arrow than me. And there's so much demand, my favourite arrows have doubled in price.'

'You're a trendsetter,' Neo said.

Before Robin could answer, one waiter slid a bowl of fries onto the table, while another needed both hands to lower a mound of seafood big enough to block Robin's view of Neo across the table.

'This looks amazing, thank you,' Neo purred, as he tucked a bib under his collar and picked up a set of metal lobster crackers.

Robin's thoughts turned to their mission as he dipped a huge tiger shrimp in melted butter. 'So we're gonna wait for *Swamp King*. Then what?' he asked. 'I was thinking maybe we could pretend to be interested in hiring it and try to get a look around.'

Neo spoke with his mouth full. 'I was thinking about the navigation system.'

Robin didn't know much about boats. 'Like satnav in a car?'

'Same function, but more complex,' Neo said. 'The delta is tricky to navigate without software, even in my little rescue dinghy. Little islands that you don't see in the dark are bad enough, but the rocks below water will rip your hull and send you down *Titanic* style.'

Robin nodded. 'I've been out on Diogo's boat. There's wrecks everywhere.'

'And when you programme the navigation, it's not just the route. You need the latest tide and weather information. That all takes time. So navigation systems tend to store the last few trips you've taken.

'As far back as two weeks ago?' Robin asked, as he split a crab claw.

'The navigation units we use on the Delta Rescue dinghies go back weeks. We also save our most regular routes on all four boats.'

Robin nodded. 'But you can delete them if you want?'

'For sure,' Neo said. 'Anyone smart would delete their navigation data after doing something illegal. But the video on your phone showed a bunch of beer-quaffing thugs who enjoy slapping the women around. So maybe we'll get lucky . . . Do you want half of this?'

Robin recoiled as Neo used tongs to raise a giant squid tentacle.

'I'll stick with shrimp and lobster,' he said.

'Coward!' Neo laughed, as he chopped off a small sucker-covered slice and dropped it onto Robin's plate. 'It's delish – you have to try.'

Robin closed his eyes as he ate his slice of tentacle and gave his verdict. 'Better than the economy sausages my dad used to serve up when we had no money.'

'So we go back to *Swamp King* when it arrives,' Neo said.

Robin nodded. 'Stick to my story from earlier and say you want to hire a big party boat for your eighteenth. Ask to have a look around. Once we're aboard, we snatch the navigation unit and leg it.'

Neo hesitated. 'We'll probably need a screwdriver to remove it. And they're not just going to stand there and let us steal it – we'll need to disable someone. Azeem has taught me enough ju-jitsu to choke a guy out.'

'We passed a marine supply shop,' Robin said. 'They'll have rope for if we need to tie someone up, and I've got a multitool that Marion got me for my birthday, but the screwdriver on it isn't great.'

'We'll buy some rope and a decent screwdriver,' Neo agreed. 'But *Swamp King* will still be here if we come back another day, so if it feels risky, we'll sneak back at night or something.'

'Definitely don't want to get trapped,' Robin said, as he nodded in agreement. 'Diogo said there's only one bridge off this island and it's too far to swim.'

# 24. BEST-LAID PLANS

Robin and Neo were stuffed as they left the restaurant with half the ocean in their bellies. They grabbed a coil of rope and a multi-bit screwdriver at the marine supply store and saw *Swamp King* approaching its berth as they strolled out.

The U-shaped walkway through the dock met the shore at both ends, and they went the opposite way from last time to avoid another encounter with Starlet McGill.

Robin had only seen *Swamp King* in the dark from across Landing Dock Y and wasn't prepared for the scale of the vessel close up. After the gangplank slammed on the wharf, forty boozed-up staff of a Capital City accounting firm came stumbling ashore. Some loud, some seasick and a few carrying bags with dead fish sticking out.

Once the accountants were clear, a three-person cleaning crew hurried aboard, while deck staff in waiters' uniforms threw off rubbish sacks filled with glass bottles and wheeled empty catering trolleys and clattering racks of used champagne flutes down the gangplank.

Robin studied a woman two decks up. She was tall and wore a white captain's uniform as she stood in the open doorway of *Swamp King*'s bridge, puffing clouds of vape smoke. She seemed familiar, but Robin wasn't certain until she yelled down at the cleaners.

'Someone's wig got sucked down the upstairs crapper. You're gonna need the big pump.'

'That captain was there the other week,' Robin told Neo. 'She had camo trousers on and smashed a woman's nose in for asking a question.'

'Nice lady,' Neo said, then tutted.

The dock had benches for passengers waiting to board. They decided the best thing was to sit and watch for a while. Neo bought coffees and freshly fried donuts from a stall by the dock's entrance, to make it look like they had a reason to be there.

'This boat has to be clean, stocked and ready to depart in an hour,' the captain shouted to the waiters, as she walked down steep steps from the top deck. 'Let's see some hustle. Has anyone seen the refuelling crew?'

The captain was yelling into her phone as she strode purposefully off the dock, sweeping past Robin and Neo without seeing them. 'I need fuel on the boat, John. I've got another cruise in an hour . . . Did you pay the last invoice? Because they're not here.'

As soon as she was out of earshot, Neo spoke quietly to Robin. 'Boat leaves in an hour, captain's gone. You fancy our chances if we sneak up there?'

Robin nodded. 'If it's lunch, she'll be at least fifteen minutes, and I can't see anyone else on the bridge.'

'I had no idea there would be so many people servicing the boat,' Neo said. 'This could be our only shot unless we hang around until night-time.'

'I think we should chance it,' Robin said. 'If we're stopped, just act confident. Say we're here early for the afternoon trip. Worst thing they'll do is kick us off.'

Neo led the way through the open gate onto *Swamp King*'s dock. The cleaners were vacuuming inside, but the catering staff had sloped off to gossip on the rear deck as soon as their boss was out of sight.

The boys ducked as they jogged along the gangplank and clambered the two flights of steep rungs to the bridge.

Neo checked there was nobody inside, but the sliding door didn't budge when he shoved.

'Locked,' he grunted.

Robin looked for another way in and saw every sliding window along the front of the bridge was open.

'I'll squeeze through if you give me a boost,' Robin said, as he took off his backpack.

Robin glanced back to check if anyone on the dock was looking their way, then Neo grabbed him around the knees and fed him through a high window. Robin reached out awkwardly, trying not to knock rows of switches as he slid down onto a control console next to the ship's main steering panel, then did a forward roll before planting feet on the floor.

Robin could hear voices and a pump thudding at the bottom of an internal staircase. He inhaled pure filth as he dashed across to let Neo in. The stench of clogged drain didn't sit well on top of seafood and donuts, and as Neo stepped by Robin held onto the sliding door and almost puked.

'That explains why the windows were open,' Neo said, pulling his shirt up over his nose as he returned Robin's backpack.

'Captain said the toilets were blocked,' Robin moaned, as he retched again.

'You keep watch,' Neo said, then scanned the control console.

Everything from the radar set to the ship's radio were modular units, designed to be swapped out if they malfunctioned. As Neo tried to keep the stench out of mind, he identified a navigation unit. It had a 25cm screen and was fixed into a console next to the ship's control stick with four screws.

'All clear out here,' Robin said, glancing about as Neo slotted a magnetic bit into the newly purchased screwdriver.

The screws were easy, and the wires linking the navigation unit to depth sounders and an outdoor GPS receiver glided out, but the power cable was hard-wired into the back of the unit and Neo couldn't get his arm far enough inside the console to unplug it.

'Can't reach the socket,' he gasped, as he lifted the navigation unit out of its slot and peered into the console's murky interior. 'Have you got a wire cutter on your multitool?'

The inside of Robin's backpack was a disaster zone, but after churning through everything from a baseball cap to the false teeth he'd found at the church hall, Robin found the multitool and opened a little set of wire cutters.

'I'll lift this up so that the wire is taut,' Neo said. 'You reach under and snip it.'

'Right,' Robin said, as he ducked under Neo's armpit and leaned on the console.

The power cable was chunky and the cutters didn't have much leverage because they were only ten centimetres long. Robin squeezed with both hands and was about to suggest they swap roles because Neo was stronger when the wire finally split.

'Got it!' Robin said.

Neo stumbled back as the cable snapped free. Robin heard rapid clicks followed by the tingling sensation of an electric shock. His hand sprang open and his multitool dropped irretrievably deep inside the console. At the same time, a quick deafening blast erupted from the ship's horn before fading like wheezing bagpipes.

'Zapped me!' Robin hissed, kicking the console furiously as he flicked his wrist to fight the pain.

Neo looked out front and realised the horn blast had made everyone on the dock look their way. At the same time everything inside the boat had gone eerily silent. No pump, ventilation or vacuuming.

'I think we fused the electrics for the whole boat,' Neo said, looking worried as he dropped the navigation unit into his backpack.

An engineer wearing the kind of elbow-length gloves you put on when your hands are going somewhere extremely nasty poked his head up from the bottom of the internal stairs. 'Hey! Who are you?'

Robin stepped out of the bridge and saw one of the waiters running up the outside steps towards him.

# 25. GETTING WET

If you can't go down, you have to go up. Robin snatched his backpack, used the handle of the bridge's sliding door as a foothold and pulled himself onto the roof, amidst radio masts and a radar dome. Neo was fit but lacked Robin's climbing skills and needed a hand up.

The waiter who'd been running up the stairs reached for Neo's black basketball boot but decided minimum wage plus tips wasn't enough to risk life and limb chasing over a slippery roof.

Mildewed plastic flexed as Robin ran towards *Swamp King*'s stern. He bounced down onto a striped canopy that extended across part of the rear deck, then rolled off the side onto a walkway near the gangplank.

As Robin landed, a big-shouldered woman in grubby engineer's overalls came at him brandishing a massive wrench. As Neo landed behind, Robin ducked and the swinging wrench made a clank and chipped paint off *Swamp King*'s superstructure.

Robin hadn't practised his judo since forever but instinctively hooked his foot around his attacker's ankle and swept out her leg. As she stumbled backwards Neo made sure she hit the deck by barging her and tore the wrench out of her hand as he charged on.

Fortunately the chefs and waiters at the back of the boat didn't want to get involved and the engineer in the long gloves had stumbled as he missed a step on the way down from the bridge.

A two-person refuelling team had arrived on the dock, but the one who thought about tackling Robin as he sprinted across the gantry to the shore bottled it when he saw Neo's sturdy frame wielding the giant wrench.

Robin started a run towards the gate where *Swamp King*'s berth met the main walkway through the dock, but two beefy security guards were storming it.

'Down on the ground!' one shouted, as she pulled a bright yellow stun gun off her belt. 'First and final warning.'

Robin glanced back at Neo.

'How's your swimming?' Neo asked, as he peered over the railing into cloudy water.

'Average,' Robin said, though his face suggested that was optimistic.

But the guards were steps from being in range to shoot metal barbs, connected to a wire that delivered 50,000 volts, so Robin vaulted the fence and splashed into water ten metres below.

Neo landed behind, holding his backpack with the precious navigation unit to his chest so it didn't flood. The eighteen-year-old had done advanced swimming and lifesaving training before being allowed out in a Delta Rescue dinghy and immediately realised Robin was shocked by the cold as a wave knocked them away from the dock.

'We're OK,' Neo said, as Robin spluttered. 'Breathe normal.'

Neo used his free arm to grip the back of Robin's shirt and pull him in close. Then he kicked expertly, ducking under a wave before guiding Robin around so he could grab one of the dock's thick wooden posts.

Robin glanced up. He saw there were cross-beams spanning the pilings that held up the pier, and two guards and several other people were peering over the railings. He climbed effortlessly up the slippery wooden post, then grabbed a cross-beam and balanced on top.

Neo looked up from the water. 'I think I'm better swimming.'

As Neo moved his backpack onto his chest and swam towards shore in a rapid backstroke, Robin went in the same direction by clambering through the dock's chunky supports.

While guards up top called the cops, Robin reached a six-metre gap where *Swamp King*'s berth met the dock's floating walkway.

Robin thought about a leap and a short swim, but the underside of the dock's wooden deck had a series of pipes that fed water, fuel and power to the boats. As Neo swam efficiently below, Robin tested the pipes for strength, then gripped the back of a thick fuel hose and went hand-over-hand with legs dangling.

It took all the grip in Robin's fingers, and he didn't dare grab or grasp because he could see the people who were looking for him through gaps in the wooden deck above. He slipped on dark green algae when he landed on one of the giant plastic mushrooms that supported the floating walkway, but after a scary couple of seconds his fingers found a protruding bolt and he steadied himself on a ledge.

Helpfully the next post had a set of climbing rungs, and Robin's head bobbed up on the far side of the footpath. After making sure nobody was paying attention, he slithered over a fence and realised he was in the spot with the benches where he'd sat eating donuts minutes earlier.

The captain had rushed back when she heard the horn blast and was haranguing her staff for letting the boys sneak on board, while one of the security guards tried to calm her down by telling her that the dock had been sealed and police were nearby.

Water streamed out of Robin's backpack and he realised he'd smashed Diogo's sunglasses as he straightened up. He had no chance of blending in while he was dripping wet, so there was no reason not to sprint.

The walkway was clear, and Robin was delighted when he glanced back and saw that he hadn't been spotted. But as he neared the shore, a body shot out from between two wooden kiosks.

Robin fell hard, scraping his knee on the wooden deck, as the woman jumped on his back. When she rolled Robin over, he saw **CHEAP DAY TRIPS** stretched across her chest.

'Caught the little guy!' Starlet McGill shouted.

She pinned one of Robin's arms, but he gripped her hair with his other hand and ripped out a chunk of hair extensions. Then as Starlet yelped, she saw Robin's algae and birdcrap-smeared hand come towards her face and instinctively recoiled.

The motion gave Robin enough space to thrust his torso upwards and knock Starlet away. She tried to get an arm around his neck as he stood, but he spun free.

Robin's relief was short-lived, because a guard tasked with blocking the dock's entrance fired her stun gun at him. But her aim was low and Robin hurdled, making the bolt shoot between his legs and clank into a rotating sign offering two-for-one swamp tours. As Robin looked behind, he saw the captain and the other two guards sprinting towards him. Robin figured it was better to fight one guard than three and charged the woman who'd tried to zap him.

The stun gun dropped to the ground as Robin collided with the guard. He thought about picking it up, but it skimmed under the side rail and dropped into the water.

He stumbled on, gasping, to the spot where the walkway met the beach. Tourists stood about gawping as he saw Neo staggering up the beach with sand coating his legs.

'OK?' Robin gasped.

'For now,' Neo answered.

But there were three people chasing from the dock, and a police van screeching to a halt by the taxi rank on the far side of the old car park.

# 26. LEGENDARY FOOTAGE

'Where are you going?' Neo shouted, as Robin sprinted purposefully across the sand. 'There's a vanload of cops up there!'

Robin's shoes squelched as he took a dramatic leap onto South Strip Archery's tall wire fence.

He yelled, 'Don't shoot!' as he leaped down in the middle of an archery range.

'I can't climb that,' Neo shouted, as two burly security guards and the captain of *Swamp King* closed in. 'What are you doing?'

'Meet me around the front, by the gift shop,' Robin shouted back.

The archery range was holding a beginners' lesson for six-to-eight-year-olds. A youthful instructor in one of the range's branded shirts planted hands on hips and yelled, 'Excuse me, young man,' as Robin sprinted towards the little archers at the shooting end.

Robin had no way of knowing the injury was minor and felt shocked. After a brain freeze, he found Neo holding a neon life jacket and tugging him up off the sandy ramp.

'Get up, put this on,' Neo yelled. Then to the attendant, 'I'm sorry I pulled the stun gun. Thanks for helping.'

'The boss can kiss my arse,' the attendant said as he gave Neo a fist bump. 'Leaving to go backpacking next week anyways.'

The two-seat ST-140 was in the water with the engine running, but there were four armed cops somewhere nearby and Neo feared a gunshot as Robin spent precious seconds taking off his backpack, pulling on the life vest and then putting the pack back over it.

'Hold on tight,' Neo ordered, as Robin straddled the back seat. 'It's gonna get bumpy.'

Robin was shocked by the power as the jet ski hit 70 km/h in under three seconds.

Back on shore, the officer with the split visor got his helmet off, and while a thirteen-year-old shooting arrows at cops wasn't everyone's idea of a good thing, the entire beach was on their feet, knowing they'd witnessed headline news.

Sarah and her two girlfriends joined a group standing on the harbour wall shouting, 'Robin Hood lives!' and 'Robin, we love you!'

A cop ordered the nervous teen to get off the jet ski. But by the time the officer had mounted it, Neo and

Robin had shrunk to a dot and he didn't like the idea of falling into the delta wearing hefty body armour.

'They're not coming after us,' Robin shouted over the engine, as the speeding craft bounced over waves.

'Don't count your chickens,' Neo yelled back. 'They'll put up drones and we're cooked if a prowler starts shooting.'

# 28. AAAARGH, SNAKES!

Two drones circled and there was a relatively harmless Skegness Island police boat in the distance as the jet ski beached on a mud bank on the mainland coast. The local heron population didn't seem impressed as the boys jumped off the noisy craft into ankle-deep water.

'You good?' Neo asked, as they waded towards dry land.

Robin nodded as he ditched his brightly coloured life vest. 'Grazed knee is all.'

Neo had landed in a spot where there were plenty of trees to give cover.

'We need as much space as possible between us and that jet ski,' Neo said.

'I've got my drone-killing gadget,' Robin said. 'Hold my bow so I can get it out.'

As Robin went to hand Neo the bow, a water snake fatter than Robin's thigh cruised through the water between them.

'Those are the deadly ones!' Neo yelped as he bolted.

Robin's heart shot into his mouth as he realised there were smaller snakes in the water around him.

'Get up here,' Neo ordered when he reached dry ground.

Robin was bricking himself as he splashed through water that got deeper before it got shallow. As he scrambled onto rocks, with a hand up from Neo, everything below his knee was coated in sticky green algae.

It was an easy jump from the rocks to dry land, but with his imagination full of snakes, Robin spasmed like he'd been tasered when a thistle brushed his shorts.

'That was no fun,' he complained, clutching his chest as they headed towards a single-track road, which helpfully had a **BEWARE OF SNAKES** sign.

Neo finally took the bow as they cut across the deserted road and onto marshy ground between tangled trees. After a few gulps from his water bottle, Robin pulled out his magic lunchbox and shook off some drips.

'Hope the water hasn't wrecked it,' Robin said, as he pushed in the loose battery.

One drone flipped and plunged satisfyingly into the swamp, while the other one kept flying in a straight line until they couldn't hear it any more. At the same time, Neo used his phone to study the local map.

'This area looks like a good tangle,' Neo said. 'Plenty of places to hide, and drones will struggle to pick us up again.'

'Just hope there's no cops over this side,' Robin said, as he glanced around.

Neo downloaded the map, then reminded Robin to switch off his phone in case the cops could track their signals. The tangle of branches and saturated ground meant they could move at a squelching walk, until they reached higher grazing land and broke into a run.

Several drones buzzed by, but nothing locked on. Robin could run all day, but after seven kilometres Neo had a red face and a stitch. They'd reached a little shopping park, with car charging points, a drive-thru Mindy Burger and a Farm Stop, part of a rural chain that sold everything from pig feed and overalls to beer and groceries.

'I need water,' Neo said, stripping off his shirt to reveal a well-muscled chest and tan lines from his Delta Rescue wetsuit. 'I'll get some snacks. Maybe a change of clothes in case they've passed our descriptions around.'

Robin nodded. 'Best if I stay out of sight.'

Beyond Farm Stop was a roundabout and a busy four-lane highway. Robin found a spot among trees. While his shirt and shorts had mostly dried out, his pocket had a ball of soggy napkins from the seafood restaurant, which he used to clean his scraped knee.

He also noticed a slimy lump where his trainer met the back of his ankle. He tried kicking it off, but it was stubborn, and when he looked closer, he realised it was a leech sucking his blood.

'Hate the delta,' Robin told himself, shuddering as he prised the leech off with a stick then squished it against a tree trunk. 'I thought Sherwood Forest was bad enough . . .'

Neo took long enough for Robin to start worrying, but came back wearing a new black singlet and carrying four plastic bags.

'Massive queue,' he complained, as he flipped Robin a bottle of icy water. 'They've got a couple of TVs in with the toasters and coffee machines. News cameras were on the beach, interviewing the jet-ski guy and that girl who kissed you.'

Robin sat up anxiously. 'Casualties? That cop I hit in the face?'

'Two officers wounded, plus five civilians. They said three were serious but not life-threatening.'

'That must be the three I shot through the knee,' Robin said. 'Why have you bought half the shop?'

'Four big bottles of water and a pack of cheap face cloths so we can wipe this green crud off,' Neo explained. 'Small bottles of water to drink. Beef jerky, M&Ms, dry socks . . .'

'I had a leech on my ankle,' Robin said, between gulps of water.

'Same,' Neo said, opening a pack of trail mix as he sat with his back against a trunk. 'Those snakes freaked me out. A bite from that big one would kill you in minutes.'

'We'd better call your mum,' Robin said. 'Taxi's too risky and we can't walk forty kilometres.'

'My mum will go bananas,' Neo said, shaking his head and looking up at the sky. 'Could you call Diogo?'

Robin laughed. 'How can you be eighteen and still scared of your mum?'

'Not scared,' Neo said. 'Just . . . You know how mums are. Going on and on about every little thing.'

'I really don't,' Robin said, a touch sad.

'Oh *damn*,' Neo said, waving his hands. 'Sorry . . . I didn't . . .'

Robin half smiled as he dug into the bag of trail mix. 'It's OK, I know you didn't mean anything.'

'My mum is the best person to call,' Neo admitted. 'But check your present before I get yelled at.'

'Present?' Robin said, as Neo threw a bag over.

'I got baseball caps, cargo shorts and Crocs, so we're not wearing anything that's on the news,' Neo explained. 'But the tank tops were ten each or three for twenty, so I got an extra one.'

Robin dipped into a bag of Farm Stop's finest fashion items.

'I think it's right at the bottom.'

'Just what I always wanted!' Robin said, laughing as he unfurled a black T-shirt.

It had a sketchy-looking surveillance photo of himself dressed as a girl when he escaped from a cash-machine robbery. Underneath it said *Robin Hood Lives.*

# 29. DOWN THE DRAIN

Robin found two leeches on the back of his leg as he wiped off sand, algae and birdcrap, then swapped the 'rich boy holidaying on Skegness Island' look for the oversized tank and baseball cap of a person who buys clothes while shopping for ground beef and poultry bedding.

Emma said she'd organise a pickup, but since the boys felt safe and there was a chance of police roadblocks, she reckoned it was best if they stayed put until things calmed down.

Neo decided to move away from Farm Stop, in case they tangled with roaming kids or someone taking a leak in the bushes. They found a sheltered spot near an open storm drain that channelled water from the highway. Beyond the traffic and the retail park, it was fields of swaying wheat in every direction.

'Did it get wet?' Robin asked, as Neo pulled the navigation unit out of his pack.

'Luckily I bought this pack for when I'm out on the rescue dinghy,' Neo said. 'It's supposed to keep stuff dry.'

'Don't you need a plug?'

'Should have a back-up battery,' Neo said, shaking his head. 'You can't risk having navigation drop out if you're cruising at twenty knots and your generator fails. I just hope it didn't get fried when we cut the wire.'

They were sitting on the slope of the concrete drainage channel and Robin shuffled closer as the unit's screen lit up. After the manufacturer's start-up screen, a yellow warning triangle came up:

**EXTERNAL GPS ERROR.**

'Tap the arrow at the bottom for a menu,' Robin urged.

'I know what I'm doing, Robin. Apart from the bigger screen, it's the same as the navs on Delta Rescue boats.'

Neo proved his point by swiping past more warning screens and locating the *Recent Trips* menu. The slider bar got close to the oldest entry as he scrolled back by date.

'That it?' Neo asked.

Robin nodded before Neo tapped **DISPLAY ROUTE**.

'Another couple of days and this would have been wiped,' Neo said, as he tapped the option to display the route map.

A 3D map popped up, showing *Swamp King* starting from out of its berth on Skegness Island, making a brief stop at a pier on the mainland and then heading to Landing Dock Y. Robin moved his face closer to the screen as Neo used the touchscreen to scroll up.

'It stops!' Neo said dramatically. 'Just after it leaves the dock with the women on board.'

'Noooo!' Robin groaned, wrapping hands around his head and kicking feet in the air. 'After everything we went through to get this . . .'

Neo smiled knowingly. 'I'm messing with you. I pressed the screen lock.'

'Butthead!' Robin gasped, shaking his head as Neo started scrolling again.

After leaving Landing Dock Y, the navigation screen showed *Swamp King* zigzagging through shallow water between several islands to reach the delta's main shipping channel. The boat then travelled upstream for thirty-six kilometres.

Neo used his phone to photograph the navigator screen showing *Swamp King*'s final destination. Then he zoomed in to see the outline of a dock built for huge tankers.

'Porthowell Dock,' Robin read from the screen. 'Heard of it?'

'You can't miss it,' Neo said. 'It's part of a massive chemical plant on the riverbank. It was built to supply the car plants in Locksley. Most of it shut down, but you still see smoke coming out of chimneys when you go upriver.'

'What if Porthowell wasn't the women's final destination?' Robin asked, as Neo forwarded the photos to his mum.

'I'm pretty sure it will be,' Neo said. 'The fishing boat unloaded the women at Dock Y, then *Swamp King* took them upriver to Porthowell. It's a lot of hassle and risk, moving seventy people against their will. If you were going to drive the women somewhere else, why not load them into trucks at Dock Y?'

Robin thought for a second. 'So why transfer the women to *Swamp King* at all? Why not take that trawler to Porthowell?'

'You can hide in the delta because it's huge,' Neo explained. 'But a foreign fishing boat with women crammed on deck would attract lots of attention on the river.'

'I guess there is a brain under that dark fringe of yours,' Robin said, as he took a bag of M&Ms out of his pack. 'You want, or can I finish 'em?'

Neo's phone rang before he could answer. 'Mum,' Neo said, then laughed. 'So now you think we did a *good* job?'

There was nobody nearby, so he put the phone on speaker.

Emma told them that footage of Robin shooting the cops and escaping in the jet ski was blowing up online, and apparently the guy Robin shot in the shoulder at the archery shop was some famous retired tennis player.

Then she told the boys what she planned to do next.

'If the bad guys figure out why you stole *Swamp King*'s navigation unit, they might try to move the women. I'm going to organise a boat and find out what's happening at Porthowell Dock tonight. If you guys think you can safely make it back to the water, we'll pick you up along the way.'

# 30. SET AN EXAMPLE

It started chucking it down as the sun dropped so Robin and Neo got another soaking as they walked back towards the delta.

Their pickup spot was a pier in front of an upscale nursing home run by a pal of Diogo's. As residents' TVs flickered inside dark rooms, Robin sat outside in a gazebo surrounded by roses and picked up the home's Wi-Fi.

He tapped on a video titled *Robin Hood: Hero or Villain?* The clip was from a trashy afternoon talk show called *Muldoon*. It was the kind of show where they book guests who don't like each other and encourage the studio audience to misbehave.

'Robin Hood is a criminal . . .' a sweating congresswoman called Enola Straight began.

Some of the audience jeered so loud she had to pause.

'Today, this hooligan child shot and maimed *six* people. Two were police officers. One was a beloved Australian tennis champion. How can this be a hero? What type of people spray Hood's name on walls and wear his T-shirts? We need to catch Robin Hood, then set an example by locking him up and throwing away the key!'

Ms Straight finished with a flourish, pounding her fist on the desk. The camera cut to a noisy audience. About a third applauded the congresswoman, but others shook their head and jeered.

A scruffy young comedian called Darrell Snubs spoke next. 'When Enola Straight's crew of muppets came to power, it was all like, yeah, we're cool! We're gonna make this country great. Fair tax, better schools, better hospitals, make everyone equal. And what did we end up with? Politicians whacking their own salaries up by half, whole towns run by criminal gangs with bent judges, and corrupt cops like the dirtbags who framed Ardagh Hood.

'The boss class in this country doesn't like Robin Hood because he didn't say, "*Yes, sir, thank you, sir,*" when the system kicked him in the arse. Hood may be a kid, but he has the guts to fight back against a system totally rigged against the little guy.'

Darrell Snubs stood up out of his chair and buttons flew off his shirt as he ripped it open to display a *Robin Hood Lives* T-shirt. Cheers and shouts erupted. The camera cut to the audience, showing screaming girls in *End Police Corruption* tops and two red-faced dudes shoving each other in the front row.

'Snubs is great,' Neo said fondly, as he stepped under the gazebo and saw the image on Robin's phone. 'I saw him live in Nottingham before he went into rehab.'

'Seems to be a fan of mine,' Robin said, feeling tired and fuzzy-headed as the clip ended.

'My mum texted,' Neo said. 'They'll be here in five.'

*Water Rat*'s flat grey hull rolled out of the dark as Robin and Neo stepped onto the care home's wheelchair-accessible pier.

'Look what the cat dragged in,' Diogo said, as the boys jumped aboard.

Marion gave Robin a big grin and a sarcastic wagging finger. 'I let you off on your own for one day, and look at all the trouble you cause.'

Diogo teased Marion as he powered *Water Rat* away from the pier. 'I thought you'd slap his face after they showed him kissing that girl.'

'She's welcome to him,' Marion said, as she settled on an upturned bucket next to Diogo.

As Robin and Neo realised it was going to be no fun squatting in *Water Rat*'s open rear cargo bay, Emma peeled back a plastic sheet she was using to keep the rain off and introduced the two women huddled next to her.

'This is Lynn, she's a journalist, and Oluchi, her camera operator.'

Oluchi, who looked about Neo's age, gave an embarrassed laugh. 'Just the unpaid intern, but I can point a camera.'

'Have we met?' Robin asked, as he gave Lynn a curious look.

Lynn smiled and spoke in her newsreader voice, 'Good afternoon, this is Channel Fourteen serving the Central Region. I'm your host, Lynn Hoapili, sitting in a boat with a very wet bum.'

'Oh wow!' Robin said, cracking a big grin. 'My dad *always* watched you when you used to do the morning show.'

'I'm as excited to meet you, Robin Hood,' Lynn said. 'My cousin Napua put me in touch with Emma.'

Emma explained further. 'Delta Rescue isn't resourced to take on smugglers that might have hundreds of forced workers, plenty of money and back-up from corrupt Customs and Immigration officers.'

Robin nodded. 'You can bet they're paying the cops off too.'

'Wouldn't surprise me.' Emma sighed. 'We'll need publicity to get public opinion on our side, and we need to document everything we witness, because CIS will use every trick to discredit us.'

'I get bored behind a desk in a studio,' Lynn said. 'So when Napua called, I told my boss I was sick and roped in Oluchi to film.'

Neo gave Robin a friendly slap on the back and grinned at Oluchi. 'I guarantee your story will get attention if you put this squirt in front of the camera.'

# 31. TWO TU

Robin sat in a puddle as the rain varied between drizzle and a blast that had to be pumped out of the open hull. *Water Rat*'s flat bottom was designed for skimming over shallow water in the delta and things got choppy as they moved into the Macondo River, which was flowing fast after days of heavy rain.

Robin decided he'd be happy to spend the rest of his life on dry land and Oluchi felt even worse, spending half the trip heaving over the side.

There was only moonlight as Porthowell Dock came into view. The river at this point was over a kilometre wide and the docks were on an epic scale, with concrete walls built to berth ships that rose ten storeys out of the water. The chemical plant behind was a cathedral of moonlit pipes, domes and storage tanks.

Since the desolate harbour had been built for tankers, they had to scale eight metres of rusty metal rungs to get up to the harbourside. Diogo stayed on *Water Rat*, ready for a getaway if things got hairy.

'Place is massive,' Robin said as he stood with his stolen bow, glancing about. 'Where do we even start?'

As Lynn Hoapili recorded a whispered piece to camera, saying where they were and who they'd come looking for, Emma switched on a heat-sensing camera, that was part of the kit Delta Rescue used to find refugees.

Robin hadn't seen a thermal-imaging camera before and was fascinated. The device was shaped like a big ping-pong bat, and as Emma swept it around, its rear screen showed areas of the plant that were being used lit up in white and orange, while cooler areas were blue or black.

Robin was amazed that the camera was sensitive enough to distinguish tiny traces of heat left by their shoes as they'd stepped off the ladder and walked around the dock.

Neo had found an old diagram of the plant online and led the way along the riverbank, walking below transfer pipes wide enough to drive a car through. Oluchi had mostly recovered from her nausea and filmed with a shoulder-mounted news camera as they walked.

Much of the sprawling chemical plant had been demolished, but three huge buildings survived. Robin, Marion, Emma, Neo, Oluchi and Lynn walked through an open gate and along a space between two ghostly buildings covered in pipes and rusted metal gantries.

The third building lay at the end of this gap. It still produced paint for cars and had been fenced off from the abandoned sections, with security cameras and floodlights.

'Could the women work in there?' Marion asked.

'Unlikely,' Emma said, as she kept sweeping the thermal camera. 'It would be hard to mix regular employees and slave labour.'

The fence stopped you going past the ends of the two abandoned buildings, but most doors were open or missing. Robin peered in through an archway big enough for a truck and saw bright dots of street lamps on the opposite side.

'I think we can cut through here, rather than go all the way back.'

He was startled as his voice echoed inside. *Back, back, baaack* . . .

Robin's shoes crunched dust and broken glass as he moved in further. Marion swung up a big torch, casting dim light over a space filled with gantries and pipes, many with missing chunks where scrappers had stripped out copper and other valuable metals.

Besides bats and squirrels, the interior hid stolen cars and several huge graffiti murals.

'Robin Hood, how do you feel right now?' Lynn asked, as Oluchi pointed the camera at him.

Robin shrugged and sounded grumpy. 'It's past midnight. I'm soaked. I've got blisters from walking in wet shoes. Right now, a comfy bed would be very nice.'

'So it's exhausting being a hero?' Lynn said.

Before Robin could answer, Marion groaned and blurted, 'Robin's ego is big enough already!'

'My friend Marion is jealous of my incredible talents,' Robin joked to camera, then flinched as Marion lobbed a big metal bolt, deliberately aiming way over his head.

'The banter between Robin and Marion is gold,' Lynn whispered to Oluchi. 'Keep the camera running.'

Marion led the way out of the far side of the building and found herself on a railway platform. The rails had been taken, but you could see the outline of the track bed through the weeds. There was even a line of railway tankers, rusted in place, with faded logos of the Porthowell Chemical Company.

Beyond the railway sidings a stretch of wet road had crisply painted markings and modern street lighting. This section of the chemical plant had been demolished and replaced with four identical metal-sided warehouses. A rooftop sign and hundreds of waiting delivery vans bore the logo of Two Tu, the online shop that brought *the world to you*.

'How about Two Tu, *using forced labour*?' Robin speculated, as Emma stepped out onto the railway platform.

Emma smiled. 'The place we're looking for won't have logos or signs.'

'This is a bust,' Robin moaned, then stretched into a big yawn before jumping off the railway platform into weeds and gravel. 'And it's gonna be way after three when we get home in Diogo's crappy boat.'

'Don't let Diogo hear you diss *Water Rat*,' Marion warned, as she landed beside him. 'He loves that crazy boat more than anything.'

Robin managed a weary laugh. 'He'll be angry enough when he finds out I smashed his good sunglasses.'

Neo jumped off the platform, but the other adults did the grown-up thing and used the ramp at one end.

Emma kept scanning with her thermal camera, but the only heat came from rats, birds and rows of little dots left by fox feet. As they neared the dock after a circular half-hour search, everyone felt tired and pessimistic.

Mostly out of boredom, Marion hopped onto the bed of a rusting, wheel-less truck trailer. As she strolled along, she glimpsed a chink of light from a door opening. It was a long building behind trees and a fence that only seemed to rise half a storey out of the ground.

'I saw a door open,' she said excitedly, as she jumped down and pointed. 'Neo, show us your map. What's over there?'

Neo opened the diagram of the site on his phone and zoomed.

'*Waste-water treatment*,' Marion read.

'Sure you didn't imagine it?' Robin asked.

'I'm not stupid,' Marion snapped back.

'See what you get with the thermal camera,' Emma suggested.

Marion jumped back on the truck bed and Emma reached up to pass the camera.

'Don't drop it,' she warned. 'They're sixteen hundred quid.'

Robin jumped up as well. It took Marion a few seconds to relocate the gap between the trees where she'd seen the door open. The thermal camera showed a distinct yellow blur.

'Does this zoom?' Marion asked.

'Big lever on the front,' Emma answered.

When Marion zoomed, the blur turned into wafts of smoke, a glowing white cigarette tip and a human-shaped figure.

'Believe me now?' Marion growled to Robin, before turning to Emma. 'Big building, no lights or signs. Isn't that exactly the kind of place you said we were looking for?'

# 32. ACROSS THE FENCE

Oluchi stood back, filming, as Emma used wire cutters to snip a hole in a rusty fence. Robin and Marion felt re-energised now they'd found something, and beat the adults to the other side by climbing a tree and dropping from overhanging branches.

Neo suggested the waste-water treatment ponds might still be used by the paint company at the other end of the plant. But the tatty fence, weed-strewn paving and lack of lights didn't give that vibe.

'Careful, you two!' Emma warned, as Robin and Marion crossed cracked paving and approached a metal door surrounded by hundreds of cigarette butts.

The bunker-like two-storey building was set in a trench with steep grass embankments along either side, while the gently sloping roof was braced with huge concrete beams. Circular water-treatment ponds stretched into the distance along one side, but the only liquid in them was puddled rainwater.

'**Danger: Hazardous Material**,' Marion read from a faded sign. '**Employees entering this building must carry an emergency respirator at all times**.'

'I guess that concrete roof is to contain a blast if something inside goes bang,' Robin said.

Marion nodded. 'Though with all these cigarette butts, I'm hoping there's something less explosive in there now.'

While Marion and Robin inspected the area by the door, Neo and Emma checked a row of giant wheeled bins. Neo peered into one and almost got flattened by the glue fumes. When he held his breath and tried again, he pulled out little triangular scraps of leather and a lattice of spongy synthetic rubber with dozens of foot-shaped holes punched out.

Robin wandered around the side of the building, peering down into the steep-sided trench in which the building was set. Narrow windows with lights on the lower floor and spinning ventilation fans suggested there were people inside. When he looked up, he was alarmed by a rooftop mast with two satellite dishes and cameras pointing in every direction.

'Loads of cameras,' he reported as he backed up to the others. 'I don't think we should stick around.'

Oluchi filmed as they retreated through the fence and regrouped next to the flatbed truck. Neo kept lookout, but there was no sign of anyone coming after them.

'Seems they're making athletic shoes in there,' Emma told everyone.

'I saw logos when we looked in the trash,' Neo confirmed. 'Designer gear, probably fakes.'

'I guess it makes sense,' Lynn said. 'I spend a fortune on trainers for my boys. But shoes are bulky, so they bring workers to make shoes, rather than the shoes themselves.'

Marion looked at Robin. 'If you saw all those cameras, why has nobody come after us?'

Robin had hacked the security system at Sherwood Castle Resort a few months earlier and knew the answer.

'There are millions of security cameras in the world,' Robin explained. 'But hardly any are watched all the time. Most only get looked at *after* an event, like a robbery or something.'

'So what now?' Neo asked. 'The women from *Swamp King* are surely in that building. But there could be armed guards and hundreds more workers.'

Emma nodded in agreement. 'The six of us can hardly launch a raid, and if we call the cops, we're more likely to end up in jail than the bad guys.'

Marion laughed. 'Especially if your name is Robin Hood.'

Robin thought for a second. 'If any of you has a laptop with a network port, I can get up on the roof, plug into their computer network and try to find out what's going on inside.'

'How?' Lynn and Emma asked simultaneously.

'IP security cameras are just devices connected to your computer network,' Robin explained. 'Like a printer, router or webcam. So, I unplug the cable on the back of one camera, plug it into the laptop and I'll be connected to the computer network inside the shoe factory.'

'How long will that take?' Emma asked.

'Getting onto the network takes seconds,' Robin said. 'The big question is, how good is their security? If they've locked down every computer and device, I won't see anything. But not many people password-protect their printer, or bother enabling encryption on security cameras.'

Marion nodded enthusiastically. 'The worst thing that can happen is Robin falls off the roof and dies. So I see no downside to this at all.'

'Two in the morning and you still manage to be hilarious,' Robin said drily, before moving on. 'Does anyone have a laptop?'

Lynn's bag of camera gear had a beaten-up video-editing laptop with Channel Fourteen logos. Robin opened it up, tethered it to his phone and downloaded a bunch of network hacking tools that he kept stored online.

Marion had become a decent archer since Robin started teaching her, so he gave her his bow and told her to keep an arrow notched in case anyone came after him.

The danger made Robin feel less tired as he climbed back through the fence with Neo, then stood on the older boy's shoulders before straddling a fragile-looking rain gutter and stepping onto the roof. But it had been an exhausting day and his brain felt fuzzy as he walked up the gently sloping roof between thick concrete braces.

He dropped to a crawl when he got near the camera pole. He'd expected that he'd have to plug into the network by disconnecting the cable coming out of a camera, but helpfully the eight cameras and two satellite dishes all fed into a weatherproof box with a network switch and two empty ports.

The engineer who'd installed the cameras had even left a spare cable she'd used when setting the system up. Robin took the Channel Fourteen laptop out of his backpack, plugged it in and stretched in a mammoth yawn as he waited for his packet sniffer program to detect all the devices connected to the computer network.

Robin had expected computers, printers and cameras, and hopefully an internet connection. But the list showed he wasn't looking at some crude sweatshop. Among more than fifty networked devices were a vacuum moulding machine, two laser cutters, an embroidery machine and several industrial robots.

The level of technology made Robin worry that there would be good security too, but although the computers were locked down or switched off, he had no problem getting a live feed from the cameras. There were twenty-six on the network, and since they had numbers, the only way to find what each one pointed at was to access them in turn.

After connecting to a couple that stared outside, Robin hit the jackpot with a wide-angle camera showing a well-lit production floor. Although it was two in the morning, more than fifty workstations bustled with women sewing and cutting leather trainer uppers.

Robin made a short recording from this camera, before flicking through others that showed a moulding machine, a huge warehouse filled with boxed shoes, a bathroom and showers that looked spotless but had no shower curtains or cubicles around the toilets, a commercial kitchen and a tightly packed dorm with triple-height bunks and sleeping women.

Most of the spaces were clean and brightly lit, but black uniformed guards and metal doors made it obvious the workers weren't there willingly.

Robin took a recording from each camera. But it would be better still if he could enable remote access to the network to see what was going on after coming down off the rooftop.

Fortunately for cybercriminals, almost nobody installs security updates on their network equipment, so after a two-minute search of the software library on his favourite hacking site, Robin downloaded a tiny program that exploited a badly written code in the factory's internet router.

After a couple of clicks to install the program on the router, Robin had a back door that would let him log in and watch the underground factory's cameras from any device with an internet connection.

Neo was waiting when Robin got back to the edge of the roof.

'How'd it go?' he whispered, as he helped Robin to the ground.

'Almost too easy,' Robin said, smiling awkwardly. 'You know when everything goes so well that you feel sure you must have forgotten something?'

# PART IV

# 33. LEAVING THE STATION

Three days after the incident on Skegness island, Robin was still in the news. For close to two months he'd been hiding in the delta, but now the whole world knew he'd been in the area and everyone would take a closer look when they saw the athletic little teen with scruffy hair.

Even more worryingly, an elderly Italian had wandered into Boston Church Hall. He looked offended when the chef asked if he'd come to join the seniors' lunch club. Then he came out with a convoluted story about how he lived nearby and was looking for two kids who'd ridden over his front lawn on dirt bikes.

The chef knew he was lying because she'd lived in the village her whole life and had never seen him before. She told the Italian she didn't know any kids with dirt bikes, then called Emma because the guy had a creepy vibe and the description fitted Ross and Mary, the two kids staying with Diogo who'd been clearing out the storage room.

Emma realised it was Dino Bullcalf hunting the bounty on Robin's head, and that meant it was time for him to leave The Station.

Robin felt sad as he took a last look back at the little room he'd slept in for the past two months. Then he grabbed a backpack crammed with clothes, books and archery gear and carried it down The Station's spiral stairs.

Marion had already brought her stuff down and sat on the floor cushions, ready to go.

'What are you wearing?' Marion said, tutting and smirking.

Robin dropped his bag and stretched out the *Robin Hood Lives* T-shirt that Neo had bought him. 'They're the height of fashion,' he explained. 'And here's the clever part: no fugitive would be stupid enough to wear a shirt with his own name on, so I can't possibly be Robin Hood.'

'Your genius knows no bounds,' Marion said, rolling her eyes. 'I'll bet any money Emma makes you take that off the second she gets here.'

Robin headed out onto the balcony to enjoy the delta view one last time. Diogo sat on the swinging sofa with Napua's head in his lap and broke into a booming laugh when he saw Robin's shirt.

'Did you ever get to twenty muscle-ups?' he asked.

Robin held the tips of his thumb and index finger a tiny bit apart. 'Nineteen yesterday. But I'm gonna get a chin-up bar in my den at Designer Outlets. So next time I come here, I'll be able to do at least fifty.'

Diogo raised his eyebrows. 'Who says you're invited back?'

'Won't you send an invite when you two get married?' Robin teased.

'You keep safe at Porthowell later,' Napua said firmly, as she rolled off Diogo and stood up to give Robin a goodbye hug.

'I'm *always* highly responsible,' Robin said, unable to smudge the tear rolling down his cheek because his arms were around Napua. 'And I've only got one thing to blow up on tonight's mission.'

'Robin's blubbing,' Diogo yelled inside to Marion. 'Get out here and do the thing where you say something sarcastic.'

But Marion felt sad too, hugging Napua, then crouching down to rap *Water Rat*'s plastic hull with her knuckles.

'I'll miss our trips on this mad thing,' she told Diogo.

A couple of minutes later, Emma blasted the horn of a big double-cab pickup truck. Neo got out from the passenger side and laughed when he saw Robin come up the beach in his *Robin Hood Lives* shirt.

'Very funny, now go change it,' Emma said, snapping fingers.

'Told you,' Marion sang.

Neo loaded their bags onto the pickup bed while Robin stripped off.

'I set up a remote server so anyone can see what's going on inside the shoe factory,' Robin told Emma, as his head popped through a polo shirt. 'Did you get the link and password I sent?'

'It works great,' Emma said, nodding. 'I already passed the link on to Lynn Hoapili and Oluchi. They're bringing a senior camera operators from Channel Fourteen too this time, so we should get good footage.'

'The more proof we get, the harder it is for government and CIS to spin our story into something it isn't,' Neo added.

'Did you show the factory footage to Srihari at the reception centre?' Marion asked, as she opened one of the pickup's rear doors.

Emma nodded. 'Of course. She watched hours of footage. She eventually spotted Bejo's mum walking to the workshop to start a shift.'

Marion smiled. 'I wonder how Bejo will react when he sees her.'

Neo sounded wary as he got back in the front passenger seat. 'There are fifty things that could go wrong between now and then.'

'It's a good plan. I feel confident,' Robin said, as he slid into the rear seat next to Marion.

They both looked out of the back window as Emma started the engine. Napua stood on the jetty waving as they pulled away from The Station for the last time. Diogo gave Napua a quick kiss before straddling his big Harley Davidson and rolling out behind the pickup.

'The Station's cool,' Marion said, as Diogo opened his throttle and accelerated past the pickup in a blaze of noise and pollution.

'Summer's been fun,' Robin agreed as he smiled at Marion. 'And now, the thrilling finale!'

# 34. AWARD-WINNING TOILETS

'Bullcalf has been sniffing around,' Emma reminded Robin, as the pickup neared Boston. 'Don't go wandering off.'

The peaceful seafront village was in a state of shock. Thirty Harley Davidson motorbikes were parked in front of the shops. A line of hairy men wearing the colours of Brigands Motorcycle Club stood eating outside the chip shop, their filthy black boots crunching around in smashed beer bottles.

The tide was way out and three bikers were blasting across open sand in a race, while another group peed against the sea wall.

'Dad!' Marion yelled, as she jumped out of the pickup.

Jake Maid, usually known as Cut-Throat, was the leader of the Brigands Motorcycle Club's Sherwood Forest chapter, and even by the standards of big, scary-looking bikers, he was big and scary-looking.

'How's my best daughter,' Cut-Throat roared, gripping Marion with huge tattooed arms and sweeping her off the ground into a hug. 'Has my old pal Diogo been looking after you?'

Diogo was in the biker crowd, growling, bear-hugging and acting nothing like the gentle giant who pottered around The Station with Napua.

'One up!' one of the younger Brigands shouted.

Robin had just stepped out of the pickup, and got a rapid introduction to One Up, a drinking game that involves throwing your empty beer bottle in the air and shouting *One Up*. If you're too slow or drunk to get out of the way, you get whacked on the head.

Cut-Throat erupted as the bottle crashed onto the pavement in front of him. 'Luke, if you throw another bottle near my daughter, you'll find out where my nickname comes from! Get over here!'

Luke was in his late teens and had the word 'Prospect' beneath the Brigands logo on the back of his denim jacket. Before becoming a full Brigands member, prospects have to spend two years getting ordered around and doing nasty jobs like cleaning toilets and polishing bikes.

'I'm sorry, Cut-Throat,' Luke said nervously.

'You're buying fish and chips and colas for Robin and Marion.'

'Of course, boss,' Luke said, then smiled when he noticed. 'That's Robin Hood!'

Cut-Throat glowered. 'Don't gawp, move!'

'I'd prefer Fanta,' Robin said, as Luke backed up and went straight to the front of the queue because he was following Cut-Throat's orders.

'So, Robin Hood!' Cut-Throat said menacingly, as he swooped down in front of the teen. 'What's going on between you and my daughter?'

Robin didn't look worried and Marion tutted.

'Dad, you make the *same* joke every time you see him.'

'Do I?' Cut-Throat said, then broke into a monstrous laugh as he hugged Emma. 'Long time no see, girl!'

'Thanks for helping out at such short notice,' Emma said. 'I can't trust the cops, and Delta Rescue doesn't have the muscle to pull those women out.'

'Helping refugees ain't exactly our thing,' Cut-Throat said, rubbing his hands. 'But the club is flat broke, and we'll make a bundle selling those knock-off shoes.'

'They're not refugees, Dad,' Marion said. 'Refugees come to a country willingly, trying to find a better life. These women were kidnapped. They'll want to go back to their families in Indonesia or wherever.'

'Believe that when I see it,' Cut-Throat grunted, as Luke came back outside with Robin and Marion's food.

'Can I get a selfie with Robin?' Luke asked.

'You'll get my boot up your arse in a minute, prospect,' Cut-Throat growled. 'Buzz off!'

'We have award-winning toilets, you know!' an elderly woman shouted from the pavement as Robin tucked into his chips. 'You should be ashamed. Grown men smashing glass and urinating on the seafront.'

'Don't worry, ma'am,' Cut-Throat told her, as he stole one of Marion's chips. 'I'll get young Luke to make sure everything is left spotless.'

Robin felt pity as the older Brigands jeered, slapped Luke on the back and mashed chips into the pavement, knowing he'd have to clean them up.

'So barbaric,' Marion said, shaking her head.

'We all did our time as prospects,' Cut-Throat said. 'If you want to be a Brigand, you have to suffer for a couple of years. You're just sour because girls can't join in.'

Marion filled her mouth so she didn't have to answer. She hated that her dad's gang were a bunch of violent, boozed-up, sexist lunatics, but loved the motorbikes and the way Brigands took no nonsense from anyone.

'You want to race?' Diogo shouted to one of the Brigands. 'I'll race you on the beach, right here, right now!'

'He's acting like a big kid,' Robin said, looking at Marion and laughing as Diogo sprinted to his bike.

Marion nodded. 'He'd never act like that in front of Napua.'

'One up!' someone shouted, as another bottle got lobbed into the air.

# 35. DEATH STAR STUFF

As Luke and another prospect borrowed brooms from the chippy and swept up broken glass, Emma led the rest of the Brigands on a rowdy march to the church hall.

Lynn Hoapili and her two camera operators were waiting inside, plus some members of the New Survivors, who'd agreed to provide buses to transport the women to Delta Rescue's welcome centre on the edge of Sherwood Forest.

Stacking chairs had been put out in rows, and Neo had set up a little video projector. This could show either a live feed from the shoe-factory cameras, or a detailed floor plan that Neo had drawn up based on the footage.

The Brigands stayed loud and tried to bait the New Survivors, first by taking the mickey out of their short hair and green polo shirts, then by suggesting that they secretly planned to kidnap and brainwash any women they rescued.

The New Survivors remained calm. They offered the Brigands leaflets and asked if they'd considered their relationship with God and would like to hear the good news about eternal life.

'I don't want to go to heaven,' one Brigand shouted. 'That's where all the boring people end up!'

The Brigands quietened down when Cut-Throat told them that anyone who didn't shut up would lose their cut of the money from selling the shoes.

'Thank you all for being here,' Emma began. 'This plan has come together in less than three days and I want to thank everyone for the work you've put in.

'After studying the video feed, we estimate there are one hundred and ninety-five women being held captive in a former chemical-storage bunker.

'At any one time there are fifteen guards in the building. Most seem to live onsite, but in better conditions than their prisoners. Guards only seem to carry batons, though there is a gun locker in the guards' break room. Therefore, our first job upon entering the building will be to secure this room before the guards can tool up.

'Of course, we have to get inside the building first. This is tricky because it was originally constructed as a storage facility for volatile chemicals. It has thick walls, few windows and airtight metal doors, along with a reinforced roof and sloping grass embankments designed to deflect any blast up and away.'

'I'm in *Star Wars*,' one of the Brigands joked. 'You know, briefing the rebel pilots before they fly off to nuke the Death Star?'

A few people laughed. 'You're sure not Luke Skywalker,' another Brigand said.

'No, he's the alien with the head shaped like a turd.'

'Let Emma speak, you cretins,' Cut-Throat roared, close to losing his temper. 'Do I need to remind you how much we need this money?'

Another Brigand shot up from his chair and lost his cool with Cut-Throat. 'Yeah, because your idiot son Flash ripped us off.'

Cut-Throat's chair flew backwards as he stood up and ripped out the machete hooked to his belt. 'I told you never to mention that boy's name!'

'Dad, no,' Marion yelled, desperately grabbing Cut-Throat's arm, and getting dragged across the room behind him.

Emma wondered if partnering up with a bike gang had been a good idea, as Diogo wedged himself between Cut-Throat and the Brigand who'd dared to mention Flash.

'There'll be plenty of time to stab each other tomorrow,' Diogo urged. 'Right now we need to sit still and listen.'

Everyone settled back down, but Marion looked close to tears and Emma sounded shaken as she resumed speaking.

'Breaking into the building will be hard, so our aim is to lure as many guards as we can into the open . . .'

As Emma got back into her stride, Diogo's phone pinged. He leaned across to Robin and whispered, 'Our toys have arrived.'

Diogo and Robin stepped out into the sun, followed by Marion.

'Did we invite you?' Robin asked.

'I read the briefing already,' Marion said. 'And my dad makes me *so* mad sometimes.'

Brigands prospect Luke jogged up to the side of the church hall, holding a padded envelope with orange hazard tape wrapped around it.

'Guy in the chip shop said you'd want it straight away,' he said breathlessly.

'Good lad,' Diogo answered, then gave the prospect a slap on the back.

Diogo ripped the package open and let Robin peek inside at four M112 demolition blocks. They looked like sticks of black Play-Doh, but were actually a mouldable explosive, typically used in mining and demolition. There was also a clear bag filled with peanut-sized impact fuse detonators.

'How did you get this stuff?' Marion asked.

'I've been smuggling in this delta for years,' Diogo explained. 'I know folks who'll get you anything, from a bazooka to a baby baboon.'

'I'll need to test it,' Robin said. 'When you add weight to an arrow you have to change your aim.'

'The beach?' Marion suggested.

Diogo shook his head. 'Way too public. We'll head up to the shops at the end of Sunshine Road.'

'Good idea,' Robin said. 'We used to park our dirt bikes there when we came into the village.'

'Before you so cruelly confiscated them,' Marion added.

It took ten minutes to get Robin's bow and arrows from Emma's truck and walk a kilometre uphill to the gravel parking lot behind the boarded-up supermarket and souvenir store. Diogo squinted as he propped his bum on a ledge, reading a sheet of instructions with tiny print.

'The impact fuse must be inserted into the explosive at the point of impact and will trigger upon a decelerative force greater than 5G,' Diogo said. 'Explosive power is 1.352 kWh per gram.'

'What does that mean?' Marion asked.

'No idea,' Diogo admitted.

'We're not that far from the village,' Marion said warily. 'What if someone hears?'

'I'll start with a bit the size of a pea,' Robin said. 'If it's not enough we'll do a bigger one.'

'Sounds good,' Diogo agreed, then tried to soothe Marion's worries. 'With the Brigands in town, nobody in Boston will worry about a little bang up here.'

It took Robin a minute to cut a slice off one M112 and mould the plastic explosive around the tip of a carbon-fibre arrow. He wasn't sure the tiny detonator would stay in place if he just pushed it into the soft explosive, so used some of the tape he carried for sticking up targets to hold it in place.

'Will that blow up if you drop it?' Marion asked.

Robin hadn't considered this and eyed his explosive arrow warily.

'It should only detonate if it slams something hard,' Diogo said. 'But probably best not to find out.'

'Aren't explosives the kind of thing you should only mess with when you know *exactly* what you're doing?' Marion said.

'I have to check my aim,' Robin answered irritably. 'We're driving up to Porthowell as soon as Emma's briefing ends.'

'You could practise shots with the explosive but without the detonator,' Marion suggested.

'I just used a tiny blob,' Robin said as he notched his arrow. 'I'm gonna aim for that big tree to the right of the supermarket.'

Robin lined up the arrow as if he was shooting normally, then nosed up a few degrees because the added weight would make the arrow pitch downwards.

'Might be a bit loud,' Robin said, then let the arrow go.

Robin aimed to hit the tree at head height, but the arrow dipped faster than expected. The blast knocked the three of them backwards in a hail of gravel as a huge orange fireball shot up through the tree, charring leaves.

They shielded their faces from heat, dust and clumps of earth as birds launched and squawked.

'That wasn't bad,' Robin said, coughing a couple of times as he walked up to inspect the damaged trunk. 'That's enough explosive. I'll shoot a couple more without the detonator to get my aim right.'

Robin got a strong smell of burning as he closed on a trunk that had been blasted to less than half of its original width. Then he heard branches rustling overhead and realised the top of the tree was listing sideways.

'Bloody hell!' he shouted, as he spun around. 'It's coming down!'

After creaking while its upper branches got tangled in a neighbouring tree, the trunk picked up momentum as Robin bolted.

He slowed down when he realised the enormous trunk wasn't going to hit him. But his relief was tempered seconds later, when the top of the tree smashed down on the supermarket building's flat roof, demolishing a side wall, shattering the boarded-up windows and showering him with glass, screws and chunks of chipboard.

He dived into the parking-lot gravel and covered his head with his arms, then rolled onto his back and found himself in the dappled light beneath swaying branches. An intruder alarm made woo-woo noises from what was left of the building as Diogo yanked Robin up.

'You OK?'

'Just about,' Robin said.

'We'd better get out of here,' Diogo said warily.

Marion looked furious. 'I love you guys,' she shouted, as they grabbed their gear and started to run. 'But at times you two are so dumb I don't know how you manage to walk upright.'

# 36. LITTLE OL' CONVOY

The Brigands blasted their bikes along the sunny delta coastline, Marion on the back of her dad's Harley, Robin declining Diogo's offer of a ride along and spending the eighty-minute drive playing with his phone in the comfort of Emma's pickup.

At the rear of the convoy were a Channel Fourteen news van and three green double-decker buses with **GOOD NEWS FROM THE NEW SURVIVORS** painted along their sides. When everyone stopped for petrol and snacks, the sun was getting low and six more Brigands joined, driving a fleet of hired trucks.

While they all stood around scoffing petrol-station junk food, a couple of the Brigands got selfies with Robin. Then Robin put his *Robin Hood Lives* T-shirt back on and got some of the guys to take pictures of him sitting astride one of the big Harleys.

'Robin, can I ask some questions for my report?' Lynn Hoapili asked.

Her two camera operators loved the shot of Robin astride the bike, but the Brigands jeered and took the mickey when Lynn dabbed foundation on his forehead.

'It's to cut the reflections with the low sun,' Lynn explained, before telling the camera operator to start rolling and asking her first proper question.

'Robin Hood, six months ago you were an ordinary pupil at Locksley High School. Now you're an internationally famous outlaw. Some people say you're a hero, some think you're a menace. What is your message to them?'

'I'm just me,' Robin said, struggling to keep a straight face and ignore Marion and several Brigands standing behind the camera doing chicken walks and dickhead gestures. 'I didn't ask for all this.'

'But do you have a message?' Lynn asked again.

'I guess my message is that the world would be better if everyone stuck up for what they believe in,' Robin said, then smirked. 'Also, I want royalties on all this Robin Hood merch people are selling.'

Lynn laughed politely.

'Now, you've drawn together several disparate groups for a bold rescue operation. But you're already wanted for a number of serious crimes. Does the thought of being captured and spending years, even decades, in jail worry you?'

Robin shrugged. 'First off, people way more organised than me pulled this together. Second, I don't plan on getting caught any time soon. Third, I've got so much stuff on my rap sheet now, it doesn't matter what else I do. I mean, the bad guys can only kill me once, right?'

When Robin said this, all of the Brigands cheered loudly in the background.

'So you feel invincible?' Lynn asked.

'No . . .' Robin said warily. 'I . . .'

He was partly thrown off by the question, but mostly because the Indonesian teenager Srihari had moved up beside the camera operator and reached out, holding . . .

'And who is this little guy?' Lynn cooed, as Robin got handed a baby wearing a striped romper suit and a little Brigands M.C. baseball cap.

'Who set me up?' Robin gasped, as Bejo settled astride his leg.

The baby didn't make a fuss and seemed fascinated by reflections in the bike's chrome handlebars. Marion laughed and even thuggish Brigands made *ahh* noises.

'I'm not exactly used to holding babies,' Robin said nervously.

'But he's part of the reason you're here,' Lynn said. 'Tell us how you met him.'

Robin was surprised by how warm the baby felt on his leg.

'So, this is Bejo,' Robin said. 'Me and my bestie helped rescue him from thugs and corrupt CIS agents a couple of weeks ago. His mother was brought here from Indonesia against her will. She's being held near here, forced to work in slave conditions making trainers. And we're about to try and get her out.'

Another huge cheer erupted, startling the baby.

Lynn nodded, then sounded extra solemn for the camera. 'But shouldn't you have called the police and left this very serious matter to them?'

'Recent events have taught me not to trust cops,' Robin said, as Bejo lurched forward like he was trying to get away. 'And we definitely don't trust Customs and Immigration.'

'Robin Hood, thank you!' Lynn said, then turned to the camera operator and made a cut gesture.

'I didn't know you were here,' Robin said, smiling as Srihari reached in and took Bejo back.

'Just now,' Srihari answered. 'To help translate.'

Robin turned to Lynn. 'Did you arrange to have her hand Bejo to me?'

'Your expression was gold!' Marion said in the background.

Lynn smiled mischievously. 'I'm a journalist, Robin. If I put out a grim report about poor Indonesian women forced to work as slaves in a shoe factory, people will reach for the remote. But a story about Robin Hood reuniting an adorable baby with his mommy will be the biggest thing ever.'

# 37. ROLL UP, ROLL UP

Emma felt more like a travelling circus ringmaster than the organiser of a covert rescue operation. But while the convoy of bikers, buses and a TV van sparked the curiosity of anyone who saw it, their intent wasn't obvious and everyone had orders to keep off social media.

Brigands ran their bikes without mufflers to make them roar, but thirty deafeningly loud bikes are useless for sneaking around, so they parked half a kilometre from Porthowell and piled into the back of a container truck along with Marion and Robin.

Last to board the truck were Tara and Hannah, two members of a New Survivors security team, wearing tactical vests that bulged with weapons.

Robin was sweating because he'd been given a military helmet and bulletproof vest. As the truck's rear doors slammed, plunging everyone into darkness and body odour, he wondered when some of the Brigands had last washed.

'Who farted?' someone joked as the truck started a wobbly ride.

There was no view out as they rode past the giant Two Tu warehouse complex, through a break in the fence around the abandoned part of the Porthowell chemical plant, then a bumpy final stretch over the torn-up railway sidings.

Emma, Neo, Srihari and the TV crew had driven ahead. As Robin and Marion jumped out into the day's final rays of sunlight, Cut-Throat told his men to squat out of sight behind the truck bed, put their phones on silent and keep the noise down.

'Team one, ready?' Emma asked sharply.

Robin stepped up to Emma, along with the two New Survivors.

Tara and Hannah's camouflage, body armour and holstered handguns contrasted with the gentle manner and green polo shirts of the New Survivors back at Boston church hall. The fierce-looking pair made Robin uneasy, reminding him what Marion had said about the cult's giant underground compound and the rumours that they brainwashed people.

Neo had a laptop set up on a rusty barrel, monitoring the live cameras inside the factory. He wasn't the greatest with computers, so he made sure Robin looked on as he logged into the factory's computer network and disabled the eight outdoor cameras.

Now that the factory guards couldn't see out, Robin grabbed his arrows, checked his walkie-talkie and followed Tara and Hannah through the fence near the bins.

Hannah gave him a boost onto the rooftop as Tara rolled a wheelie bin up to the wall. The women then used the bin as a step to climb onto the gently sloping roof and sat on a concrete beam directly above the black metal exit door.

Two days observing the factory's comings and goings had revealed that this door was used more frequently than the main entrance around the front. Sometimes it was for a guard to smoke, but Neo was watching a larger group on the laptop feed.

'Coming your way,' he warned over the radio. 'Three women, sandwiched by guards.'

Robin, Hannah and Tara heard the door's hinges squeal. A guard led the way, then the three women. They were scruffy, barefoot and each struggled to push a huge wheelie bin filled with factory waste. Last out was another guard, who jabbed the third woman with his baton and growled something sinister.

As the three bins rattled over the rough pavement, this second guard stayed by the door and took a cigarette from his top pocket. Tara leaped down and coshed him across the back of the head. Robin kept an arrow locked on the first guard in case he tried to run, but Hannah tackled him, taking him down before he knew she was coming.

Robin watched from the roof as the three enslaved workers froze in shock and several Brigands came in through the fence, along with Srihari.

'Please keep quiet,' Srihari whispered in Indonesian, as she pointed to the fence. 'We're here to help you. Come this way, quickly!'

As the three women stared nervously, four Brigands dealt with the flattened guards. Emma had instructed them to restrain guards with plastic zip ties and take them away with a minimum of fuss. But the Brigands couldn't resist swinging their boots as Tara reached in to snatch a big bunch of keys hooked to one guard's belt.

# 38. THE BIG BOSS

Hannah and Tara's next task was to move stealthily through the factory building, entering the guards' break room and securing the gun locker. As the pair strode through the black door, Robin sprinted across the factory roof.

The plan called for Robin to do this alone, but as he began a hundred-metre dash, hurdling the thick concrete support beams, he saw Channel Fourteen intern Oluchi giving chase with her shoulder-mount camera.

The squat building had been built to store dangerous chemicals, so cooling, heating, and other systems that might start a fire if they went wrong were located in a separate utility building.

Robin went down on one knee, looking from the edge of the roof across a steep grass embankment and three rows of parking spaces towards the utility building. This was a perfect metal-sided cube, apart from three big chimney ducts rising out of one end.

'Hood in position,' Robin told his radio.

'Let me confirm,' Neo answered, as he stood outside the compound flicking through the camera feeds. 'Hanna and Tara have the break-room weapons secured. You're free to shoot.'

'Nice,' Robin said, then looked back at Oluchi, who'd crept up close with the camera. 'Keep low if you don't want your eyebrows singed.'

Robin had only shot one practice arrow, so he'd fixed explosives and detonators to three more, giving him extra shots if he missed. He used the same routine as earlier, lining up his shot on a metal cooling vent. Since his shot at the tree had gone low, he made a larger upwards correction so that the dangerous end almost pointed at an emerging moon.

As Robin let go, he thought the shot might skim clean over the target building. But it lost height rapidly and vanished into gloom. As Robin had the horrible thought that he might have to use the second arrow without even knowing where the first one went, he heard a deep thud.

With as much luck as skill, Robin had hit his target. The building had muffled the explosion but the metal wall bulged out, and dense grey smoke began spewing from one of the chimneys.

'I think I got it,' Robin told his radio.

'I'm in the guards' break room,' Hannah replied. 'We're on emergency lighting, all the machinery has stopped.'

'Camera feeds are down too,' Neo added. 'Looks like you've done it.'

Robin and Oluchi peered over the edge of the roof as the building's main entrance swung open. A guard and an engineer with a toolbox strode purposefully up the steep grass embankment towards the plant building to see why the power had failed.

They stopped walking when they saw the billowing smoke, then got scared as a swarm of Brigands spilled from behind a low wall at the end of the parking lot and began a charge down the embankment towards the main entrance.

Oluchi filmed as several confused women wandered out through a side door, while Brigands poured in.

'They felt that!' Robin said, as Cut-Throat sent the guard and engineer rolling down the embankment with an enormous double headbutt.

As the remaining guards got dragged outside by Brigands, they were thrown down, frisked for weapons, then made to lie face down as their wrists and ankles were bound tightly with plastic zip ties.

The Brigands weren't about to win any awards for gentle handling of prisoners, but were pussycats compared to some of the freed women, who picked up batons stripped from their former captors and used them to settle scores.

After a hefty chain was snapped with bolt cutters, a gate swung open and the four green buses rolled into the car park. Srihari and two of the women they'd rescued by the bins were shouting frantically in Indonesian, encouraging the nervous barefoot women to board.

A lot of the freed workers were confused, maybe because bikers don't fit most people's image of what good guys are supposed to look like. New Survivors who'd stepped from the buses in their neat green polo shirts did a better job, by holding up laminated cards printed in Indonesian:

> **We are here to help.**
> **Please board our buses**
> **quickly and quietly.**

'Check that,' Oluchi said, nudging Robin's arm and pointing down.

Robin peered down over the front of the building at suit trousers and polished shoes dangling from an upper-floor window. A small, grey-haired man in a suit jumped five metres. He landed awkwardly, then grabbed a briefcase he'd thrown out first.

The man's knee kept buckling as he limped up the grass embankment. Robin recognised him as the guy with designer luggage he'd seen get off the trawler at Landing Dock Y.

'I bet he's the boss,' Robin said, as he realised that nobody down below had spotted him.

'Wait,' Oluchi said, as Robin scrambled off along the roof.

While it had been easy to climb up the side of the building, here at the front the drop was fifteen metres. So Robin ran across the roof until he saw a drainpipe, then swung out over the side and mixed clambering and sliding to get down.

Robin lost sight of the limping man as he ran up the steep embankment, but when he got to the top he sighted him at the far side of the car park, heading for the water treatment ponds and Porthowell Dock beyond.

Robin thought about shooting an arrow as the man clanked up steps onto a metal observation gantry that spanned one of the empty concrete pools.

Fortunately he didn't have to. It was almost dark now and scrappers had stolen a circular manhole cover from the middle of the walkway. When the man's front foot went through the hole, his forward momentum saved him from a ten-metre drop, but in doing so he banged his already weakened knee, then face-planted into the walkway, bursting his nose.

As Robin closed warily, in case the man had a weapon, he heard someone running behind and saw Luke, the teenaged Brigands prospect.

'I saw you chase him,' Luke said, slightly breathless. 'You OK?'

'Pretty sure he knocked himself out,' Robin said, pulling a torch from his pack and shining it along the gantry at the slumped figure.

Emma's orders were to tie up anyone they caught and hope the cops did something more than set them free when they were found. The Brigands had been given heavy-duty zip ties to do this, though before Luke bound the unconscious man's wrist to the gantry railing, he stripped a gold Rolex watch.

Robin was more interested in what the man had chosen to stuff in his briefcase before fleeing. Popping the lid revealed a half-eaten bag of Pickled Onion Monster Munch, a swanky miniature laptop, some papers that looked like they'd been flung in hastily and a fat brick of £100 notes in an elastic band.

'I'll give the case to Emma,' Robin said, as Luke extracted a wallet from inside the man's jacket. 'Could be evidence. For all we know, there are loads of factories like this.'

Luke's eyes were locked on the money. 'We're not giving her that,' he said firmly.

Robin had seen how much abuse Luke took from the older Brigands and thought he deserved a break.

'Our little secret,' he said, splitting the money into two and passing the slightly smaller half to Luke. 'Sixty–forty in my favour, since you got the watch.'

# 39. HOLD THE BABY

While Robin dealt with the businessman, Lynn, who had lost both camera operators in the chaos, struggled to make her report, Emma was desperate to get the women away from Porthowell before cops or CIS showed up, and Cut-Throat wanted the four buses to clear out so he could bring in trucks and start loading thousands of pairs of knock-off trainers from the warehouse.

Srihari spotted Bejo's mum heading towards a bus. As the two young women shared a tearful hug, Marion snatched up a snoozing Bejo from Emma's pickup and jogged across the car park towards them.

'I need that on camera!' Lynn screamed when she saw what was about to happen. 'Steve, Oluchi, where are you? Marion, can you please hold back the baby reunion for five seconds?'

But nothing was going to stop Bejo's mum when she saw her baby, so Lynn scrambled to capture the moment with her phone.

Bejo was moody after being woken up and, as his mum scooped him up for kisses, the eight-month-old furrowed his brow crossly, as if to say, *Where did you run off to?*

'I hate to spoil this party,' Emma said, approaching as the first busload of women pulled off in the background. 'But double-deckers won't outrun cop cars, so we have to clear out of here.'

Robin and Luke jogged towards the gathering, though Luke kept going because he needed to help the Brigands.

'Where have you been?' Marion asked suspiciously.

'We cuffed a guy to a gantry over a pond,' Robin explained, slightly breathless. 'He's the boss, I think. Emma, I've put his ID and briefcase in the back of your pickup. There's a laptop and phone. I can probably get information off them when I have time.'

'Good work,' Emma said.

As Srihari, Bejo and his mum headed tearfully towards the last bus, Hannah and Tara approached.

'Great work in the guard room,' Marion told the security officers. 'We were watching on camera when you splattered the three guards.'

'Cheers,' Tara said, then looked at Emma. 'Some of the women speak English. They're saying they've got things in their dorm. Clothes, medication, wedding rings.'

'A lot of the women are also saying that their children were taken away when they arrived,' Hannah added.

Emma sounded stressed. 'Missing kids, more slaves in more factories, corrupt CIS officers. Who knows how big this scandal could get?'

'Some of us New Survivors would like to go down to the women's dorms and gather their personal items,' Tara said. 'I'd also like to smash some of the expensive factory equipment so they can't set up another factory.'

'Happy to help,' Robin suggested, as Marion nodded in agreement.

'If I ever find my camera people, I'd like to film inside the factory too,' Lynn said, glancing about.

'I *must* leave with Neo now,' Emma said. 'I've got extra volunteers but it's going to be chaos when two hundred women turn up at a welcome centre designed to handle twenty at most. You adults can do whatever you think best, but remember, cops could arrive at any time. Robin and Marion, you're travelling back to Sherwood with Cut-Throat, yes?'

Marion nodded. 'We'll spend the night there, and my dad'll take us back to Designer Outlets tomorrow.'

'But you've got our luggage in the pickup,' Robin said. 'We can't carry all that on bikes.'

'You might have to wait a few days, but you'll get your stuff,' Emma said. 'And I'll go remind Cut-Throat not to leave without you.'

'I'm his daughter,' Marion said indignantly. 'He'd better not.'

'Ten minutes inside the factory,' Emma warned as Robin and Marion ran off. 'Don't get left behind!'

# 40. PACKING UP AND MOVING OUT

After watching the factory through security cameras, Robin felt weird seeing it for real. It had seemed clean and well lit, but as Oluchi filmed him walking along a corridor with dim orange emergency lighting, Robin was struck by fierce heat and a throat-burning stench from glues and chemicals that weren't properly ventilated.

Robin worked out where he'd seen the boss man go out the window and found an office with three desks and laptops.

'If I took this, could you get it working for me?' Marion asked, as she eyed a laptop. 'My computer is older than I am.'

'I could sort you out for a modest fee,' Robin said cheekily.

She put the slim laptop in her bag and another for her family. There were shelves full of files. Some might have valuable evidence on CIS corruption and how the factory operation worked, but they faced a long trek through

Sherwood Forest to get back to Designer Outlets, and now Emma and the pickup were gone, they'd have to carry anything they took.

They walked down steps to the factory floor. Oluchi broke away to film machinist tables with half-finished shoe uppers that women had been working on as the Brigands stormed in.

Tara had crawled under a laser cutter designed to turn leather hides or vinyl into shoe parts and was using her stun stick to fry the circuit boards. Hannah took a more athletic approach, battering the control panel of a bonding machine with a fire extinguisher.

'These lights are on battery back-up,' Robin warned them. 'I doubt they'll last much longer.'

The last stop on Robin and Marion's tour was the women's dorm. Three New Survivors swept efficiently through a space that reeked of sweat, waving torches, lifting mattresses and dropping personal items into plastic tubs.

Robin couldn't walk between the triple bunks without turning sideways and he could barely imagine what it must have been like packed with women, who used the bunks in shifts while the rest worked.

'Do you need help?' Marion asked.

'We're good,' one of the New Survivors said. 'Almost finished.'

A rat jumped off a counter as Robin and Marion crossed a dining area with half-eaten plates of rice on the tables.

'This place is depressing,' Robin said. 'If nobody needs our help, we might as well get out of here.'

'I wonder how long some of them were stuck here,' Marion said.

'The computer network was installed four years ago,' Robin said, as he started up a flight of stairs. 'So it could be as long as that.'

There was a happier scene as Robin and Marion pushed through a fire door at the top of the stairs, exiting into a huge warehouse space with long rows of metal racking.

Moonlight shone through open shutters at the far end and, considering their alcohol intake and dislike for rules, the Brigands were making a surprisingly efficient job of loading boxes of shoes into the trucks outside.

A couple of them had warehouse experience and expertly used forklifts to pick pallets of shoes from the higher shelves. The rest of the Brigands worked the lower shelves and piled shoes onto trolleys and wheeled them to the trucks by hand.

'I bet they haven't got any in my size,' Marion joked.

'My trainers are all knackered, but I've got enough to carry,' Robin said, as his eye caught a shelf stacked with rolls of fake clothing tabs and clear tubs filled with embroidered designer logos. 'Didn't realise they made these here.'

Marion dropped three small pots into her bag. 'I can sew these on everything,' she joked. 'Even my crustiest undies are gonna have designer labels.'

Robin laughed. 'Your brother Matt's crew are into branded gear. You could probably sell them to them.'

They almost got mown down by Diogo pushing a powered handcart as they headed between shelving stacks towards the open shutters up front.

'Sorry! I can't see over all the boxes,' Diogo explained. 'If you're going to find Cut-Throat, tell him the last truck should be loaded in ten minutes.'

One truck was already leaving as they stepped outside. Cut-Throat was ending a call and looked the happiest Robin had ever seen him as Marion relayed Diogo's message.

'There's three times more gear than we can fit in the trucks,' he said cheerfully. 'And the quality is great. Only an expert could tell this stuff from originals.'

'Any sign of cops or CIS?' Robin asked.

'Not a squeak so far,' Cut-Throat said. 'I've got lookouts all over.'

'We're in the middle of nowhere,' Marion pointed out. 'We wandered around for forty minutes before spotting this place.'

'Six trucks, seven thousand pairs per truck,' Cut-Throat calculated. 'Fifteen pounds a pair from the wholesaler Diogo knows . . .'

'Only fifteen?' Marion said. 'Aren't these brands like a hundred in the shops?'

'You'll be lucky to get twenty per cent of retail price for stolen gear,' Cut-Throat explained. 'But it's still six hundred thousand for the gang. As leader, my whack is over fifty.'

'Did I mention you're the best daddy in the whole wide world?' Marion said, looking up with her huge blue eyes, trying not to smirk. 'You'll receive my list of gift suggestions shortly.'

# 41. ROADSIDE LEAK

Convoys are conspicuous, so each truck left as soon as it was full. With the New Survivor buses long gone and still no sign of cops, Cut-Throat told Robin and Marion to grab the passenger seats on the fourth truck.

A silver-haired Brigand named Zoot plugged his phone in to play Johnny Cash tunes as he drove west through a drizzly night. Robin slumped against the passenger side door and watched the road markings blur as he nodded off. Marion was in the middle seat and fell asleep nestled against him.

Neither of them saw the sign that said:

> You Are Now Leaving Delta Country
> Drive Safe & Come Back Soon

But Robin and Marion knew they were back in Sherwood Forest when Zoot woke them up. It was pitch dark and the truck had stopped in the front courtyard of a storage unit off Old Road, the deserted highway that had been Sherwood's main north–south route until Route 24 opened.

Robin saw 02.33 on the truck's dashboard clock as he blinked tired eyes. His mouth was dry and there was something weird on his tongue, which disappeared when Marion moved.

'You chewed my hair!' Marion complained. 'Gross!'

'You're gross,' Robin shot back. 'Falling asleep with your grubby hair over my face.'

'End of the line, kiddos,' Zoot said.

'Eh?' Marion said, yawning.

'Truck's unloading here,' Zoot explained. 'Looks like it'll be a while. Then I gotta take this lump back to the truck hire place and pick up my Harley.'

Robin saw they were in a line of trucks waiting to get unloaded. As he picked up his bow and pack then jumped out, a van with Two Tu branding pulled up behind.

'Looks like they blagged a couple of extras,' Marion laughed.

'I hope they killed the tracking devices,' Robin said warily. 'All big companies use them.'

'I wouldn't worry,' Marion answered. 'Some of Dad's crew have been thieving vehicles since before we were born.'

The pair walked past the trucks to a line of motorbikes. Everyone was helping to unload, apart from Diogo, Cut-Throat and an elderly woman with lots of jewellery and frizzy hair.

'I can only pay ten a pair,' the woman was saying, as Robin realised they were haggling over the price of the extra shoes in the Two Tu vans. 'With this kind of quantity, I can't get the same price.'

'How about we split the difference?' Diogo said. 'Twelve fifty?'

The woman was mulling this when she saw Robin and Marion and turned into an over-attentive grandma.

'I know this little guy!' she announced warmly. 'Are you cold, sweetie? Do you need the bathroom? There's a machine for hot drinks and banana bread if you're hungry.'

'I could use the toilet,' Marion said, stifling a yawn. 'Thank you.'

'Old Road is flooded south of here,' Cut-Throat told the kids. 'But we contacted Will Scarlock. With the water so high from the rains, he's sending a boat to pick you up.'

'Seriously?' Robin said, grinning because a boat ride was a million times better than a two-hour trek through the forest.

'I can sleep in my own bed,' Marion said happily, then looked at Diogo. 'Not that there's anything wrong with the one at The Station.'

Cut-Throat checked the time on his phone. 'We're only a ten-minute ride from the river, and your boat won't get here for a couple of hours. You two can sit inside and chill.'

Price negotiations resumed as Robin and Marion stepped into the warehouse, weaving between guys carrying shoeboxes.

'There's no other stock here,' Marion noted, as they headed for a rest area at the back with plastic tables and a broken vending machine. 'I guess the buyer will move the shoes straight on somewhere else.'

Robin laughed. 'Would you trust the Brigands not to steal them back after they get paid?'

He liked the look of the banana cake sat under a flyproof dome on the table, but his hands were black from crawling around the factory roof, so he decided to wash them before eating. Marion followed the toilet sign into a corridor and Robin followed her.

The bathroom was cramped, with one cubicle and a tiny sink. As Marion locked herself in the stall, Robin rested his bow and pack against the wall and turned on a tap that spat brown water before settling down.

He had to pump several times to get soap, and as the lather on his hands turned grey, the main door swung open, hitting his bag.

'We'll be out in a tick,' Robin said as a man edged in.

It took Robin a second to realise who it was, by which time he'd been yanked powerfully into the hallway. A tattooed hand clamped over Robin's mouth and a gun was pushed into his cheek.

'Gotcha!' Dino Bullcalf said.

# 42. ONE GOES BANG

The toilet flushed as Marion stepped out of the stall.

*Idiot left the tap running*, she thought, but then saw Robin's backpack and bow on the floor.

'Robin?' Marion asked curiously.

She leaned out of the door and said it louder, then saw that a fire door at the end of the corridor was ajar and thought maybe he'd gone outside to pee.

'Robin?'

It was dark and the area behind the building was a tangle, but Marion's heart sped up as she saw a path trampled through the weeds.

'I think someone got Robin,' Marion shouted as she scrambled back into the warehouse. 'Hello? Dad? They got Robin!'

Marion decided she couldn't waste time running to the front of the warehouse to raise the alarm. She stumbled back into the bathroom, grabbing Robin's bow and the four arrows sticking out the top of his backpack.

'I'm going after Robin,' she shouted, but there were blokes bantering and boxes crashing so she had no idea if anyone heard.

Following, or avoiding, tracks was a life-or-death skill in the forest and Marion had no problem following trampled plants. When she reached boggier ground there were drag marks and man-sized boot prints.

The trail of prints continued away from the building, but Marion heard a shuffling noise to her right. It seemed unlikely that any large animal would come so close when there was light and noise coming from the warehouse, and since the guy must have tracked them here by following the truck, Marion figured he'd have to move away from the warehouse before circling back towards a car parked near the road.

The branches were too dense to run, but Marion was confident in her shortcut as she walked fast. After a hundred metres she'd closed enough to sense movement among the branches ahead. Another fifty and she heard breathing as the trees thinned out.

Marion wished she was wearing proper forest gear, as her trainers flooded and branches scraped her bare arms and legs. She kept low as she neared a dark clearing with the outline of a parked car. There was a flash of orange indicator lamps as Bullcalf used a plipper to open the doors of a tiddly Honda hatchback.

Robin groaned in pain as the elderly man opened the passenger door and shoved him inside.

'Don't move a muscle, brat.'

Bullcalf kept the gun aimed at Robin as he marched around the front of the vehicle to the driver's side.

Marion was relieved to hear footsteps running behind her, but Bullcalf was already in the driver's seat. She kept low as she moved to the edge of the clearing and notched an arrow.

Marion shot as Bullcalf started the Honda's engine. The carbon arrow passed clean through the front driver's side tyre and wedged in the noise-insulating foam packed around the wheel arch.

Bullcalf didn't get what had happened, as he tried to drive but just heard the arrow shatter inside the wheel arch as the front bumper ploughed into the gravel.

'I'm over here,' Marion shouted behind her, as the footsteps got closer.

'Marion,' Cut-Throat shouted, 'is Robin with you?'

Bullcalf knew he was a sitting duck in a car that wouldn't go. He opened his door, rolled out holding a handgun and glanced about.

'Bullcalf has Robin in the car,' Marion explained, as her dad and Diogo arrived, both carrying rifles.

But the sound of two men arriving gave Marion's location away. Now Bullcalf knew where they were, he used the car as a shield while dragging Robin out of the passenger side.

'If anything moves, I'll blow Hood's brains out,' he shouted, as he backed up towards the trees.

Marion looked at her dad and whispered, 'Robin looked floppy when he put him in the car. His hands are tied and I think he's drugged or hurt.'

'I'll flank around the side,' Diogo said, then tapped Marion. 'Maybe you should back up.'

'The hell I will,' Marion said furiously as Diogo began creeping around the edge of the clearing.

'Let Robin go,' Cut-Throat said, half standing up. 'It's a big forest – you can move faster on your own.'

'Biker scum!' Bullcalf shouted, then bobbed from behind the car and took a shot that almost parted Cut-Throat's hair.

'Jesus!' Cut-Throat blurted, firing a wild shot into treetops as he fell backwards and squashed Marion in the mud beneath his enormous back.

Marion was soggy and her arm covered in the insides of a massive squashed bug as she crawled out from under her dad. She notched another arrow as Bullcalf kept backing out of the clearing with his gun to Robin's head.

Bullcalf sighted Diogo moving around the edge of the clearing and took a shot at him.

'I was the top marksman in my unit,' he warned.

Before Bullcalf could point the gun back at his head, Robin scooped a mix of gravel and mud with his tied hands and flicked it into the elderly Italian's face. Then he braced both feet against the side of the car and used it as a lever to push free.

Robin's right arm hung uselessly as he stumbled through the dirt. He kicked out at the car door behind him, hoping it would knock Bullcalf. But the old man was swift and did a backwards roll before springing up, martial-arts style.

Diogo was still stumbling after being shot at and Cut-Throat's gun was waterlogged from landing in the puddle, so it was down to Marion as Bullcalf took aim at Robin's back.

'You're worth more alive, but I'm not a greedy man,' he warned, as Robin scrambled.

Hitting a man's chest from ten metres was an easy shot, so Marion was horrified to see her arrow pitch down and wedge in the dirt between Bullcalf's feet.

She worked out what had happened a microsecond before the explosive in the arrow's tip went off. Robin was moving fast and low. He felt a searing heat up the back of his shirt and screamed in pain as the blast knocked him forward into bushes, landing on his injured arm.

With the explosion erupting between his boots, Dino Bullcalf took the full force of the blast. As the car crumpled, he got thrown eight metres into a tree, then crashed down through branches as his clothes burned and clumps of hot debris pounded him.

When Marion dared to look up, she saw the car on its side and Diogo racing across to check on Robin.

'Are you OK, pal?'

'It's just my arm,' Robin moaned, as Diogo sliced the parachute cord around his wrists with a little pocket knife. 'I think he broke it when he yanked me out of the bathroom.'

'Is Bullcalf dead?' Marion asked, as she stumbled towards the smouldering, mangled Honda behind her dad.

'His legs are over by the car and the rest of him's stuck in a tree,' Cut-Throat said, as he peered up through clearing smoke. 'So if he ain't dead, he'll be sore in the morning . . .'

# 43. NURSE DIOGO

The explosion brought twenty Brigands charging from the warehouse. Cut-Throat was already happy after pulling off the biggest score of his life, but Marion's stunt had sent him into ecstasy.

'My little girl is ruthless!' Cut-Throat boasted to anyone who'd listen. 'Barely thirteen years old and she blew the guy to smithereens!'

'Dad,' Marion said, scowling and batting his arm. 'Killing someone isn't something to be proud of.'

'Depends who you kill, in my book,' Cut-Throat roared. 'Hunting a kid for bounty money? I say death is too good for him.'

'We helped rescue two hundred slaves,' Marion said. 'That is something I'm proud of.'

'I wish someone had recorded it,' Cut-Throat said deliriously. 'Life is too good right now.'

Marion tutted as she backed away. 'I'm gonna go see how Robin is.'

While the leader of the Sherwood chapter of the Brigands Motorcycle Club enjoyed himself, Robin was in agony as Diogo carried him back to the warehouse.

'I need painkillers,' he said, trying not to cry. 'It hurts *so* much.'

A small crowd gathered as Diogo entered the little break area at the back of the warehouse, kicked two plastic dining tables together and laid Robin on top.

'Can you clench your fingers, open and closed like this?' Diogo asked, as he demonstrated the action.

Robin opened and closed his fingers as Marion dashed in.

'How's he doing?'

'Better than Bullcalf,' a Brigand in the audience joked.

'Can you raise your arm above your head?' Diogo asked.

'I can't lift it at all,' Robin said, as Diogo felt along his arm. 'Stop prodding me.'

'We won't get his shirt off over his head, and my pocket knife is blunt,' Diogo said. 'Does anyone have a sharp knife?'

Several Brigands pulled out massive zombie knives and machetes. Diogo went for a medium-sized cleaver.

Robin shuddered as Diogo used the cleaver to slice up the front of his *Robin Hood Lives* T-shirt, then cut away both sleeves.

'Maybe I should wait and see Dr Gladys back at Designer Outlets,' Robin suggested.

Diogo looked at Robin's shoulder joint now it was bare. 'Does this hurt?'

'OWWWWWWWWWWWW!' Robin bawled. 'I already told you it hurts.'

'Nothing's broken,' Diogo announced.

'How do you know?' Robin asked angrily. 'And do we need eight people watching like I'm a freak show?'

Most of the Brigands went back to unloading shoes but Diogo asked Luke to stay.

'Your shoulder popped out of its joint when Bullcalf yanked you,' Diogo explained. 'It's less serious than a broken arm, but way more painful.'

'Are you sure?' Marion asked.

'I did two years of nursing school before I took to bikes and smuggling. It takes strength to pop a shoulder back, so they always got me to do them.'

Marion grimaced. 'So you can fix it?'

'Will it hurt?' Robin added.

'Your choice,' Diogo explained. 'Put up with this pain on a bumpy two-hour boat ride back to Designer Outlets, where they'll dose you up with painkillers before fixing it. If I pop it back now, it'll hurt bad, but you'll feel better straight away.'

Robin sighed, then nodded. 'Do it.'

Diogo looked at Marion. 'Wedge something in his mouth so he can't bite through his tongue.'

Diogo looked at Luke. 'I need you to clamp your hands around Robin's chest so he doesn't move. Don't push down or you might crack his ribs.'

'Open wide, cream puff,' Marion said as she gave Robin a piece of his torn T-shirt to bite down on.

She pulled out her phone to record as he gripped the edges of the plastic table.

'Hey, you can't film,' Robin protested, but with the T-shirt stuffed in his mouth, all anyone heard was, *Mff mff marp mmm*.

'This'll teach you to break my good sunglasses,' Diogo joked. 'One, two, three.'

There was a crunching sound.

'OWWWWWWW.'

# PART V

# NEWS UPDATE

'Good morning, this is News 24 broadcasting from Capital City, with Hanlon Cardinal.

'Our top story is that Eastern Delta police are investigating after the discovery of sixteen men tied up at a disused chemical production facility in the early hours of the morning.

'Footage has been released showing activists, including Robin Hood, removing workers from the plant, which appears to have been a secret factory making counterfeit sports shoes.

'The controversial Delta Rescue group claims it liberated two hundred young women being held in slave-like conditions, and the organisation's chairperson, Emma Scarlock, claims to have proof that Customs and Immigration officers were involved in smuggling the women who worked there.

'In a statement, the CIS Commissioner for the delta region has described the claims made by Scarlock as absurd. He told News 24 that the women are illegal immigrants and that the raid was probably staged in order to steal the shoes, which have a retail value of more than five million pounds.

'We'll be bringing you updates on this rapidly developing story throughout the morning, but just in the last few minutes it has been announced that this channel will be replacing tonight's seven o'clock news hour with a special documentary.

'Hosted by our Central Region correspondent Lynn Hoapili, it will feature an exclusive face-to-face interview with Robin Hood, along with incredible insider footage from last night's alleged rescue operation.

'That special programme – *Robin Hood: What I Did on My Summer Holidays* – will be broadcast at seven this evening, right here on News 24.'

# 44. YOU CAN ONLY KILL ME ONCE

Weeks of heavy rain had changed the landscape around Sherwood Designer Outlets. As the sun rose, Robin and Marion were able to approach the abandoned mall in a little motor launch, piloted by Lyla Masri, with her sister Azeem keeping a machine gun handy in case they came under attack.

Over a hundred mall residents lined the rooftop, banging pots and cheering as Robin and Marion jumped off the boat. There were even a couple of fireworks as they waded through the shallow water that now engulfed most of the mall's enormous car parks.

Marion's mum Indio and her partner Karma stood waiting at the mall's main entrance. Marion's pain-in-the-butt brothers Matt, Otto and Finn were there too, but before Marion could say hello, Karma handed her a five-week-old bundle.

'Zack Robin,' Karma said proudly. 'Meet your big sister, Marion.'

'Hello, Zack,' Marion said, raising her newborn brother up to her face and falling instantly in love with his red face and the incredibly fine hairs dusting his tiny head. 'You can never have enough little brothers with four-letter names.'

'Did you bring us presents?' three-year-old Finn asked, as he hugged Marion's wet leg.

'That is for me to know and you to find out,' she teased.

Will Scarlock tried to hug Robin, but he backed away. 'Shoulder feels better since Diogo popped it, but no squeezing!'

So Robin shook hands with Will, Sam, Mr Khan and a few others before Marion gave him a turn with Zack.

'I'm flattered you gave him Robin as a middle name,' he told Karma.

'You're part of our family too,' Karma said.

As Robin moved closer to the entrance, people offered him a free haircut, a massage and meals in their rooftop eateries before a girl he'd not seen before took a selfie as she gave him a kiss.

'I've got you on my tummy,' Finn said, proudly showing off a kid-sized *Robin Hood Lives* shirt.

It had a cartoon Robin on a motorbike, chasing a fat policeman with arrows sticking out of his butt.

'I might get one of those myself,' Robin told Finn.

Marion tutted. 'If you get another stupid shirt with your name on, I'll burn it.'

'We can all have breakfast together if you like,' Indio suggested, as they headed inside. 'Or if you're tired, you can rest.'

'Sleep first,' Marion said. 'I don't mean to be rude, but I am *so* wiped.'

Robin nodded in agreement, as he breathed the mall's familiar muggy tang. 'I slept for an hour in a truck, that's all.'

When they got to the sports outlet store, with the Maid family's living quarters downstairs, and Robin's den on a mezzanine level at the top of a dead escalator, Marion stayed back chatting with her brothers while Robin went upstairs.

Indio had got things ready for Robin's return, with clean bedding, iced water and a fan running to clear the musty air. He glugged a big glass of water, then sat on a little sofa beside his backpack.

He wanted to put the stack of money, the last explosive arrow and the M112 demolition blocks somewhere safe, before one of Marion's little brothers got hold of them.

As he rummaged through the overstuffed bag, churning everything from water-damaged targets and his drone-killing device to the set of false teeth he'd found at Boston church hall, he noticed **Robin Hood Form 7E** written in the lining.

It made him feel nostalgic, remembering the days when he carried the backpack around Locksley High School and the only deadly things inside were his unwashed gym socks.

But Robin realised the real reason he felt sad was because Marion was downstairs with her family. And as great as Indio, Karma, Will, Emma and everyone else at Designer Outlets had been to him over the past few months, Robin's real family was a dad in prison and a half-brother he couldn't be with.

He took his phone out of his pocket, checked he still had battery and opened an app that routed him via a virtual network and made his calls untraceable.

'Speak,' Little John said, after a couple of rings.

'It's me,' Robin said. 'Safe to talk?'

'Hang on,' the sixteen-year-old said quietly. 'The maid is around. I'll lock myself in my bathroom.'

'How's life?' Robin asked his brother, as he heard a bolt snap.

'Could be worse,' John said. 'It's school holidays, so there's not much going on. You?'

'Same,' Robin said. 'Very quiet.'

John laughed noisily. 'Yeah, right. My mum was complaining about you over breakfast this morning. She was supposed to be flying to Capital City this afternoon for some big interview on News 24. They've cancelled it for the one-hour Robin Hood special.'

'There's a special?' Robin said.

'How can you not know?'

'I knew I was being filmed,' Robin explained. 'Lynn Hoapili said it was a news report, not a whole programme.'

'Mum was already furious with you. Sherwood Castle has been losing heaps of money. Rich customers don't feel safe since you lot broke in and shot her most prestigious clients up with paintballs. She's worried she'll get fired from the board of King Corporation if she can't turn it around.'

'Does it matter?' Robin asked, only half joking. 'Won't you be moving to the presidential palace in a couple of years?'

'My mum announced that she won't stand for a fifth term as Sheriff of Nottingham. But she'll need King Corporation money to pay for a presidential campaign, and if things don't turn around, they're more likely to fire her than fund her.'

Robin laughed. 'So instead of President Marjorie, she could end up with nothing?'

'And all because of you and your forest pals,' John said. 'Which is why she chokes on her bacon if your name comes up at the breakfast table.'

'Nothing is what that evil cow deserves,' Robin said sourly. 'She tried to have me killed.'

'True,' John said. 'But I was here to tip you off.'

'Have you heard from Dad?'

'I nagged until Mum agreed to let me visit him once a month,' John said more cheerfully. 'You obviously can't visit him without getting busted, but I was thinking – if you record a video message, I'll play it next time I see him. And I can get Dad to record one back to you.'

'Awesome idea,' Robin said, cracking a big smile.

'I'm seeing him next week.'

'And Dad seems OK?' Robin asked.

'As well as any guy in prison can be,' John said. 'He's teaching IT classes, just like he did on the outside. Your mate Cut-Throat told the bikers to protect him, so he doesn't get bullied.'

'That's good,' Robin said.

'Are you OK?' John asked. 'You don't sound like your usual cocky self.'

'Busted my shoulder and dead tired,' Robin said, but then tried to explain the real reason. 'You know what's weird, John?'

John laughed. 'Your face?'

'Seriously,' Robin said, irritated. 'Like, to the world I'm either this big hero, or Sherwood's Most Wanted. There's graffiti with my name, now a TV documentary, and *so* many T-shirts. Right now I'm sitting in this room on my own, and I feel like the same person I always was. But no matter what I do, I can't ever go back to being ordinary.'

'You're brainier than me,' John admitted. 'If you can't figure it out, I've got no chance.'

Robin laughed as he ran a hand through his hair.

'So stressed and tired after last night,' he said, as he broke into a big yawn. 'I'd better go. I'll call for a longer chat when I'm less knackered, and I'll send you that video message for Dad.'

'Don't overthink,' John suggested. 'Take things one day at a time.'

'Love you, bro, but I gotta go,' Robin said, yawning again.

'Try not to get killed,' Little John said.

Robin Hood threw down his phone, lay across the little couch and was asleep almost before his head hit the cushions. He dreamed that he was blasting across the delta aboard *Water Rat*. Marion wore a captain's hat, and his brother and his dad sat in the back. The sun was warm, the water was calm.

Maybe it would happen some day . . .

Look out for

# ROBIN HOOD

## DRONES, DAMS & DESTRUCTION

Read on for an extract . . .

# 1. YOU STEPPED IN SOMETHING

Record-breaking summer rain had flooded vast tracts of Sherwood Forest, and for the first time in decades the Macondo River ran deep enough to take a boat the three hundred kilometres from Lake Victoria to the Eastern Delta.

The rains had continued into October and Robin Hood was sick of it, from emptying drip buckets in the night to stop his den flooding, to the mushroom stench of mould and clinging humidity that made him sweat through clean clothes in the time it took to tie his boots.

Robin sat in an open-hulled boat, trying to read a book with damp crinkled pages, while rain pelted a thick tarp that covered him up to the neck. Lanky trees blocked most of the daylight as an outboard motor moved the boat at a crawl.

Lyla Masri had been charged with keeping Robin and his best friend, Marion Maid, out of mischief. She sat on a plank at the boat's rear, steering. She had a Russian assault rifle propped between muddy legs and kept a careful eye on the deck compass. It was easy to lose the river's path on the flooded plains and this was one of many spots where satnav signals didn't reach the forest floor.

Robin's head felt fuzzy. His brain refused entry to the words on the page and he'd read the same line four times when Marion's boot nudged his ankle. She sat across from Robin, sharing the big tarp, her head protected with a wide-brimmed rain hat whose goofy neon strap looped around her chin.

'That your chemistry homework?' Marion asked.

Robin thought about holding the book up so Marion could see the cover, but moving risked draining puddled water from the tarp into his lap.

'I downloaded crib notes,' Marion continued. 'You can copy my answers if you like.'

Robin sounded grumpy. 'It's not homework. It's a book about the Magic Cheese.'

Marion looked baffled. 'Magic *what*?'

'Magic Cheese were legendary computer hackers back in olden times. They did wild stuff. Developed the first computer virus, built the first scorpions to track mobile phone signals. They almost wound up in jail, but the CIA recruited them to hack the Chinese.'

Marion wasn't a big reader and looked unimpressed. 'I don't know how you get through . . . what is that? Five hundred pages?'

Robin slapped the book shut. Marion wasn't the reason he'd read the same paragraph six times, but he blamed her anyway.

'How can I read if you keep interrupting?'

'My first words in half an hour,' Marion growled back.

As Robin rolled his eyes, Marion pulled a pack of chocolate-covered peanuts from her backpack. She tipped a dozen into her palm and put on a show, dropping them into her mouth one at a time as Robin pretended he wasn't interested.

'Want some, grumpy guts?' she asked, as she rattled the bag.

As Robin leaned forward, Lyla steered the open-hulled boat between an embankment and a huge lightning-charred trunk.

'Ta,' Robin said.

But as he tried to take the chocolates Marion flicked her boot up, spraying him with rainwater pooled on the tarp.

'What was that for?' Robin gasped, as it went in his eyes and trickled inside his hoodie.

As Marion cracked up laughing, Robin flicked wet hair out of his eyes. He realised Marion had put serious thought into the prank because she had her phone filming it.

'Turn it off!' Robin said, as he made a grab.

'Got you in glorious slow motion,' Marion said. 'Your expression was gold!'

As Robin tried to get Marion's phone she burrowed under the tarp and started crawling down the wooden hull towards the rear. But Robin managed to dig fingers down her trailing boot and yank her back.

The boat was too large for the wrestling to make it unstable and Lyla smirked as she watched them tussle under the tarp.

'Delete or I'll dunk your head!' Robin yelled.

But Marion got free by pulling her foot out of the boot.

'It's going online,' Marion yelled, as she crawled down the boat. 'I'll call it "Buttface Gets a Soaking".'

'What did you step in?' Robin said, making a gagging sound. 'This boot reeks!'

Lyla watched Robin reach out of the tarp and try to dangle Marion's boot over the water. But Marion straddled his chest and snatched it back.

'Get your bum off my face!' Robin demanded.

'Fart's a-coming!' Marion said. 'Inhale my breakfast, loser.'

As Robin escaped and clattered into a stack of empty cargo boxes Lyla decided they were getting too crazy.

'Enough!' she roared as she grabbed the tangled tarp and stripped it away.

The two thirteen-year-olds were sprawled over empty boxes. Breathless, soggy and smirking.

'We're still a couple of hours from Locksley,' Lyla continued. 'I'd better not hear either of you moan that you're cold or thirsty, or . . .'

Lyla stopped abruptly because she was only twenty and realised she sounded like her mother.

The teenagers straightened their clothes and stacked the boxes they'd knocked over. Robin reached for a plastic tub and used it to bail rainwater over the side, while Marion realised she really had stepped in something nasty and leaned over the side, washing the sole of her boot in the spray coming off the bow.

'I need a snack and my shirt is itchy,' Robin said, putting on a baby voice to wind Lyla up.

At the bow, Marion shot upright. Her dripping boot twirled by its laces and she looked alarmed.

'Did you hear?' she blurted.

'What?' Robin asked, as he shook drips off his Magic Cheese book.

'Gunshot,' Marion said.

Lyla looked doubtful, but she couldn't hear much of anything sat near the outboard motor.

'Sherwood's full of weird noises,' Robin said dismissively.

They couldn't risk ploughing into bandits, so Lyla cut the motor. The forest soundscape of birds, bugs and lapping water went uninterrupted long enough for Marion to feel stupid, but as Lyla reached around to restart the engine there was a squeal from a tiny human.

'Mummy, she's hurting me.'

Something muffled the little voice and Robin felt queasy at the thought of anyone harming a little kid. The echo in the canopy made the sound hard to pinpoint, but it wasn't far away.

Robert Muchamore's books have sold
15 million copies in over 30 countries,
been translated into 24 languages and
been number-one bestsellers in eight
countries including the UK, France,
Germany, Australia and New Zealand.

Find out more at
muchamore.com

Follow Robert
on Facebook and Twitter
@RobertMuchamore

**Discover more books and sign up to the Robert Muchamore mailing list at muchamore.com**

# HOT KEY BOOKS

Thank you for choosing a Hot Key book.

If you want to know more about our authors and what we publish, you can find us online.

You can start at our website

**www.hotkeybooks.com**

And you can also find us on:

**We hope to see you soon!**